# Pent

## by Steve Wallin

*With thanks to all those I owe a drink for their help.*

Other titles by the same author:

The Disappearing Hands: An Inspector Copeland Mystery.

Twelve Dead Monkeys: An Inspector Copeland Mystery.

# 1. DAY ONE.

## EASY RIDERS.

Another tour of a local town had left Keira Starr in a dark mood. Who knew being an organised crime boss could have such long hours or be so competitive? When she had decided on her new career she had not envisaged it being such hard work, or envisaged making so many enemies. Yet despite everything she had done to improve the lives of the town's inhabitants they still did not seem happy. Despite the special offers on crack and meth, the special payment plan for business protection and the payday loans being a mere twenty percent interest per week, the people still seemed miserable. But Keira knew that would all change soon. Soon they would be happier than ever. Once they had the new wonder drug.

She eased the throttle of the 1000 c.c. Vincent Black Shadow as she approached the gates of her stately home and slowed almost to a halt. The gates were open, the security guards nowhere in sight. Only the moon and her headlamp cast any light. She stopped for a moment before she revved her motorcycle and warily continued through the gates. The engine purred as she rode her Vincent between the vast lawns and made her way nearer the house. All three floors of the main house were in darkness, as were all the floors of both the east wing and the west wing. She halted the Vincent near the high double entrance doors, kicked the stand in place and turned the engine off. She listened. Far away, an owl hooted as it hunted under the full moon.

Dismounting, Keira Starr removed her black helmet and shook her long black hair so it fell over the shoulders of her black leather cycle jacket. She sighed, strode towards the entrance and pushed the doors open to look into the moonlit entrance hall. She did not question where either the security guards or the servants were because she knew very well what was going on – another group of assassins had chosen this night to try their luck. She hoped they weren't upstairs. Many items in her antiques collection on the top floor were fragile.

Choosing not to climb the grand staircase in front of her, nor to go into the visitor waiting room, library or great dining room on her left, she chose to enter the ballroom on her right where the doors had been left open, as if inviting her in. She stopped at the open doorway. The moonlight through the front doors had partly illuminated the great hall but the ballroom's high, heavy velvet curtains were drawn and she could barely make out the four high pillars down each side of the room. She wrapped the motorcycle helmet strap around her palm, gripped it tight and walked into the ballroom. She was barely five paces inside when the first assassin leaped from behind the nearest pillar and swung a Samurai sword at her head.

Minutes later, the ballroom lights flicked on. Walking the length of the ballroom, the light switch operator said, 'That didn't take long.'

'Are these the best we have, Konrad?' asked Keira Starr.

'Well, they were, My Lady' replied Konrad. 'But that one seems to have a broken leg and that one has his own sword in his shoulder, but I suppose the two unconscious ones should be up and about soon.'

Keira Starr handed him her motorcycle helmet and said, 'This really won't do, Konrad. Our strike teams will have to be better than this if we're going to get past Ania Rose.'

Far to the south, Inspector Larry Copeland asked, 'Who's Ania Rose?'

'She's the best confidential informant Department C has, Larry,' replied Director Wendy Miller from behind her desk. 'Rich, beautiful, smart and half our age, but let's not hold her being perfect against her!' Director Miller grinned. 'But if she offers you any…Never mind. You'll find out.' She smiled to herself and reached for a notepad.

While his boss wrote down the address Copeland ran his fingers back through his thick silver hair and said, 'Is this about the so-called pentagram murders? I gather there's been another one.'

Wendy Miller stopped writing. Surprised, she looked at Copeland. 'You've actually read a police report for once, Larry?'

'Of course,' Copeland indignantly lied. He was sure the report probably said little more than he had heard on the radio news anyway. What was the point of reading another report? What more could the new confidential police report say that the others had not said? Body found with a pentagram carved onto his forehead, nothing to link the victims, etcetera, etcetera, except they were all missing a heart. Black magic ritual ruled out (at this stage). Okay, the police had kept things quiet and the news had not reported the missing heart, the carved pentagram or the (no) connection to the black magic thing, but it had reported the latest man was the tenth in the space of four weeks to be found dead, blaming everything from gas leaks to internet suicide pacts, and that was enough for Copeland to avoid reading another vacuous police report and proof enough the murders were organised, somehow, and clearly a job for him: he was so desperate to escape the drab, stifling, temporary Slough office he was even willing to do some work and track down a serial killer, as long as good pubs and long lunches were factored in.

Director Miller got over her surprise and continued to write. 'No, Larry, you're not going about the so-called pentagram murders. They're still the concern of the regular police,' she said. 'This is about a new drugs gang taking over in the north. The word is they're making a powerful new designer drug. Ania Rose has got us some crucial information. You have to fetch it.' She handed the paper over her desk. 'That's directions and Ania's address, Larry. I'd assign someone younger like Natalie but she's still off training our new recruits in the Brecon Beacons. Ania Rose is old school and still prefers things on paper and even you can't mess up collecting a file and bringing it straight back to me, can you? Destroy that address once you've memorised it. Don't use a satnav or Google or anything internet linked to find it. That's an order. Our informant's address must remain top secret.'

Copeland stared at the address. Even without the written directions he had a good idea where it was. He knew Bricknall well, even the well-heeled northwest outskirts. He could pretty much name every pub within a ten mile radius of it. He looked across the desk at his boss. 'This is all very hush-hush even for us, Boss. What do you want me to do with this piece of paper once I've memorised the address? Eat it?'

*You eat everything else, Copeland,* mockingly laughed a voice inside Copeland's head: it had once been Copeland's conscience but had evolved into something far more sarcastic.

Wendy Miller also laughed, but it was the full, deep laugh of someone built like an Olympic weight lifter. She slapped her hands together and said, 'I thought you said you were trying to eat less, Larry,' and laughed again.

'I am,' Copeland said seriously, patting the robust stomach protruding though his open jacket. 'I've cut down on snacks between meals.'

'But you have seven meals a day, Larry,' pointed out Wendy Miller, grinning.

'I hardly think a couple of Danish pastries for elevenses and a few scones with afternoon tea constitute proper meals, Director Miller,' Copeland defiantly said. 'And I only eat *one* chunk of cheese with *one* box of crackers for supper.'

Wendy Miller pulled her face straight. She sighed deeply. 'Well, except for the stomach, you're looking good for your age, Larry, I'll give you that. You'd pass for fifty! It must be all the stress you work so hard to avoid.'

Copeland tugged his jacket down, resenting the implication he had not done much work since joining the new Department C a few months before. He had solved two cases, or at least half solved two cases, and had done a lot of work with the new recruits. He had spent nearly a whole day preparing his seminal lecture on infiltrating organised crime gangs and it had been so good a few of the recruits had still been awake at the end. His revised lecture had been more succinct, amounting to: 'The moment you think they suspect you of being the law then run away,' and he had then shown the raw recruits the best way to get information was to go to the bad guys' local pub. He had conducted many field trips with the recruits to demonstrate this point. After twenty pub lunches they had information about a corrupt business cartel selling machines to North Korea to enrich uranium and although the ringleader was still on the run many arrests were made, which was annoying because the pub did a very good lunch.

Snapping out of his daydream, Copeland saw a glaring Director Wendy Miller pointing to her door as she said, 'Go! Fetch that file!'

Soon free of the office, Copeland was getting his Nissan Micra motor running and heading out on the highway, not looking for adventure and hoping the slightest thing would not come his way. Unless it was a Danish pastry. He pondered the pentagram murders and the northern drugs gang as the breeze blew through his silver hair from the open window. There was one thing he knew with absolute certainty. He needed to get the car's air conditioning fixed.


## FREYA AND HER CAMERA.


Camouflage clothed, Freya Noyor once again ascended the grassy knoll overlooking the Longbeck Estate of Keira Starr. Before she reached the summit she crouched and took her small rucksack from her shoulder, laid it on the bank and took out her binoculars before smearing her face with more dusty soil, pulling her camouflage hat low and dragging the rucksack behind her as she crawled up to the crest.

Staring at the corner of a stately home through binoculars was not what Freya Noyor was used to. Nor was twenty kilometres north of Sheffield the sort of place she usually spent her time, though her tent, hidden in the nearby woods, had been five nights of comparative luxury compared to many of the places she had slept in. Painstaking research had led her north and whispers and rumours had told her of a new, well-funded group calling themselves 'The Dark Stars'. They were taking over organised crime in one northern town after the next. From a frightened man, who had once boasted he controlled half of Newcastle, Freya had learned there was another rumour that no one would hardly dare speak of – the Dark Stars were funded by none other than Keira Starr. Even then, finding their base had taken weeks before Freya had discovered Keira Starr owned Longbeck House.

Lying prone on the top of the knoll Freya waited for dawn and scanned her binoculars across the grounds of the grand stately home, the extensive lawns and orderly gardens. The day began like every other hot, dry day. Gardeners began mowing and pruning, armed security guards with dogs sauntered the perimeter, the minibus ferrying white shirted servants arrived and left. It was as if nothing unusual had happened the night before when Freya had been watching from the same spot with her night-vision binoculars. She had been about to leave when a single motorcyclist sped from the estate so quickly Freya had no time to use her camera. Hours later, and minutes before the motorcyclist had returned, all the security guards had disappeared and every light on the estate had blinked off. Freya had waited to see the lights come back on and the security guards return a few minutes later, as if nothing had happened.

Armed security guards were one thing but what appeared every morning at nine was another. And here *they* came again. Between Freya and Longbeck House, almost a kilometre away, the vast lawns either side of the main drive were being filled by over a hundred, mostly young, men and women dressed in black judo outfits and at least double that number in white outfits. On the huge lawns either side of the drive, each group was going through their jujitsu or kung fu or whatever-it-was motions in unison. Freya called them the karate kids. Soon they would get out their wooden swords and start thrashing about with them as if they knew what they were doing.

To her left, a delivery van arrived at the iron gates. There was nothing unusual in that. She had seen many delivery vans come and go. Usually they unloaded food for the many servants and wannabe Bruce Lees, sometimes they were there to collect the rubbish and recycling, but they always arrived early, before the rows of karate kids had assembled on the lawns, and they were always stopped at the gates. The only vehicles allowed straight through were the minibuses arriving with the many new recruits or those leaving with the few who had somehow failed. But this new vehicle was being waved straight through. Freya followed it with her binoculars. Although it was the size of a supermarket delivery vehicle, it had no logos on the outside. It was completely black. Freya reached for her camera as the truck approached the house. The telephoto lens might capture what they were about to unload, even at this distance. She dragged the camera in front of her and placed the binoculars to one side. The truck had veered to the right in front of the house and had stopped nearer her, where the newer restaurant and gift shop used to be before the estate had been sold. Freya trained her camera lens and prepared herself to take the photos that would expose exactly what was going on. She felt sure whatever was in this delivery van would give her the answers she was after. It had to be the new designer drug. Why else would the delivery be met by the huge blond, bearded man they called Konrad?

Something was wrong with the camera. Most of the screen seemed to be filled with red. Freya turned the camera. It was fine when she pointed it at the security guards at the gates. She tilted the lens towards her to examine it. There was nothing wrong with the lens, but there was a red spot on the back of her hand. She watched the spot move from her hand. It crawled towards her prone body, where only her eyes and camouflage hat were exposed above the crest of the hillock. Her eyes widened. She dropped the camera and rolled to one side. A cloud of dry earth erupted near where her nose had been. A cracking noise followed close behind. Freya rolled down the bank before the second bullet split her abandoned camera in half.

Besides two shots being fired from a third floor window, the first Konrad knew something unusual was going on was when a squad of black uniformed security guards came rushing out of the house. Konrad noticed they were wearing their side-arms and watched them until they revved up their motorcycles, sped down the main drive and on beyond the gates. Disapprovingly, Konrad shook his head. He disliked guns and disliked the noisy motorcycles, but he guessed there had been yet another spy spotted on the knoll. Were none of the henchmen of these other organised crime bosses bright enough to realise the trees had been cut down so the knoll gave the perfect view over the estate as the ground sloped away to the main house? Were none of them bright enough to realise it had been done on purpose to provide the perfect vantage point and the place where the security teams would keep watch for spies? Shaking his head again, Konrad went back to organising the unloading of the airtight plastic boxes from the rear of the truck.

Freya had seen none of what Konrad had seen but she guessed security guards would be on their way. After one more roll she got to her feet and, still crouching, ran down the grassy knoll. She burst through the woods, ignoring branches scratching her cheeks. She was soon back at her car and glad she had taken the daily precaution of taking her tent down, strapping it to her larger rucksack and throwing it onto the car's back seat. She had been in enough perilous situations where she had needed to move quickly and had learned not to take anything for granted.

She reckoned she had a few minutes start at most and drove recklessly down the rutted track back to the road, sending up a cloud of dry earth when she met the tarmac and swung the wheel. Freya had spotted the row of powerful black motorbikes on day one of her vigil of the stately home and knew then if she was spotted she would never outrun them. She was in no doubt what they expected her to try to do, just as she was in no doubt they had expected her to take up the only possible viewing position to spy on the estate, but it had been the only place to observe the stately home from so she had found herself with no choice. Deep down she was quite pleased it had taken them five days to spot she was even there. She was also quite pleased with her getaway plan. They would never expect her to be stupid enough to drive *towards* the house, but that was exactly the direction she had swung the car in as soon as she hit the access road. She rammed the car into third gear and hoped she had guessed right, that she would have just enough time before the motorcycles appeared around the curve. She switched on the four wheel drive and rammed on the brakes as she swung the wheel hard left. The car bounced over tree roots as it squeezed between thick trunks and scraped under branches. Freya accelerated, juddered over roots, bounced off a trunk, and skidded to a halt in the hideaway she had built the first day she had arrived.

Gripping the wheel and trying to calm her breathing, Freya heard the roar of the motorcycles as they shot by on the road less than fifty metres away. She wound down the window and heard them fade into the distance. She warily climbed out of the car and dragged over the branches she had piled nearby, using them to make sure the rear of her racing green Mini Paceman was soon as disguised as the rest of it. After briefly admiring her handiwork she circled round to the front of the makeshift hide, crawled through a gap, gave the car a loving pat on its roof and retrieved her rucksack from the back seat. Staying with the car was too risky. With the rucksack hoisted onto her back she trudged deeper into the woods where she knew it would be safer until the flurry of searching had died down.

## COPELAND VISITS ANIA ROSE.

'Ania Rose?' asked Copeland for the second time that morning when the door opened.

'No, I'm Simon,' smiled the white shirted, dark haired young man who looked like he would not be out of place adorning a poster on a teenage girl's wall.

Larry Copeland was not in the mood for time wasting. He was not in the mood for anything much except a cool glass of beer. Even lager would do. It was the hottest June day he could remember and Director Wendy Miller had ordered him to keep his jacket and tie on for the visit. Climbing the two stone steps to the door had sapped his energy and he was leaning against one of the marble columns flanking the entrance when he looked up and frowned at the well-spoken, door-opening man calling himself Simon.

'Sorry, Inspector Copeland,' said Simon, becoming sombre. Copeland would have wondered how he knew his name already but he had just had to say it into the intercom so the electronic security gates would be opened. 'Please come in,' Simon said, standing aside. 'Miss Rose is waiting for you in the sitting room.'

Copeland's frown turned into curious surprise as he entered the building. After the security gates and the hundred metre drive to park his car, Copeland had assumed the building contained perhaps ten or more self contained apartments, but now he was not so sure. Smelling jasmine and hearing silence, he followed the door-opening Simon across the wooden flooring through a nearby door on his left. He found himself in a white-walled room as large as a tennis court. A tall, striking woman with long red hair greeted him with a Julia Roberts smile and a firm handshake.

'Please sit, Inspector,' Ania Rose said, gesturing to the far white armchair wedged between the slate fireplace and a man-size cactus. Copeland duly sat, concerned an arm of the cactus was trying to share his armchair's arm-rest. Ania Rose, looking a lot cooler in her white silk blouse and white designer trousers than he was in his suit, sat on the long white sofa pulled to the edge of the plush white rug in front of the fireplace and said, 'Simon, please organise refreshments befitting Inspector Copeland's first visit to my humble abode.'

With a short bow Simon responded, 'Of course, Ma'am,' and proceeded past Copeland into the other, empty half of the lounge and out through a door which Copeland presumed led to a kitchen.

Assuming the other half of the lounge was some sort of as yet unfurnished extension, Copeland found his voice to ask, 'Is this is all yours, Miss Rose?'

'All what, Inspector? Oh, the house? I hope so. I've been living here since I had it built a few years ago. Successful business and all that. Only six guest bedrooms besides the two servants rooms, though. The third floor is just offices, a home cinema and my personal rooms.'

'Very nice,' commented Copeland, feeling unable to compare the scale of the Olympic swimming pool size house with his little semi-detached in Leyton.

Ania Rose smiled enigmatically and said, 'I'm curious. May I ask why you are still an inspector, Inspector Copeland? Your Department C title should surely be Agent Copeland.'

'Just a paperwork hold-up,' shrugged Copeland, holding his hands wide before noticing Ania Rose's eyes had fixed on his generous stomach. He folded his arms over it again. 'Er, as you know, Miss Rose, I'm here because Director Miller says you have some important information about a dangerous organised crime gang in the north which you feel has to be imparted in person rather than over the internet.' He was tempted to say how Wendy Miller had gone on to say Ania Rose was the best informant the new Department C could possibly have, but he couldn't be bothered. He knew where this was going, or more accurately, where *he* was going and he couldn't say he was all that keen. Tackling an organised crime gang alone had almost got him killed once before and he did not want to repeat the experience, especially if it meant going all the way up north.

'Straight down to business I see Inspector,' smiled Ania Rose and said, 'But please assuage my curiosity further and tell me, Inspector, how did you get a confession out of the culprit in that Devon lab case? You had no real evidence.'

*Er, Copeland…How does a mere informant know about a confidential case?* asked an inner voice

Copeland tried to loosen his sticky shirt collar and carefully answered, 'The perpetrator was just following orders from higher-ups in the food chain. The confession closed the case and they got off. In this game, minor wins are better than no wins, Miss Rose.'

'I understand,' nodded Ania Rose, winking a crystal green eye at Copeland. 'I'll fetch the file for Wendy.'

'Isn't that it?' Copeland asked, pointing at a red folder on the sofa next to his host as she stood up.

She turned to look down at the folder as if she had forgotten it was there. She laughed as she turned back to Copeland. 'Oh, no. This is just a personnel file for the P.R. company I own. I'm trying to select two employees to represent us in a silly competition against other companies owned by some old acquaintances. It's become something of a tradition. I'll get your file. I'll be back in a minute.'

Left alone, Copeland rubbed his hands together and huffed. He sidled further away from the uncomfortably close giant cactus. He looked about. His eyes fixed on a delicate bronze sculpture of a rose sitting on a small table next to the other armchair on the far side of the slate fireplace. He settled back into the chair and waited for Simon to emerge through the doorway. A young woman with thin arms extending from the short, puffy white sleeves of her black satin maid's dress complete with white apron appeared with a tray instead.

'Good afternoon, Sir,' she said as she approached Copeland. 'Simon has prepared tea and a home-made chocolate muffin for you.' She stooped, placed the tray at his feet, flicked a strand of cinnamon hair from her forehead and looked up at him with hazel doe-eyes as she said, 'I'll just get a little table for your tray, Sir.'

'Thank you,' Copeland said and an observant inner voice commented, *She's a pretty girl, isn't she, Copeland?* Adding, *Very slim too*, just as Copeland was thinking she looked like she needed a few helpings of pie and chips.

The maid averted her eyes as she stood, said, 'You're welcome, Sir,' and crossed over the plush white rug to remove the small rose sculpture from the low table it stood on and lowered it carefully onto the wooden floor. She carried the little table across to Copeland and placed it on the cactus side of his armchair. She lifted the tray onto it before she gave a little curtsey and left. 'Thank you,' called Copeland as she disappeared back through the door she had entered by.

Copeland chose to attack the muffin before the cup of tea and lifted it for closer inspection. Home-made chocolate muffin, eh? Copeland hoped it tasted as good as the last home-made muffins he'd eaten. He bit into it. It was undoubtedly not the same recipe. He grabbed a paper serviette and emptied the contents of his mouth into it. Seeing the door to the hall move he rammed the remainder of the muffin into the serviette and stuffed it into his jacket pocket.

'Aha!' said Ania Rose as soon as she entered. 'I see you've already eaten one of my special chocolate muffins. Wonderful aren't they? It's vegan chocolate, you know.'

*Note to self, Copeland...* began a voice in Copeland's head.

'So, Miss Rose…' began Copeland's more audible voice as Ania Rose handed him the black file she had brought back with her and cut him short with, 'I suppose you want to know how I get all this information to pass on to you spooks at MI5, don't you Inspector?'

'Department C is only sort of MI5,' Copeland protested. 'We have a limited remit – organised crime, corruption…'

'Contacts,' asserted Ania Rose, ignoring him as she sat back on her sofa. 'I have a lot of contacts who pass on information. Your boss, Director Miller, sometimes gives me the heads up on some people and I get my contacts to ask discreet questions. It amazes me how much people give away over a business dinner or at the dentists or when having a facial or...You get the picture. As it happens I'm hosting a dinner party next weekend and… Well never mind about that, eh?' Her smile radiated confidence. 'As a matter of fact your boss has just phoned to ask if my people can keep their ears open for any information about these dreadful pentagram murders. Serial killers are scary, aren't they? There was one stalking Cambridge when I was doing my degree.'

'Finding a killer is always about finding their motivation,' said Copeland, trying to sound as if he knew what he was talking about as he wriggled uncomfortably in his seat to avoid a cactus arm. He smiled back, balanced the black file on his lap and lifted his cup of tea. He hoped it would wash away the taste of the muffin. Still looking at Ania Rose, Copeland drank. He looked at the cup he held near his lips.

'Camomile and Rosehip,' announced Ania enthusiastically. 'Green tea unspoiled by milk, of course.'

Copeland considered spitting it back into the cup. He told himself he had tasted worse things, though his memory struggled to remember when. Fortunately, Ania Rose had sat on the red folder and half stood as she turned to move it. Copeland quickly spat and poured the tea into the pot of the providentially nearby giant cactus, hoping it would not kill it. By the time Ania Rose sat facing him again he was replacing his empty cup on the saucer and smiling. 'Thanks for the tea. I think I'd best be off then,' he said, standing with the file under his arm.

'Of course, Inspector. No doubt Director Miller is keen to get that file,' Ania smiled as she also stood.

*You want to go so you can go to a pub for lunch on the way back to HQ, don't you Copeland?*

Copeland smiled. Ania gestured towards the door and followed to watch him crunch across the gravel drive to the Nissan Micra Director Miller had got on eBay for him when he had complained about the size of his Fiat 500.

As Ania raised a hand to bid Copeland farewell a voice at her shoulder whispered, 'Director Miller will send him up north to investigate, won't she, Ma'am?'

'I expect so, Alice,' replied Ania Rose to the young woman in the maid uniform.

'Did you tell him about the last two you sent there, to warn him, Ma'am?' asked Alice.

'Why ever would I do that, Alice?' said Ania. 'If Director Miller does send him north I'm sure he'll be fine – no doubt Inspector Copeland is a highly competent professional.'

## KONRAD BRIEFS KEIRA.

Chief of Staff Konrad approached the high-backed, black wooden chair where his leader sat, her head down with the light from the flickering candles shimmering off her raven-black hair. He guessed she already knew what he was going to tell her. He knew she was displeased because she was stroking the pendant hanging from her neck more forcefully than usual. Konrad made his customary bow before he said, 'Your shot destroyed the camera but the spy eluded our security, My Lady.'

Keira Starr looked up. Konrad knew that dark stare. He felt like his soul could be ripped from his body. He knew she was more than displeased. She let go of the pendant, lifted the hem of her long black skirt, stood and folded her slender arms. She said, 'As my chief of staff, Konrad, you should know the head of security will be summarily dismissed. He'll prove more useful fertilising the gardens. We need someone who can better motivate the guards. I'll soon be appointing a new head of security. In the meantime, Konrad, I would like you to be at the ready in case this spy reappears. From what I saw down the rifle's telescopic sight when I destroyed her camera, I believe it is a woman. I would like to know who she works for. I want this one alive. You understand me, Konrad?'

Konrad bowed low to show his understanding and said, 'On a brighter note, My Lady, now your empire grows, we have thirty new recruits this week alone.'

Keira frowned. 'I hope they prove to be better assassin material than the ones in the ballroom last night. How are they, by the way?'

Konrad winced. 'They'll recover, My Lady. Eventually.'

'Good,' nodded Keira. 'Tell Kurt to prepare another strike team for me to test to see if they're good enough to get around Ania Rose. So…Thirty new recruits? That's satisfactory, but how many have we lost Konrad? Not those lost fighting for our cause, but those who have chosen a different path?'

Konrad smiled. 'Actually, Lady Keira, none have died expanding your domain this month. All victories have had no fatalities. At least not for our side. But, in the last seven days, six more recruits and two Dark Stars have chosen to leave, have been found wanting in their loyalty or have transgressed. The usual, appropriate arrangements are being made for them. They will be taken care of.'

Keira Starr walked to the large round table in the centre of the room. She ran a long black nail along the shape carved into it. She nodded and said, 'Good. Send more of my Dark Stars to Nottingham in readiness for a final push there. And make sure those who have failed my Dark Stars are taken care of appropriately, Konrad.'


## COPELAND GETS AN ASSIGNMENT.

After a quick two hour pub lunch and restricting himself to two pints, Copeland delivered the black folder from Ania Rose into the hands of the Department C Director, Wendy Miller. She asked him what he thought of Ania Rose and when Copeland replied he thought she looked a little pale Wendy Miller gave him a frown, a quizzical look, a shake of the head and told him he needed to get out more. He thought she was obviously unaware he sometimes went to see Leyton Orient play **and** he visited the golf club occasionally for Sunday lunch. When he mentioned the awful tea Ania Rose had given him Director Miller laughed. When he mentioned the terrible muffin she laughed louder and said she was glad she had stopped herself from warning him how bad they tasted. Thanks a lot, thought Copeland.

While Director Miller read through the folder he'd brought back, Copeland had a chat with Janet, Director Miller's personal assistant and currently the only other living thing in the run-down office, not counting the mould on the wall and the woodworm in the second hand teachers' desks. Janet had refused to retire out of loyalty to Wendy Miller and had vowed to stay at her side until they vacated the previously disused and airless office near the Langley roundabout of the M4 and moved into their plush new central London office block near The Gherkin. But The Onion, as it was being commonly called, was well behind schedule and it looked like Janet would be staying at Wendy's side for some time yet, or at least until new admin staff had been appointed. Janet had sifted through hundreds of highly qualified applications. She had high standards. No applicant had yet made it to the interview stage. Yet Janet had soldiered on and had not only continued as secretary, PA, office manager and chief administrator but had also continued to claim the salaries for all four posts.

And why would Janet want to retire? The government had moved the goalposts for her state pension age to an entirely different pitch and her husband had passed away quite suddenly a few years before. Sadly, it had been during their holiday of a lifetime in Kenya. Having paid no attention to the warnings to never leave the safari camp at night, he had gone for a little walk to have a cigarette and had discovered the warning that 'smoking kills' was true when he was joined by two prowling lionesses looking for a late evening snack. Fortunately, there was enough left to identify his remains. Unfortunately, Lord Insurance Ltd. refused to pay out because he had 'been engaged in hazardous activities not covered by the policy'. Janet could not argue with that. Her husband had indeed been involved in hazardous activities as soon as the lionesses leapt on him.

Interrupting Janet's work was not an unusual occurrence for Larry Copeland. He often chatted to her when he gave her the occasional bottle of Prosecco and cream cake in return for keeping the paperwork that would change his title from 'Inspector' to 'Agent' in her desk. He had no idea why she always giggled and blushed when he did though.

Copeland was soon summoned into Director Miller's office where he was sat down and had the black folder placed in his hands. He flicked through the first few sheets. He wished he had not left his reading glasses at home. He glanced up at Director Wendy Miller on the other side of her desk and gave her a weak smile.

Wendy Miller drummed her fingers on the table. 'So, Inspector Copeland,' she said, drumming more forcefully, 'your mission is to gather as much information as you can about this organised crime syndicate calling themselves the Dark Stars.'

'And find out who the brains behind this new designer drug is before they can start mass producing it, I suppose,' nodded Copeland, drawing on what he'd heard when he'd been sitting on Janet's desk and Wendy Miller's voice had come through the intercom telling Janet to, "Find out where sodding Copeland is and send his big arse in here to talk about this new designer drug." Copeland was glad he was on the good side of Director Miller. He had learned it was best to placate his boss whenever possible, especially since he thought she was quite capable of losing her temper and throwing her solid wooden desk at him, probably with one hand.

'Yes, Larry, foiling these Dark Stars' new designer drug is the key to stopping them,' said Wendy Miller. 'Now, I know you're a bit past it to be going undercover but the new recruits we're training aren't ready for this yet and it's a time-urgent case. If we don't find out who this Walter White is then these new drugs will be swamping the whole of northern England before we can blink.'

Confused, Copeland squinted and tried to read the summary on the last page of the folder. He was still confused. He had to ask. 'Er,' he began, sure he had possibly missed something, 'you want me to find out who the brain behind making these drugs is, but you already know his name is Walter White?'

Wendy Miller slowly shook her head. 'You don't watch much TV, do you, Larry? He's a character in a contemporary classic called Breaking... Oh, never mind. Just get up there and find out who this so-called Professor is.'

'OK,' Copeland said confidently with a thumbs-up. 'Find the Professor! Right, Boss! Up where?'

Moments later Copeland vacated his boss' office before the desk was hurled in his general direction. Behind him he heard shouts about him putting his (expletive) glasses on.

Copeland was soon back in his hotel room in nearby Slough. The hotel was his home during the week so he did not have to commute across London to get to the office. It was his last few days there before the three months of Department C funding for his room ran out. He knew he would miss the especially comfy toilet seat and was getting maximum use from it while he flicked through the black folder. It read like an American self-help book and had thirty pages when three would have been enough. Did it really need step by step instructions about how to get to the secret, designer drug making lab located somewhere near Hadrian's Wall? Did it really need ten pages to tell him how this new group calling themselves Dark Stars were systematically disposing of the leaders of other organised crime gangs and taking over their territories? The two page comparison to cutting the head off the hydra and taking over its body by replacing all the street sellers was particularly long and he particularly did not like the implications that the police were either taking bribes or at least turning a blind eye to the spreading tentacles of the Dark Stars gang. Copeland knew the police would *never* take bribes, would they? Although there were maps galore there was only one long range photo of the large drug making complex. It had been taken by a drone and a footnote told Copeland the drone had subsequently crashed after encountering some sort of electronic jamming device. The footnote was the only clue Copeland got regarding the author of the file. The footnote had the letters HRH after it. Clearly, file author HRH had been out to impress Ania Rose with how thick a file he or she could produce and Copeland wondered if one of the Windsor's was thinking about a new career.

Copeland packed his bag and ate alone in the hotel restaurant, readying himself for the long drive north the following day by moderating himself to only a single bottle of red and one double brandy.

## THE POSTMAN ALWAYS RINGS TWICE.

Rupert Jennings sighed deeply, put the video game on pause, tossed the controller onto his sofa and went to answer the door. He'd ignored the first ring but the caller seemed persistent.

'Delivery is for you,' said the man in the light brown uniform when Rupert opened the door.

'Thank you,' smiled Rupert as he took the large parcel with both hands to scrutinise the address on something he could not remember ordering while the delivery man got out his machine for Rupert to sign. Rupert said, 'I don't remember ordering OUCH! You just jabbed me with that pen! I feel...'

The delivery man winced. He always did that when they fell backwards and hit the floor. A shorter man in a grey suit and grey hat appeared at his side carrying a grey sports bag. He slapped the delivery man on the shoulder and quietly said, 'Well done again, Mr. Green. Let's drag him further inside so we can close the door and get down to business.'

Within moments the door was closed and Rupert's comatose body was lying in front of his paused video game. Anesthetised Rupert had little choice but to wait patiently while his two visitors took their white protective suits from the bag and put them on, tugged plastic coverings over their shoes, pulled the white hoods over their hair and snapped their surgical gloves on.

'Why you bother, Mr. Grey?' moaned delivery man Mr. Green. 'You sit on ass while I do all work.'

'I did turn the computer game off,' responded Mr. Grey, seating himself as far from Mr. Green and the unconscious Rupert Jennings as he could.

'I suppose it my turn again, then,' continued to complain Mr. Green as he took the knife from the bag and knelt down on the floor next to unconscious Rupert. He placed the tip of the knife against Rupert's forehead.

'Stop!' commanded Mr. Grey. Mr. Green stopped and looked up. Mr. Grey waved a finger at him. 'Go round to the top of his head and do it from there. It's always so unsymmetrical when you do it that way up. Be neat, young man!'

Mr. Green groaned and shuffled round to the top of Rupert's head. He placed the knife between Rupert's eyes and began to carve the symbol. 'You is right, Mr. Grey!' he smiled, looking up and giving a nod to the smaller man who was literally twiddling his thumbs in the chair on the far side of the room. 'Is much easier from top. Look, Mr. Grey! Very... er... very not what you said others were. Un-simmy-something.'

'I always like to help anyone from the Russian motherland,' said Mr. Grey. He was surprised to see Mr. Green spit on the floor. It was a heartfelt spit.

'Russian?' shouted Mr. Green, perhaps unwisely given the fact he was in the act of committing a murder. 'I no Russian! I hate Russian. I Latvian. We kick out Ruskies.'

'My apologies, Mr. Green,' said Mr. Grey in his refined accent based on the 1939 BBC Radio voice which had once informed the nation that Mr. Neville Chamberlain had decided 'we' were at war with Germany, though Neville never showed up at Dunkirk.

'Ended,' announced Mr. Green, kneeling up and admiring his handiwork. Mr. Grey went over to inspect. 'A decent enough job of an upside down pentagram,' he complimented.

'What iz this upside down? It done right!' baulked Mr. Green.

Mr. Grey nodded and returned to his seat. He was starting to think Mr. Green was a liability. Perhaps his saliva on the latest victim's carpet would be his undoing once it was DNA tested. Mr. Grey could only hope.

In the meantime, Mr. Green was on a roll. 'Now I do how what you showed me. Cut open here, yes?'

'Quite right, Mr. Green,' said Mr. Grey, wondering how this young idiot could still ask after he had done it over a dozen times.

Mr. Green was about to plunge the knife just below napping Rupert's rib cage when he stopped and leaned back on his ankles.

Here we go again, thought Mr. Grey. 'Listen, Mr. Green, I've told you countless times the victim won't feel a thing. The injection from the pen puts them totally unconscious. It's just like an operation. There's no need to feel any guilt.'

Mr. Green continued to stare at Mr. Grey. 'Why am I green?' he asked. 'I know you grey because you grey. Not just suit and hat but your skin grey and wrinkly. Mr. White is Mr. White 'cause all hair white. But I not green. I want be… Mr. Pink!'

'So,' mused Mr. Grey, 'you think Mr. Orange is orange?'

'Maybe,' said Mr. Green. 'Mr. U.S. president is.'

Mr. Grey considered this. 'It's not up to me to decide these things, Mr. Green,' he said, brightening up as he saw a new way to get someone other than a Russian hating Latvian as a new Mr. Green. Mr. Grey said, 'Hmmm…You are pink. You may have a point.'

'Yes, I got knife,' agreed Mr. Green, showing him.

'No, Mr. Green. I meant you should talk to Mr. White about it. He's the boss and decides things like our code names. If I were you I would threaten him with going to the authorities with information about these murders he's paying us to do.'

Mr. Green smiled. 'Yes! I will so do!' he beamed.

Good, thought Mr. Grey. That should ensure you are replaced forthwith with someone who does not hate Russians. He watched Mr. Green return to his task. He put his hands on his ears. He was not squeamish but he never liked this bit. The bit after Mr. Green put the knife down. It was the squishing and glugging bit Mr Grey found somewhat off-putting. The bit where Mr. Green reached up inside the ribcage and tugged. And did he always really need to hold it up like he'd just received an Oscar?

It was time for Mr. Grey to play his part. He took a plastic bag over to Mr. Green. It was a large, sealable, freezer bag, both air and blood tight. Mr. Green dropped Rupert's heart into the bag and Mr. Grey promptly sealed it.

'This guy on floor,' said Mr. Green. 'He will be much annoyed when he wakes up, no?'

'Pardon?' asked Mr Grey, who had retreated a safe distance from any red seepage and begun to take his protective clothing off.

'Well,' said Mr. Green, joining him to do the same. 'Man will wake up and have no heart bone. I think he may have walk all stoopy over.'

Mr. Grey slowly shook his head. 'I'm sure he will not be troubled by a stoopy walk, Mr. Green.'

'Good,' said Mr. Green. 'Grandmamma had stoopy walk. Mama said Grandmamma had no heart. So I know no heart means people have stoopy walk.'

With raised eyebrows, Mr. Grey said, 'You exhibit impeccable logic, Mr. Green.'

## 2. DAY 2. THURSDAY.

### ONE CRAWLED UNDER THE CUCKOO'S NEST.

An idea struck Freya Noyor. She had been shot at and hunted but all was not lost. Not yet. Besides the photographs she had already transferred to her laptop before her camera had been shot with a sniper bullet, she now had new knowledge: the Longbeck stately home occupied by the Dark Star gang was getting deliveries of their new illicit drug from somewhere and it was being delivered in a black, Tesco home-delivery size van.

Climbing out of her sleeping bag, Freya drank some water and headed back to the narrow road leading to the stately home lair of the Dark Stars. She detoured to check her car was still undiscovered and found it still shrouded by the branches she had constructed its hideaway garage with. The walk was finally warming her up. Listening for the faintest cracking twig huddled in a sleeping bag under a tree all night was not as warm as it might have been and at times she had been tempted to risk putting her tent up. She seemed to feel the cold more now than when she was younger, but even back then she had always been keen to get near a fire whenever a chilly wind blew. She wished she was somewhere warmer than Yorkshire. Somewhere like Damascus again, or Libya, or Sudan or even Serbia. That was a strange one, Serbia, she thought as she warily approached the road.

After three hours crouching in the bushes Freya's hope was fulfilled. A black van identical to the one she had seen the day before drove past, heading for the gates of the stately home. All she had to do now was wait until it came back. Then she could follow it back to where the drugs were being made. Once the van was out of sight Freya stood, intending to fetch her rucksack and her car, wait near where the narrow road met the B road and see if the truck went west or east. She stopped in her tracks and fell to one knee while she considered her plan. How could she follow the van for miles along quiet roads without being seen? What if she had to follow it all the way to Leeds? They would be bound to spot her following them. *Damn it, Freya!* she scolded herself. *These people are an organised crime gang. They're bound to be watching out for someone following them*. She came up with an alternative plan. She could get into the back of the truck when it went past. She thought about how she might do this. It had worked in The Congo when she leapt into the back of that truck to track down the rebels' base, but that had been an open back truck crawling along a dirt road. Was she really going to wait for the black drugs truck, run behind it at twenty miles an hour, leap onto the back, open the doors and climb inside? And how would she get out undetected? Wait for the driver to open the door, give him a smile and a little wave and say, 'Hi, I'm just here to find out where you make all your illegal designer drugs?' It sounded a little too risky. Another thought struck her. She did not need to know which way the truck went – only where it ended up. With a new spring in her step she found her way back to her car.

Removing the branches of the car's camouflage shelter and reversing back through the trees took some time but Freya was finally in position near the narrow asphalt road. She risked a brief exposure and reversed onto the road to turn the car round, listening for any sound of approaching vehicles. She sat and waited, trying to work out what to do if a patrol of security guards on motorbikes came along, perhaps still looking for her and finding a proverbial sitting duck at the side of the road, but she knew it was either this or give up and go back empty handed.

Freya smiled. Her gamble had paid off. That was the sound of a distant truck and it was heading towards her and, more importantly, away from the house. The drugs had been unloaded and the truck was on its way back to wherever they were making them. Even if it ended up parked in some garage somewhere, she knew sooner or later it would go back to the drugs factory. She pulled the car forward, stopped, took out the keys, opened the door and dashed into the bushes.

Hidden behind a fallen tree trunk, Freya watched as the van approached, slowed and stopped. Two men got out and looked at her car blocking the narrow road in front of them. They were not wearing the usual, apparently mandatory black uniforms of Dark Stars, but simple open neck shirts and jeans. One of them started shouting, 'Hello? Is anyone there?' until the other punched his shoulder and said something Freya could not hear. Their next move was to check the car and find the doors unlocked then, after one more look around, to begin pushing it off the road and out of their way. Freya seized the moment. She broke cover and ran to the back of the van, opened the door, slid her phone deep inside, closed the door and ran back to the cover of the woods.

A new sound made her throw herself flat behind the fallen trunk. Motorbikes! She had not anticipated someone in the truck radioing their base and a squad of security guards riding out. Why hadn't she thought of that? She knew why. She had become obsessed with getting results and did not have anyone to tell her she was taking too many risks. Now here she was, a few metres from the road and less than thirty from the rear of the black van with six armed security guards arriving to see what was going on. Freya's head sagged when she saw one of the black uniformed guards was none other than Konrad himself.

When the drone of the motorbikes ceased Freya risked a glance over the fallen trunk. Her face was soon down again, but she knew what she had seen. The truck driver and his colleague had got back in the van and the Dark Star security squad were off their bikes and peering into the woods. She heard the truck engine start. She heard the truck pull away. Any minute now the security guards would be searching the woods with their guns drawn. Freya waited. She listened to her own breathing. Birdsong returned to the trees. A cuckoo called somewhere above her head before, abruptly, motorcycle engines roared to life, roared as they revved and roared as they accelerated away. Freya lay still. She waited five minutes, then ten, then fifteen. She risked a glance over the fallen tree trunk. She saw nothing except her car, tilted into the wood at the side of the road. She crawled forward, slowly rising to her knees to scan the woods and road. Crouching low, she stepped over the trunk.

Staying in the woods for cover, she soon saw her car had all four tyres thoroughly slashed. She turned and started making her way back to where she had left her rucksack. It was only a twenty mile cross-country hike to Sheffield. She thought she might make it there before dawn. She had not gone fifty paces before she stopped, slapped a palm to her forehead, cursed her own stupidity and punched the nearest tree.

Keira Starr was finishing the remains of her smoked salmon and salad lunch when Konrad returned. He knew she would be in the great banqueting room, sitting alone at the head of the far end of the table, awaiting his return.

'Well?' said Keira Starr when Konrad had finished his purposeful walk along the length of the table and stood where he belonged, at her right hand. Konrad's eyes flashed towards the servants. Keira waved a hand and they hurriedly left.

As soon as the doors were closed Konrad nodded and said, 'All went according to your plan, My Lady, but how did you know the spy would..? Stupid question. Forgive me.'

Slowly placing her cutlery on her plate, Keira stared at him. She smiled broadly.


## MR. GREY MAKES A CALL.

Speaking into his phone Mr. Grey said, 'It's done, Mr. White. Another one off the list.'

A voice too close to Mr. Grey's ear for audible comfort shouted, 'Tell boss man on phone – Valdis now want be Mr. Pink and no more Mr. Green,' which prompted Mr. Grey to scowl menacingly at Mr. Green. It made no difference. 'And ask Mr. White boss man if Valdis still have job when finish list of men winning stars on heads,' shouted Mr. Green.

'Sorry, Mr. White, I didn't quite hear that,' said Mr. Grey into the phone.

'And tell man boss we need crutches,' yelled Mr. Green.

Mr. Grey stared at him. 'Crutches? Why the f... Yes, Mr. White. Sorry.'

Mr. Green was determined to have his say. 'Need crutches for men with stars on heads!'

'Yes, Boss. I understand. I await your email.'

'Starry head men wake up and be all stoopy without heart bone,' persisted Mr. Green as loudly as he could.

Clenching a fist in Mr. Green's general direction, Mr. Grey tried to listen to the voice on the phone. His jaw fell. 'Mr. White! You cannot be serious!'

About to make a further point, Mr. Green stopped short when he saw Mr. Grey take the phone from his ear and tap it to end the call. Now Mr. Grey only had his voice to listen to, Mr. Green moderated his volume to something merely approaching bellowing. 'What man say?' he asked.

Shaking his head as if he had just seen a flying pig, Mr. Grey said, 'He's sending another eight names and addresses of people he wants us to visit.'

'Aha!' exclaimed Mr. Green. 'That why your face look like tractor squash your rabbit!'

'No, it's because Mr. White said you can be called Mr. Pink,' said Mr. Grey, feeling like he would never get rid of his Russian hating Latvian sidekick. But he was not going to be downhearted. He was sure he would find another way to get rid of Mr. Green, er, Mr. Pink.

# 3. DAY THREE. FRIDAY.

## COPELAND ARRIVES AT THE DRUGS FACTORY

With no intention of being stupid enough to try to infiltrate a drug gang's remote factory to find out who this mastermind 'Professor' was, Copeland had driven up the M1 and across half of England to within striking distance of the drugs factory. He imagined a crime gang might not be too pleased to find him lurking outside their factory and he could hardly drive up to it and say, 'Hello. I'm here from Department C, sort of a section of MI5, and I'm here visiting your new illegal designer drugs factory to do a health and safety inspection.' It was the sort of thing that might be prone to getting him shot. Instead, Copeland had decided gathering intelligence was the first priority, and Copeland had always found the best way to do that was to extract it from the ordinary workers, and the best way to do that was in their local pub over a pint.

Doing that sort of subtle interrogation was just what Copeland needed. The long drive north had exhausted him. It had taken almost ten hours. It might have taken less if he had not stopped for coffee and cake twice each side of lunch, then again for high tea somewhere along the A69 before he turned off towards the B road running parallel to part of Hadrian's Wall as it stretched from the west to east coast. He was glad to arrive at the guest house he had booked. It was near the nearest pub to the drug factory's location and a stone's throw away from an old Roman fort near the middle of Hadrian's Wall. The guest house lounge was full of retired Americans from Kentucky, all awestruck by how just one man had built such a big wall and all disappointed it had "kinda fallen down." Even so, they intended to let The Donald know there was this English guy called Hadrian who was really good at building walls.

After checking in, Copeland had been further exhausted by the long walk to the pub for his evening meal. It was all the way up the guest house three car length drive, all the way over the road, past the bus stop and all the way around the side of the pub to get to the entrance. Copeland had enjoyed a pint of ale while he waited for his food to arrive and enjoyed another when it did. He had gone for his usual – meat pie, chips and three veg., minus the veg. The pie was both delicious and filling. Copeland simply could not face ordering pudding. Not before he had ordered a second helping of the pie. He had later been unsure at first about the apple crumble and needed a second portion to decide whether it merited a nine or a full ten. All he could manage afterwards was a fourth pint while he played darts with some of the locals, but none of them worked at a local factory and gave him blank looks when he said he was going there to do a health and safety inspection. His interrogations of the locals thus required a fifth pint while chatting to the bar staff, who were also unaware of the existence of a local factory, or even a large shed that made illegal designer drugs. On reflection, Copeland thought he perhaps should not have mentioned the drugs.

Still feeling half full of pie and beer when he went down for breakfast, Copeland only had porridge, a Full English and three rounds of toast before he was on his way to drive stealthily in front of the nearby drug gang's secret factory where he intended to definitely not risk trying to get in to find what they were up to. If the worst came to the worst, he would drive past and do a blurry video on his phone, go back to HQ and check everyone he filmed on the new facial recognition thing once Janet had showed him how to use it and, with a bit of luck, he would still be doing that when Natalie and the recruits returned from their survival training, then they could do some secret agent type stuff, like parachute onto the drugs factory roof or something.

With his new plan, Copeland set off for the nearby factory. After three hours and nearly one hundred miles he stopped to check his bearings. He had driven around single track roads to find the allegedly nearby hidden drugs factory and was rapidly coming to the conclusion it was not called 'hidden' for nothing. His satnav was proving useless in the middle of nowhere where a single post code seemed to cover twenty square miles. He knew he had taken the correct left turn off the B road – it was the only one that went anywhere – and had followed that road through a gap in old Mr. Hadrian's wall, so where the hell was the secret factory?

His more observant better self was being less than supportive with comments like, *You've messed up again Copeland! That sign said Welcome to Scotland!*

Copeland turned round and was virtually back at the gap in the Roman wall when he had an idea. He would stop and have a look at the folder Ania Rose had given him. Sure enough, the exact instructions, down to the last metre, supplied by the mysterious HRH, were still there. Copeland committed them to memory and set off. An hour later he was knocking on the door of a farmhouse.

A stout woman in an apron answered. Copeland gave her a smile and said, 'I may be a little bit lost. Is this Butterburn?'

'Butterburn is a burn, dear,' replied the woman wiping her hands on her apron. 'You know – a burn. A stream, a rivulet, a brook, a tributary, a pain to get the tractor over. You want to get to the burn?'

'Er, no,' said a hot exasperated Copeland still attempting something that might pass as a smile. 'I'm actually looking for a factory that makes illegal drugs.'

'Hmm,' said the woman as she theatrically stroked her chin. 'You must want the place over the road. The place that has all those black trucks coming and going. How they don't end up in a ditch on this little road I'll never know. Still, there's more passing trade for our farm shop now. Did you want to buy something and then I can tell you exactly how to get there?'

Copeland suspected he was being scammed. The suspicion grew when the woman added, 'Perhaps a few things costing somewhere in the region of fifty pounds?' Copeland turned his head, looked across the road, saw endless flat fields peppered with an occasional tree and went to his car to fetch his wallet.

Carrying the most expensive half eaten packet of biscuits he'd ever bought, Copeland returned to his car with exact instructions to find the drugs factory. To be fair to the farm shop lady, she had offered him a potato for his fifty pounds but he had declined her generous offer, accepted the half eaten biscuits from her cupboard and handed over the cash.

*Don't miss the left turn where this road swings right this time, Copeland. Put those biscuits down and look out for it.*

Following the narrow road a few hundred metres further north, Copeland ate the last of the biscuits and pulled into an even narrower road, just wide enough for a tractor. Like the road in front of the farmhouse, this road also had grass verges flanking it, but these were well-worn with thick tyre tracks and Copeland knew he was finally closing in on the secret factory, no more than a few fields from where he had first started. A cow lifted its head over the nearby stone wall and gave him a look. It made Copeland remember something important. He pulled the car onto a track in front of a metal bar gate leading into the cow field.

*Good idea, Copeland. Leave the car here and reconnoitre the factory on foot. Why are you looking at your watch? Why are you turning the car around? You're going back to the pub for lunch, aren't you?*

After a light lunch of a repeat of the beef pie, chips and crumble, washed down with a couple of pints, Copeland found the minor road off the minor road off the minor B road quite easily. He was soon tentatively driving slightly upslope, passing the cow field and wondering if he had just eaten one of their relatives. He decided when he got to the top of the rise he would stop to survey the scene and try to find a good spot to use his phone for a few photos. He would be back in London before… Ooops.

Copeland had two choices. He could stop and turn around or he could carry straight on. Since the road was only just wide enough for a tractor and Copeland was not that good at reversing when there was a possibility of stranding the car in a roadside ditch, Copeland chose to go on. He gave the two security guards emerging from their shady little hut a wave. They did not wave back as they took up position in front of the red and white hooped barrier. He tried a smile as he drove the last few metres to where they were clearly not smiling back while taking black things with barrels from holsters at their hips. Copeland stuck his head through the open car window and said, 'I'm here to do a health and safety inspection.'

# FREYA SPOTS A WEAK SPOT.

After a brisk walk to Sheffield, Freya had hired a car, purchased an inferior camera, a reconditioned phone and blurry binoculars. When she had finally stopped cursing her own stupidity she plugged her tablet in, placed it on the passenger seat and connected to the 'find my phone' app. It had led her to the remoteness north of Hadrian's Wall.

With the car left in the car park of a farm shop (which charged twenty pounds a day for parking) and her tent pitched between isolated rocky outcrops, Freya trekked across the parched, barren landscape to see exactly where the black van had taken her phone. It was not long before she was climbing over a stone wall into a cow field. At first the cows eyed her curiously. They herded together and walked towards her. They waited until she was halfway across the field before they broke into a trot. Freya broke into a run. Being chased by cows is more terrifying than anyone might realise. Though not in the same league as crocodiles or aspiring to the 665 thousand killed by mosquitoes, cows move pretty fast and kill many more people than sharks do every year. Freya did not have these facts to hand but ran for her life anyway. She went over the stone wall much quicker than she had the first one and landed on her back in a muddy ditch. She looked up to see cows peering over the wall, looking innocently down at her.

Raising herself to look over the edge of the ditch, Freya saw she was within a hundred metres of her phone. A row of three black vans stood outside the narcotics factory. Except it wasn't one factory. It was a group of three low buildings. Two modern glass-fronted square buildings with sides as long as four buses faced each other across a narrow strip of tarmac road. The black vans were beside a third building at the end of the tarmac road. This building was an older, windowless, concrete structure and bigger than the other two buildings combined. Freya took all this in with the quickest of glances. She had also spotted the security guards at the barrier across the road leading into the compound and felt fortunate they were busy talking to the driver of a small Nissan car.

Easing up to the rim of the ditch Freya glanced at the distracted guards and was about to launch herself across the open, dusty soil towards the vans when she stopped, slid back down into the ditch and, with her eyes at dusty soil level, she looked more carefully. Ankle high metallic towers and small mounds of dry earth told her a run across the open ground would not be undetected. Invisible lasers from the low towers and pressure pads under the soil would be impossible to avoid and, no doubt, a host of security guards from the buildings would soon emerge. Freya suspected the Dark Star drug gang's guards might not invite her in for tea and cake but might instead find her a shallow grave. She slunk back down the bank of the muddy ditch, rolled onto her back and stared disconsolately at the cloudless sky.


## KEIRA WATCHES CCTV.


Over a hundred miles south, on the third floor of Longbeck House, inside a room resembling NASA control with rows of monitors, Keira Starr sullenly folded her arms across her black Alexandre Vauthier silk top. She stared intently at the screens while Konrad hurried the team working at keyboards who were frantically trying to find out who the new visitor to the secret Butterburn facility was. Keira did not like having her afternoon interrupted, but she knew if Konrad had sent for her then it was serious. She poked a black fingernail into the shoulder of the black shirted man sitting on the swivel stool in front of her. He got the message and zoomed the camera in on the unwanted guest, whose appearance had been unusual to say the least. Anyone who actually found the secret Butterburn facility usually tried to gain entry unnoticed, but this man had driven straight up to the barrier and claimed he was there to do a health and safety inspection. He was either very bold or very stupid.

Keira heard Konrad say, 'Put it up on the big screen.' She lifted her gaze from the monitor to see what one of the computer geek team had found. It confirmed what she had suspected. This tallish, silver-haired man with a ridiculously large stomach was clearly not stupid and had intentionally arrived at the barrier. It explained why he seemed so calm when the two armed guards had got him to get out of his car and place his hands on its roof.

What she did not know was why he kept shuffling his feet. She suspected it was some sort of code to another security service agent watching from a distance.

Konrad joined her, stood at her side and looked down at the monitor. He laughed. 'Looks like the old chap needs a toilet.'

Keira gave him a look and his face turned to stone. 'This new Department C is a threat, Konrad,' she said, staring back at the information on the big screen. 'A new branch of the security services set up to tackle organised crime.'

They continued to glance from the monitor to the big screen, where newer information replaced the old. It told them Department C was so new it was barely functioning out of its temporary, disused offices not far from Heathrow, but still... It was an arm of MI5 and Keira still suspected the tall, tubby, jiggling man was doing some sort of coded shuffle to an accomplice who was possibly filming the entire scene. She knew they could not take the risk of treating him like the others who had been caught straying too close to things she did not want anyone to know about.

She said, 'Tell them to let him in. The Professor can give him a guided tour and show him we have nothing to hide in our facility.'

Konrad took a step back and looked aghast at her. 'But, My Lady…' he began, stopping short when Keira held up a long, straight finger and levelled a black painted nail at him. She whispered, 'Listen and hear, Konrad.'

Konrad stared at the pointing nail. He stared at her dark eyes. He smiled, nodded, dropped his head to stare the long, long way to his feet and said, 'My Lady is most wise, as always. We shall let the Professor show him we have nothing to hide *in* our facility.'

Keira smiled. 'I'm glad you caught up, dear Konrad,' she said, sidling closer to him and whispering, 'Assemble yet another strike team in the grand ballroom for me to test. Ania must be close to choosing and we need to be ready.'

'Yes, My Lady,' Konrad said, hesitantly. 'On a different note…We have the name and address of our recent spy from her car number plate. Her name is Freya Noyor and she lives in London. I think we should send Kerry to, erm, *visit* her.'

'Kerry? Ah! A good choice,' Keira nodded. 'Make it so.'


## COPELAND MEETS THE PROFESSOR.

A vintage analogue walkie-talkie crackled into the ear of one guard while the other pressed his pistol into Copeland's back. As a glass half-full type of person, Copeland felt pleased he had gone back to the pub for lunch and wouldn't have to die on an empty stomach. On a less positive side, the guards had forced him out of the car and made him put his hands on the roof and the metal was pretty hot.

Walkie-talkie guard had read from Copeland's Department C identity card and spoke into the old radio. The wait for a reply lasted so long clouds began rolling in from the west and Copeland began to hope they would at least let him use a toilet to vacate his lunchtime beers before they shot him. As clouds released the first spattering of rain and Copeland sympathetically had a minor leak of his own, walkie-talkie guard's radio crackled as a vaguely audible voice spoke. The guard raised his eyebrows and said, 'They've given you clearance to see The Professor. They say to tell you the management take health and safety issues very seriously.'

Two more black shirted guards arrived to frogmarch Copeland to one of the low glass buildings where he had to hand over his phone, sign in and get a visitor pass on red ribbon hung around his neck even before the guards let him inspect the desperately needed men's room. With hands thoroughly washed in case the Chinese had accidentally unleashed another new virus like SARs they marched him back past reception to an office at the far end of the building.

Wearing a sceptical look and a white lab coat, The Professor was leaning back on an office desk, waiting.

'Health and safety inspection?' asked The Professor. 'Is that the best you could come up with?'

Almost lost for words, Copeland replied, 'I had to think on my feet. Not literally, I suppose, because I was sitting in the car at the time but... Beth? *You're* The Professor?'

Beth Spencer strode across her office as she said, 'It's a sort of nickname,' and threw her arms around Copeland's neck. The guards retreated and left them to it when Copeland's arms tentatively went around The Professor's shoulders.

As they broke the embrace and stood apart clasping elbows, Copeland smiled and nodded. 'You look well, Beth,' he lied. She had the same short hair and had reverted to blonde again, but she looked pale and sallow compared to when he had last seen her. It was the way with workaholics.

'You look well too, Larry,' said Dr. Beth Spencer as she released his arms and stepped back. 'Actually, Larry, you look *very* well indeed. At least ten years younger than the last time I saw you at your police retirement do. And I know why!'

'You do?' said Copeland, feeling uneasy.

'Yes! You've given up smoking, haven't you?'

'Ah, that. Yes. So I have Beth,' smiled Copeland.

Beth turned and pressed a button on her desk. 'And working for those super secret Pickfords must have done you good too, Larry. Though I don't see how all that travelling around the world assassinating dictators, crime kingpins, other assassins and so on could have been so stress free.'

'I had a desk job, Beth. And for your own safety I need to remind you The Pickfords don't officially exist. Just because you met my old friend Beryl who happens to be the current Pickfords boss and just because I told you she had offered me a job doesn't mean an ultra secret organisation like The Pickfords actually exists and it definitely doesn't have a secret HQ above a bank in Kensington, which was a hell of a tube journey from my house in Leyton and oh, tea. Good.'

'Thank you, Kylie,' said Beth to the short, blonde pony-tail woman who entered the office and placed the tray down on Beth's desk. Beth sat in her high-backed leather chair and indicated Copeland should sit on one of the comfy-looking guest chairs opposite.

'So sorry about the security people, Larry. We're all paranoid about industrial spies. Their guns are only tazers really. We have a special license because we make them.

They're only five thousand volts,' said Beth as she poured the tea after putting a little milk into each cup while Copeland helped himself to the biscuits. 'So you work for MI5 now?'

'It's not like the real MI5, Beth. We just do organised crime and corruption and take all the bad guys assets without the need to go through the courts so we can pay back the money all the private sponsors put into setting up Department C and the milk should really go in after the tea not before so it doesn't scald,' explained Copeland.

Beth nodded thoughtfully and said, 'Perhaps you can tell me all that again once you've swallowed the two jammy dodgers you just put in your mouth. But, frankly, I'm more interested in whether or not you've seen Tom. I'm not sure he and I have ended our relationship on the best of terms…'

Gulping some tea and thanking the gods it was proper English tea, the biscuits were quickly washed down. Copeland pretended not to see tears in Beth's eyes and said, 'I saw Tom a few months ago. He told me you'd got a new, plum job up north. I suppose this is it. But Tom's fine, Beth. He's made friends with Jesus.'

'Jesus?' Beth said, wiping the tear. 'Tom's found religion?'

'Jesus lives in the box-room in the little house someone has made into bedsits for about ten people, counting Tom Benson and the kids in the family downstairs,' Copeland explained, clearly distracted by the remaining biscuits. 'His real name is Brian, but he thinks he's Jesus, and Tom has a new job just outside London working for a PR and management company.'

'Did he mention me?' asked Beth, leaning anxiously across her desk.

'Well, sort of,' said Copeland, picking up a biscuit and inspecting it. 'He said something about you never answering his calls and how he'd got the message and moved on without you. Does that help?'

Beth sighed. 'They gave me one of those new solar powered phones and a new number. Something to do with the Chinese listening in on the old one. I meant to call him. I was so busy. Then weeks became months and I couldn't work out what to say. When I did phone, the number was dead. I finally went back to Lincoln to see him. He'd gone and his phone was down the toilet. I knew he'd given up waiting for me when I saw he'd taken all his books about aliens, JFK conspiracies, magic tricks and secret societies with him. He even took the one he had about Elvis sightings. And his Yoda poster...' Her voice was cracking.

Copeland wanted to say something consoling to support a clearly emotional Beth. 'That's life,' he said, with feeling.

'He was so charismatic,' sighed Beth, making Copeland consider if they were talking about the same Tom – the little thin one with the balding head, buck teeth and squat nose who resembled a skinny garden gnome and had somehow ended up living with an extremely attractive thirty something genius doctor named Dr. Beth Spencer, now apparently also known as The Professor.

Copeland allowed Beth to wipe her eyes again and blow forcefully into a tissue before he swallowed another jammy dodger and said, 'I'm here because we heard you're making drugs, Dr. Spencer.'

Beth Spencer coughed, put her elbows on her desk and narrowed her eyes. 'So we are, Inspector Copeland,' she said, intensely. 'And a lot more besides. The least I can do is show you round Butterburn before we... get rid of you!'

Copeland stared intensely back, maintaining eye contact without blinking while his hand slid surreptitiously across the desk to grasp another jammy dodger. Beth Spencer laughed.

## MR. GREY.

Mr. Grey couldn't take it anymore. He asked himself how he had ended up working with an imbecile like Mr. Pink, but remembered it was because he needed the money to hire an anonymous contract killer to kill Larry Copeland.

Mr. Pink rammed his foot on the brake. He turned to stare at grey Mr. Grey. Mr. Pink's mouth fell open as he said, 'You say they no need crutches because they no wake up?' Mr. Grey nodded slowly. Mr. Pink ignored the drivers pulling around him, blasting their horns and giving him a full variety of rude gestures. He looked at the road ahead for some time. He seemed oblivious to the traffic warden placing something on the windscreen. He seemed blind to the pigeon hopping across the bonnet. He shook his head and turned the windscreen wiper on. The parking ticket flew away in the breeze. The pigeon tried to fly but crashed to the ground. He turned to Mr. Grey again and whispered, 'You mean they dead? They dead when we take out heart bone? But Mamma said Grandmamma had no heart and she wasn't dead.'

'Yes! They're dead!' growled Mr. Grey. 'Why do you think the boss pays us five thousand for each one? They are very dead. Very, very dead. The English have a saying – they're as dead as a dildo!'

Mr. Pink considered this. 'You mean dodo? I go once to Natural History Museum and…'

'They're dead!' screamed Mr. Grey.

'So crutches no needed?' Mr. Pink tried to confirm and thought the look on Mr. Grey's face meant probably no crutches needed. 'OK,' said Mr. Pink, 'Fair enough. Who next on list?'

## FREYA.

The torrential rain brought good news and bad news for Freya Noyor. Hiding in a muddy ditch as it filled with water was not how she would have chosen to spend most days but the good news was the guards stationed at the road barrier had retreated into their little wooden hut and, occluded by the rainstorm, she could slip away. Taking the long way round, along the ditch and around the field, seemed a better route than going back over the wall and risking the wrath of the herd of psychopathic cows.

Armed with plan B, or possibly plan E since she was starting to lose track, Freya was soon shivering and dripping as she sat in her hired car outside the farm shop and waited. And waited.


## COPELAND INSPECTS THE INFAMOUS DRUGS LAB

The tour of the allegedly nefarious drug gang facility started with Beth telling Copeland how the building she was responsible for had triple-glazed, solar power glass, state of the art equipment and the most brilliant young scientists working in three separate labs. The first of these was the drugs lab. As far as Copeland could understand it the drug was chewable so it could also be absorbed through a usually neglected but important thing expert scientists called 'the mouth'. Beyond that he thought it all sounded like boring technical stuff about alpha and beta globulins along with a newly discovered transferase enzyme, but he got the main idea: the drug worked well because it had other stuff in it that made it work well.

'So, let's get this straight, Beth,' Copeland said hesitantly as he held an amber tablet the size of a ten pence coin in his palm. 'The new designer drug about to hit the streets of British cities is a vitamin tablet? And you've registered its trademark name as ChewiVit?'

Beth huffed. 'I've already told you, Larry, I've no idea where this designer drug rumour came from. They've been thoroughly tested on a large sample of people and they're completely safe. And if what you call hitting the streets means being sold in pharmacies and health shops, then yes, it's hitting the streets. We're mass producing them at the rear of the labs. The first batch has gone for packaging.'

'So this in my hand is a vitamin tablet?' asked Copeland.

'For the millionth time! Yes! But not just **any** vitamin tablet. It works really, really well.' Beth flexed her fingers as if preparing to wrap them around Copeland's neck, took a couple of deep breaths instead and said, 'Because we've added digestive enzymes it gets absorbed properly, which most other tablets don't, and then the vitamins, and minerals, get transported effectively around the body because we've added the boost of this new transferase enzyme we found in blood. We retro-synthesised it. My team wanted to call it spencer-transferase after yours truly, but I've decided on vit-transferase. Test subjects say they felt like they had renewed energy, though we've had to change the flavour from orange to honey after the market research. You can try one.'

Copeland shook his head. 'I only have natural things.'

Beth grinned. 'Like meat pies, chips and beer,' she said.

'Quite,' said Copeland, but succumbed to Beth's look, popped the tablet into his mouth and chewed. 'Mmmm... honey,' he said.

'Synthetic taste so it's vegan friendly, of course,' said Beth, spoiling the moment.

The rest of the tour was fascinating, providing you were some sort of nerdy scientist rather than someone looking constantly at their watch and wondering how long it would take before they could just leave and drive somewhere civilised for an evening meal and a bottle of red.

Another of Beth's three labs was working on a new sort of synthetic skin for burns victims made from a new gel which reminded Copeland of strawberry jelly, which he'd never been keen on. The third and final lab was where the animal experimentation was taking place. Beth pointed to a large fish tank. Copeland put his glasses on and still saw nothing inside. Beth scooped some water and put it on a slide, focused a microscope as long as Copeland's arm and brought an image up on a screen.

'It's so cute,' cooed Copeland, taken totally out of character by what he saw on the screen. 'Like a Michelin-man roly-poly cuddly toy hippo with six legs and a trumpet for a nose.'

'Tardigrade,' announced Beth. 'Sometimes called a water bear. And they have eight legs. A fifth of a millimetre long and that trumpet nose is really its mouth. It's a voracious eater and if you were algae or a small invertebrate you wouldn't think it was cute. And if it really was hippo size those claws would be long enough to go straight through you.' She looked at Copeland's stomach and reconsidered. 'Through most people. Tough creatures, tardigrades. You can freeze them, boil them, squash them and they bounce back to life. More importantly, they can be dormant for who knows how long and you can blast them with radiation and they shrug it off.'

'So why..?' ventured Copeland.

'Space travel,' answered Beth. 'If humans are going to Mars and beyond we need to get some of their genes inside us.'

'So astronauts will look like roly-poly hippos?' asked Copeland.

Beth Spencer laughed loudly. 'Gene splicing. CRISPR. Cutting and pasting genes to people like you who didn't do **proper** science degrees, Larry. We're trying to identify which genes give them their abilities.'

'And you're testing the tardigrade genes on those baby mice?' Copeland asked, pointing to glass tanks which, to be fair to him, did look like they were occupied by tunnels teeming with baby mice.

Beth laughed again. 'Heterocephalus glaber, also known as naked mole-rats, Larry,' she smiled. 'Perhaps even tougher than tardigrades. Creatures their size should live about three years but they live over thirty before they die of who-knows-what. We don't. They shrug off UV light damage and every known toxin doesn't bother them either. They seem to boost the genes that stop damaged cells dividing. We're trying to identify those genes. We think we have the same genes somewhere in us. They're just dormant. We just need to find them and switch them on.'

'For space flight?' asked Copeland, almost slightly interested.

Beth did not laugh. She said, 'To cure cancer, Larry.'

Following a brief tour of the ChewiVit® production line and the tidy storage area packed to the ceiling with empty airtight plastic boxes, Copeland found his tour of the equally elaborate research block the other side of the narrow tarmac road even less inspiring than 'The Professor' Beth Spencer's labs. He met the other labs' own techno-boss, Dr. Cynthia (call me Cyn) Wood. All her teams seemed to be wasting their time making robots, developing a quantum computer with advanced AI capabilities to go one better than Google or IBM, and, much more interestingly, building a new generation of virtual reality headsets. Copeland wanted to know if he could put a headset on and do something like he had done at that London exhibition where he had put one on and really believed he was flying a fighter jet. He had found flying the VR fighter jet quite exciting and had needed a few medicinal whiskies afterwards. He thought this virtual reality set-up looked better than the one in London, mainly because it did not have a massive queue, so was upset to find it was currently linked to the AI quantum computer for trials of experimental virtual brain surgery techniques. Disappointed, Copeland went on to view the technology block's workshop, full of robot parts and laser torches, and the neatly boring, packed to the ceiling, storage area at the rear.

But there was one more building left to see. The older, concrete one at the end of the road. The one that was bigger than the two enormous triple research labs combined. Beth got brollies from Kylie at reception and was walking Copeland over when he stopped and pointed. 'You've got pyramids over there,' he said, indicating a ridge beyond the field of cows. 'If Tom was here he would tell you they're landing pads for alien spaceships.' He laughed. Beth stopped a few paces in front. She did not reply. Copeland caught her up.

The rain pelted on their umbrellas, thudding relentlessly. Beth's face was wet. She turned to face Copeland. She said, 'If you see Tom, tell him I still…' She turned away. Copeland heard a loud sigh before she said, 'They're water vapour extractors. The pyramid things. Prototypes. One of Cyn's team's finished projects. They take water from the air and the solar panels power the pumps. That's why this dry land has a field wet enough to grow enough grass for thirty cows in a single field. Sub-Sahara Africa could become the breadbasket of the world. The Arabian Peninsula could have roaming herds again like it did thirty thousand years ago. Keira is trying to get Namibia interested. Let's go.'

As Copeland followed in Professor Beth's wake he began to think this may not be an illegal designer drugs manufacturing place after all. He thought making synthetic skin for burns victims, curing cancer, space flight, turning deserts into farms and even making robots was probably all fairly legal. Then they went into the concrete building and he doubted what was in there was legal at all.

For a start, the restaurant had an almost all-vegetarian menu. The gym looked like hell on earth. And the cinema was showing Mamma Mia! The staff accommodation consisted of little more than rooms with a double bed, wi-fi, TV, the usual furniture and an en-suite. Adding an occasional window might have been nice. But at least there was a separate bar to the one in the noisy disco (which Beth informed him was called a night club since the 1990s) and the games room did have two pool tables.

***And to be fair, Copeland, it does have lifts down to the basement and the sub-basement***, pointed out his inner voice, which had been strangely silent since a black shirted security guard had pressed a gun into his back and had consequently not been encouraged to break its silence by Beth saying the guns were really tazers with '*only* five thousand volts.'

Beth took Copeland to the room she had ordered to be prepared for him for the night, told him the 'special' would be steak pie made from local produce and promised she would make an exception to her evening swimming pool and gym routine and join him with a few co-workers for an orange juice in the free bar afterwards. Any doubts Copeland may have had about staying evaporated with the words *free bar*.

Alone in his underground room, Copeland got into his shower feeling like he was missing something. When he had finished washing his thick silver hair he was absolutely certain he was missing something. He realised what it was. Where was the Silver Shine hair conditioner?

His inner voice had something to say about this. ***Hells bells, Copeland! Missing something? Above the door into this building was a bloody big red pentagram!***

While showering Copeland thought he heard his guest-bedroom door close. He poked his head out of the en-suite and saw someone had left clean clothes on his bed. Shirt, trousers, sweater, socks and underwear were all there and all black. Nearly all black. The sweater had a red logo the size of a fifty pence coin.

***Ooh! Look Copeland! What a coincidence. It's another red pointy pentagram***, commented his inner voice.

But Copeland had already noticed.

The lab workers and security guards had somehow got it into their heads that Copeland worked for MI5 as some sort of procurement officer and he was treated like royalty in the restaurant and then the bar. He thought everyone seemed very friendly and may even have still thought that even if the food and wine had not been free. Because they thought he worked for MI5, and not a privately financed offshoot investigating things the real MI5 felt beneath them and the police did not have the resources for, and because they thought he was there to buy things for HM Government, Copeland had plenty of people offering him drinks and telling him how he should buy whatever their particular lab was making. Some still eyed him suspiciously and only talked about how often they did fire drills or electrical equipment checks and would not believe he was not really a health and safety inspector.

Beth had tried to give him some attention as she sipped her soft drink and looked disdainfully at his meat pie while she ate her salad, but she was called away to attend to some crises or other and Copeland ended up sitting with diminutive technology guru Dr. Cynthia Wood, who proved to be as excellent a drinking companion as the others who joined them in the free sub-basement bar after their meal.

A few more bottles of wine had been brought over to their table when Copeland finally asked, 'So, Cyn, Beth mentioned someone... red again for me, please... someone name Keira. Who's that?'

The previously rowdy table fell silent.

Dr. Cyn sipped her wine, placed it carefully on the table, looked at Copeland and answered, 'Keira Starr, of course.'

'Oh, Keira Starr,' Copeland nodded knowingly, adding, 'And who's Keira Starr?'

Mouths dropped around the table. Heads were shaken. There was some staring. The adjoining table joined in.

'*Lady* Keira Starr?' said Cyn.

Receptionist and part-time security guard Kylie explained. 'She's not *really* a Lady. They say an ancestor of hers was given a lordship but another king took it away again when he chopped his head off. They say she likes to be called Lady Keira to be ironic. She owns a big estate near Sheffield called Longbeck and... What? Why are you all looking at me like that?'

Copeland noticed the way the others looked at her. He thought the looks she got were a bit much. Kylie might be an Australian but she seemed quite friendly anyway.

Cyn cleared her throat and turned back to Copeland, smiling. 'Keira Starr funds this whole facility. She's quite well off. She owns a few magazines.'

'A few?' blurted Kylie, adding emphasis with, 'A few?'

Copeland clarified with, 'So she owns quite a few then. Well, good for her for using her money on things to help people. That's what I say! Pass the bottle over, Big Kris, I need a refill.'

After an audible sigh of relief the chatter started again and continued for some time until Big Kris and Little Kris helped Copeland find his room and, just in case he accidentally wondered out of it, they stayed outside his door all night.


## TOM BENSON.


As fate would have it, at about the same time Dr. Beth Spencer was telling Inspector Larry Copeland how much she missed Tom Benson, Tom Benson was, in actual fact, not thinking about Beth Spencer at all. The former partner of Beth Spencer and frequent passing acquaintance of Larry Copeland was extremely busy with an urgent and important matter of life and death and giving it his full concentration. But no matter what he did, the photocopier still refused to work: Tom Benson's employment prospects hung by a thread if he dared miss his deadline. After using his slightly used handkerchief to mop his mostly bald head and clean his NHS plastic spectacles he bent his knees slightly so he was at eye level with the insides of the infernal machine and tried to tug the concertinaed piece of paper out. After several attempts and more brow mopping, old Mary, who did the cleaning, took pity on him and used a finger and thumb to pull it free.

The jammed photocopier was one of the many reasons why Tom Benson was late with the file on the potential new client his big boss had demanded. The other reasons were mainly to do with him not having a clue about his new job. He had no idea why this particular file had to be on paper and delivered personally to the company's owner and not emailed to his supervisor as usual, but he vainly tried to make up for lost time by exceeding the speed limit slightly so he was less than two hours late when the sun was starting to set and he parked his old VW in front of his boss's home.

Perspiring in his jacket and tie and fully expecting to be fired from his new job for missing his deadline, Tom Benson had not expected to have the door opened by the Big Boss in person, or to be almost instantly asked his opinion even before his boss had seen the file on the new client. He did not expect to be given a drink, to be invited to stay for dinner or be offered a lucrative new post and other perks if he answered some questions correctly and agreed to be the representative of Rose P.R. and Management in "an insignificant contest against some other companies."

Tom thought the questions were rather unusual for a job promotion interview, but felt he must be getting them right because Ania Rose nodded increasingly enthusiastically and her smile grew and grew. After that it was all plain sailing – chatting, soft music and dessert – and Tom Benson signed the provisional contract without a second thought about why he'd had three medical examinations during the last week.


## ANOTHER ONE BITES THE DUST.

While Mr. Pink demonstrated his improving pentagram carving skills Mr. Grey stopped twiddling his thumbs in the armchair and took his buzzing phone from his grey jacket pocket. He held it next to the grey hairs growing from his ear.

'Mr. White! What a pleasant surprise!' enthused Mr. Grey as he inwardly groaned at being bothered by amateurs. He pretended to smile as if Mr. White could see him while Mr. White spoke.

'No, no, Mr. White. Mr. Green – I mean Mr. Pink – is here as well. He's just doing his latest masterpiece. He's becoming a regular Van Gogh.'

Mr. White spoke.

'No, Mr. White. It's definitely pronounced Van Gogh.'

Mr. Grey momentarily held the phone away from his ear.

'Using coarse language does not change the fact it is pronounced…Tell you what, let's just say Mr. Pink is becoming a regular Vincent, shall we? He's got very good at this. Best thing since sliced toast.'

Mr. Grey listened. 'I'm sure it's toast, not bread, Mr. White. What?'

(Pause.)

'Yes, Mr. White, we did the Forest Road job. Number 34A. Mr. Willmott, wasn't it?

(Pause.)

'Yes, I know we've been paid, Mr. White, but I assure you… What? Really? Oh, I see. We killed Mr. Jennings in number 34, not Mr. Willmott in 34A. How silly of us.'

(Long pause.)

'You're right Mr. White. Silly was a silly word to use given the circumstances. Er, hang on a moment. Mr. Pink needs a sealable bag before the floor gets any messier.'

Mr. White paused while he heard a glup sound and a bag being sealed, followed by a voice younger than Mr. Grey's loudly asking, 'Who da man?' and then somewhat more quietly, 'Why crazy Americans say that, Mr. Grey?'

Mr. Grey smiled, thinking there was still hope for Mr. Pink and he could yet become a good Soviet citizen once again, given time and a Russian invasion to rightfully reclaim Latvia. With his phone back to his ear Mr. Grey reconsidered, thought

Mr. Pink might not have much time at all and whispered, 'Shall I dispose of Mr. Pink since it seems he pressed the wrong doorbell and we killed the wrong person?'

Mr. Grey watched Mr. Pink still in the kitchen taking his protective clothing off and waited for a response. He got one.

'What do you mean, Mr. White? We're not getting paid for the next two men we kill? And what do you mean by it takes two to tango? Surely you mean it takes two to salsa? And why is it my fault as well? I didn't press the door-bell. It's Mr. Green – er, Mr. Pink who should be eliminated for... Oh, ah, yes, all finished changing then Mr. Pink?' Mr. Grey quickly switched his phone off.

Mr. Pink looked at him and frowned. 'Mr. White not happy? What eliminated mean?'

Mr. Grey knew he had two choices. He could tell the truth about them not being paid for the next two kills because they had inadvertently killed the wrong person or he could lie. Telling the truth had never been one of his better traits so he erred on the side of caution. 'Eliminate is an English word meaning a pay cut, Mr. Pink. The five thousand we would have got for our next four murders is only half that, I'm afraid, but, as these English say, a problem shared is a problem doubled.' He slapped Mr. Pink on the back as he thought, *It's half for you because I'm still getting my full share! Aha! Hang on... Half of the next four is...*

Mr. Grey gave up, knowing his mind was sometimes not what it once was. But he still knew there were plenty more potential victims on the list and he would soon have enough money to get his revenge and take out the biggest ever assassination contract on that back-stabbing Larry Copeland.

## KEIRA REVIEWS THE CCTV FOOTAGE.

Konrad had put together a two hour montage of CCTV footage before he texted Keira to join him in front of the monitor. She swished in wearing her customary long black skirt and with her raven hair flowing. Konrad thought she looked as sultry as always despite her growing concerns. He was not so pleased to see Kurt, the Master of Hounds, trail in behind her and loiter near the doorway, but guessed Kurt had followed Keira from the grand ballroom after watching his latest A-grade anti-Ania strike team be humiliated by Keira.

Standing beside the seated Konrad, Keira nodded and Konrad pressed the playback button. Keira watched with her arms folded, but soon pressed fast-forward and folded her arms again. She remained silent for a few moments afterwards and said, 'Is that it? Beth Spencer took him on the tour and only showed him what was **in** the facility, as instructed, then he got intoxicated in the bar with Cynthia and some others? It looks like we were right to let him in. He appears to be a total incompetent. Who does he work for again?'

Konrad handed Keira a file. She skimmed through it. 'Department C is a department of MI5 which can seize criminals' assets? It's sponsored by private companies? What is this country coming to, Konrad?'

'Please look at the sponsors list, My Lady,' suggested Konrad, stroking his blond beard.

Keira read aloud: 'Uroboros Rejuvenation Ltd., Sunflower Hotels, Quill Flooring, Daffodil Estate Agents, Tulip Holdings, Buttercup Gyms... Am I detecting a suspiciously botanical connection here, Konrad? And what exactly might the Deadly Nightshade modelling agency be?'

Konrad smiled as he gently relieved Keira Starr of the folder and replaced it with another. 'Oh,' said Keira flicking through it. 'So this Copeland character appears to be a tubby, bumbling Inspector Clouseau, but he has a past, doesn't he?'

Konrad swivelled in his chair and looked up at Keira. 'Yes, he does, and he cleverly waited until everyone had been drinking before he asked about you, My Lady.'

Keira handed the folder back and stared down at her extremely broad right hand man. She placed one hand on his shoulder while her other stroked the pentagram pendant hanging from her neck. Eventually she said: 'This Inspector Copeland may be a genius. Or worse, he may be lucky. Either way we do not want him investigating secrets we want kept secret. We'll need to do something about him, Konrad.'

'There's something else, My Lady,' Konrad said flicking a switch to get the playback from previously unseen footage of the bar. He zoomed in.

'What's her name?' asked Keira.

'Kylie,' said Konrad.

'She gave him information? She told him I own Longbeck? I take it she did so without authorisation?'

Konrad nodded.

The Master of Hounds, Kurt, cheerily called from the doorway: 'Shall I send for her so we can feed her to the dogs, My Lady?'

Keira turned to look Kurt in the eye. She sighed resignedly. 'It's the twenty first century, Kurt. Feeding people to dogs is not an option.' She laughed. 'The animal rights people would be down on us like a ton of bricks. We need to be more subtle. Have this Kylie brought here. She can sit on the seat.'

Keira ignored the sudden draining of blood from Kurt's face and turned back to Konrad. 'Do you think that's too severe for divulging information to a stranger, Konrad? Mentioning this location is unforgivable! Make sure all of my Dark Stars know Kylie is to be sat on the seat for a week so they know what punishments may be expected for transgression.' She smiled down at Konrad and watched him turn as pale as Kurt had.

Konrad swallowed hard. His deep voice cracked. 'A week?' he croaked. 'A whole week on the naughty seat? My Lady, surely not..?' Keira gave him a look. Konrad bowed his head, took a breath and said, 'As you wish, Lady Keira.'

# 4. DAY 4. SATURDAY.

## COPELAND LEAVES THE DRUGS FACTORY

After a tolerable breakfast Copeland signed out and got his phone back in exchange for his visitor pass. Kylie was not on duty at the reception desk. Beth appeared and walked Copeland to his newly polished and valeted car. She looked like she had not slept all night. She told Copeland she had been unable to join him in the bar because there had been a problem with the ChewiVit production, but as he gave her a farewell hug she admitted she had also been in her room crying and only pulled herself together around dawn when she had gone for a short two mile swim and a quick five mile run. Copeland could not understand the need for exercise but could guess why she had been crying. 'If I see him again, I'll give your best wishes to Tom,' he said.

'Work to do!' said Beth, stepping back and clapping her hands together. 'I suppose you can keep those clothes as recompense for eating the pie last night.'

Copeland frowned. 'The pie was great.'

'Nothing to do with me, Larry.' Beth held up her hands and smiled. 'Before my time. Making beef tasting substitute from grubs is still killing animals as far as I'm concerned.'

'Grubs?' queried Copeland, starting to feel a little queasy.

Straight faced, Beth said, 'They churn them out in the lab's basement. They can make them taste like any sort of meat. Nearly all the local pubs are on the supply list.'

'Grubs? Local pubs? Meat substitute?' muttered Copeland.

'I thought it best not to show you the basement grub vats since you'd be eating them later. Have a good journey, Larry.'

Copeland replied to her parting wave with a raised hand and slowly lowered himself into his car, determined to get through the red and white hooped barrier before he thought about what might have been in his breakfast sausages. He dared not think about the pigs pudding.

A voice said, ***Errmm… Sorry to interrupt your nausea, Copeland, but you might have missed something…again.***

Copeland arrived back at his little house in Leyton feeling happy despite the prospect of spending the whole weekend packing and leaving his little house behind. Beth had left a note on the passenger seat of his car wishing him well, telling him to lose his stomach and urging him to exercise and eat better. To support her case she had placed a pile of ChewiVits on top of the note. Having tried one already and having discovered they tasted like those honey throat sweets he had consumed a packet of in one day five years ago when he had a slightly sore throat, Copeland had chewed on three ChewiVits between his stops at motorway service stations. During his last stop he had received a thoughtful text from Wendy Miller telling him to be careful because Ania Rose had told her she had already sent two other people to scout the lab and they had never been heard of again. Copeland thought they were probably still driving around country lanes somewhere.

Once home, he hung up his suit and was considering taking his new black, pentagram logo sweater off now he was down south again where it was noticeably warmer under the blanket of smog when he heard a knock at his door. It prompted him to wonder if he should put new batteries in the doorbell before he moved out. Still considering the battery replacement conundrum Copeland opened the door and barely saw the fist before it connected with his jaw.

He regained consciousness with his hands taped behind his own kitchen chair and his ankles taped to the chair legs. He tried to focus. That was possibly a face in front of him. That was possibly a knife pressed under his chin. One out of two, he thought, as he looked down and saw a blurry knife. It looked almost ceremonial.

*Like a Satanist would use to inscribe a pentagram on your forehead and then cut out your heart!* said his inner voice, a bit too enthusiastically for Copeland's liking. He breathed a sigh of relief when the knife was withdrawn. His assailant punched his jaw again.

'Ow,' said Copeland.

'Slime-ball!' cursed his assailant, which made Copeland think whoever this was had probably met him before.

Working his bruised jaw, Copeland tried to focus again. The person hitting him looked like a mud monster, or perhaps more of a medium size mud woman in need of hair shampoo. She punched him again.

After four ChewiVit tablets Copeland knew he should be feeling pretty good. He concentrated. He forced his hands apart to break the tape binding them. Less than not much happened. Except he was punched again.

Copeland had suffered enough of this. 'Shouldn't you be asking me questions or something?' he asked.

'Should I?' replied the female voice from the muddy face. 'I thought I would hit you a lot first and then ask questions.'

'Fair enough,' said Copeland. 'But exactly why are you hitting me? Are you one of the prospective new tenants who got turned down? Finding accommodation in London is awful, isn't it?'

The side of his jaw was punched again. He was called a slime-ball again as well. He thought it was all getting a bit unnecessarily repetitive.

'Admit it, scumbag! You work for Keira Starr! Your little suitcase with wheels was full of mind-bending designer drugs you've brought back to sell in London! Where have you hidden them?'

Copeland reeled as another punch was thrown but he had time to appreciate being a scumbag rather than a slime-ball before he said, 'What are you talking about?' and got punched again.

The assailant held the strangely adorned knife to his throat and said, 'I was there, hiding in a ditch. I was chased by cows. I saw you. They let you in. I waited in my car at the farm shop. I was soaked. I waited all night – you owe me twenty pounds for extra parking – and then I followed you here. All those stops on the motorway for tea and cake and toilets! You're a drug running scumbag, aren't you? You have her emblem on your sweater!' She poked the sweater's pentagram logo into Copeland's man-boob.

Copeland took exception to the accusation. He looked at the mud caked into the wrinkles around his assailant's eyes and proudly stuck up for himself. 'I only had cake twice,' he said. 'Once was Danish pastry and once was burger and chips.' He got punched again.

'Who the hell are you?' shouted Copeland.

'I'm John Smith,' said his assailant.

'That explains it,' said Copeland. 'I thought you were a woman, but no woman could knock me out with a single…' He got punched again. 'What was that for?' he asked.

'I *am* a woman,' said John Smith.

'Oh,' said Copeland. 'Oh, sorry. I see… But my generation isn't very up to date with all this sort of thing, you know. Born in the fifties, we were. Live and let live was our motto. We didn't worry about all these new fangled gender things. Didn't need them in my day, everyone just did what they felt…' He got punched again.

'I'm a woman!' cried John Smith.

'OK. Fine. You have the right to be a woman if you want, John, and I think your hair looks very nice, though it's a bit in need of a wash and... Ow! Stop punching me!'

'Where are the drugs?' demanded John Smith. 'Admit Keira Starr is behind the Dark Stars gang. Tell me which city they are targeting next!'

'Why?' asked Copeland, feeling he was definitely getting the upper hand.

'I'm John Smith!' bellowed John Smith and punched him again.

The penny dropped. Somewhere deep inside Copeland's head, the penny dropped. The penny may have been helped on its way by an inner voice shouting, *It's John Smith!* but Copeland remembered who John Smith was. His eyes widened as he said, 'You're John Smith!' just before another punch landed.

After pausing to run his tongue along his lower teeth to check they were still there, Copeland said, 'You're the investigative reporter, John Smith!'

'Bloody right,' said Freya Noyor as she punched Copeland again.


'I'm so sorry,' said Freya a short while later. 'Why didn't you tell me you were MI5 before I found your ID card, Inspector Copeland? And by the way, you have a melted chocolate muffin in one of your jacket pockets.'

'Department C isn't really MI5, it's... Oh, forget it. No harm done, John,' said Copeland, rubbing his jaw.

'I was holding back,' said Freya.

'I could tell, John,' said Copeland.

'Call me Freya,' said Freya.

'If that's the name you've chosen, then I will, John,' said Copeland.

'I keep telling you, Inspector Copeland, I *am* female,' said Freya.

'I understand, John. Everyone should be free to choose whatever gender they feel they really are, irrespective of their anatomy,' said Copeland.

'Once again, Inspector… John Smith is my alter ego so I can go into places like Damascus, Beijing and Pyongyang or get information about corrupt officials and no-one knows I'm really the journalist John Smith,' said Freya.

'Hmm… I see. You're Freya Noyor the woman when you're gathering information and John Smith the man when you write the stories for the newspapers. Like a split personality? You know they say split personalities don't really exist?'

'Aaargh! I need a bath!' screamed Freya. 'Then we'll get your laptop and I'll show you the photos of Keira Starr's Dark Star hideout near Sheffield. You don't happen to have some clean clothes I could have, do you, Inspector?'

Copeland thought about this. He had not touched his parents' room since they had passed away. Their clothes were just as they had left them. But the wardrobes and drawers had to be emptied before the new tenant moved in. The clothes would end up stuffed into black bags and taken to a charity shop. He said, 'You can help yourself to my parents' clothes. Did you want my mum's or my dad's?'

Left alone, Copeland tidied up the remnants of the tape that had bound him and picked up the knife Freya had held to his throat. He looked at the ornate handle. It had the words A GIFT FROM SPAIN written on it. As letter openers went it was too blunt to be of any use. He put it back on its little gold stand on his mantelpiece and decided to put what meagre food he had left into boxes ready for the move to his new rental place in Slough.

Freya appeared an hour later wearing a flowery dress and a faded tan cardigan Copeland's mother had worn the day he went to university in 1974. Freya's fringed, shoulder length hair was a less dishevelled mousy brown and the mud had disappeared from the lines around her eyes, though she had kept the lines. She had even found some peach lipstick to broaden her lips. Copeland thought whatever hormones they were giving John looked like they had started to work, but thought John should ask for a bigger dose next time.

Having decided to respect John's gender choice and thinking his guest might need a compliment, Copeland said, 'You look very clean, Freya.'


## DEAL OR NO DEAL (PART ONE)

Mr. Grey loved this new way to do banking while 'on the go'. 'On the go' for Mr. Grey involved swiping and tapping his phone while ignoring the constant complaints of, 'Why me Mr. Pink do all work again Mr. Grey?' He knew he would have to get the bag ready again soon and really wanted to see if... Yes! His monthly bills to the Russian mafia could be paid and he would still have enough money to take out the kill-on-sight contract on the traitorous Larry Copeland.

Mr. Grey had already tracked down an individual calling himself 'The Broker' on the Dark Web. The Broker would arrange a contract killing for the small arrangement fee of twenty five percent and had assured Mr. Grey that Mr. Lawrence Copeland would be eradicated from the face of the earth for a mere ten thousand pounds, plus another twenty five percent commission. But because of the inexplicable disappearance of nearly half of the hit-men advertising on the dark web a few months before it was currently a sellers' market and Mr. Grey would, unfortunately, not get the very best for ten thousand pounds these days. The Broker had offered a special two for the price of one deal for a mere fifteen thousand pounds, but, with this current job almost in the bag as it were, Mr. Grey had the ten thousand and no more and he really wanted Larry Copeland dead and gone ASAP. Mr. Grey had already forwarded his deposit.

'Need bag for heart-bone,' shouted Mr. Pink, doing his look what I've got in my hand victory salute.

'Just wait!' snapped Mr. Grey.

'It making mess on man's nice carpet,' protested Mr. Pink.

Mr. Grey glanced up from his phone. He could not see how a few more drips could make that much difference to the carpet at this stage. Just one more tap and the rest of the money would be transferred to The Broker and that would be that. Tap. Mr. Grey smiled contentedly for a few moments then frowned at what appeared on his phone screen.

Mr. Pink called, 'Really need bag now, Mr. Grey.'

'I'm reading! This is important,' snapped Mr. Grey. 'It's my bank.'

Mr. Grey read and answered out loud. 'Question one. No, I have not received an unsolicited phone call. Question two. Do I know the recipient is really who they say they are? I hope so. I'm paying them enough commission to get me someone to assassinate someone. Three. Has my phone been tampered with in the last month? If someone had tampered with my phone would they be inclined to tell me? Four. Have I given my bank log-in details to anyone else? Now that would be a stupid thing to do wouldn't it? Five. Has the recipient told me they can make more interest with my money than the annual zero point two percent interest currently offered by our Supersaver account (click on right for details and move your money for a fixed five year term now)? Er, no to that one. Six…'

'He moved!' screamed Mr. Pink. Mr. Grey looked up to see Mr. Pink standing and pointing down at the body. 'You say they dead when no have heart-bone! You lie, Mr. Grey!'

Mr. Grey sighed. 'It's just his involuntary nervous system,' he said.

'So Mr. Cunard nervy system still alive?' Mr. Pink cried apoplectically as he jigged and sprayed red liquid around the room.

'Calm down, Mr. Pink,' soothed Mr. Grey. 'Mr. Cunard will stop twitching in a few moments. Now just let me tick this little box to say I've just read all thirty pages of these terms and conditions and… Who's Mr. Cunard?'

'You right, Mr. Grey,' said Mr. Pink. 'He got over his nervy twitch now. What? Oh, this Mr. Cunard. He signed while I was getting out other pen to jab him. I sort of forgot I wasn't real delivery man anymore.'

Mr. Grey lowered his phone onto his lap and said, 'This is number fifty seven isn't it, Mr. Pink?'

Proudly, Mr. Pink replied, 'Yes, Mr. Grey. I double check number before I ring bell this time.'

'Fifty seven Windermere Drive?'

'Yes. Fifty seven Windermere Lane.'

Mr. Grey thought it was true, certainly in Mr. Pink's case: you could lead a horse to water but you couldn't make it think. He considered his future bank balance and tapped 'cancel transaction'.

## COPELAND AND FREYA

How the photos Freya had taken of Keira Starr's stately home seemed to be on his laptop confused Copeland. Emailing things to oneself was not something Copeland had thought possible, but prided himself on being open minded about all these new-fangled ideas, like emails.

Freya talked him through the photos and look – she could even make some parts of them appear bigger on the screen. Just like in sci-fi films like *Blade Runner*. Amazing! He saw the stately home of Keira Starr brought close even though it was almost a kilometre to where the armed, black-uniformed guards patrolled with their Hounds from Hell, or possibly dogs cross bred from Dobermans and Rottweilers. Freya grumpily complained about how she had already discovered the Longbeck Estate was registered as a gun club so the Dark Stars were actually ***allowed*** to carry firearms on the estate, but she cheered up when she showed Copeland her favourite shots of the rows of black and white clad would-be ninjas doing their practising with sticks and she glowed with pride when she showed him one blurry night-time photo of someone riding into the estate on a very large motorbike. Freya expanded the grainy image, enthusiastically pointed at the screen and proudly told Copeland there was ***not one*** single photograph of Keira Starr on the whole internet ***but*** she believed this photo was of none other than Keira Starr herself*!*

'Hmmm… Great photo,' said Copeland, tactfully.

What interested Copeland most were the expanded photos of the security guards in their unisex black shirts and black trousers. They all wore a red armband. When expanded to full screen Copeland could see the red armband had a white circle, and inside the white circle was a black symbol. The symbol was a five pointed star, also called a pentagram.

Freya explained how she had taken photos of the black van being unloaded and how that camera had been shattered by a bullet. She explained how she had managed to get her phone into the back of a similar van so she could track it when it left. Copeland was completely absorbed, inwardly thrilled to find out there was a way to find his phone when he'd forgotten where he'd left it. He also thought it was a good job Freya had one of those new solar charging phones, otherwise, after she had camped out for days, the battery would have run out long before she had tossed it into the truck.

They ordered pizza, opened wine and Copeland found himself telling Freya all about his visit to the remote research place near Butterburn and how it was funded by none other than 'Lady' Keira Starr.

Freya had a theory. The tablets *may* well have been vitamin tablets when they left the Butterburn research facility, and Dr. Beth Spencer *may* have been truthful, as Copeland believed, but once they got to the stately home the tablets were taken into the old restaurant and gift shop building where they weren't just packaged, but something was added to make them into dangerous street drugs. Copeland considered this as he ate the last slice of his family size pepperoni and thought it might be a little out of the ordinary for Keira Starr to cut out the middle man and sell new designer drugs to end-point consumers at health shops and pharmacies. He thought it more likely the ChewiVits were just ChewiVits and if there were any street drugs being made they were being made somewhere inside Keira Starr's stately home. After all, he'd eaten some ChewiVits on his way back from Northumberland and he felt fine.

In fact, Copeland felt so fine he tried hard to finish the last few bottles of wine before his imminent move to Slough. He was happy to share and stay up to listen to his guest's stories of how freelance journalist and photographer Freya Noyor had travelled the world to expose a range of human evils and later write them up under the name John Smith – or, if you were Copeland, hear how John Smith had travelled the world to expose a range of human evils disguised as Freya Noyor.

At the end of their fourth bottle of cheap Merlot Copeland told Freya something he knew he shouldn't have. Something the police were bending over backwards to keep quiet. He told her about the seemingly random pentagram murders. Freya shot upright, snapped her fingers and, wide-eyed, told Copeland about how the Dark Star failures got shipped out in minibuses – would Keira Starr risk them telling the world about her illegal operations, or would she perhaps send them somewhere and have them quietly silenced?

Excitedly, Freya exclaimed, 'The victims *must* be Keira Starr's ex Dark Stars! Pentagrams carved into the victims' foreheads *surely* prove Keira Starr is behind the murders!'

With two bottles of wine sloshing about his blood stream, Copeland thought Freya's "kill the failed Dark Stars" theory had some merit but also thought an evil genius leading an expanding criminal organisation might perhaps just kill people without advertising the killings by carving her emblem into victims' foreheads in their own homes. Unless the evil genius wanted to show there was nowhere to hide for those who turned their back on her…

An inner voice made an astute observation: *Great! Well done, Copeland. You've just told an investigative journalist about a series of murders that will cause mass panic if it gets out. Just great!*

## 5. DAY 5. Sunday bloody Sunday.

<u>ROSS</u>

Temporary Commander Ross held his hat under his arm and uncustomarily stood to attention. He had said, 'Yes, Sir,' and 'No, Sir,' several times before he ventured to ask, 'So I'm off the case, Sir?'

'I've just told you that three times, Ross. Home Office orders. The NCA is not meant for investigating random murders.'

'But, Sir! The pentagrams carved onto their foreheads and the removal of their…'

'Enough! No more of this Satanic cult nonsense, Ross. Everyone knows Satanists sacrifice virgins.'

Refraining from suspecting his superior's main source of evidence was entirely cinematic, Ross said, 'They might have been virgins, Sir.'

'What? Twelve men over the age of consent all virgins? And I suppose this…where's the list…this Rupert Jennings fellow was still a virgin as well? Are you suggesting he hadn't consummated his marriage after two years?'

'It happens, Sir,' said Ross and wished he hadn't.

'You're off the case Ross. People like you from SO15 see conspiracies everywhere. Spent too long chasing terrorists and can't see the wood for the trees anymore. This is just some nutcase and has nothing to do with organised crime. Besides, there's been a leak to the press. The Times asked for a comment. We've shut them up with the offer of an exclusive when it's all over, but The Commissioner thinks the leak must have come from one of your team. Anyway, we have more cutbacks now this new Department C is taking over most of the NCA's role so we'll let them and the local police forces look into these murders.'

'Very well, Sir,' sighed Ross. 'I suppose my team has a new assignment then?'

'Well, in your case, it's more of a reassignment. Like I said – cutbacks. Plus the Home Office wants a more visible police presence on the streets again so more resources are going there, which probably means you can put money on a general election soon.'

Ross had only heard one word. 'Reassignment, Sir?'

'Ah, yes. You're useful with a firearm so it's protection duty for you, Ross.'

Ross thought. Ross smiled. Ross beamed. 'So is my promotion into Royal and Specialist Protection or into Parliamentary and Diplomatic Protection, Sir?'

'Er, sorry to tell you this, Ross. Honest. But the truth is the Commissioner is pointing the finger directly at you for the press leak. You're lucky not to be suspended, so it's not exactly a promotion.'


## COPELAND MOVES


Copeland woke up feeling pretty good and put the radio on while his ancient toaster thought about turning bread browner. He felt like music and switched the radio to his favourite classic music station. As one of his all time favourites began he felt his feet start to shuffle.

Emerging from the bathroom, Freya feared the Dark Stars had tracked her down when she heard Copeland's cries. She rushed down the stairs before abruptly halting at the kitchen door. Why were Copeland's arms waving like snakes above his head? Why were his hips gyrating from side to side? Why was he shrieking something about a lion and a jungle? Why was he repeating the shriek with: 'In the jungle, the quiet jungle, the lion sleeps alright' and then going into a chorus of 'Runaway, runaway, runaway' unendingly?

'Oh, hi!' Copeland said cheerily when he saw Freya. 'This chorus is my motto.' He swayed again. 'Runaway, runaway, fancy some lovely honey on toast, John? It's all I've got! Ha, ha! Nice day for moving house, isn't it?'

Wide eyed, Freya nodded and left the kitchen quickly when OooooH! The Macarena! came on.

The boot and back seat were full but Copeland was still disturbed by how everything he possessed could be loaded into a Nissan Micra. The furniture and appliances left in the house were his, of course, but all that was staying and would still be there when he came back in a year's time when Department C finally moved out of the temporary offices near Slough and into the new ones in The Onion (being built near The Gherkin). The cost of the hotel he was staying in during the week was too much according to Wendy Miller, but Copeland didn't really mind leaving his little house in Leyton for a while. He was renting it out for double what he would be paying in rent in Slough and the Daffodil Lettings Agency were doing all the hard work so it was all just one more tick to add to his reasons to be cheerful list.

Copeland was glad of Freya's help and noticed how well the old pair of his mother's jeans fitted despite the physiological differences. In return for being allowed to 'crash out' (as she called it) on his parents' old bed, Freya had offered to travel with him and help him unpack the car at the other end.

A text from Director Wendy Miller disturbed what would have otherwise been a happy journey singing along to his Best of Blondie CD. Copeland held the steering wheel between his knees while he responded to the text and turned the music off.

'Got to take a folder back,' he said. 'On a Sunday… And jacket and tie in sweltering weather again.' He smiled. 'Oh, well! Worse things happen at sea!'

*Are you feeling alright, Copeland?* asked a concerned inner voice. *You're not your usual miserable self.*

Copeland was glad Freya was there to unload stuff into his new ground floor, one and a half bedroom flat. It gave him chance to shower and spruce himself up before taking back the file about the new not-really designer drug lab. Of course, he had already phoned Wendy Miller when he got back to tell her driving north of Hadrian's Wall had been a complete waste of time but, for some reason Copeland couldn't fathom, Director Miller still wanted a full report. And she wanted it typed.

*Typed? Good grief, Copeland! That'll be our whole week spent typing or another present for Janet for typing it for us!*

Wearing his usual dark blue suit and light blue shirt and with the now unusual dark blue tie, Copeland waited for the electronic gates to open and pulled into Ania Rose's drive. He parked the Nissan between a red Ferrari and an ancient black VW, picked up the black folder from the passenger seat and merrily crunched across the gravel drive to the front door. It opened as he approached the three stone steps. The maid stood in the open doorway, first looking him up and down with her arms folded across the white cotton pinafore of her short-sleeved, black satin dress, then holding out the sides of the dress and bowing her head as she gave her little curtsey. Without a word, she turned. He followed her through the door on the left into the sitting room.

Ania Rose did not stand when he entered. She remained on her white sofa reading a red file. She was wearing all-whites. She looked ready for tennis. Copeland wondered if her servants were going to put a net across the middle of the room for her to play in there but caught her steely green-eye gaze and the nod of her red-haired head and gathered he was to sit on the seat between the slate fireplace and man-size cactus again. He crossed the plush white rug and sat, perceiving the cactus looked somewhat less green than on his previous visit and suspected someone might have poured something into its soil that could harm it. The maid stood in front of him, relieved him of his black folder and curtsied again. Was it anger or sadness he saw in her doleful hazel eyes? Her petite frame and cinnamon hair had gone before he could decide.

Copeland waited. He hoped the maid had not gone to get that awful camomile and something tea or one of those disgusting muffins. He waited. He smiled at the top of Ania Rose's head. Unlike the last time he had visited, the sofa was a long way away, pushed back against the far wall under what looked remarkably like a Constable landscape. Copeland thought it looked... colourful. Much better than the one above the fireplace with the boats and swishy fog painted by someone name Turner.

Ania turned another page of the red file on her tennis skirt lap. Copeland cleared his throat and said, 'Ahem, I... Erm...' Ania Rose softly but distinctly said, 'Shhh.' Copeland waited. He looked right to where the twenty centimetre high bronze rose sculpture sat on the small, low table next to the other armchair. He looked left, around the cactus, to examine the empty half of the massive room, the snooker table wide conservatory the other side of the sliding French window, and the football pitch size lawn beyond the patio.

*You're not doing all those sports comparisons again are you, Copeland? You hate sport!* complained his inner voice. Copeland resisted the urge to argue, but could have reminded his annoying alter-ego how he had spent many happy hours watching Leyton Orient get promoted and reading golf magazines.

His shirt had begun to stick to his spine when Ania Rose forcefully closed the file. He stopped peering into the garden and looked at her. She looked serious. With the file in her hand she stood and walked across the wooden floor and over her deep-pile white rug towards him.

As Copeland watched Ania Rose approach in her tennis skirt and tight white vest top, the ever-observant inner voice noticed something. It said, *That's a short tennis skirt, Copeland!* Copeland wriggled to unstick his shirt from his back. Ania Rose stood in front of him. She looked tall. He smiled. She did not smile back. She handed him the folder, meaningfully gave him a single nod and returned to her sofa.

Copeland stared at Ania as he turned the cover of the file. He took his reading glasses from his top pocket. The first page was blank – except for his name. Lowering his eyes he scanned through the first dozen pages of his life. He had forgotten he had got a totally unfair grade E for physical education when he was twelve and thought there were many better wedding photos than the one on page ten. The cold facts presented on page thirteen triggered memories he had locked away for almost thirty years. He placed a hand to cover the page, stared at his knee and recalled the events that began one March evening in 1991…

Just before midnight Copeland returned home in a blood splattered suit. It was not his blood. Not mostly. Only the blood on his shoulder and shirt collar was his. He needed a drink.

The evening had turned noisy when the four surrounded Albanians refused to have either their suitcase of heroin confiscated or be arrested and had chosen to open fire with automatic weapons instead. Young Detective Constable Ross had been determined to be a hero and had got himself shot, leaving it up to a huffing Copeland to break cover and drag Ross back behind the car. An Albanian's bullet had merely grazed Copeland's scalp but all the same there had been a lot of blood. Once the suitcase of heroin was as full of police bullets as the Albanians, Copeland had gone with young Ross in the ambulance, then waited until Ross was out of emergency surgery, and eventually left for home once the doctor had told him Ross would be fine. The waiting around had given him time to rinse most of his blood from his hair and object to a doctor insisting on stitching his scalp.

Copeland closed his front door as quietly as he could. He *really* needed a drink, but climbed the stairs stealthily to peer through Emily's bedroom door. He wished he could sleep as soundly as his three year old. He sighed deeply and went back downstairs to get his much needed drink. He had just put the kettle on when Helen came into the kitchen, scanned his blood stained suit, scolded him for going upstairs with his shoes on (again) and thrust the divorce papers into his hands. Copeland read them while he drank his tea. Later, he stared motionless at the ceiling above the sofa for the rest of the night.

The court case for the custody of Emily was brief. At first he had been surprised Helen was demanding he had zero access to Emily. Helen's lawyer argued he was a danger to Emily because he associated with armed criminals and terrorists. Copeland knew it was true. He knew he had a choice. He chose his job, told his lawyer not to contest anything and walked out of the courtroom. The following day he volunteered for undercover work in Northern Ireland.

A month later Inspector Larry Copeland was Larry Campbell from Castle Douglas. The Dumfries accent was one he could master easily after spending several summers with his grandmother there, though he had never got round to asking her why she had moved to Scotland to open a flower shop. Not even drivers on their way to the ferry at Stranraer bothered to detour off the nearby A75 to visit Castle Douglas. It was safer for Copeland to pretend to be Scottish than an Ulsterman. Anyone from Belfast could not only tell which side of the 'divide' you belonged to but which street you were born in simply by listening to your accent, and it was easy to pretend to hate the Catholics and the English just as much as the Loyalists did if you were Scottish.

Extolling this even handed hatred in the pub near his cramped flat above the greengrocers soon got Larry 'Campbell' noticed. He had never heard of the CDB but according to its leader, Ronnie, it was the greatest loyalist paramilitary in Ulster and, since his job was to infiltrate the loyalist paramilitary, Copeland became an enthusiastic recruit. He soon discovered the CDB, or more fully the Crown Defence Brigade, met in a small disused warehouse and consisted of five members. He was the fifth. Besides Ronnie, there was Michael, Mike and Mickey. Once Copeland had passed the initiation ceremony, which consisted of holding aloft a gold painted cardboard crown and swearing eternal allegiance to the monarch as long as she (or he) remained protestant, he discovered the CDB had a wide sphere of control, stretching from the street outside all the way to the pub on the corner and halfway down the street beyond. Their main source of income was protection money from local shopkeepers: more specifically the greengrocer shop above which Copeland lived. For convenience, since he only had to go downstairs, Copeland was tasked with collecting the weekly protection money from Mr. Boyce the greengrocer. When Mr. Boyce had to raise Copeland's rent to cover the costs of the protection money Copeland accepted the increase understandingly.

The other main activities of the CDB consisted of collecting unemployment benefit and drinking in the pub on the corner. It was called The Crown so it fitted their political agenda quite nicely and since it was the usual watering-hole of the CDB it was, of course, exempt from being extorted for protection money.

The five members of the CDB were having their usual Friday night pint or five in The Crown and Copeland was considering moving on to join a more prominent loyalist paramilitary group when everything changed. Four balaclava masked men carrying baseball bats and knives burst into the pub, announced themselves as the UPF and threatened the barman come manager come owner, Fat Freddie, with all sorts of nasty things unless he started paying them a whole fifty pounds every month. The old adage of never taking a knife to a gunfight was proven true when Ronnie produced a revolver and pointed it at the four intruders. Moments later they had dropped their knives and assorted battering implements and were pleading for mercy on their knees. Ronnie took pity on them, mainly because Fat Freddie protested he did not want to clean guts and brains off his floor, and they were marched back to the CDB headquarters in the old warehouse.

The UPF members duly had their hands tied behind their backs while they tried to negotiate some sort of deal with Ronnie. They explained they were the famous UPF – the Ulster Protection Front; not to be confused with the Protectionist Front of Ulster, the Ulster Popular Front or even the Ulster Peoples Protection Front – and they controlled the streets down the other side of the block, including the lucrative newsagents. Leader Ronnie listened attentively and gave them a reasonable choice. They could renounce the UPF and join the CDB or die. Three of the members immediately volunteered to join the CDB and Gerald, Gerry and Gez were added to the CDB ranks. The UPF leader, Barry, remained defiant and stated he would rather die than join a two-bit bunch of gangsters like the CDB, which he had never even heard of. Ronnie spent a moment admiring the bravery of his counterpart then handed Copeland the revolver and told him to shoot their rival.

Stunned, Copeland looked at the revolver placed into his hand. Amid shouts of 'Go on Larry!' from Michael, Mike and Mickey, along with similar urgings from the new Gerald trio who seemed to have no love for their former boss, Copeland considered the options. The best one seemed to be to point the revolver at the assembled 'loyalists', back out of the warehouse and get the first flight back to London. Then Ronnie pulled a second pistol from the back of his belt and pointed it at Copeland. Copeland's options had changed.

This would not be the first person Copeland had killed. Well, probably not. He was pretty certain he had hit one of those Albanians directly in his heart. Or that might have been a police sniper and his shot may have hit the heroin suitcase. But, either way, this was not the same. Holding a revolver to the back of someone's head while they knelt with their hands tied behind them on the concrete floor in some shabby run-down warehouse was not the same as shooting at someone who was shooting at you. He reconsidered his options. Option one was to pull the trigger. Option two was to not pull the trigger. Option one would result in brains splattered over the floor and someone needing a mop. Option two would result in no need for any mop at all and Barry carrying on with his life. Except it wouldn't. It would result in Ronnie shooting Barry and Copeland being drummed out of the CDB for cowardice or, **much** more likely, Copeland being the next person to be on his knees with his hands tied behind his back. Barry would be dead anyway and Copeland would either be out of the paramilitary or out of future.

Copeland pulled the trigger.

*That wasn't a nice thing to do,* his long dormant conscience commented before Ronnie stared at the blood and splattered brains and promptly vomited. At the time, Copeland did not realise the significance of Ronnie's distaste for blood.

After that things changed. Besides Copeland not sleeping terribly well, the CBD now controlled four whole streets and they were soon visited by Libyans who offered a wide variety of pistols, rifles and plastic explosives. Unable to afford any of these things, the Libyans put them in touch with some friendly Columbians who had connections with Bulgarians who had connections with Russians who had connections with Afghans who grew poppies. Copeland was initially surprised how many people living on just four streets needed heroin, but remembered the deprivation they were living in, not to mention the constant intimidation from the CBD, and found it quite understandable they should spend what little money they had seeking some form of escape.

Armed with slightly rusty Russian AK-47 rifles the influence of the CBD grew. It absorbed other loyalist factions and even the UVF left them alone for a reasonable monthly fee. However, Ronnie had no understanding of quid quo pro. How could he? He did not speak Latin. And so it was that a prominent UVF leader ended up with his hands tied behind his back, kneeling on the floor in the middle of the old warehouse (which was still the CBD headquarters for sentimental reasons). Copeland was again chosen to do the honours and put a bullet in the back of the unknown man's head so that the glorious and righteous CBD defenders of Ulster could take over a few more streets, sell heroin to its needy inhabitants, buy more guns and take over a few more streets, etc., etc. Copeland sometimes had the nagging suspicion that Ronnie had lost his moral compass and was acquiring a modicum of personal wealth, just like most of the other paramilitary leaders on both sides of the sectarian divide.

Copeland was about to close his eyes and pull the trigger when Ronnie stopped him. Ronnie said he did not want the nice clean warehouse spoiled by blood and brains. Copeland wondered which bit of the warehouse Ronnie was referring to. He surmised the sight of blood and brains was what Ronnie really wanted to avoid. Instead of using the warehouse, Ronnie insisted the victim was taken out of the city and 'finished off' in some woods somewhere. He presented the keys of his spanking new Mercedes to Copeland and the un-named UVF man was bundled into the boot.

Copeland drove out of the city with young Mickey in the passenger seat. Copeland liked Mickey. He was almost completely uneducated. But he was far from dumb. As Copeland tried to come up with a plan to avoid murdering someone else in cold blood, Mickey had an idea. It was simple. They would find a phone box and call the police and demand a ransom for the captured UVF leader. They could pocket the money and Ronnie would never know.

Copeland saw several flaws with this plan. The Royal Ulster Constabulary was not known for its discretion and, secondly, news that a local UVF leader was back at the helm may not go unnoticed. Subsequently, the powerful UVF might become a bit aggrieved one of their own was kidnapped for territorial gain and seek some sort of revenge, which would probably involve killing everyone associated with the upstart CDB, including Mickey and Copeland. But Mickey's idea gave Copeland his own idea and he suggested they sell the UVF man to the British security forces instead. Mickey shrugged and agreed. He looked a little suspiciously at Copeland when they stopped at a phone box and Copeland phoned a number he seemed to have in his head, but Mickey's suspicions were short lived once Copeland told him the deal was done and MI5 had agreed to pay £500 pounds for the man in the boot of the Mercedes. Mickey clapped his hands with joy when Copeland explained that it was £500 **each**.

Mickey said nothing when Copeland fired his revolver into the air in the middle of a remote wood and four balaclava SAS men appeared from the shadows. Mickey was more interested in the large brown envelope they tossed to him before they carted the UVF man away. Copeland was disappointed his envelope contained a wad of cut-up newspaper.

It was the start of a beautiful relationship. With Ronnie determined to grab increasing amounts of territory, Copeland and Mickey's visits to the woods became increasingly frequent. Ronnie even gave Copeland an old Ford to transport the 'victims' into the woods to be executed, probably because he did not want the terrified victims odorous bodily fluids staining the boot of his Mercedes again. Copeland had no idea who most of the kidnapped men were, usually because their heads were covered with a sack, but he got the gist from whether their title had a 'U' or a 'R' in it – Ulsterman or Republican. The reach of the once insignificant CDB stretched further and further. Ronnie sometimes got annoyed the CDB was never named in the news and Copeland didn't have the heart to tell him it was because he was telling the security services to make sure the group was never mentioned so Ronnie was suitably motivated to capture an increasing number of rivals to his ever-growing extortion and drugs empire. To be fair to Ronnie, he had shown entrepreneurial flair and had branched out into gambling and prostitution after attending a swanky seminar in Miami organised by the Mafia.

Some people have questioned why Prime Minister John Major rarely used his country retreat at Chequers. The general consensus was he had to work 24/7 because he had so much trouble with members of his own Conservative Party trying to overthrow him. (No one knew about his 'friendship' with Edwina Curry at the time.) The dissident fringe of his Conservative Party believed Prime Minister Major was insane to believe being a member of the EU was a good thing. They thought Britain would be better off on its own, cut off from the rest of Europe. At the time he called them 'bastards', though everyone else at the time just called them nutters. But the real reason 'Honest John Major' rarely used his Chequers country retreat was because it was full of Irish paramilitary leaders. At least the nuclear bunker underneath Chequers was. Copeland and Mickey had been steadily filling it to breaking point and that breaking point eventually broke. Sanitation and sleeping arrangements were the catalysts for the discontent. The inmates of the nuclear bunker demanded use of the quarters reserved for the UK Cabinet – or more specifically those Cabinet members the Prime Minister deemed worthy of surviving the nuclear holocaust. (A significant reason why many Members of Parliament always suck up to any Prime Minister.) The desire for extra lavatories inspired the paramilitary inmates from both sides of the sectarian divide to do what they did best. They formed a committee. The committee persuaded the powers that be to open the HM Cabinet Members Only dormitories and washroom facilities. The new toilets flushed them with success. The Loyalists and

Republicans continued their joint committee and worked together with a new found common purpose, finding they had more that united them than divided them, such as cable TV and substantial amounts of weekly beer. And so it was that the embryo of The Good Friday Peace Agreement was born.

Sleeping in his flat above the greengrocer shop and apathetically visiting an increasing number of other establishments to collect protection insurance, Copeland knew nothing of the bonding occurring beneath Chequers. While Ronnie and others snatched paramilitary leaders off the streets, Copeland's main source of job fulfilment was being given the new trading estate as part of his weekly collection schedule. Most of the proprietors paid up promptly but one gave him excuse after excuse. At the end of his tether and fearful the young man would soon have his kneecaps blown off, Copeland tried to tell young Jeffrey his business idea would simply never work. No one had even heard of this new internet thing, so how could they buy things on it? And what sort of name for a company was Jeffrey thinking of when he called it Amazonian anyway? Young Jeffrey got the message and relocated back to the USA. Copeland sometimes wondered if Jeffrey had ever pursued his idea and had perhaps managed to make some sort of a living out of it.

Beer at The Crown continued with the original members of the CDB every Friday night. Ronnie sometimes opened his bulging wallet and bought the whole pub a beer, confident in the knowledge that for every beer he bought everyone would buy him at least two back or risk getting their home torched. Copeland's other diversion happened on Sundays. Lunch with Mickey, his wife and their three kids started as a rarity and soon became the norm. After receiving countless brown envelopes containing increasing numbers of twenty pound notes straight from the British security services, Mickey had a new car and new furniture and was taking his holidays in Greece. Copeland warned Mickey not to be so extravagant and maybe use the money he got from handing over terrorists in the woods to quietly pay off his mortgage rather than trying to keep up with the Jones's and then overtaking them. Mickey tried to reign himself in but his heart always got the better of him – and Copeland could not blame Mickey for wanting his wife and kids to enjoy life and have nice things and be happy amid the chaos that was Belfast.

After a pleasant Sunday afternoon laughing with Mickey and his family Copeland walked into the old CDB warehouse as usual on Monday morning to collect his list of collection addresses for the week. He was met by Ronnie and a metal bar. The metal bar was significantly harder than Copeland's skull.

When Copeland regained consciousness his wrists hurt. He looked up and saw why. They were inside two bench clamps. The clamps were attached to a chain. The chain was attached to a metal roof girder. Ronnie was quite innovative and had cobbled together a rather effective contraption to hoist Copeland by his wrists and dangle his feet several inches above the concrete floor. But to show he was not all bad, Ronnie had apparently taken all of Copeland's clothes to Oxfam. He had also taken all of Mickey's and found more G-clamps and chain to hoist Mickey off the ground alongside Copeland. Copeland gave the naked, shivering Mickey a sideways nod and smiled. His suspicion that someone, somewhere had screwed up was confirmed when Ronnie enquired why the wife of one of the IRA members they had supposedly disposed of in the woods had recently received a letter from her husband.

*Uh-oh, Copeland,* sighed an ever-alert inner voice.

At first Copeland found the torture not too painful at all. This was mainly because Ronnie started with Mickey. Phase one of the torture consisted of Ronnie administering a rather heavy handed pedicure with a pair of pliers. After two of his toe nails had been shaken free of the pliers, Mickey confessed to everything and, as a reward, he was lowered from the ceiling and, without further ado, shot in the back of the head.

Ronnie rushing out to vomit gave Copeland time to think. He had to come up with a new plan before Ronnie returned from regurgitating his breakfast. He needed a plan B. When poor Mickey had confessed and had been lowered down to be executed Copeland had devised plan A. He thought its simplicity bordered on sheer brilliance. He would confess as well and be promptly shot in the head, thus avoiding the unnecessary extraction of his toe nails. He had known the risks when he took the job and if a summary execution was what the Universe had planned for him then so be it. Why give the Universe the added pleasure of the toe nails pedicure thing first? The trouble was poor young Mickey had tried to bargain for his life at the last minute by telling Ronnie and his fellow henchmen that Copeland did not get paid by British security for delivering all those blokes in the head-sacks: he had seen what Larry had got in his brown envelope and it was just cut up bits of newspapers.

***Damn, Copeland! That means...*** had begun the inner voice, only to be cut short by a very loud bang and Mickey's naked body crumpling onto the concrete floor.

When Ronnie returned from putting his head down the toilet and wondering how bit of carrots had come up with his cornflakes Copeland still held out the vague hope that he could still stick to his original plan and admit he worked for Special Branch. But Ronnie wanted to know things Copeland was never going to divulge, such as who his contact was and what had happened to all those IRA, INLA, UVF, UDL (and so on) men he had taken into the woods. Copeland refused to tell Ronnie anything, mainly because he did not know any of the answers. He toyed with trying to explain his contact was 'some guy at the other end of the phone' but thought that might just slightly annoy Ronnie even more. Instead he tried to point out that since he served HM Government and worked for the Crown and the CDB believed in defending the Crown then surely they were on the same side? Ronnie confusing the Crown in Buckingham Palace with The Crown pub on the corner did not really help so Copeland gave up and accepted the situation stoically as Mike and Gerry held his legs while Ronnie got his pliers. On a scale of one to ten, Copeland expected a pain level of about eleven and was fully mentally prepared. The stoicism lasted for a full five seconds. The pain level from just his little toe was at least a twenty. Copeland tried to distract his mind from the pain by making up a new scale going up to a thousand.

His inner voice was its usual supportive self with comments like, *You're really hurting my ears with all this screaming, Copeland!*

At least his wrists and shoulders got some relief when the tenth toe nail was extracted and he was lowered to the ground so an equally heavy-handed manicure could be performed. He gained some respite when his thumb started to bleed profusely. Ronnie went pale and had to go outside for some fresh air. Copeland groaned and shivered in a ball on the cold concrete, but Mike thoughtfully kept him from getting bored by occasionally kicking him. He knew he was getting to the limits of his endurance. It had been hours of torture and, worse, he was desperate for a cigarette. But what could he do? Ronnie kept firing questions at him he did not know the answers to. His best bet was to stick to the truth and keep telling Ronnie he did not know in the hope Ronnie would get bored and do the on the knees and back of the head thing.

As he was being hoisted off the ground again Copeland remembered all he had to do was hold out for about forty eight hours. Once he did not check in at the usual time the SAS would storm the old warehouse. Had he told his MI5 contact about the warehouse being the HQ of the CDB? He was sure he had. Several times. They had even bugged the phone in the back office even though it was out of order.

*Oh, what! Cold water! They're just taking the piss now Copeland!* objected the ever-alert inner voice as Copeland's eyes shot open to see Ronnie with an empty bucket, looking somewhat displeased and saying something about what would happen to him if he did not tell them everything. As far as Copeland was concerned he quite clearly told them he did not know anything, but it may have sounded like a series of incoherent grunts to the assembled audience gathered around his dangling torso. It still had the desired effect. Ronnie announced they would let Larry ponder his predicament while they all went to the pub. Copeland thought telling him that was just spiteful when he hadn't had a pint all day.

Ronnie's creative ingenuity reached new heights the next day when he led in a troop of the CDB carrying car batteries. Besides telling Copeland he had used the money from Copeland's wallet to buy the batteries, Ronnie added insult to injury by connecting all the car batteries, sparking the leads together in front of Copeland and placing them on his skin. Ronnie had obviously spent the night planning this and started by placing the leads on each of Copeland's nipples. It may not have been quite so bad if the electricity was just coming through wires, but did Ronnie really have to secure the leads with those enormous crocodile clips? During a break when a dud battery had to be replaced, Copeland objected that it was inhumane for Ronnie to use clips with metal teeth on his nipples. Surprisingly, Ronnie agreed and found another part of Copeland's anatomy to attach the clips to.

*Any more complaints, Copeland?* asked the inner voice as Copeland's legs flayed about.

Eventually, Copeland achieved a moral victory when the charge in the batteries ran out and an exasperated Ronnie led his troop to the pub again. This time he left Mike to keep an eye on Copeland to make sure he did not get the luxury of sleep. Copeland usually needed two pillows and a nice snuggle down under his quilt so he thought he had little chance of sleeping while dangling naked from the roof. He told Mike this and said he need not put himself out on his account but Mike apologised and explained, just as every good SS man once had, he was only following orders. Unlike Ronnie, Mike was not squeamish and had a sharp knife. Copeland was glad Mike sterilised the knife by heating it to a glowing red before he placed it on Copeland's buttocks. When the gas in the blowtorch ran out Mike found a second use for his knife. Being at the most convenient height, Copeland's thigh lost a significant amount of skin before the sunlight appeared through the glass roof again and Copeland had enough sense left to realise a) the forty eight hours had passed and he was still dangling and b) there needed to be some sort of streamlining for paperwork at MI5.

On days three and four Copeland knew he was getting the upper hand. Ronnie had to give up on his pliers and batteries and resort to using a baseball bat. The scientific side of Copeland was truly amazed by how many bones could be broken in just one ankle. When Ronnie got worn out swinging the baseball bat, Copeland was further intrigued to discover just how many body parts could be placed in a bench vice. Thankfully, Copeland's nose was spared because Ronnie wanted Copeland's body to be easily recognisable as a warning to others who betrayed him.

Day five was even better. Ronnie got really annoyed by Copeland refusing to tell him where all the paramilitary leaders had been smuggled to and threatened Copeland with being left hanging there until he starved. Copeland knew this was a complete bluff. He knew he would never starve to death. He knew his organs would shut down through dehydration first. Or possibly hypothermia would win out if it got any colder.

*Good thinking, Copeland! A sudden frost in August and we'll be off to the Pearly Gates!*

Copeland knew his inner voice was a complete idiot and he would be off to somewhere far warmer where some chap with a pitchfork would make Ronnie seem quite nice. Copeland smiled to himself. This prompted Ronnie to smash his kneecaps with the baseball bat.

By day six Ronnie had done some research, worked out how to rig the light fittings and Mr. Sparky was back with his friend, Mr. Crocodile Clips. Copeland really missed the nice steady voltage from the batteries for a short while but he had developed the tendency to flip into unconsciousness quite frequently. Between bouts of oblivion Copeland had a thought. All he had to do was simply block the pain. Perhaps some self-hypnosis might work?

*Oh, yeah, that's bound to help, Copeland! Let's see how good THAT works the next time Mr. Sparky sends two hundred and forty volts through your dangly bits!*

Copeland had an hour or two finding out before the SAS arrived.

Lots of reconstructive surgery and lots of morphine later and Copeland was up and about trying to learn to walk again. His only visitor in hospital was recently promoted Detective

Sergeant Ross, who still seemed to appreciate Copeland dragging him from the line of fire of the Albanian heroin entrepreneurs, though while in his morphine haze Copeland sometimes had the feeling a small, frail, Miss Marple-like woman with her hair in a bun was standing beside his bed.

Eventually he returned to work, replaced the morphine with whisky and earned the reputation for tackling every sort of bad guy head on. Literally. His superiors warned him he would get himself killed if he carried on charging into hails of bullets, and where would his pending promotion to Chief Inspector be then?

When the Special Trade Attaché from the Russian Embassy, Vasily Goraya, spoiled Copeland's Thursday night pub visit and told him about the rogue Russian Mafia who were trying to take over a dockland area from the Official Russian Mafia, Copeland was sceptical and went alone to check out the dockland warehouse where the supposed rogue Russians were allegedly storing their cocaine.

Copeland hated this warehouse almost as much as the one in Belfast. Five Russians shooting at him while he hid behind a fork-lift truck was not his most enjoyable evening ever and he tried to make his point by sticking his pistol out and randomly firing back now and again. Back-up was on its way but Copeland knew all the bad guys had to do was outflank him and he would be toast. Copeland thought about this. He liked toast. He was just inventing whisky flavour marmalade when a bullet ricocheted near his head. The promised back-up would arrive in ten minutes but the Russians had realised they could outflank him and ten minutes might be a tad too late. (In those days a tad was about nine minutes.)

*Might be too late? MIGHT?* cut in the inner voice, which Copeland was beginning to regard as his more rational self – the one that did not drink a bottle of whisky every night or run headlong into bullets or wander alone into warehouses occupied by rogue Russians. Copeland poked his Browning around the front of the fork-lift and pulled the trigger. The Browning quietly said, 'Click.'

Oh shit, thought Copeland.

*Oh shit*, thought his rational self. Adding, ***You do have spare bullets, don't you, Copeland?***

Copeland shook his head and repeated his previous thought. He closed his eyes and waited. He heard a shot. He heard a scream. He heard a Russian curse. He waited some more. More screaming. As if someone had been hurt. He heard shouting. Frantic Russians were shooting but none of their shots were anywhere near him. He breathed a sigh of relief. Great! The armed response team had arrived nine minutes early. But why hadn't they done the usual, "Armed police! Lay down your weapons and come out with your hands up!" thing? Another shot rang out. That's a sniper rifle Copeland thought and opened his eyes as he heard more screaming in Russian. Copeland knew two things for certain. Firstly, there were four, or possibly five, or maybe six, Russians, and secondly there was a guardian angel in the warehouse. Fortunately, the guardian angel had brought a sniper rifle.

'Vasily Goraya!' Copeland said aloud as another shot rang out and there was more screaming in Russian. 'He's followed me and is picking off the rogue Russians. He's saved my life!'

***Yes, Copeland! Yes! He wants to make sure only government sanctioned Russian Mafia sell cocaine here!*** Copeland smiled. It was the first and probably the last time his 'better' self had agreed with him.

When the firearm squad arrived they found one cowering Russian and four writhing, wounded ones. There was a lot of back slapping, amazed looks and pain from his metal kneecap. There was soon the promise of a medal and that promotion. Neither materialised.

Two months later Copeland was suspended. Copeland had taken bribes from a member of the Russian security services, namely Captain Vasily Goraya of the Russian SVR. Now the Soviet Union had well and truly fallen, the SVR was the new Russian Federation's equivalent of MI6 and specialised in foreign interventions of every sort as long as they led to the Russian president making money. OK… Bribery charges… It was true. On their first meeting, Copeland had accepted a pint from Captain Goraya. But he had bought Goraya a pint of Guinness in return, and they had continued to employ this reciprocal beer purchasing system on the many nights they had gone out drinking together since. Bribery charges seemed somewhat extreme.

*I don't remember you getting twenty thousand pounds, Copeland!* remarked an inner voice during Copeland's first disciplinary hearing. *Was it when I was having a nap?*

For several weeks, Copeland wandered about in the little semi-detached his late parents once lived in. How could he have known they would both die while he was undercover in Northern Ireland? Throat cancer and sepsis from a simple scratch could have waited one more year surely? Visits to the local pub and trying to cheer on his beloved Leyton Orient failed to stave off Copeland's boredom. Meat pies and pizza helped. So did the red wine before the whisky.

Although Copeland's accuser and clever planter of a wad of notes in Copeland's desk was exposed as the real turncoat and Copeland was given a partial apology, his file still contained the words, 'Bribery allegation. Insufficient evidence.' Copeland did not get his promotion. Recently promoted Inspector Ross was almost crying when he squeezed

Copeland's shoulder and said, 'Sorry, Larry.' He was being promoted to Chief Inspector instead of Copeland.

'So,' said Ania Rose, 'did the self hypnosis work?'

'What?' said Copeland, startled and looking up from the red 'This Is Your Life' folder to see Ania Rose sitting cross legged on the floor, inches from his feet, right in front of him. On the wall beyond her, the colours of the Constable painting seemed less vivid. His remembrances had sucked every drop of his previous happy mood out of him.

*Good! You're back to your normal self again, Copeland!*

Staring up at him intently, Ania said, 'The details of what happened to you in that warehouse are sketchy, but you told people you resisted the torture by using self hypnosis. I'm very interested in self control, the mind controlling the body – all that sort of thing. So what I want to know is… Did the self-hypnosis work?'

Copeland half laughed. 'To be honest, Miss Rose, I never really got much chance to…' He trailed off. He shuddered. 'Can we talk about something else, please? Such as how you got this information?'

Ania Rose nodded and completely ignored the question. 'I hear you got lots of compensation for your injuries and more to stop any sort of litigation against the security services for not responding earlier when you didn't check in. Several hundred thousand pounds, wasn't it, Inspector?'

'I'd rather not talk about that either, thanks. Confidentiality agreements and all that,' Copeland said, folding his arms and pretending not to notice he had dropped the folder on the floor.

Ania Rose pretended not to notice either. 'Mickey's family…' she began. 'I heard they moved to Scotland. To Castle Douglas, in fact. Wasn't that where your Grandmother moved to when you were a child? I hear Mickey's wife somehow got enough money to buy a rather nice house and open a florist shop there too.'

Copeland shrugged. 'The town needed a new florist and there's a nice park for the kids to play in. It has a great fish and chip shop too. Anything else, Miss Rose?'

Ania nodded knowingly. Copeland ignored the usual twinge in his knee and stood. Ania shot up in front of him, raised a finger to hold him in place and said, 'Please sit. Let's talk about the unfortunate failure to find evidence of illegal drug production at Miss Starr's reprehensible science compound, Larry.'

*Er, Copeland, how does she know..? Director Miller told her? And when did it become Larry?*

Copeland sat down again, having now guessed how Ania Rose had obtained his confidential information: the link between Ania Rose and Wendy Miller was clearly more than Director Miller had led him to believe. He sighed. 'The thing is, Miss Rose, I think they must be making them at her stately home. I suppose all I can do now is…'

With a finger raised to stop him, Ania cried, 'Wait!' which was exactly the word Copeland was about to say. Ania clasped her hands together and turned round, deep in thought.

*Er, Copeland… That really is a short tennis skirt!*

She turned back again. 'You're right, Inspector. I suppose there's nothing else for it. Again, you show exemplary bravery! I'll tell Wendy how impressed I am that you've volunteered to infiltrate Keira Starr's stately home estate.'

*Oh, bugger!* said and inner voice, sensing Copeland was lost for words.

'Listen, Larry,' said Ania, squatting down in front of him and looking up into his eyes. 'Some of us know you are some sort of extraordinary genius. Either that or Lady Luck always rolls the dice in your favour.'

*It's not the genius one, is it Copeland?*

'I suppose I'm lucky,' admitted Copeland.

Placing her hands on his knees Ania said, 'You're so modest, Larry. I do so want to help you get Keira Starr under lock and key, along with all her misguided followers, but climbing up a drainpipe, silently subduing her guards, cracking open her safe and paragliding away with the evidence to arrest her isn't an option.'

*I think she's confusing you with James Bond, Copeland*, sniggered an inner voice.

Gripping Copeland's knees, looking concerned, Ania continued, 'No matter how brave you are, infiltrating Keira Starr's Longbeck estate would be suicide. I've already lost two of my... my informants who tried. One was brainwashed into joining Keira Starr's Dark Star army and the second lost his mind when she had him... interrogated.'

*I think we should give visiting there a miss then, Copeland. Don't you?*

Copeland found himself nodding.

'Wait!' exclaimed Ania Rose excitedly as her hands moved to squeeze Copeland's thighs. 'I know someone who might be able to help, Inspector. She might have the information you need to arrest Keira Starr, but...' She suddenly stood, wrung her hands and winced. 'No, I couldn't,' she said, with a shake of her long red hair. 'It would put her in danger...'

Copeland felt deflated. For a fleeting moment he thought he was gaining a new way to get evidence on Keira Starr, without the unnecessary risk of sneaking into her home, but that moment had just as quickly dissolved. 'Miss Rose,' he pleaded, 'you have to let me talk to this person if she knows something that could lead to us breaking up this drugs gang.'

Ania Rose looked at him, turned and paced across her plush white rug a few times, wringing hands and shaking long red hair as if torn between two choices. She stopped at the far side of the fireplace, turned to Copeland with a pained look and said, 'I would need your promise of full immunity if I arrange for her to speak to you.'

Copeland nodded, 'As long as she hasn't committed any murders, I promise her immunity.'

*Are you sure you can do that, Copeland?*

'I presume,' continued Copeland, 'this poor woman used to be a member of the Dark Stars and is fearful for her life.'

'Oh, no…' said Ania with a frown. 'She's Keira Starr's younger sister – well, half sister to be precise. If anyone can tell you where you can find evidence to arrest Keira Starr, then Louise can. She and I go back a long way, but I'll still have to persuade her to talk to you. Give me a few days.'

'Er, okay,' nodded Copeland.

Now standing in front of him, Ania said, 'Good. I'll be in touch if Louise agrees. Now, could you do me a favour in return?'

*Tread carefully, Copeland. This sounds suspicious.*

'Er, it depends,' said Copeland.

'Would you come to my dinner party on Saturday evening, Larry?' asked Ania. 'There'll be about twelve of us.'

'It's kind of you to ask,' replied Copeland, 'but I'm not a very social sort of person.'

*That's a great British understatement if I ever heard one, Copeland.*

'It's not social,' Ania informed him, leaning forward, placing her hands above his knees, bringing her face close to his and whispering. 'I need you here to arrest someone. You'll get a full confession on tape before the night is out, Larry.'

*I think she's one of those touchy-feely people, Copeland.*

'Well…' said Copeland looking into Ania's eyes a hand width from his and forcing his spine back into the chair.

Ania quietly said, 'I understand you get bonuses. When someone is arrested don't you get ten percent of their confiscated assets?'

'It's five percent now. The new office block is over budget,' Copeland explained as calmly as he could. 'And once our recruits pass their probationary period it gets shared out. And there are checks and balances. Three judges have to agree there's enough evidence for the arrest. A taped confession should do that. You're really very close to me, Miss Rose.'

Ania smiled. 'This person has UK assets of over thirty million and may well have over fifty million on his person.'

***Er, Copeland, we'd get five percent…We'd be rich!***

Copeland considered. Looking straight into Ania Rose's rather nearby eyes he said, 'Money doesn't interest me Miss Rose. But will there be a cheeseboard?'

Ania smiled her enigmatic Julia Roberts smile, stood upright and clapped her hands. 'That's settled then!' she beamed. 'We'll have a room ready for you to stay over. Now, if you'll excuse me, I have tennis practice arranged with Simon so I have some chance of beating Alice one day.'

Still somewhat confused about whether or not there would be a cheeseboard, Copeland mumbled, 'Alice?'

Ania smiled. 'Yes, Alice. The young lady who let you in.'

'The maid?' asked Copeland, raising his head.

Ania Rose frowned. 'What makes you think she's a maid?'

'Er, possibly the maid's uniform?' said Copeland, craning his neck to look up at Ania.

Repressing laughter, Ania said, 'You amuse me, Larry. You simply *must* call me Ania from now on.'

Sounds reasonable, thought Copeland. He said, 'Okay, I'll call you Ania.'

*Copeland… you need to be careful here…*

Ania headed for the French windows as she called, 'Time for tennis. See yourself out, Larry!'

Copeland watched her leave. He had to admit his inner voice was right. It was a short tennis skirt.


## DEAL OR NO DEAL (PART TWO).

Mr. Grey had the larger size, super-seal plastic freezer bag ready and waiting but was confused. He would have been flummoxed but he had never been taught that word. How could he use the 'one time passcode' the bank were about to text him when he was already using his phone to do his online banking transaction to The Broker so Larry Copeland could be terminated by a hit man? Or hit woman – Mr. Grey was not particular about who actually killed Copeland as long as they killed him.

A few metres away, Mr. Pink was pleased with himself. 'Best pointy star thing Valdis done everest!' he exclaimed, happily pointing at the latest victim's forehead.

'No names, Mr. Pink,' reminded Mr. Grey, who had himself once been known as Vasily Goraya of the Russian SVR. 'It's safer that way in case we ever get caught.'

Mr. Pink thought about this while red droplets dripped from the tip of his knife. 'So…you mean… Mr. Pink should forget his name is Valdis? Wow! That super clever, Mr. Grey. If I arrested they not know who I am!'

Mr. Grey looked at him. 'Quite so,' he said and went back to looking at his phone. Mr. Grey had acquired a recent new respect for Mr. Pink. The latest victim was a rather large gentleman and Mr. Pink had dragged him all the way from the hall without Mr. Grey having to do anything except watch him struggle.

Mr. Grey tried swiping the image on his phone, fearing it would disconnect him from his bank details and he would have to go through the tedious process of remembering his log-in details again. There indeed was the OTP text message, along with a text from The Broker. Mr. Grey was glad he had not transferred the money. There was a 10% off special offer for contract killings where the method of death was not specified in advance. Unaware he could have specified the method of demise the traitorous turncoat back-stabbing Larry Copeland should receive, Mr. Grey texted to accept the offer and waited for his new bill to arrive.

Mr. Pink interrupted his important waiting with, 'Might need bigger knife for this one,' and Mr. Grey looked up to see Mr. Pink had made his usual neat incision, but the victim's natural blubber was proving thicker than the blade length, which was considerable. Mr. Grey nodded his agreement, suggested, 'Try the kitchen, Mr. Pink,' and went back to his vital business while the vitals of the oversize victim were sorted by Mr. Pink.

Indeed, Mr. Pink soon proved most resourceful and returned from the kitchen with an assortment of long knives which he tested methodically on the thick upper abdomen of Mr. Blobby and Mr. Grey was free to scowl at his phone when the conditions for the 10% offer appeared. Besides requiring the home address of the potential prey for the soon to be hired hit-man, the offer also required a photograph, the completion of a questionnaire about why he had chosen 'The Broker' and a promise he would complete a customer satisfaction survey once the job was done. Mr. Grey could not accept such terms. He did not have a photo of Copeland.

'Ta-ta!' announced Mr. Pink holding up his latest trophy. Mr. Grey tossed the sealable bag in his general direction and went back to where he started, logged on, and tried to remember which primary school he had put down as his extra security question. He plumped for the one he had been assigned to in Moscow when he was seven, after he had impressed the KGB by showing such early promise with his playground extortion racket of the nursery kids.


## KEIRA AND KONRAD DISCUSS COPELAND.

Keira Starr did not like to be disturbed when she was thinking. She knew some of her Dark Star followers regarded it as brooding when she sat on her high-backed black throne on the raised dais in the room lit only by flickering candlelight. She had given orders to the guards stationed at the door to let no one interrupt her, with the exception of Konrad. He was her strong right arm. He had been at her side since before she had decided to found the Dark Stars and change the world by taking over organised crime in one town after another. Konrad could have been Thor's stunt double and his forty-something appearance added an appearance of maturity to the leadership team. He rounded the large table, sank to one knee and bowed his head before the feet of Keira Starr.

Still resting her elbows on her knees and her chin on her fists she said, 'What is it Konrad, my loyal Viking?'

Konrad smiled to himself. He liked it when His Lady called him a Viking. It made him think about growing his blonde beard longer again. He looked up into Keira's sultry dark eyes and said, 'The Grimsby strike squad is ready, My Lady, and the gangs of Derby have asked for peace on our terms. Other strike squads have met with initial successes in the Lancashire towns in readiness for your takeover of Manchester. Tonight's initiation ceremony for recruits to demonstrate their loyalty to you and convert to Dark Stars is fully prepared and Kurt has assembled a new squad ready to raid Ania's home as soon as we discover its location. However, your governor of Leeds has requested more Dark Stars to quell some local problems.'

'Send them,' said Keira with a flick of her hand. 'This place is overflowing and we have more recruits every week. We can spare fifty. In fact, send a hundred once we have plucked the Grimsby thorn from our side. But tell my loyal Governor of Leeds we want fifty back next month for our push into Manchester. But why are you bringing this to me, Konrad? You usually confer with the head of human resources – that strapping ginger woman who looks like she's descended from Viking stock herself.'

'Kirsty, My Lady,' said Konrad. 'And I have discussed it with her, My Lady, but…'

Keira sat up. She tapped her thigh with one hand while her other twiddled with the pentagram pendant dangling from her neck. Konrad knew it was not a good sign and he should get to his real concern sooner rather than later. He gave a little cough, and said, 'May I stand, My Lady?'

'Is my stone floor hurting your knee, Konrad?' asked Keira. No answer came. She gripped her pendant and said, 'Dark Stars should be able to endure anything to show their loyalty to our cause. You above all know that. The guards would think me soft if I let you stand in my presence. Your impertinence requires recompense, Konrad.'

Konrad bowed his head again. 'Yes, Lady Keira. I will self-flagellate later to remind my body it feels no pain.'

'Self-flagellate? There's really no need for self-flagellation, Konrad. Get the stout ginger Kirsty woman to do it for you. I hear many of the mares she rides have tasted her whip, so she should be good at it. In fact, put her in charge of staff discipline. Now get to your point.'

'Yes, My Lady. I was thinking about Copeland, My Lady. We know he works for this new branch of MI5 called Department C, and it is privately financed by rich sponsors and seems to have Ania Rose as one of its main sponsors…'

Keira was on her feet. Her dark eyes narrowed. 'You think Copeland is another of Ania's spies?'

'Well, possibly. I think Copeland may not be knowingly working for Ania Rose, but as a member of Department C and however indirectly a member of MI5… Perhaps we should speak alone, My Lady?'

Keira Starr clapped her hands. 'Guards! Leave us!' she commanded. The guards hurriedly left. Keira Starr stared down at the kneeling Konrad and whispered, 'You can get up now, Konrad. The guards are gone and the door is closed.'

Standing, Konrad said, 'Copeland might have useful information, Kee… I was thinking kidnap and torture.'

Keira stepped down from her dais and approached Konrad. 'You're right, Konrad. Copeland could be useful…Hmm… This requires subtlety. I may have another plan that doesn't involve kidnapping,' she whispered as she slipped her arms around Konrad's waist.

Placing his arms around her shoulders and, with his face bent close to hers, Konrad smiled and whispered, 'So am I forgiven? Do I still have to report to Kirsty and her whip?'

Keira smiled back. Her lips got closer to his as she huskily whispered, 'I can think of an alternative punishment, though you may not regard it as a punishment at all, my strong Viking.'

Copeland picked up the file from his feet and flicked through the last few pages of his life. His retirement from SO15 was noted, as was his minor stroke, along with details of the two cases he had worked on since joining Department C a few months before, but at least his time working for the super secret Pickfords was only referred to as a sabbatical so he knew Wendy Miller had stopped short of divulging information that might get her removed from her post, or worse. The vigilant Pickfords were very determined to keep their very existence unknown. Copeland was sure Wendy Miller had divulged the other information in the file to Ania Rose but the question was why would she do that?

*Duh!* remarked his inner voice. *How is Department C funded, Copeland? Who's got oodles of money, Copeland? Here's a clue... Look at the paintings in this room!*

As much as Copeland hated to admit it, there was the possibility that a ridiculously wealthy person like Ania Rose might be one of the private sponsors of Department C – a concept which the Home Office had thought a splendid idea to save taxpayers money. Copeland was under the impression it was a purely financial arrangement where Department C would use money confiscated from criminals to pay back the loans from the sponsors, not be in the sponsors pockets. Pondering, Copeland left the file with almost every detail of his life on the chair next to the pale looking cactus. He got to the front door to show himself out but stopped to ponder some more. Copeland continued to ponder until he was sure he knew what he had to do, and that was to do what any sane man over sixty would do and use the bathroom before he left.

Relieved he had made the right choice Copeland emerged from the bathroom at the top of the stairs and looked to his right. Two closed doors were a few paces away, before the corridor-come-landing continued round to the foot of the stairs leading up to the top floor. To his left the corridor resembled any hotel corridor, passing three doors on each side as the red carpet stretched away into the swimming pool length distance.

*Please, Copeland… Don't start the bloody sporting comparisons again*, pleaded the inner voice.

Copeland resisted the urge to snoop and look in the rooms, mainly because it would have meant a longer walk than he felt like. These stairs are exercise enough in this heat, he thought as he descended back to the hall. As one hand reached for the front door his other went into his jacket pocket for his car keys. It came out again with a ChewiVit. He had forgotten he had dropped them into his pocket when he had got back from Butterburn. The vitamin pill had fluff on it, but with a bit of flicking it was soon alright and Copeland popped it into his mouth. As an excuse, he told himself it was more like a honey flavoured sweet than a health pill. Chewing happily, he reached for the front door again.

*Copeland! Did you hear that?*

No, thought Copeland. Then he thought: Damn – I did hear it that time, and I know cries of pain when I hear them!

He knew he had to investigate. Instead of opening the front door to leave he turned to his left and opened the door facing the sitting room door. Stunned by what he saw, he walked through the door.

The room was as big as his old primary school hall. (*I was worried you were going to use a bigger than a badminton court comparison for a moment there, Copeland.*) Copeland stared, dumbstruck, at the torture chamber. It was full of diabolical contraptions. He had heard about such places. He had even heard that masochists paid good money to subject themselves to the fiendish contrivances he could see in front of him and, even worse, to pay money to others to subject them to sessions of personal torment. For there, beyond the square of blue rubber matting, were exercise bikes, treadmills, and, horror of horrors, a weights machine. He had heard such places were known as 'gyms'. Director Wendy Miller, in one of her more sadistic moods, had insisted all members of Department C should join one. Copeland had complied, found a local gym, signed the enrolment forms and dutifully shown Wendy Miller his membership card. He was glad she had never said he had to go there ever again and, strangely enough, he had decided never to set foot in the place. It was a good decision if the shrieks of torment coming from the man lying on his back on the bench and trying to bench-press the weights bar above his chest were anything to go by. An Amazonian woman with muscles on her muscles was standing over him shouting, 'Push! C'mon fella! No pain, no gain! Push, you pathetic feckin' toe-rag!' Copeland's keen hearing detected an Irish accent – not the usual lilting sort, but the sort adopted by aggressive, bitter spinsters wielding brollies at buses, though the woman in question looked a very young spinster. Copeland crossed the mat to approach her and her victim as the poor horizontal soul tried again to raise the bar until his arms were fully extended. The two could not have appeared more different: his legs were white matchsticks emerging from his short red shorts, hers were bronzed tree trunks emerging from hers; he was skin and bone, she had an eight pack below her very full red bustier; she had frizzy, dark, ponytail hair swept back from her severe face, he hardly had any hair.

*Oh, NO!* cried Copeland's inner voice. ***It's HIM again!***

Copeland stood next to the woman, who had given him no more than a glance and his stomach no more than a long stare as she continued to shout, 'Come on! That's eighteen! Jest two more now, Tom. No pain, no gain!'

Copeland looked down at the prone, sweating, struggling Tom Benson and said, 'Isn't he supposed to have weights attached to that bar?'

'We're feckin' buildin' up to 'em. Nineteen! One more, you weedy little shite, Tom!'

'Are you two friends?' asked Copeland as the last of the ChewiVit slid down his throat and he rummaged in his pocket to pop in another. The muscle-woman glared at him. Tom Benson managed his twentieth bench press and panted with the steel bar resting on his bony chest.

'I'm Larry,' said Copeland, turning to extend his hand to the keep-fit slave-driver. He felt his fingers overlap as she squeezed his hand and said, 'I'm Lucy. I'm a personal trainer. I'm twenty eight next week and I can bench press a hundred kilos 'til the cows come home.'

'Nice to meet you,' said Copeland. 'Happy birthday for next week.'

'This thing's crushing me! Help!' implored Tom Benson. Lucy raised her thick eyebrows and lifted the bar off his chest with one finger.

Sweaty Tom Benson sat up and peered through misted spectacles. 'Larry?' he panted. 'It is! Larry Copeland! What are you doing here? Or should I say, well met, well met, Antipholus!'

Copeland shook his head. 'Still quoting the old Bard, eh, Tom? I've just delivered something to Ania,' he said. 'But, besides lifting a metal rod, what are *you* doing here?'

'You've met Lucy?' Tom beamed. 'She's wonderful. I think she's the most beautiful woman ever. She's my barbarian princess!' Lucy blushed. Copeland rolled his eyes. He knew Tom thought any woman who actually bothered to speak to him fell into the category of 'the most beautiful woman ever', including the woman on the checkout at Tesco and traffic wardens. As far as Copeland was concerned, Tom Benson's relationship with Beth Spencer had either been a statistical anomaly or Beth had an undiagnosed vision defect.

Now Tom Benson had sat up and the thick lenses in his plastic frame glasses had begun to clear, and now Lucy was no longer barking at him but wiping his bony shoulders with a towel, Copeland detected something between them. He ventured to ask, 'Are you two..?'

Lucy's laugh almost deafened Copeland.

'That reminds me,' said Tom, taking the towel from Lucy and wiping his sweat from his shiny dome, 'Erica wanted to thank you for clearing her name so she got her modelling contract. I was seeing her quite often.'

Copeland was trying to keep up. 'You and Erica? Erica, the model? Ex pole-dancer, Erica? **You** and Erica?'

'She's a client. Well, her modelling agency is. With Rose Public Relations and Management,' said Tom. 'It's Ania's company. I'm in the publicity department now. It's one of the perks for agreeing to be one of the company's contestants.' Tom wiped his face and stood to his full five foot two inches, took Copeland's hand with his little sweaty one and warmly shook it, saying, 'Good to see you again, Larry.'

'A contestant?' said Copeland.

'A sort of inter-company thing. Rose PR against other companies. Ania chose me. That's why I'm training. For the contest against them. I do mornings with Lucy doing the body building stuff, afternoons with Alice doing yoga and meditation and office work in the evenings. I've escaped that overcrowded house. I'm living here now. Ania has found my friend Jesus – I mean Brian – somewhere better to live too. You met him. The guy who thinks he's Jesus. No harm in it really. Him moving to somewhere nicer was one of the extras Ania offered if I agreed to be her company's contestant.'

Copeland sought clarification. '*You've* been chosen to be in a contest? You? Against other companies? What is it? Paintballing or something?'

'The little fella'd be bang on for that,' laughed Lucy. 'When he turns sideways he's as thin as a sheet of paper. They'd never hit him!'

Tom Benson smiled at her as friends do when they tease each other. 'Maybe it is paintballing,' said Tom. 'We don't know yet, but I think I've been chosen for my quick thinking.' He winked knowingly at Copeland. Copeland looked at Lucy. She shrugged her muscly shoulders and said, 'C'mon, Tom, time for our sauna and cold spa before your massage.'

Copeland winced. 'Sauna? Cold spa? Massage?'

Tom Benson pointed with a thumb over his shoulder. 'Down the other end. They're through those doors. The other one on the left goes down to the basement. Hey, Larry, you'd love the wine collection down there!'

Copeland nodded. He murmured, 'Basement.' He cried, 'The basement! She said the grubs were in the basement! I've got to go! Bye!'

Copeland knew he needed to talk to Director Miller. He turned and rushed towards the door.

***Steady on, Copeland! You almost broke into a jog there.***

Alice was waiting outside, still looking very much like a maid in a uniform and pacing the gravel between the front door and Copeland's car. She turned to him with a look of concern in her big hazel eyes. She curtsied, stood and, with hands nervously clasped, said, 'I'm glad you made it back alright from Butterburn, Sir.'

'Er, thanks, Alice,' said Copeland, 'but I really must…'

Alice stood between him and his little car. 'I shouldn't be telling you this but…But you thanked me for the tray of tea and muffin, Sir. No one ever thanks me. So I wanted to tell you Miss Rose has sent four people north to spy on Keira Starr and the Dark Stars – two to where you went and two to her Longbeck home. None of them came back. Harry used a drone to get the information in the Butterburn file you had. I'm glad you're back alright, Sir, especially after all the pain, agony and suffering you've been through already. I've just read your file.'

Copeland did not want to be reminded of his time in Ireland again so brushed the comment aside with, 'What's a few days being tortured and months of excruciating operations, eh, Alice? Now, I need to…'

'I meant not seeing your daughter since she was three, Sir,' Alice said. 'I wasn't much older when I was separated from my parents twenty years ago, Sir.'

As much as Copeland would have loved pointlessly comparing family stories he needed to get off to see Director Miller, but he had to say: 'Ania implied you're not just a maid, Alice.'

Alice looked down at her shiny black shoes. She flicked an errant strand of her cinnamon hair from her forehead. In a quiet voice she said, 'I'm just a maid, Sir, though I'm quite good at tennis… and croquet.'

'Right, whatever,' shrugged Copeland. 'I really have to go now. Thanks for your concern, Alice, but I've heard my daughter is doing okay. She's a sculptress.' He held out a hand to shake with Alice. She looked at it and stepped back. Still with her head down, she did her curtsey and whispered, 'I don't do touching, Sir. They call it haphephobia, Sir.'

'Jolly good name,' said Copeland. 'Er, you can get up from your curtsey again now.'

Alice lifted her face and stared up at him. Without expression she whispered, 'Stay away from Keira Starr, Sir. She's evil incarnate,' and stood and walked briskly back into the house.

*A very pretty but very strange young lady, that one Copeland*, commented an inner voice and Copeland found himself nodding.


## MR. GREY: DEAL OR NO DEAL (PART THREE).

Mr. Grey got the impression Mr. Pink was not happy. Doing three murders in one day so Mr. Grey could get extra cash for the hit-man contract on Larry Copeland was taking its toll on Mr. Pink. Mr. Pink was clearly stressed, which was hardly surprising: the London traffic had been horrendous. Mr. Pink was so stressed his pentagram artwork was starting to fall below its usual high standards. Quite unsymmetrical, in fact. But at least Mr. Pink had learned how to open the airtight bag with one hand and then seal it with his teeth. This allowed Mr. Grey to get on with replying to the constant stream of emails from The Broker. The first one had started with the words 'Reason for killing of (type name here)' and Mr. Grey had thought The Broker perhaps needed his software updated, especially when the third question was, 'How long have you wanted to kill this man/ woman who jilted you?' (The second question was a fairly standard one: How did you hear about our people termination service? Was it: A. Word of mouth, B. TV advertising, C...) What really upset Mr. Grey most was he was being charged an extra 50% because, no matter how poor The Broker's algorithmic AI questioning was, it seemed to have been good enough to do some internet searching and find Larry Copeland was some sort of minor secret agent for HM

Government and, as such, had an extra levy placed on any contract to kill him. Mr. Grey thought this was nonsense. Anyone who was not a computer knew Department C was not a **proper** part of the security services, just an understaffed bunch of mostly naïve newbies funded by **private** do-gooding sponsors. Still, what could Mr. Grey do? Since he wanted Larry Copeland dead for his treachery **like yesterday**, all he could do was accept the 50% extra increase plus the extra commission for The Broker and choose to go down-market with his choice of hit man. His ten thousand pounds now bought him a professional killer in the 'will probably succeed' category. Unlike many punters, Mr. Grey was thorough and scoured The Broker's dark web website to find the word 'probably' was defined as over 50% likely. It was better than the three categories below it. Mr. Grey felt so relieved when he finally accepted the terms and conditions and transferred the money he even took the Russian hating Latvian idiot, Mr. Pink, to a pub for a pint of Guinness.


## COPELAND VISITS WENDY MILLER.

Director Wendy Miller leaned forward with elbows on her desk, locked her fingers together and rested her chin on top of them. 'Let me get this straight, Larry,' she said with an uncertain tilt of her head. 'You wanted us to meet at the office in person, on Sunday, at lunchtime, when the pubs are open, because you think they might have planted some sort of listening device in your phone when you went up to that research place near Butterburn and handed it over?'

Copeland gave a single, uncharacteristically enthusiastic, emphatic nod.

'And you think Dr. Spencer was trying to tell you something when she saw you off?'

Copeland grinned and gave a single, emphatic nod.

'Because she told you they were breeding grubs in vats in the basement to make them into burgers and other sorts of whatnot and when she gave you the tour she didn't take you into any basement to see the grubs you later ate in a pie?'

Copeland gave a single, less emphatic nod.

'And you think they'd disguised the labs' elevators behind storage stuff and this new Dark Star drugs gang might be making their designer drugs in the basement, presumably next to the vats of grubs, and the whole thing is bankrolled by Keira Starr who owns some magazines.'

Wide-eyed, Copeland gave two very emphatic nods.

'And there was a pentagram symbol above the entrance to the living quarters and on the sweater they gave you, and it's also the symbol for this Dark Star gang according to your informant who goes by the name of John, so you think this Keira Starr and her Dark Stars are also behind the pentagram murders? That they're killing off people who left the Dark Stars? So you… you! … actually **want** to take on **more** work and look into the pentagram murders as well?'

Copeland was not sure how many emphatic nods that required so he played safe and did several.

'And you also believe these new designer drugs are being transported to Keira Starr's stately home estate in secret when they pretend to be only transporting innocent vitamin tablets called ChewiVits. Is that what you're eating now?'

Copeland nodded less emphatically.

'And Ania is arranging for you to meet with Keira Starr's half-sister, Louise, who may well be able to give you enough dirt on Keira Starr to get a conviction?'

Copeland did not nod emphatically. He was trying to get a bit of ChewiVit out from between his teeth.

'Well, Larry, I'm pleased to tell you, the pentagram murders case is all yours. The police have given up on it and passed the buck to us anyway. I think The Commissioner wants to show the Home Office we're not up to the job. So if you don't get a conviction we'll need a sacrificial lamb. You know how it is. And you can guess who the sacrificial lamb will be.'

Copeland nodded very un-emphatically.

'I'm glad we're clear, Larry,' said Wendy Miller. 'Now, I do have one question.'

Copeland nodded uncertainly.

Director Miller's eyes narrowed. 'Why has Ania Rose invited you to her dinner party and not me?'

Copeland had no answer to this, other than telling Wendy Miller that Ania Rose thought he was a genius, but that would only lead to both Wendy Miller and his inner voice laughing for the next hour. Fortunately, his phone pinged. He took it out of his pocket and looked at its case. There was a ChewiVit stuck to it. He pulled it off and popped it in his mouth, flicked the phone case open and looked at the text message. He passed the phone across the desk to his boss. She read it. She rested back in her chair and read it again.

'It looks like you were right about your phone being tampered with. How else would Keira Starr know the number of an MI5 registered phone?'

The inner voice had a theory: *It could be because you swapped numbers with Beth Spencer and Keira Starr asked her for it. What do you think, Copeland?*

Copeland said, 'They must have bugged my phone. I can't think how else she would have the number. Honest.' His eyes grew wide. 'But this is brilliant, Boss! Keira Starr is personally inviting me up to her stately home! We can't look a gift horse in the mouth. It's a chance to find out if the drugs are being transported there or made there, and possibly find a link between her and the pentagram murders.' He was on the edge of his seat. 'What better way to find the truth than to infiltrate a crime baron's stately home full of armed guards!' Copeland's fist punched the air. 'Yes!'

Wendy Miller slowly handed the phone back and said, 'Have you had a blow to the head, Larry?'

'No, I feel great, boss,' grinned Copeland. 'Really great!'

'Hmm... You'd better leave one of those ChewiVits with me so I can send it for analysis. I know they've been cleared to be sold and you trust Dr. Spencer, but even so...'

Copeland rooted into his pocket, pulled a fluffy tablet out, looked at it lovingly, slowly handed it across the desk and said, 'That's my last one.'


## THE BATTLE OF GRIMSBY.

Known locally as 'Fish-hook' Ramsden for the habitual way he displayed his rivals' heads, the Grimsby crime lord felt confident about his future tenure of the town. Despite the influx of another hundred of his new enemy he still controlled the docks and the all-important mushy pea factory. Even after the initial attempted bribes offered by this new upstart Dark Star gang nearly half of his men had remained loyal. True, he was down to his last handful of men after another recent swathe of desertions and disappearances but he had plenty of ammunition for the final confrontation to prove the town and all the drugs in it were still under his control.

Ramsden checked his pistol, pulling the magazine out, tapping it on his desk and replacing it before clicking the safety catch off. He stood, threw out his chest and went through his office door to join his men in the main part of the building that masqueraded as a tyre garage. His underlings held their pistols at eye level. They were all pointed at the barricaded double metal doors. The underlings' hands were shaking, except when they twitched every time something large rammed against the doors.

As the door lock cracked open and a sliver of light came between the doors Ramsden bellowed, 'Cummon, lads! They don't even have guns! We'll blast them into next week!'

'There's about two hundred of 'em, Fish-hook,' pointed out one of the last remaining underlings. Fish-hook Ramsden shot him and asked, 'Anyone else have any defeatist remarks?'

The new second in command slapped his ear and said, 'That was bloody loud, Boss. Aargh!'

Fish-hook Ramsden held his hand up and said, 'Sorry about that, Trevor. I jumped the gun a bit there,' after he had put a bullet in Trevor's leg. 'Ha! Get it? Jumped the gun! You see, I've got a… That's bloody noisy wailing, Trevor.' Another shot sounded and Trevor stopped wailing.

'Excuse me, boss,' tentatively said one of the few remaining henchmen. 'This is just a question. But what's that sticking through the crack in the doors? It looks like a…'

Ramsden watched the henchman fall and answered, 'It looks remarkably like a crossbow bolt. Let them have it lads!'

Trevor was probably glad he had already left so his ears were not hurt by the extremely loud banging that came repeatedly from the multiple shots fired. Someone Ramsden knew as Underling Six was hit by a bullet ricocheting off the metal doors. Ramsden shouted, 'Hold your ground lads!' and ran back into his office to hide behind his desk.

He waited with his pistol poised. The gunfire became sporadic and then ceased. Ramsden waited. He risked a look above his desk through his open office door. Chunks of the corrugated roof littered his lovely drugs distribution centre. Ramsden ducked down again, disappointed these Dark Stars did not know how to play the game. They had cheated and cut holes in his roof when all his lads' firepower was directed at the door. They had compounded their dishonesty by not using guns like proper organised crime gangs and had decimated his men from above with arrows and those ridiculous ninja throwing stars. Only Underling Four had been lucky enough to have not been hit by one of their weapons. A section of the corrugated roof had sliced him in half.

Ramsden reached his hand above his desk, pointed his gun in the general vicinity of his open office door and pulled the trigger again and again. He took an extra clip of ammunition from his desk drawer, rammed it into the pistol and fired again. He repeated this process for nearly an hour. Then he ran out of ammunition.

Ramsden waited behind his desk as minutes ticked by. Inspired by a new idea, he slid open the bottom desk drawer and took out the long fish-hook he had intended to use on his former adversary, Stan the Skewer, but Stan had run away from Grimsby when the black uniformed Dark Stars first appeared. Now he would show these Dark Stars what a formidable weapon a fish hook could be in the hands of someone who knew how to use it. He told himself it would be easy – he had a fish-hook and there were only a couple of hundred of them and they only had crossbows and samurai swords. He told himself this again to see if it sounded any better the second time round.

With his fish-hook in his clenched fist, Ramsden shouted, 'Come and get me if you think you're hard enough!' and stood up to decimate his foes. For a moment, his office seemed to spin around. Then it went blurry. Then someone turned the lights off.

'Hello, Mr. Ramsden,' said Keira Starr as she circled around Ramsden's desk and wiped her blade on his backside. She nodded at the floor and a nearby Dark Star picked up Fish-hook Ramsden's head. 'Put it on his desk,' Keira Starr instructed, 'and hold it steady so I can make my mark.'

A flourish with the tip of her sword inscribed her signature pentagram symbol on Ramsden's forehead so that all the crime lords who were yet to be defeated would be more inclined to take her offer or run for the hills instead of wasting her time with futile resistance. Just to make sure everyone got the message, Fish-hook Ramsden's head was suspended by his own fish hook in front of his drugs distribution garage.

(A local newspaper headline on page 4 subsequently read: Heroin Gang Killed By Collapsing Roof. No Civilians Hurt Say Police.)

## COPELAND HAS A GUEST.

After his longest chat ever with Director Miller about his forthcoming visit to Keira Starr's Longbeck House stately home and being fitted out with a camera disguised as a tie pin and a watch that was really a powerful transmitter, Copeland was lucky to arrive safely back at his nearby, one and a half bedroom ground floor flat in Slough. Being a dancing John Travolta as well as doing the falsetto with the Bee Gees singing *Stayin' Alive* while simultaneously steering with his knees might have been okay most of the time, but possibly not when going around a motorway roundabout. Copeland thought all those drivers crashing into each other should learn to drive better.

Half skipping from his car to his new front door, Copeland stopped. His new home was wonderful, as in full of wonder. He thought the trees were much greener, the sky was bluer, the breeze felt cooler, the birds sang sweeter, the pollution smelled stronger.

Copeland Saturday Night Fevered to his front door and put the key in. He felt great. The truth struck him. The ChewiVits weren't just vitamin tablets. They were much, much more than that. They were vitamin tablets that really worked! Beth was right!

He shimmied down his hall and did a twirl before realising he had missed elevenses and, on recollection, lunch as well. He went to his new fridge and opened it. Great! It was full. So was the freezer underneath, mainly with pepperoni pizzas. Great! There was even a stuffed crust one. Great! The cupboards were the same – full! What a great landlord, Copeland thought, but only for a moment because he heard the front door opening. If the landlord was coming to check he was okay that was one thing, but letting himself in? Not acceptable! Copeland resolved to write a very strongly worded letter of complaint to the Daffodil Lettings Agency. He marched into the hallway with his hands on his hips and demanded, 'What do you think you're doing?'

'Coming back from a run,' replied Freya (aka John Smith). 'I took the spare key.'

Copeland stood aside as Freya sidled past him to go into the kitchen and help herself to a glass of **his** tap-water. He followed her in, uncertainly waved a forefinger in the air and said, 'I thought…'

'No, I got someone from the car hire company to collect the car. I told them I couldn't because I'd been run over by a bus,' said Freya, finishing her water and having the nerve to help herself to another one.

Copeland could not help noticing that in running shorts and running vest, John Smith's hormone treatment was possibly more effective than he had previously thought. The inner voice almost agreed with, *And the shorts are snug... Maybe he's also had the surgery... I don't think I want to think about that...*

'I went shopping,' said Freya, putting her glass on the draining board. 'I got some new clothes and got us some food.'

'Thanks,' said Copeland. *Hang on...* said a wary inner voice.

'These new contactless cards are great, aren't they, Larry?' enthused Freya with her rhetorical question. 'I just went round a few times so everything cost less than thirty pounds each time.' She laughed. 'I suppose it's only fair that they stopped doing just chip and pin. It's the egalitarian dream really, isn't it? Now a thief can steal your card and redistribute wealth by using it to treat themselves on anything costing up to thirty pounds. And in as many shops as they like. Not that I'm a thief, Larry.'

*Hang on*, said an inner voice.

'I thought,' said Freya, 'since we're in this together, you wouldn't mind me using one of your credit cards.'

*Double hang on*, said the inner voice.

'So I bought enough food for both of us,' said Freya. 'Oh, and extra bedding for the single bed in the guest room.'

Hang on, thought Copeland.

'I'm going for a shower,' said Freya, leaving the kitchen.

*Hang on!* exclaimed inner voice in a tone that superseded all previous 'hang ons'. *Was that a kiss on the cheek on her way out? Have we just been kissed by a woman with dangly bits, Copeland?*

Copeland was in a quandary. He had always accepted LGBTQ people on their merits as individuals and had once even thought about trying to find out what the letters stood for. He fully supported the rights of those he called 'those transgender people' to express themselves however they sought fit, as long as it wasn't in public or, worse, on the BBC. And his support had *even* extended to transsexual people, providing their hormone treatments and operations weren't paid for by the NHS. He was very mainstream on the issue. He had always supported them fully! At least he had always *thought* he did. He had a very broad mind about all things like *that,* just as long as no animals were involved, with the possible exception of sheep. Suddenly, he wasn't so sure how broad minded he really was now Freya was suggesting she, or he, was going to live with him. For longer than he could remember, Copeland had told himself he didn't want to live with anyone. Still, he thought, why let someone moving in uninvited and using his credit card spoil his good mood?

By the time Freya emerged from her shower in a new red dress Copeland had prepared vegetable curry with rice and mixed salad and, without a word, Freya helped him carry plates and cutlery from the kitchen, past the bathroom and bedrooms, to the table in the bay window of the lounge.

It was not until Copeland poured both of them orange juice that Freya said, 'I suppose you want to know why I've moved in with you, don't you, Larry?'

Copeland did want to know. He was hoping it wasn't because John Smith had taken a liking to him and was relieved when Freya explained how, by using her car to block the road for the black truck as it left the Dark Star estate so she could smuggle her phone inside it, she had unwittingly played into the hands of Keira Starr. They had her car. They had the registration number. And, if rumours were to be believed, they had friends on their payroll in the police force. They would have discovered her home address in no time and probably already had people watching her house awaiting her return. No doubt Keira Starr had been surprised Freya lived in London and was not a spy for one of the rival northern drugs gangs and, while Keira Starr might never guess Freya Noyor was really John Smith the journalist, it was still too risky for Freya to use her bank cards in case her location could be traced since she had hired the car in Sheffield.

Copeland understood. 'So you're hiding out here in my new flat and using my credit card to buy things with?'

Freya nodded and reassured Copeland with, 'It's only until Keira Starr and all her henchmen and henchwomen are arrested, sent for trial and put behind bars.'

*Oh, it's just for a few years then, is it Copeland?* his inner voice said. Copeland didn't care. The world was bright and happy and he was glad to have someone to share his flat with and the teamwork kicked in again when they cleared the table together and discovered Copeland liked washing up and Freya liked drying. It was a perfect arrangement as far as Copeland was concerned, as long as John Smith didn't try to kiss him again.

The platonic bliss was spoilt as the last of the cutlery was put away. As he turned to go down the hallway, Copeland remarked, 'That doorbell is pretty loud. I expect it's someone from the letting agency checking I've moved in OK.'

Freya doubted a lettings agent would arrive after seven on Sunday evening to check the new tenant was all hunky dory. Had Keira's Dark Stars somehow tracked her down? Or more likely, tracked Copeland down? She grabbed Copeland's arm. 'Whoever it is, call me… Diana. I'm your partner, right?' she whispered urgently. Copeland frowned but nodded, understanding the need for secrecy.

Copeland opened the door to the last person he could keep secrets from. It was the last person *anyone* could keep secrets from. 'Er, hello, Beryl,' he said, wondering what he had done wrong now to put the safety of the Crown at risk. (The one on the head of the Monarch, not the pub on the corner.)

'I've brought these as housewarming gifts, old friend,' smiled Beryl holding out a bottle of red with a fancy label in one hand and a tin of chocolates in the other.

'Cadbury's Roses!' enthused Copeland, relieving Beryl of the tin. 'I love Roses!'

'I had them left over from Christmas,' said Beryl.

'Who is it darling?' came a voice from the nearby lounge. Everything was nearby in Copeland's new flat. 'Do hurry, darling, we said we'd have an early night. Remember? An early night *together*?'

Beryl gave Copeland a half quizzical, half astonished look.

'It's my partner, Beryl. No, not Beryl. You're Beryl. His name is... I mean her name is... er...got it! It's Dana.'

'Can I come in?' asked Beryl Pickford, the pocket-size, grey hair-in-a-bun Miss Marple-like supremo of the ultra-secret security service agency known only as The Pickfords. They were known as The Pickfords because they were in the removal business, which was unfortunate if you were an international terrorist leader, South American drug baron, a foreign dictator or anyone else The Pickfords deemed might destabilise the order of things. A 'removal' by The Pickfords tended to be permanent. Copeland had known Beryl when she was Beryl Welsh, long before she had taken the title *Pickford*.

'What?' said Copeland, looking down at Beryl.

Beryl smiled. 'I asked if you were going to invite me in, Lawrence. I'd love to meet your partner. It's the first relationship you've had since your divorce isn't it? And you hardly had that many when we were at university, did you?'

'Yes. Right,' said Copeland, stepping back, holding the door wide for Beryl to enter and relieving her of the bottle of wine in the process. 'Yes. Come in. I'd love you to meet my partner…er… Deidre.'

Copeland followed Beryl across the hall into the lounge in time to see Freya's false grin slowly descend and her jaw gradually drop. Beryl greeted Freya with, 'Hello, John. So how's the investigative journalism game going these days?'

Having to share a bottle of wine with an expensive label brought as a housewarming gift only slightly upset Copeland because he managed to drink most of it while Freya and Beryl were busy talking.

Sitting between them at the round dining table was not the best move he had ever made. They could really talk. Copeland began to suspect John Smith really was a woman. For most of the time Copeland phased out, but he got the general gist of the conversation since they both seemed to be talking to him. It had apparently been nearly ten years and three months since Freya had begun to investigate the existence of The Pickfords. It had been ten years and two months since she had found herself in the boot of a car with a sack over her head, being transported to some unknown country location to be interrogated by Beryl and several other Pickford agents.

Beryl had offered a deal to Freya. It was not the habit of the Pickfords to assassinate members of the press, unless it was a last resort. Apparently, Freya had strayed into last resort territory and consequently readily agreed to Beryl's deal. In return for Freya sending information about people she came across during her journalistic investigations, The Pickfords would let her live – providing what she had uncovered on them remained as secret as ever. Freya had lived and had sent information about 'unpleasant' people to The Pickfords, who then decided their fate, which usually meant them having an unfortunate and fatal accident and their assets mysteriously disappearing into the Pickfords bank account.

Copeland had a lot of questions which he had given a lot of thought to while Beryl and Freya were filling him in about their past dealings. The main one was: what possessed me to eat that awful salad with the *vegetable* curry? Followed by: has it gone cold or have I got a bit of man-flu coming? And lastly: what had Freya/ John Smith found out that was more unusual than the other reporters who had dug around? Reporters usually got a quiet word in their ear from one of the less secret security services like (the real) MI5 or a quiet visit from the SAS in the middle of the night. MI5 and the SAS were usually the ones who 'explained' to journalists that The Pickfords did not exist in any shape or form and the newspaper's proprietor would be sacking them the following day if they persisted with their ludicrous enquiries. Copeland knew that was the way it usually worked. He knew this because he had phoned MI5 several times himself to ask for their co-operation when he had spent nearly three recent years working behind a desk for Beryl and the Pickfords. MI5 had always been keen to help, usually because any head of MI5 who had ever hesitated to help the Pickfords ended up being replaced within days. It had been the way of things since The Pickfords were formed as an off-the-books, ultra-secret, combined branch of MI5, MI6, Military Intelligence and the forerunners of GCHQ during the height of the cold war.

Copeland asked the question. What had Freya found out that called for such drastic interference with the free press? Copeland hoped Beryl would not resort to claiming it should remain secret because it was 'in the national interest'. As far as Copeland could tell, 'the national interest' usually meant helping the people who held power keeping that power at the expense of the millions who did not have any power. He and Beryl had experienced a fundamental disagreement on this and it was one reason why he had left The Pickfords to work for the new Department C, knowing the issue was starting to divide their long, long friendship. The other main reason he left was because he would get longer lunch breaks.

'You're asking me what I found out, Larry?' asked Freya. She looked across the table at the seemingly harmless, older, frailer, Beryl Pickford. Freya swallowed and said, 'I didn't find anything out.'

Beryl reached across the table and put a hand on Freya's bare forearm. Copeland noticed Beryl wore a large ring.

***Correct me if I'm wrong, Copeland, but isn't that the ring our old friend Beryl once said contained a little needle that could deliver an instantaneous deadly toxin? I might be wrong, but...*** the inner voice trailed off.

'You can tell him,' said Beryl.

Freya swallowed hard again. She looked at Beryl's ring. Then she told him.

'Is that it?' huffed Copeland when she'd finished. 'So what if the Pickfords were previously known as Ye Honourable Friends of Ye Crown and were set up by Henry the, which number was it, the seventh? He was really paranoid after that Wars of the Roses thing, so it's not surprising really, is it? And taking the chance to come out of the woodwork and call themselves The Pickfords during the cold war so they could cherry pick talent from the other services isn't really that mind-blowing, is it?'

'What about causing the reformation so the Crown could be independent of Rome?' asked Freya.

'Who cares?' said Copeland. 'Ancient history. Just like bumping off that Bloody Mary woman, causing James II to abdicate, running the East India Company and founding the

British Empire. Oh, wait! Two of those chaps were monarchs. I thought the whole reason for the Pickfords was to support the crown?'

Beryl removed her hand from Freya's arm now she was content Freya had not said too much. She nodded and said, 'Of course it is, Lawrence, to an extent, yes...After her father went a bit over the top and her dear brother Edward mysteriously died young and Mary gained the throne, Queen Bess gave us special powers so we could steady the ship and get rid of her half sister. It was for the best really after Mary did all those burnings at the stake and started taking land back from us we'd only just taken from the monasteries. Queen Bess made us vow the crown and not its current wearer was our priority when it comes to maintaining stability.'

'Whatever,' said Copeland, standing. 'We need more wine and I need the toilet and to find my phone to check if Ania Rose has arranged for me to meet with a new informant yet and see if Keira Starr has replied to me accepting her invitation to visit her stately home, though don't ask me why I've agreed to travel all the way to bloody Sheffield.'

Aghast, Beryl said, 'You're not going to stay with Keira Starr, surely!'

Aghast, Freya said, 'You're not letting Ania Rose do you a favour, surely!'

Copeland sat down again.

'Shouldn't your worries be the other way around?' he asked as he shook the last few drops from the wine bottle into his glass. 'I mean, you, Freya, think Keira Starr is a new drug lord who's having people killed if they dare leave her gang, while you, Beryl, should be concerned Ania Rose seems to have undue influence over Department C.'

Beryl spoke first. 'The Pickfords have always found Ania Roses to be supportive of stability and the crown, while Keira Starr is a dangerous vigilante socialist.'

'National socialist, more like!' cried Freya. 'As in Nazi Party National Socialist!'

Beryl raised her eyebrows and calmly said, 'Perhaps I misread the memo. But frankly, Keira Starr and her Dark Stars are not our concern, even if she might be murdering those who leave her cult. Organised crime in the UK is now Department C's concern while we Pickfords look to re-establish the influence of the crown abroad now we are finally freeing ourselves from the shackles of the EU. We're focusing on regaining our former colonies in America first. They love the British monarchy.'

'Just a second, Beryl,' said Copeland. 'You just said…'

'Ania Rose is a spider!' retorted Freya, unable to contain herself and slapping her palm on the table. She had Beryl and Copeland's attention. 'She weaves webs and draws people in like flies,' Freya continued with clenched teeth. She looked at Copeland and Beryl staring. She thought she should explain. 'I'd heard she has a finger in more pies than Sweeny Todd so I started investigating her business dealings but then I had to go to West Africa to get a story on Foreign Minister Mozawinga and the blood diamonds scandal, then to Serbia, then the Dark Star thing came up…Anyway, I learned enough to know Ania Rose indirectly controls lots more businesses than just her little PR agency. Be careful, Larry, I heard she lures people into her web with an offer they can't refuse.'

Copeland sat up very straight, folded his arms, grinned like a schoolboy being appointed head boy, and resolutely said, 'Don't worry, Freya, there's **nothing** Ania could offer **me** that I'd be interested in.'

***How about that cheeseboard, eh, Copeland?***

'Well,' said Beryl to break the tension, 'as far as we Pickfords are concerned, Ania Rose is a stalwart of the community and a great benefactor to charities and the arts.'

It was time for Copeland to look at Beryl and do some eye-narrowing of his own. 'She's singular again, is she?' he said, 'You called her Ania Roses before…You said…'

'Slip of the tongue, Lawrence,' said Beryl. She glanced at her watch. 'Goodness! Is that the time? I really must go and leave you two lovebirds to it. Try not to get yourself killed by Keira Starr, Lawrence. I won't always be there to be your guardian angel with a sniper rifle. Byeee!'

Copeland wondered how someone as old as he was could move so fast, but Beryl had grabbed her old mustard cardigan and was out of the door before he could say another word.

'I'm worried about you too, Larry,' sighed Freya. 'Okay, Ania Rose may exploit people for her personal gain, but visiting Keira Starr? Why would Keira Starr invite you to her home unless she thought you'd seen something when you were at Butterburn and means to silence you?'

'No worries, Freya,' beamed Copeland, feeling his mojo returning now he was not being scrutinised by Beryl Pickford. 'It'll be as right as rain. Wendy Miller and I know **exactly** why Keira Starr has invited me to her Longbeck stately home.' He noticed Freya had placed her hand on top of his.

So had a vigilant inner voice. It said, *Uh-oh, Copeland!*

Copeland was marched across the marble floor of the stately home by four black-shirt guards wearing pentagram armbands. He found himself in a room where even the flagstones beneath his feet were black. Only the circular grey stone table disturbed the blackness. Lady Keira Starr, like some teenage goth, was clothed in black. Beneath her centre-parted long raven hair, her dark eyes were circled with black paint, as if she was prepared for war.

Copeland was forced to sit on the black wooden chair across the wide stone table from her brooding Ladyship. She glared malevolently at him while cowering servants brought in a huge cauldron and placed it in the middle of the pentagram carved into the stone table. Unsurprisingly, the cauldron was black, as were the deep bowls placed in front of him and Keira Starr.

A servant ladled contents from the cauldron into the bowls. Copeland looked down to see what was on the menu. In his bowl was a beating, human heart. He watched as Keira Starr plunged a hand into her bowl, lifted out a pulsating heart and took it towards her black lips. He watched as her mouth opened and her teeth grew fangs before they tore into it.

Copeland screamed, 'Holy shit!' and fumbled for his bedside light switch. Sweat trickled down his body. His hair was soaked. He found the light switch. His head collapsed back onto his pillow while his heart pounded in his chest, which he did not mind because it told him it was still there. For some reason, as is the way with dreams, he was sure the heart Keira Starr was devouring was his own.

# A MEETING AT KEIRA'S.

It was almost midnight. In The Black Room, lit only by the five candles in the tall candelabra, Keira Starr and three of her Dark Stars were gathered around the large grey stone table inscribed from edge to edge with a black pentagram. They sat on black wooden chairs at one of the pentagram's points. The fifth point had a vacant chair. It was for Him Who Was Yet To Come. The bringer of pain and despair. The One who brought The Darkness. On this night, as on many others, they had waited for him for so, so long. But now, at last, they knew The Master drew near. The rotten stench preceded him.

Keira, Konrad, Kirsty and Kerry sat motionless as The Master entered and approached the seat set aside for him. Keira broke the total silence with the time-honoured greeting. She stood, held her arms wide and proclaimed, 'You're a whole bloody hour late again, Kurt. I despair!'

'Our backsides are killing us on these seats,' added Kirsty.

'No! Kurt! Don't!' cried Konrad. 'Now you've gone and knocked the damn candles over again! We can't see!'

'And you've still got dog shit on your shoes,' piped in Kirsty. 'The stink is awful. We could smell you coming! How many times do we have to tell you, Kurt?'

'Sorry,' said Kurt as Keira found the torch she kept handy for such a repetitive occurrence and shone it in Kurt's face.

'*Master* of Hounds, indeed,' laughed Kirsty.

Kurt sat down and pointed a finger at her. 'Shuddup, Ginger! At least I'm not a turncoat, Miss Head of Human Resources. And what sort of title is that? What the heck's human resources?'

'People!' snapped Kirsty. 'I manage our people. I look after their well-being and morale.'

'HA!' scoffed Kurt, Master of Hounds. Kurt's title should have been Head of Training but Keira Starr could not bring herself to call him the head of anything. She thought he excelled in teaching the recruits their combat skills, but he had the organisational skills of an ant. She rethought this. That was unfair. Ants were pretty organised, especially compared to Kurt. He never made a staff meeting on time, never got the 'occupational hazard' from the dogs off his shoes and invariably knocked over the candles. Kurt had good days, but more often bad days, and ever-reliable Konrad always brought a lighter. Konrad had already picked up the candelabra and lit the candles again during the friendly banter across the table: friendly bantering which had sometimes ended with friendly battering before now. Keira Starr allowed this, knowing all large organisations had their rivalries, especially when they were organised crime organisations. She had seen The Godfather movies. In truth, the bickering was one reason she called these meetings to discuss petty issues. It amused her.

Hiding her amusement, Keira glared at Kirsty and Kurt. They fell silent. She looked around the table and said, 'Right. Down to business. Item one on the agenda is…'

'What's she doing here?' interrupted Kurt, pointing at Kerry. 'And where's Kato?'

'Kerry is item three,' said Keira. 'Kato has been dismissed as head of security and is fertilising the flower beds. Now, item one is Kylie.'

'Which one?' asked Kirsty. 'We have eight now, Lady Keira. It's not my place to say but…'

'I will name the recruits when they graduate to Dark Stars as I see fit,' snapped Keira. 'It's a symbol of them leaving their old lives behind. I happen to like names beginning with K. Do you have a problem with that, *Kirsty*?'

'No, My Lady… It's just, well, we seem to be running out of names. We have over thirty five Kevins.'

'That's enough!' Konrad said, banging the side of his fist on the table. There was silence.

'Good,' said Keira. 'Now, Kurt, is Kylie where she should be? On the naughty seat?'

'Yes, Lady Keira,' answered Kurt. 'You were right not to feed her to the dogs. Skinny little Australian isn't much of a meal for them anyway. Actually, she's already screaming. Actually, she was screaming long before we sat her down on the seat. Actually, she's been screaming since I told her she'd be there for a week.'

Kirsty's fingers were wiggling above the table, hovering over her pentagram point. Unable to contain herself, she said, 'Do we really call the worst possible punishment imaginable the naughty seat? And surely that was a personnel issue? Is Kurt already taking over my new role for staff discipline now? And… What?' Everyone was staring at her. Everyone waited. Kirsty jumped. 'I meant to say, **Lady Keira**. I did. Honest. I would never forget to address you properly, My Lady.'

Keira cleared her throat. 'Again, we jump ahead. Kurt's role is item five on the agenda.'

'Is it?' asked Kurt, wondering where he'd put his agenda before he had a mild panic attack and said, 'I mean…Is it, My Lady?'

Keira nodded her forgiveness, looked down again and said, 'Item two…We are having a guest. His name is Inspector Larry Copeland. He is a member of a new branch of the security services called Department C, a branch of MI5 set up to deal with organised crime.'

'Like us,' noted Kurt, having a rare astute moment.

Everyone gave Kurt a look and waited for him to address Keira Starr properly. Kurt smiled. Everyone shook their heads, knowing Kurt's astute moment had gone again.

With a sigh, Keira said, 'We will extend Inspector Copeland every possible courtesy.'

Kirsty raised a finger. 'Ahem, My Lady Keira… May I just ask why a member of the security services is coming here as our guest? If he was our prisoner then I would really enjoy…'

Keira quietened Kirsty with a raised finger. 'Your dedication does you credit, Kirsty, and I may well hand him over to you in due course, but first we will treat him as an honoured guest and provide him with everything he may require. He may prove useful. I will handle him personally.'

Kurt raised a finger and Keira gave him the nod. Kurt asked, 'Who is it who's coming again?'

Rolling her eyes, Keira said, 'Let's move on to item three and a trickier situation. It seems our most recent spy did not fit the usual stereotype. As you know, we usually let spies from other drug dealers, organised crime groups, etcetera, etcetera, watch us for a few days, see we are hundreds strong, well armed and well disciplined so they go back and scare the living daylights out of their bosses, who often then capitulate to our benevolent over-lordship, abscond to Spain, or seek police protection. Some spies we capture and then we, er, *re-educate* them about the justness of our cause before sending them back so they **really** scare the living daylights out of their bosses. Our recent spy was different. After she evaded capture she blocked one of our new drugs vans on its return journey. Fortunately, Konrad had the good sense to let her escape.'

'How was that having good sense?' sneered Kirsty.

'Because,' said Konrad, 'we have her number plate. Those sympathetic to our cause…'

'You mean the police we bribe,' said Kirsty.

'…Have given us her name and address. Her name is Freya Noyor and she lives in London.'

'Oh!' said Kirsty.

'So?' said Kurt.

Keira explained. 'It means, Kurt, she may work for one of the London gangs who have noticed our growing influence. We don't want that. They need to know we have no designs in attacking the south. We won't need to if everything goes according to plan. Kerry is here because I've decided to task her with going to London to find this Freya Noyor. Kerry will meet with her bosses and explain we are not a threat.'

Kirsty pointed out, 'That's suicide, My Lady,'

'Why?' asked Kurt.

Keira smiled. 'Yes, they will probably just kill Kerry to warn us off, perhaps after a great deal of torture to find out more about us, but Kerry is ready to die as horribly as necessary for our cause, aren't you Kerry?'

'Whenever you tell me to, Lady Keira,' answered Kerry, bowing her head and knowing the mission was a test. Kerry knew she had been invited to the meeting around the stone pentagram table to indicate she was being considered for a higher office. Either that or, despite her efforts to disguise it, they had perceived she had been trained in combat by Ania and wanted her dead.

'Good luck, Kerry,' said Keira. 'And remember, Dark Stars endure anything for our cause. Now, Kurt, regarding your new role…The grounds have been littered with dog mess lately and we need someone with your particular skills to…'

## 6. DAY 6. JUST ANOTHER MANIC MONDAY.

### COPELAND AND FREYA

Blaming his poor night's sleep on a dream where he had inconveniently been served a main course of his own heart and Keira Starr growing fangs, Copeland woke feeling as weak as a kitten with a hangover. He swung leaden legs out of the bed. He forced weary arms into a dressing gown. He Quasimodo-staggered to the bathroom and switched the shower on. He watched the cascading water, couldn't be bothered, and sloped into the kitchen. The thought of food made him nauseous so he settled for coffee. He had just taken the first sip and spat it back into his mug when from the doorway Freya less than encouragingly stated, 'You look awful, Larry.'

He turned to see Freya did not look so good herself, with her mousy hair frizzed out and dark rings under her eyes. He noted Freya was wearing his father's old dressing gown and one of his old stripy pyjama tops. 'I had a bad dream,' Copeland said with a shrug.

'I slept great,' said Freya, leaning against the doorway into the narrow kitchen. 'Staking out Keira's mansion then sleeping under a tree then sleeping soaked through in a car then staying up late talking with you all caught up with me. That's the best sleep I've had since I stayed in a great hotel in Croatia on my way to check out that Serbian village where everyone died, probably from some sort of flesh-eating toxin.'

'I missed that story,' said Copeland, making her coffee.

'Not surprised,' huffed Freya. 'My agent said the photos of the unmarked helicopters and the troops in grey protective suits loading up body bags looked like they were doctored on

Photoshop. I still think they were Russian. But the only place my story appeared was in *Gloom and Doom Monthly*.'

'I can't say I've heard of that one,' admitted Copeland as he handed the coffee to Freya. 'Three spoons of coffee granules, black, same as yesterday.'

'Thanks,' said Freya, taking the steaming coffee in both hands. 'It's one of Keira Starr's magazines. It's even worse than all her others – all those celebrity gossip ones and stuff like *Cosmomopolis* and the even worse ones with the pseudo-science stuff in like Psykology Tomorrow. As if psychology spelled with a K isn't blatantly aimed at people who don't know any better!'

'I bet *Gloom and Doom Monthly* doesn't sell very well,' chuckled Copeland wearily as he poured his coffee down the sink.

'Not compared to most of Keira's other magazines,' said Freya. 'It's aimed at those complete nutcases who live and breathe conspiracy theories. It only sells about five million world-wide.' She sidled from the hall doorway to the end of the sink unit and leaned against the back door.

'I'm going for a shower,' said Copeland. 'No matter how lousy I feel, I still need to go and see an acquaintance...' He paused. '...To go and see a friend. I have a message for him from his ex-partner who's apparently still in love with him for some strange reason. I should have passed the message on yesterday but got sidetracked.'

As Copeland wearily padded out of the kitchen into the adjoining bathroom, Freya called, 'Did you know Keira Starr makes about ten pence from each magazine she sells?'

Copeland stuck his head round the bathroom door. 'That's not much.'

'Really?' huffed Freya. 'On average, worldwide, she sells about three hundred million magazines every week.'

Copeland nodded sagely and headed into the shower with his brain adding a zero and moving decimal points to try and work out how much profit Keira Starr made each year. After a few attempts, then a few attempts more, he concluded it was probably quite a lot.

By the time Copeland had used his new toilet seat, shaved, applied his new Shining Silver for Stylish Seniors conditioner, showered his other parts, dried himself and chose a dark blue suit more presentable than his other dark blue suits he felt so exhausted he had to sit down on his bed. When he had recovered enough he added a dark blue tie to compliment his light blue shirt and carefully attached the tie pin with the miniature camera, hoping to get some practice. He expected Freya to be using the bathroom but found her in jeans, tee-shirt and much straighter hair working on a laptop on the table in front of the lounge window.

He walked in to see what she was working on and realised it was *his* laptop. Surprised, he said, 'How did you get into my laptop? It had a password! Hang on... Is that the police data base?'

Freya did not take her eyes off the screen, waved the back of her hand at him and, as if entranced, said, 'No. Finished with that. This is the MI5 one.'

Copeland was a little surprised. 'How the hell did you hack into that?'

Freya lifted up the base of the laptop with one hand and pointed with the other.

*See, Copeland! I told you not to put those stickers with your passwords written on them on the bottom of your computer.*

Copeland could only hope his internal 'better self' would soon catch whatever summer cold bug he had. He shivered and said, 'Using my passwords was a bit naughty, Freya.'

She stopped dead for a moment, turned and looked up over her shoulder. She looked like she had seen a ghost. Copeland thought he probably looked as bad as he felt. She said, 'I thought you'd already left.'

Copeland was about to say, 'That's your excuse?' in a fairly firm way but really couldn't be bothered so said, 'Don't tell anyone or you might get in trouble.'

'No, I won't,' Freya laughed. 'I'm only looking at the files on these pentagram murders to see if I can help. It looks like all the victims lived alone – except for Mr. Jennings. How would the killer know that if it they hadn't just left the Dark Stars? I'm hoping to find something so you won't need to visit Keira Starr.' She shuffled in her seat to look at him earnestly. Softly she said, 'Otherwise, Larry, tonight might be our last night together before you go.'

*Uh-oh again*, said an inner voice.


## 'MR. GREY' : DEAL OR NO DEAL (PART FOUR).

What was Mr. Grey to do? To him it seemed totally unfair that the money he had transferred for the contract killing of Larry Copeland was non-refundable. Mr. Grey remembered a time, back in the good old days, when it was all cash on delivery. A hand or a head was the usual delivery item in exchange for a bag of money in those long-lost, carefree, happier days. He was almost tempted to get rid of Larry Copeland himself, but he thought better of it and reminded himself he needed to keep a low profile and not expose his real, General Vasily Goraya, identity to anyone who thought he was in a Siberian salt mine. An unknown contract killer was still the better option so no one would know he was behind the killing. Many people wanted Larry Copeland dead, such as nearly everyone who had ever met him, so no one would have Mr. Grey near the top of their list.

'You Mr. Black now?' asked Mr. Pink, enjoying his pentagram art-work, which he was taking increasing pride in. He had even bought a new knife especially for forehead engraving, as well as a longer bladed one in case they came across another victim as impervious as Mr. Blobby's stomach was to a shorter one.

Mr. Grey looked up from his phone. He gave Mr. Pink the sort of long hard, meaningful stare that had once made villagers in the furthest reaches of Mother Russia shit themselves. Slowly, intensely, he said... 'Pardon?'

'Valdis say...' said Mr. Pink and Mr. Grey sighed and decided not to remind Mr. Pink about the not using names thing again. 'Ooops,' continued Mr. Pink, finishing the fifth point of the forehead carving and looking pleased with himself, 'Not Valdis say, but I mean Mr. Pink say, you are Mr. Black now, Mr. Grey?'

Mr. Grey stared at Mr. Pink as he had once stared at young KGB recruits as they knelt and trembled before him. 'Oh! You mean the new hat!' he said.

'And new coat,' said Mr. Pink. 'Why you need coat on hot day like little talking bear from Paddington?'

'No, I'm still Mr. Grey,' said Mr. Grey, going back to tapping his phone and hoping Mr. Pink would just get on with it already and plunge his hand up behind the sternum of whoever this was lying unconscious on the floor so Mr. Grey could get a better bank balance. 'I like black,' said Mr. Grey, distractedly as he tapped his phone. 'It's what I always wore when I was in the KGB and then the SVR.'

A few taps later and Mr. Grey realised there was none of the usual glugging sounds associated with the next phase of the terminal heart surgery. He looked up to see Mr. Pink pointing the new carving knife at him and seemingly a little put out as he asked Mr. Grey if he was a *(content censored)* Russian and then used some more very extreme English words that Mr. Grey did not know Mr. Pink even knew existed. Mr. Grey's face remained impassive, as always, while he thought quickly and said, 'I am Ukrainian. The despicable Russians took me from my home and my loving parents and tried to make me into their KGB tool to oppress the free peoples of the old Soviet Empire.' He thought that should do the trick, unless Mr. Pink knew his geography and asked him which part of the Ukraine he was from and then he would have to admit he was from a part of Ukraine the glorious Russian Federation had rightfully reclaimed as its own, in which case he would have to kill Mr. Pink with his own knife.

Mr. Pink said, 'Oh, okay, you Ukrainian,' and swapped knives, thinking how clever he was to know what 'despicable' meant. He guessed Mr. Grey did not know the 'Despicable Me' animated movies were his favourites and his childhood aspiration had been to become the most famous villain of all time and, once he had got some real-life experiences by killing people, he would one day fulfil his ambition by going into politics.

Mr. Grey went happily back to tapping his phone again. He knew he had a couple of moments of undisturbed peace, at least until Mr. Pink broke the calm ambience with a few glugging noises and his usual euphoric *ta-ta!* moment when he held his new prize draw trophy aloft.

What had got Mr. Grey's goat was the complete failure of the hit-man who had gone to Larry Copeland's home to eliminate the pesky, silver-haired tubby man once and for all so he would no longer be the bane of Mr. Grey's life, the shadow on his shoulder, or, as he had learned the English called it, to stop Copeland being a complete pain in the gum. Why would the intermediary known as The Broker be stupid enough to give a contract killing to someone who had religious qualms about killing? And what sort of hit-man gets into a house and fails to pull the trigger because he's a Christian? And what had Larry Copeland said that utterly convinced the killer he was a man of God and not the spawn of Satan the hit-man believed all his other victims to be?

Mr. Grey tapped the email link to show the photograph of what should have been Larry Copeland's last moments. Mr. Pink cried *Ta-ta* as he showed off his latest throbbing, heart shaped withdrawal. Mr. Grey studied the blurred photo on his phone and wandered if Larry Copeland had lost weight, grown long hair and a beard and had taken up amateur dramatics to currently play the lead role in a production of the classic Webber and Rice musical, Jesus Christ Superstar.

Before he paid more money for another hit-man, Mr. Grey decided he needed more information about the failed assassination attempt, along with a much better photo.


## COPELAND JOINS BENSON IN THE GARDEN.

The servant called Simon who looked like Michelangelo's David with a more handsome face let Copeland in and proceeded to lead him through the length of the (tennis court size) lounge of Ania Rose's lavish house, passing a very pale looking giant cactus on the way. Copeland was glad Ania was at her PR company's office.

As Simon led Copeland towards the conservatory he said, 'Mr. Benson is taking tea in the garden with Miss Mithali, Sir.

She is the personal assistant of a Bollywood executive and has come to check the menu for Saturday's dinner party will be appropriate for his religious convictions, after which she got into a discussion with Mr. Benson. I believe they are discussing if nishkam karma can lead to moksha.'

'What's that, Simon?' asked Copeland as they passed through the conservatory.

'Whether selfless actions can lead to enlightenment and liberation, Sir,' answered Simon.

'Sorry, Simon. I meant what's Bollywood?' said Copeland just before he groaned when he saw how much further he had to walk across the lawn to reach Benson sitting in white pyjamas at a far-off wrought iron table.

Simon was quietly laughing. 'What's Bollywood? Very droll, Sir,' he said and, when they finally reached the garden table, 'Inspector Copeland to see you, Mr. Benson, Sir.'

The slim young Indian woman in a turquoise embroidered sari with swirling ink patterns down the side of her flawless face rose to her feet, placed her hands together and bowed to Copeland. He did the same. Fortunately, Simon was able to help him upright again. Copeland held his back, feeling like he'd been run over by a steamroller and deciding he had all the symptoms of the worst ever man-flu.

Mithali turned to Tom Benson. She said, 'You're right, Tom. Your friend is amusing, like your Benny Hill, but I didn't believe your description of his stomach until now. I hope we can conclude our talk on Saturday and you can tell me more about aliens building Atlantis, Elvis really working in a chip shop in Cardiff and about magic tricks, but I really need to go now.'

Tom stood with an index finger aloft and said, 'If we meet again, why, we shall smile. If not, this parting was well made.'

Mithali smiled. 'Brutus in Julius Caesar,' she said and kissed Tom's cheek.

*What is it about this guy, Copeland?* asked an astonished inner voice.

Mithali smiled briefly at Copeland as she passed and stared intently, almost longingly, at Simon, who offered to walk her out, promising to return with more tea.

'Your look awful, Larry,' observed Tom as he sat.

'I'm getting that a lot today,' Copeland groaned as he gingerly lowered himself onto a white, wrought iron garden chair. He nodded towards the departing Mithali. 'Another romantic conquest, Tom?'

Benson laughed. 'Mithali? No. Didn't you see the way she looked at Simon? But hopefully another client for Rose PR if she puts in a good word with her boss. Doing the UK publicity for a Bollywood film studio would be great.'

'Oh, Bollywood is a film studio! *Another* client? You're doing well at your new job then, Tom?'

'Yes. If Ania lets me have them they could be my second client. I already have someone called Mandy Gilmore who's trying to be an interior designer. Poor woman. Her husband's on the run for selling stuff to North Korea. But I hope to get another really special client at Saturday's dinner party.'

Copeland raised his eyebrows. 'You get to go to posh dinner parties as well now, eh?'

'Er, no,' said Tom, frowning. 'And I'll be working as a waiter on Saturday. Helping out when required is part of my new contract.' He leaned intimately towards Copeland. 'It was over thirty pages long. All in really small print.'

Copeland nodded. 'I suppose there's a lot of confidentiality clauses when you're dealing with publicity,' he said, gazing down the garden to the tennis court over fifty metres away.

'Not the PR company contract, Larry,' tutted Benson. 'My contract to be one of our company's contestants.'

Copeland looked at him quizzically.

'Oh, come on, Larry!' sighed Benson. 'I told you about how Ania had asked me to represent Rose PR and Management, remember? In a competition against other companies? Fitness training and saunas with Lucy and yoga and meditation with Alice?'

Half raising an apathetic finger, Copeland said, 'Oh, yes, sort of. Paintballing or something wasn't it? How is your Barbarian Princess Lucy? Shouldn't she be here training you instead of you lounging around drinking tea in your pyjamas?'

'It's my karate outfit,' said Benson. 'They had trouble getting one to fit until they tried children's sizes. And Lucy is, well, out of favour with Ania. She spilled something on Ania's favourite rug. The one in front of the fireplace. I think she did something else as well but I'm not sure about that. Ania was livid. Lucy was threatened with being sat on the naughty seat, which I think is their phrase for being sent to Coventry – Lucy's clients are mainly business acquaintances of Ania's who form this sort of network and call themselves The Roses and Ania threatened to tell them all to find another personal fitness trainer. Lucy would have had to start from scratch. She would've even lost her afternoons at the retirement village working with the really old people over fifty five – no offence Larry – because I think Ania part owns it or something.'

'Ah,' said Copeland. 'So now you get mornings to lounge about then Tom?'

'No, that was considered work,' Tom said, shaking his little balding head and pushing his plastic rimmed glasses back up his nose. 'I hardly get any free time at all. My new contract is 24/7 until after the contest against the other companies.'

It was Copeland's turn to shake his head. 'Sounds like you've sold your soul for a better salary in the publicity department, Tom.'

Benson leaned over to speak confidentially. 'Not my soul, Larry...Just my body. Literally. The contract was very specific...' He sighed. 'And it's not a better salary. I work on commission only, all based on my clients' profits. In theory I could make a fortune. Shame I haven't a clue what to do. *But*, I do get to live here instead of that grotty dump across town, *and* my friend who thinks he's Jesus has his new place *and* healthcare now thanks to Ania, and as part of my *new* deal I got Lucy off the hook – she's just having to make up for whatever she did by giving a whole week of free personal training to Ania's next door neighbours about ten minutes walk down the road.'

Copeland thought it was time to mention he'd met Beth Spencer and how much she was missing him. He swallowed hard and said, 'Actually, Tom, the reason I'm here is to tell you... Oh, thanks, Simon. Tea and a muffin, eh? Just the tea thanks. I think I might have a bit of a cold coming and I've lost my appetite. It's not camomile and vomit tea again, is it?'

Simon and Benson grinned. Simon said, 'The tea I served when you first came is what Miss Rose calls the *test* tea, Sir.'

'Test tea?' Copeland asked, lifting the lid of the teapot to check the tea was proper tea and Simon wasn't trying to pass off some of that Earl Grey stuff as real tea this time.

'Yes, Sir. Test tea,' confirmed Simon. 'Miss Rose likes to see if people drink it, and eat the awful muffin too. If they don't, they fail her test.'

Copeland checked there was milk in the jug Simon had placed alongside the pot before looking up at Simon to say, 'I presume the test is to see if people have any taste buds?'

'The test is a test of character, Sir,' Simon said seriously. 'You passed the test by eating the muffin – in record time apparently – and drinking the tea in one go, which was also a rare feat, Sir. I think it is fair to say, Sir, Miss Rose was extremely impressed. More than once she has said your resolute strength of character should be an example to us all. '

Copeland was nodding in agreement and wondering if he'd ever get the muffin unstuck from his jacket pocket and suspecting the cactus looking a little on the pale side might have something to do with him pouring tea into its soil.

'Ania says,' added Tom Benson, 'it's a test of self-control, to see if you can overcome your revulsion and eat the muffin and drink the tea. Self-control is very important to Ania.'

'Well put, Sir,' said Simon, pouring the tea. 'Control leads to liberation, Ania says.'

'Yes,' grinned Benson exposing his rabbit teeth, 'after Ania endlessly spouts on about Nietzsche's Beyond-Man Übermensch thing, she usually bangs *on* and *on* about *total* self control being needed for liberation, whatever that's supposed to mean, and then she usually churns out some endless crap about the realisation of your higher self thingy and evolving into a better human.'

'Not quite so well put, Sir,' said Simon as he picked the muffin plate up and withdrew to a discrete distance as he meaningfully said, 'Ania is very wise.'

Copeland was astonished at Simon. He simply could not believe someone like Simon, who seemed so educated, could never doubt what he heard. How could he take things at face value? How could he believe such nonsense? Was he really the sort of person who could be duped? How could he possibly have been led astray so easily and put the milk in *before* the tea? It was tantamount to tea sacrilege! Copeland bit his lip, took a deep breath and said, 'Anyway, Tom, about the reason I'm here. It's because I met...'

Benson held his hand up. 'Before you say anything else, Larry, I just wanted to apologise for the last time we met – not in the gym just before Lucy and I went in the sauna together, but when I lived in that other grotty place on the wrong side of town. I was a bit down then because of Beth – you remember her? Beth Spencer? The doctor? The one who disappeared north for a new job and dumped me? She didn't even phone to tell me. But I've realised now that she was all work and exercise. We used to turn in for bed before nine every night, but we won't go into that. Anyway, I just wanted to tell you I've moved on. I suppose Beth and I could be friends again someday, but if she had the nerve to get in touch with me now to suggest we got back together then I wouldn't even want to talk to her ever again. I'm happy with my new job and all the other stuff.'

'Er, fine,' said Copeland, finishing his first cup of normal tea after finding it had tasted comparatively OK despite the scalded milk. 'So, Tom, the reason I'm here is because...'

Benson held up his other hand. 'I know why you're here, Larry. You're here to tell me you know someone in the SAS or something and they will help with my fitness training for the contest, but don't worry, Alice is filling in until someone new starts next week. Alice is great even though she doesn't do the massages because of her not touching anyone thing, but she's brilliant with everything else, especially this self defence stuff.'

'Alice?' said Copeland, finally deciding it best not to mention the message from Beth and grimacing as Simon put the milk in the cup first again. 'Alice, the maid?' asked Copeland. Simon repressed a laugh as he added the milk scalding tea.

Copeland folded his arms, stared at Simon and had a little chesty-cough fit before he said, 'Alice isn't just a maid, is she Simon?'

'No, Sir,' said Simon, as serious as ever. 'She's the house steward.'

'Who knows karate?' said Copeland.

'She and I are both adept at all forms of martial arts, Inspector Copeland, Sir, though she's much better at tennis than I am. I was merely the all-England public school's champion.'

Putting on his best telephone voice, Copeland asked, 'And why, pray tell, young Master Simon, do servants need to be adept in all forms of martial arts?'

'To protect Mr. Benson, Sir,' was the reply. 'And he needs to learn some in case they get past us, Sir.'

'Protect me? Me?' gasped Benson, gripping the side of the table. 'Who from?'

Simon looked down at Tom Benson with a deeply furrowed brow as he said, 'I thought you were told before you signed the contract, Mr. Benson, Sir. Representatives from the two adversaries in the contest may wish to try to thwart your physical well-being by underhand means. In vulgar general parlance, Sir, they may try to nobble you.'

Benson wagged a finger in Simon's general direction as he quoted, 'A man I am, crossed with adversity! That's from *Two Gentlemen of...* You know, I was beginning to suspect this contest thing was a bit more serious than I first thought.'

Copeland added, 'Probably not paintballing then?'

Simon shrugged his shoulders. 'Who knows, Sir. As I understand it, the exact nature of the contest is yet to be decided by the organisers. All I know is that you, Mr. Benson, Sir, will be Ania's male representative. I believe your female team-mate is yet to be chosen.'

'Hmm,' hummed Copeland. 'Sounds like this contest is for high stakes if the other teams are prepared to nobble their opponents.'

Tom Benson snapped out of his thoughts and shouted, 'It's like the Hunger Games! Only one survivor!'

Simon laughed as he said, 'I doubt it, Sir. I suspect there may well more than just a few million at stake but Miss Rose is a caring person and would never put you at risk, of that I'm sure, Mr. Benson, Sir. Now, I'm sorry to say but you really should get to your karate training session, Sir.'

Leaving Tom Benson none the wiser about Beth, Copeland started feeling a little more like himself after the tea and decided he had better do some actual work now the pentagram murders case had been handed over to him. He supposed he should show willing and arranged a visit to one of the crime scenes.

## ANIA PHONES LOUISE.

Ania Rose had put a lot of thought into planning her phone call. In the privacy of her Rose PR office she considered her opening line with great care and phoned Keira Starr's sister.

'Ania! Darling!' gushed Louise, answering her phone. 'Please tell me you've changed your mind and you'll help me out.'

It was not how Ania had planned it. Sighing, she said, 'Lou, that's not why I'm phoning. We've been all through that. I'm not lending you any money.' While she was speaking, Ania heard something being poured into a glass, followed by a single gulping sound.

'Please, Ania…' implored Lou. 'Lend me two contestants then. Just this once. Please…You know the rules – without entering two contestants I'll lose what little I've got left…'

'Lou! Stop it! You know I can't just let you have two of my people to represent you in the contest. For heaven's sake, I'm one of the people you're supposed to be trying to beat. It's supposed to be *my* two contestants, *your* two contestants and the *other* company's two contestants. You have to use your own people. That's the whole point of it being a contest between the three of us.'

More swallowing and, 'Please… Pretty please, Ania…'

'I'm really sorry, but it's pointless, Lou. What if you did have two of my people? They'd have divided loyalties, wouldn't they? How could they try to beat their own side?' reasoned Ania. 'They would know if they even *tried* to win for you then their whole careers with my organisation would be over, and it's not like you're in a position to give them anything is it, Lou? Most of your companies have gone bust and the last one you own is only hanging on by a thread.'

'I know. I'm just a complete failure,' groaned Lou. More whisky glugged into a glass. 'Everything I do is so hopeless. But…Ania, dearest… I was thinking…How about if you just loaned me some money to hire some people? Not much, just enough to hire two reasonable contestants to represent me and a team to train them,' suggested Louise.

'You know I can't do that either, Lou,' sighed Ania.

'Please, Ania. Just a little,' implored Louise. 'Just a hundred million?'

'I'm not loaning you a hundred million pounds, Lou,' Ania said, sternly. 'You never paid back the last hundred million I loaned you.'

Lou thought of a compromise and asked, 'How about a hundred million dollars, then?'

'No, Lou!' barked Ania. 'Loaning you money is technically against the rules too. I'm not risking it again. What if *they* find out?'

Lou said, 'Come on, Ania. How would the contest organisers find out? Neither of us would tell them would we? Hang on. I just need to open another bottle… Okay. All topped up…'

Concerned, Ania asked, 'How much are you drinking, Lou?'

'Not enough!' laughed Lou. 'My employment agency is on its very last legs, I've sold my mansion for something cheap and I'm down to my last four servants. And one of them is Harmony and she's completely useless. I'd use her in the contest but she'd just embarrass me.'

'Use Melody then,' suggested Ania.

Louise baulked. 'Melody? I'm not risking *her*. She's the only one who can mix a decent cocktail. And my two male servants are working for just their board and keep so they'd be off like a shot if I asked either of them to be my contestant.'

'I'm sure you'll think of something, Lou,' Ania said, encouragingly. 'You've always come through in the end, haven't you?'

'I'm not so sure this time, Ania,' groaned Lou. 'It looks like the end of the line. The contest is going to have to be a two horse race. I hope you don't lose, dear Ania.'

After a pause, along with some clearly heard clinking of ice, more pouring of whisky and some swallowing, Ania said, 'I need you to do something, Lou. I need you to tell someone about your sister.'

'Which one?' asked Lou and began to giggle.

Shaking her head, Ania said, 'I think you should put the whisky away now, Lou. I want you to tell someone all about Keira.'

Lou spluttered into the phone. 'All about Keira? You can't be serious! She'd kill me!' Louise had a coughing fit.

'About her illegal activities, Lou. About her drug dealing, her extortion rackets – all about her organised crime activities with her so-called Dark Stars.'

Lou swigged another whisky. 'She'd kill me,' she repeated.

'The thing is, Lou,' continued Ania, 'Keira has crossed the line this time. There's a series of murders where a pentagram is being carved onto the forehead of the victims…'

Lou tried to make her point for a third time. 'She'd kill me… Pentagrams carved on foreheads? Really?'

'And the removal of the victims' hearts,' said Ania.

'I don't know anything about that, Ania. Removing hearts and leaving her signature trademark? Sounds like Keira has lost it!' Lou said. 'I'd better get another couple of bottles. Are these your people she's killing?'

'No, Lou, they're not,' Ania said resignedly. 'The theory is they are men who have left her Dark Stars gang and she is silencing them in case they go to the authorities. But you're right. She's out of control, Lou. Are you still there, Lou?'

'Sorry, Ania, just downing a really big one after hearing that news,' said Lou. 'You're right. It sounds like she's finally flipped. Someone else in the family is loopy besides me, eh, Ania?' Louise laughed.

'Lou!' scolded Ania. 'This is no laughing matter! Put the whisky down and tell me you know something that could get her arrested and put an end to her crime spree.'

'I suppose I do,' admitted Lou, sinking back into her depression. 'But she'd kill me.'

'So you do know something?' Ania said excitedly. 'Good. Look, I know she's your elder half-sister, but you can't just stand by while she builds this organised crime empire and murders anyone who won't bend their knee to her, can you?'

Uncertainly, Lou said, 'I suppose not. But she'll kill me if she finds out.'

'Listen, Lou, you can have the authorities protect you. The person I want you to talk to is someone called Inspector Larry Copeland. He's a member of an offshoot of MI5 called Department C and...'

Lou interrupted with, 'Isn't that the thing you and your friends sponsor? Department C?'

'Yes, Lou. I'm glad you remember me telling you we were setting it up to fight organised crime. We had the Pickford's approval, so don't worry. When you tell this Inspector Copeland everything you know so they can arrest Keira and her cronies Department C will give you witness protection for as long as you want.'

With a trembling voice Louise said, 'Keira will still try to have me killed for betraying her, Ania. She has as much sisterly love for me as I do for her. You know that. No, Ania. I can't do it.'

'Damn it, Lou!' shouted Ania down her phone. 'Keira is causing chaos. And it's spreading. She has most of the north under her sway. Manchester and Liverpool will be next! How many more people does she have to order the deaths of?'

'It's too risky,' murmured Lou.

Only breathing was heard down the phone.

Ania broke the silence. 'Do you still want two contestants for the contest Lou? And perhaps twenty million to tide you over?'

Lou haltingly whispered, 'I'm a little intoxi.. intoxi... pissed, Ania, but are you offering me two contestants and twenty million if I tell this Inspector Larry everything I know about Keira's illegal activities?'

'You have my word, Lou,' said Ania.

Silence was followed by sobbing. The sobbing was followed by more drinking. 'Make it thirty million to cover my debts and two contestants and I'll do it,' snivelled Lou.

Ania considered. 'Very well, Lou,' she eventually sighed.

'Thank you, dearest Ania. This calls for a celebratory drink! If you transfer the money I'll let you know where and when for my chat with your Inspector what's his name. You don't know how much this means to me. I can take part in the contest again and I won't lose what little I've got left after all. I'll be forever in your debt, Ania. I love you like a sister.'

'I love you too, Lou,' said Ania with a lump in her throat. 'And I give you my word that if Keira does kill you I'll kill her for you.'

'Oh, Ania… You're *so* thoughtful…'


## MR. GREY.

The list of targets supplied by their boss, Mr. White, required them to travel to do their job so having a central location suited Mr. Grey and Mr. Pink. Being near Birmingham in a house where the landlord accepted cash and did not ask any questions for lots more cash had many advantages. They were near an interlinked motorway network that went north, south, east and west so they could travel to different parts of the country, albeit at an average speed of fifteen miles an hour unless it was three o'clock in the morning. Mr. Grey often thought he should have gone into the lucrative roadside cones making business. And what fun he could have had if he had been one of those people who closed off lanes on long sections of motorways for three years at a time for road works without any actual road workers ever being seen.

Still, he was not in a salt mine in Siberia and, as the saying went, he had no reason to upset the apple tart, especially when there was only *one* rat scuttling across the living room floor eating the remnants of the canned spaghetti Mr. Pink had tried to eat off his lap while he watched something called 'Strictly' on something called 'catch-up'. Mr. Grey had started watching it, expecting something called 'Strictly' would have something in it to remind him of the good old days when schools taught proper discipline, used the cane liberally and were unafraid of parental complaints when they used capital punishment. But Mr. Grey had found this British version of 'Strictly' was nothing more than people dancing wearing costumes which Mr. Grey considered to be extremely pornographic, so he was not happy to have to avert his eyes from the TV to his phone when it pinged.

His phone said The Broker had finally managed to get a full explanation of the aborted hit on Larry Copeland. Apparently, Hit Man Cecil had turned up at the correct address in Leyton and the door had been opened by Larry Copeland who had taken one look at the gun in Hit Man Cecil's hand and invited him in for tea. Mr. Grey read the next part twice and he still did not quite understand how the tea drinking had led to a discussion about the voices Hit Man Cecil heard in his head and his recurring gout. Mr. Grey was unsure whether Larry Copeland had cured Hit Man Cecil of the voices in his head, his gout, or both, but it had seemed to involve some sort of foot massage in a bowl of water and a recommendation to eat cherries. In any event, Hit Man Cecil had left, believing Larry Copeland was some sort of messiah. Hit man Cecil had since dropped out of the Honourable Guild of Hit Men (and Women) to go back to being a social worker.

There was no better photo accompanying the report, still just a blurry one of the slimmed down, long haired, bearded

Copeland wearing what looked like a bed sheet, but there was another invoice which Mr. Grey reluctantly paid knowing he could afford it by using the money Mr. Pink was keeping in a Tesco bag under his bed.


## COPELAND VISITS A MURDER SCENE.


Everyone knew who was responsible for the pentagram murders, didn't they? But the more Copeland thought about it the more he doubted Keira Starr's sister would have enough evidence to put Keira Starr behind bars for murder. As he sat with his chin on his arms and his arms on his steering wheel, he doubted everything. He asked himself questions like does everyone see green as the same colour as I do and aren't dolphins smarter than us because they don't have to go to work and what the hell happened to music since 1979? He rubbed his eyes and rested his head against the car window, watching a little bird as it hopped happily along as free as a bird and wishing he too could be a bird and not... *That cat came out of nowhere, didn't it Copeland? Poor little bird...*

Copeland tried to buck himself up out of his malaise. He reminded himself even if this sister of Keira Starr did not come through with enough evidence he knew how to play the waiting game when it came to tracking down serial killers. It was just a matter of getting inside the killer's head and waiting until they slipped up. Waiting had always been one of Copeland's strengths and, while waiting, he had got friendly with many bartenders. Even with the prospect of talking to Keira Starr's sister Louise being dangled before him, Copeland knew catching the actual murderer and getting them to confess they were working under the orders of Keira Starr was still the easiest route. As a member of a department that was sort of part of the security services, Copeland was sure he could offer the murderer a deal if he admitted to being hired by Keira Starr, perhaps something like reducing his sentence for multiple homicides to something like a hundred and sixty years.

The police officer outside the entrance to the crime scene scrutinised Copeland's Department C identity card in its new leather, flip open wallet and signalled his approval by silently lifting the yellow tape across the doorway. Copeland entered what had once been the home of Mr. Cunard and recalled he had received the forensics report and the photos that went with it. They were still inside one of those little pictures of a folder on his laptop screen which he was supposed to have clicked on.

When Copeland entered the lounge where the grisly deed had been done the first thing he saw was the previous investigating officer looking at his watch and shaking his head. Then he saw the previous investigating officer look up at him and continue to shake his head. Copeland thought he recognised him from somewhere, a suspicion borne out when the previous investigating officer groaned, 'Hello, Larry.'

Copeland recognised him. 'Hello, Chief,' he said, knowing his name would come to him sooner or later.

They shook hands and DCI Ross said, 'I heard you went to work for…' His eyes darted left and right. He put his finger to his lips and whispered, '…The Pickfords! Scary stuff, eh? I didn't know you'd recently transferred to MI5.'

Copeland said, 'Well, Department C isn't quite like the real… Ross. That's it!'

*Well done, Copeland! That was a tough name to remember considering you worked with him for about thirty five years off and on.*

163

Ross looked about. 'That's what, Larry? Don't tell me you've spotted something we all missed!'

'Hmm...' said Copeland, stroking his chin, slowly looking around the room and occasionally doing a little sage nodding in a meaningful way until he pointed and said, 'I suspect the body was found right there.'

Ross joined in with the slow-motion nodding and said, 'You mean where the lime green carpet is now dark red? I think it stands a chance, Larry. Fibres from his slippers suggest he was dragged from the region of the front door so it looks like he was administered the powerful sedative there.'

Copeland nodded, said, 'Powerful sedative, eh? Of course, er...' *Has Ross got a first name?* '... er... Ross, I'm familiar with the report.'

Looking sceptical, DCI Ross said, 'The killers were careful and didn't leave us anything. We got some saliva from one of the sites but the DNA doesn't match anything on file. My theory is that at least two people were here. We've scoured the victims' phones and computers but they have nothing in common. The killers must be keeping tabs on them so they could kill them when they were home alone. Other than some sort of Black Magic Satanists, we have no theories.'

Copeland looked up from the stained carpet, turned to Ross and said, 'Oh, I think I know who's behind this. What's the body count?'

'What...? It's twelve, Larry, but... Who..?' said a surprised Ross.

'There's more,' said Copeland. 'We just haven't found them yet. We've only found the ones where someone reported the victim missing because he hadn't turned up for work and they couldn't contact him or something. There are a lot more single dead men out there in little bedsits waiting to be found.'

'Single?' said Ross. 'But Mr. Jennings was married.'

Copeland nodded. He presumed Mr. Jennings was a murder victim. 'Probably a mistake,' said Copeland. 'I'll tell you all about the Dark Stars organised crime gang killing members who deserted their ranks in the pub. You can buy me a pint for saving your life with those Albanians that time.'

'*Another* pint?' asked Ross.

'Yes, another one,' said Copeland. 'Maybe lunch as well. I also want us to put our heads together and work out how we would get a sedative into someone on their doorstep without any signs of a struggle.'

'OK,' said Ross. 'Another pint and another lunch it is – but only if you stop tapping that blasted tie pin camera.'


## T.B. PHONES HOME.


'Anyway, Thomas, enough about me and shopping trolleys with wobbly wheels and telling you how you should have hung on to that nice Doctor Beth. Tell me how things are going down there in the big city.'

'It's going great, Gran,' replied Tom Benson into the receiver of the white desk phone in his little third floor office. 'Living in a really nice house with my boss Ania is great – don't worry, it's not like that. She's great and the deal I did agreeing to be her contestant is working out too. I've already got one client and Ania's teaching me some new magic tricks and she's already found a place in Leyton for that friend I was telling you about. You know, the one who thinks he's Jesus. And you won't believe this, but all that exercise I told you I was doing means you can see the start of a muscle on my arm now. The meditation is going well but I can't get the hang of this yoga thing and my martial arts are awful.'

'So when's this contest against other companies, Thomas?'

'To tell you the truth, Gran, the date seems to be at the whim of the competition organisers, but the further away the better as far as I'm concerned. I'm being treated like a king here. I have to exercise, meditate, do the yoga, the publicity work for clients and help around the house, but I get a good twenty minutes a day free time to use the toilet and I get almost anything I want. Yesterday I even got a new cloth to clean my glasses with. Is that dad I can hear?'

'It's your son, Colin,' said Gran.

'Hello son. Great to speak to you,' said Dad. 'How're the kids?'

'It's your other son,' said Gran in the background.

'Oh, *that* one,' said Dad. 'I suppose you're phoning me up to borrow money again, Thomas?'

'That was five pounds to pay for *your* parking and it was ten years ago and I paid you back, Dad,' said Tom Benson with a sigh.

'Don't you sigh at me, Thomas,' said Dad in a very dad-like way. 'I was hoping it was your smarter brother phoning. The one who's got a proper job and has got round to giving us grandchildren – grandchildren who are smart enough to just get an all expenses paid scholarship to a top school awarded by something called The Rose Foundation! You didn't know that did you? Of course you didn't. You never give your niece and nephew a second thought, do you? Ha! But there's no chance of someone like *you* giving us any grandchildren, Thomas, let alone smart ones, or helping me for that matter. I've got a major problem here.'

'What's that, Dad?' asked Tom, instantly wishing he hadn't. The last time his dad had a problem was when he was trying to work out how to take photos on his 1990s phone.

'Well, Thomas, since you're asking, the TV remote has stopped working.'

'Have you tried putting new batteries in?' asked Tom.

The suggestion did not please Dad. 'I'm not stupid Thomas!' he growled. 'TVs don't have batteries. You plug them in. Here's your mother. It's your **other** son, Lillian. The gnome-face midget we brought home from the hospital by mistake.'

'Hello Thomas.'

'Hello, Mum. Gran says you were putting rat poison down in the garden. Is there a problem?'

'There certainly is, Thomas. But if that neighbour's dog gets through the fence again it'll be the last time, won't it? Now, your Gran tells me you were a bit worried about taking part in this contest thing. It's no good worrying, Thomas. Worrying won't stop you coming last like you always do.'

'I'm not so worried now, Mum,' said Tom Benson. 'I've been told it's a sort of series of tests... Probably like puzzles and things with maybe a bit of running from one to the next.'

'Like The Crystal Maze? Or Krypton Factor? That used to be a good programme. We always watched that,' said Mum.

'Yes, Mum, probably something like that,' Tom said, then lowered his voice and whispered, 'I don't know who these other two companies are, but there's a lot of money at stake. And if my boss, Ania Rose, says there's a lot at stake then it must be millions because she's loaded. She has eight cars in her garage. And it's so important the other companies might try to nobble me!'

'Don't be silly, Thomas!' said Mum. 'You can't get eight cars in a garage. It would have to be bigger than half our street. Anyway, we have to go shopping now. Your dad wants to get a new light bulb for the loft so he can sort out all your brother's stuff for him and throw your old magic stuff away.'

The landline phone in Tom Benson's hand said, 'Brrrr...'

# COPELAND RETURNS TO FREYA.

Copeland returned home to find his new house guest drinking a glass of water and still hunched over his laptop. He was not pleased. He knew it was a well known rule that liquids should be nowhere near a computer in case they are spilled into it. It was a rule Copeland had discovered after he had knocked a glass of wine over the keyboard and his laptop refused to work again. Coincidentally, neither did the replacement one or the one after that. As a consequence of this learning curve Copeland never drank while working on his laptop, having vowed to adhere religiously to this rule by never again working on his laptop. This reminded him he owed the one and only Department C secretary Janet another gift for the report she was typing for him about his Butterburn visit, as well as reminding him he should reply to her text inviting him round to see the gift she had asked him to get for her in return for typing his report on the Peter Gilmore sales to North Korea case.

*That was the gift you bought Janet online while you were drinking a bottle of Merlot, wasn't it, Copeland?* his inner voice reminded him.

Before he could admonish Freya for her careless laptop proximity water drinking habit, she whirled, looked at him and said, 'Advertisements for scanty women's underwear and slinky night gowns keep popping up on your screen with suggestions about what you should buy next. Just so you know, I'm totally OK with whatever you want to wear around your own home, Larry.'

Copeland replied with, '…Janet…'

Freya turned back to the screen and said, 'Fine. I'll call you Janet if you want. But forget that for now. I did more research on Keira Starr. Did you know the crime rate in the cities and towns her Dark Star gang controls has fallen? Some of the Dark Web forums calls her a vigilante. Then I thought I would see what the MI5 database had on Ania Rose. There's not much and like the rest of the web there's not even a photo, though it does suggest she's a top informant because she has a network of people who call themselves...'

'Let me guess...Roses,' said Copeland, pausing to think and adding, 'Where's that tin of chocolates Beryl brought? Apparently, the pentagram murderers inject the victims with anaesthetic first, so I need to eat chocolates while you get cracking on that laptop to see if any hospitals have had any stolen. Anaesthetic – not chocolates. Chief Inspector Thingy Ross and I have been putting our heads together, Freya!'

'The name's John,' said Freya.

*Told you so, Copeland!*

'Okay,' said Copeland. 'Putting our heads together, John.'

'No, I meant Chief Inspector Ross is name John,' said Freya. 'We've helped each other from time to time when he was working anti-terrorism. He was the one who tipped me off about the possibility of a flesh eating thing in Serbia possibly being a new bio-weapon – possibly something developed by the Russians during the cold war called Nosoi which fell into the hands of Chechen terrorists. The Pickfords wanted me to check it out too. Beryl herself called me on that one. She said something about missing scientists as well.'

'Hmm,' said Copeland. 'Flesh eating terrorist bio-weapon called Nosoi, eh? Named after the nastiest things to come out of Pandora's Box, or more accurately Pandora's Jar, eh? On second thoughts, forget the Roses Chocolates. We'll search for stolen anaesthetic later. I'm feeling a bit better and a bit peckish so let's go and find my new nearest pub. Get your shoes on, Freya.'

A few drinks and burgers later and they were laughing together as Copeland told Freya all about Tom Benson and his ludicrous ideas about aliens and pyramids and the JFK assassination, and how such ideas were tempered by Tom's obsessions with secret societies and magic.

'You know,' giggled Freya, 'I'm sure Tom Benson has written some articles for *Gloom and Doom Monthly*. I think one was about JFK and who really fired the fatal shot – from the grassy knoll of course. Tom Benson wrote about how he could prove it was really Elvis. I think he wrote another about how aliens built Atlantis and another about how a super secret group he called The Family really runs the world.'

Copeland laughed. 'That's Tom Benson. Who would have thought the little conspiracy nut would end up as some rich woman's champion contender in a contest that's probably got millions of pounds riding on it?' he said, with a roll of his eyes and a wry smile.

Freya looked at him then stared at her white wine and soda, a drink which Copeland considered added insult to injury. She swished the drink round in her glass and distantly said, 'A contest worth millions? Tell me more, Larry. This might make a good article my agent could be interested in.'

'Well…' began Copeland, nodding sagely to buy time as he realised he didn't know all that much and said, 'I'll tell you everything I know, but first things first. It's your round, Freya.'

'Sure,' said Freya. 'I've still got your credit card.'

They laughed.

*Very funny, ha, ha, **and bloody ha***, mocked an inner voice.

# 7. Day 7. Tuesday.

## COPELAND ARRIVES AT KEIRA'S

A sense of déjà vu hit Copeland as he was marched through the tiled great hall by four black uniformed Dark Stars sporting their red pentagram armbands. He was not terribly surprised the start of his disturbing dream was playing out in real life. After all, he had visited quite a few Georgian stately homes with ex-wife Helen back in the day. They were all pretty much the same, although this stately home did seem to be about three times larger than most with its added Victorian wings and Helen hadn't taken him to any with armed guards. Copeland hoped he wasn't going to be fed his own heart while seated at a round, stone table inscribed with a pentagram while Keira Star turned into a vampire. He doubted it, but hadn't ruled it out.

Instead of being marched to a cannibalistic meal he was marched up the great stairway, along a dim corridor with ageing carpet and into a room that would have been a feature for any olde-worlde hotel – huge four poster bed, two wardrobes, new burgundy carpet, bookshelf, big window with a sit-on shelf, en-suite with shower and separate stand-alone bath, and YES! a really comfy looking toilet seat with a furry cover for extra warmth. Copeland tapped his tie-pin camera so the photo would remind him to get one for his own toilet.

The guards left and two more appeared with his case and suits, along with two women half his age, looking like waitresses in white blouses and knee length grey skirts. The blonde one introduced herself as Linda. The dark one introduced herself as Ruth. They explained they were his maids until dinner and should there be anything he desired they had been instructed to fulfil his every whim. Copeland looked at the two attractive maids and thought about this carefully before he asked if there was any possibility they could, you know, get him some tea and scones. After giving each other a look, Maid Linda duly left to fetch some while Maid Ruth began to unpack his things. Copeland had a panic, but managed to grab his toiletries bag before the maid person saw his Silver Shine conditioner and jumped to the conclusion his shiny silver hair was really dull grey. Taking the toiletries bag into the oversize bathroom, he placed it beside the sink and noticed a small, ornate gold dish sitting on the glass shelf beside the complimentary shampoo and soap. It had three ChewiVits on it. Copeland took one to keep him going until the scones arrived.

Maid Linda placed the tray of tea and scones on the little table against the wall. Copeland had always wondered why hotels had those tables with the headed notepaper and pens and now he finally knew. They were for your tea tray. He would have enjoyed the two nice large scones with nice jam and nice cream, but there was no jam or cream. He would have *really* enjoyed the nice tea from the nice cup poured from the nice tea pot...***but*** the maids sacrilegiously poured the milk in before the tea.

***Heretics! Arrest them all, Copeland!*** demanded his inner voice, adding a snigger.

The milk first was bad enough but the maids hovering and periodically lurching forward to wipe his mouth or retrieve crumbs from the floor simply made matters worse, but, feeling slightly less hungry and a little more refreshed than he had for a couple of days, Copeland finished the last of the scones and realised he had less than an hour to change for the dinner with 'Lady Keira' which the tall blonde bearded chap whose name he couldn't remember had told him about when he arrived. He thanked the maids for the light refreshments, told them he thought he would have a bath and went into his king-size en-suite. The maids were in there before he could close the door. They seemed offended when he asked them to leave, but Copeland was determined to show he wasn't *that* old and could still bathe himself, thank you very much.

Dinner with Keira Starr was nothing like his dream. There was no giant cauldron with meat floating in it, or any meat anywhere else for that matter. The first course was what the waiter called 'a Korean delicacy'. It had tentacles moving on the plate. Copeland thought it was okay but would have preferred a meat pie for his starter. Eating moving tentacles was one thing, but he drew the line at drinking the accompanying white wine. A bottle of very expensive looking red was produced and, determined to keep his wits about him, Copeland took very small sips, just in case the next course was human hearts floating in a cauldron.

Copeland leaned to one side so he could see over the dishes of untouched vegetables and around the four candelabras to make sure Keira Starr was still there at the other end of the table. A telescope would have helped. He gave her a thumbs-up while he pointed to the wine. One of the many servants brought another bottle which he didn't complain about but it did suggest distant Keira Starr had got the meaning of his message no better than he'd got hers when she had shouted about 'something underwater' and 'something sponges' and 'something made' to him. He had no idea what she was saying but pointed to whatever was on his plate and gave her a thumbs-up anyway. The delicacy from Korea could well have been a sponge with tentacles for all he knew.

The next course was definitely fish. He knew this because it still had its head, tail and skin. The fish was looking at him. Copeland was immediately put off by its accusing stare and pushed it aside. The main course was whole crab. He'd once heard there were parts of the male crab that were poisonous – the parts the male crab used for making babies. This had put Copeland off eating crab, unless it came in one of those little pots and he could spread it on sandwiches. The crab was also staring accusingly at him, possibly because its ability to make baby crabs had been curtailed by being boiled alive. Copeland made do with sipping a second bottle of wine.

After the crab was cleared away, along with the servants, Keira Starr finally sashayed down the length of the table in her long, off the shoulder, low-cut dress (in her favourite colour). She eventually got to Copeland's end, sat, smiled and said, 'I'm glad you enjoyed your big bath, Inspector.'

'Very relaxing,' said Copeland, shuffling to his right so his tie-pin camera pointed at Keira Starr. 'Now can you stop fiddling with that pendant thing in front of your face so I can take your... I mean so we can get down to business?'

'And what business is that?' asked Keira, leaning forward with elbows on the table, continuing to fiddle and noticing that while Copeland's right hand continuously tapped at his tie pin, his left arm was suddenly thrown across his body so his watch was almost under her chin. She raised a dark eyebrow and waited for him to tap the watch's face and say, 'Testing, testing...'

'Well,' said Copeland, far too loudly, 'I know you've invited me here so you can... You know, apart from the black eye shadow and black lipstick, you remind me of someone...'

Keira laughed as she sat upright. 'Is that your usual opening line with women, Inspector? It needs improvement. I'm sure I don't resemble anyone you know. The only person I even vaguely resemble is my grandmother, and that's only because of the eyes and black hair. I've no idea who I inherited this chin from. It's so pointy, isn't it?'

'It is very, very pointy,' agreed Copeland, diplomatically. 'But the rest of you looks okay. Now, where were we? Ah, yes, you're going to bribe me, aren't you?'

Keira Starr gave him a long hard stare before she said, 'Don't you mean *try* to bribe you?'

'Er, yes, quite right,' said Copeland.

'Would you accept a bribe?' she asked.

'Of course not,' retorted Copeland. 'How much?'

'How would half a million sound, Inspector?'

'I was just curious, Lady Starr.'

'How about a nice, round million then?'

'Tempting, but no thanks,' said Copeland. 'I don't really need any more money than I have.'

'Good!' said Keira, slapping the table. 'A perfect answer. I haven't invited you here to bribe you, Inspector, but to recruit you!'

'Recruit me?' coughed Copeland. 'Recruit me?'

The inner voice woke up with, ***She's another one for the psychiatrist couch if she wants to recruit YOU, Copeland!***

'Yes, recruit you, Inspector Copeland. Why else? The state room, the extravagant meal, the expensive wine, the VIP room service...All to show you how your life could be if you worked for me. Your deepest desire could be yours.'

***You're going to ask for a three hour lunch break, aren't you, Copeland?***

'Hmmm... What you really mean,' harrumphed Copeland, 'is you want me to train your Dark Star minions to infiltrate other drugs gangs and bump off other crime-lord kingpins so you can take over their patch, don't you, Miss Starr?' He folded his arms and added, 'Is there any desert?'

'Yes, there is desert, Inspector!' snapped Keira with clenched teeth. She stood, took a breath and said, 'We'll discuss this further tomorrow when I personally give you a

175

full tour – and show you how wrong you are about me!' She swished back towards the far reaches of the other end of the dining table.

*Oooh! Get her! She doesn't like people saying no to her, does she, Copeland? You are going to say no, aren't you..?*

While being escorted back to his room by two athletic, black-uniformed Dark Stars Copeland remarked, 'That chocolate fudge cake and ice cream was good. Really good. And that local cheddar cheese was excellent. Is that legal? To call it cheddar when it's made in Yorkshire? Do you think it's something I could arrest you all for? And that Henderson's Relish stuff goes with anything, doesn't it? I could have doused it on those wriggling tentacles.'

'A great local delicacy,' Dark Star guard escorting him back to his suite Kamille informed him. Copeland's brow furrowed. *Local delicacy?* He knew he might be wrong after consuming three bottles of wine, but was sure the servant chap had said the wriggling tentacles were a Korean delicacy. He had a mild panic attack as he tried to remember flying to North Korea. He stopped. He considered the possibility that he was a bit tipsy so probably wouldn't remember being bundled onto a plane anyway. He vaguely recalled a plan to stay in control and sip the wine. He thought the plan might have worked better with fewer sips, but it was very agreeable wine with and aromatic plum bouquet and a full bodied...

*Copeland! Stop! Don't pretend you have a clue! You only ever buy wine that's under a fiver!*

'Er, right,' said Copeland, starting off again and balancing the ice-cream topped cake in the dish carefully, which was hard because he had a bottle of red in his other hand. 'Where did Keira go?' he asked, looking back down the grand staircase and glad someone grabbed his elbow.

Dark Star guards Kamille and Kamilla shot each other a glance before Kamilla said, 'I think she went to bed, Sir. It was when you asked for a second cheeseboard and a fourth bottle of wine that costs over four thousand pounds a bottle.'

Copeland froze. He pointed the neck of the wine bottle at Kamille. Wine sloshed out. He said, 'You look like someone!' He sloshed the wine bottle neck at Kamilla. 'And so do you!'

Pushing Copeland by his elbow, Kamilla said, 'We're identical twins, Sir. We always do everything together.'

'Wow! Got it!' cried Copeland. 'You look like each other!'

'Here's your room,' Kamille said, opening the door wide.

Copeland was disappointed to see the maids were not there. He tottered a little as he turned to either Kamille or Kamilla and said, 'No maids? I was really hoping they'd still be here. The night is still young!'

Kamille and Kamilla looked at each other and sighed. One of them said, 'We're here to attend to your requirements all night, Sir. Any requirement at all, Sir, for Lady Keira's guest.'

'Really? Great! Anything? Great! What I really want you two lovely young ladies to do is… hic… to attend me in my boudoir and… hic… bring me a brandy and some more of that cheese,' Copeland said, beginning to *really* feel like his old self again now he'd survived the evening alive.


FREYA.


Keen to show her appreciation to Larry Copeland for letting her stay at his new flat, Freya busied herself again on his laptop as soon as Copeland left. Having all his passwords to top secret databases really helped. She told herself it was all to help Larry and not because she saw the prospect of some really good stories. Honest. Selflessly motivated, Freya considered which story – oops, which 'help Larry' issue – she should tackle first. She decided the best way to prioritise would be with her journalist hat on and consider which story her agent would sell most easily. Serial murders always made good headlines so she began by searching the police and hospital databases for stolen anaesthetics. The message that popped up on the screen within moments surprised her. It said the search was complete. She clicked OK and was presented with a list of no fewer than seven robberies, but none of them amounted to more than petty pilfering. Freya smiled when she saw she was looking at the results of a previous search which the highlighted bar at the bottom of the screen told her had been authorised by Chief Inspector Ross. Freya began to suspect that when Copeland had told her he and Ross had put their heads together it had been more a case of Copeland picking Ross's brains.

The screen asked if she wanted to view results of the related search. Related search? Why not? She clicked OK. Clever, thought Freya. Ross had realised the hospitals had been relieved of nothing more than usual so had used the database to investigate robberies from vets. Who would have thought vets kept so much anaesthetic on site? Five vets, all within ten miles of Birmingham, had reported break-ins and significant quantities of drugs taken, including anaesthetics. Freya clicked the links to the West Midlands Police reports. She scanned each one. They all told the same story: professional job, alarms neutralised, no forensic evidence.

Freya blew hard as she leaned back, placed her hands on her head and wondered what to do next. She clicked her fingers and typed. The screen asked if she wished to resume another previous search. Freya knew this was where Ross had got to – reviewing footage of CCTV cameras in the vicinity of each robbery to try to spot the same vehicle. For a moment

Freya felt cheated. Copeland had known exactly how far Ross had got but had led her to believe they would be starting from scratch before suddenly changing his mind and suggesting they went to the pub, then she realised Copeland had purposely incited her curiosity so she would follow this path and carry on from where Ross and his team had left off. No doubt Ross and his team were, as usual, short staffed and had found it difficult to wade through hours of CCTV footage from countless street cameras. But Freya was Freya. She hadn't got where she was today by not understanding computer software. She made a few adjustments to the search. She was soon viewing scenes from six CCTV street cameras simultaneously. Even so, she knew it would take her hours, or perhaps even days, so she doubled the playback speed a few times. She tutted when it wouldn't let her double it again.

By lunchtime she had the same van frozen in all six images. All she had to do after lunch was enhance the images to get the van's two occupants' faces and identify them on the police and MI5 databases, and, of course, link them to Keira Starr and her Dark Star gang. After that she could get on with the other three tasks she had set herself for the day – using the MI5 database to see if there were any other front page stories, find out more about Ania Rose and ordering some presents for Larry Copeland to say thank you. She still had one of his credit cards and she was sure he would appreciate some more slinky underwear.

# TOM BENSON PHONES HOME.

Tom Benson watched the dial of the vintage desktop phone whirl back, heard the ringing tone and heard a voice say, 'Stoke five zero one eight. Mr. Colin Benson speaking.'

'Hello Dad,' said Tom Benson.

Dad enthusiastically replied, 'Hello, Timothy!'

'It's Tom, Dad,' said Benson.

'Oh,' said Dad, all enthusiasm evaporated. 'You again, eh? Committed any more murders recently? Phoned to tell us it wasn't you *again* I suppose.'

'It wasn't me the last time, Dad. Or the time before that.'

'We had the press camped on our doorstep because of you, Thomas.'

'I know that, Dad. You sold my story to a tabloid. You got them to call it *My Son the Killer*. They paid you, so you can't complain.'

'I damn well can, young man!' retorted Dad. 'I only got half the money because they stopped printing the story. They said no one wanted to read about someone who had failed at school, gone to some third rate university, which I can tell you used to be called a polytechnic back in my day, and whose less than dazzling career took him all the way up to being a lowly junior hospital administrator. Your boring life cost me money Thomas.'

'You sold my story again though, didn't you Dad? When they arrested me a few months ago for the other murders and you got them to call it *My Son the Serial Killer*.'

'And you spoiled that one as well, Thomas. You had to go and get yourself released before they ran the story. I blame you entirely for the police releasing you.'

'They found out I was innocent, Dad.'

'Well, Thomas, next time you're arrested for murder admit it before they find out someone else did it and let you go. You can deny it all once I've sold your life story to the papers.'

'I'll bear that in mind, Dad, and, as always, thanks for your advice, but is Mum there?'

'Hello, Thomas,' said Gran. 'Don't listen to your dad. Never admit to a murder. That's always been my motto. Now, your mother said if you phoned to tell you she was too busy to speak to you. She's out in the garden burying next door's dog before they spot it's missing. So I suppose you'll have to tell me all your latest news.' Gran took a deep breath. 'So how's all the keep fit and stuff going, Thomas? Do you have any muscles worth mentioning yet?'

'Actually, Gran, it's not going too bad. I was worried at first when the contract was slightly amended after I did a deal to help my new friend Lucy. But giving all rights and privileges for all actions concerning my physical form to Ania Rose, as the new contract puts it, isn't so bad. I did have a bit of a problem with an itch on the end of my nose. I'm not allowed to scratch without permission and Ania said it would be character building for me to use self control and block it out and if I scratched it before she said I could then she would tie me to the tree next to the ants nest so I could experience what real itching felt like.'

'Hmm,' said Gran. 'So how were the ants, Thomas?'

'Not as bad as I thought they'd be, Gran, not after the first hour or so. But you know I told you about this dinner party Ania's having on Saturday? You should see the guest list. It's amazing. That Hollywood actor, George thingy is coming.'

Gran showed some interest. 'George Clooney?'

'Er, no… the other George one. He does all those romantic comedies. They call him the next Richard Gere.'

'Oh that one,' said Gran, still sounding slightly interested.

'And that Brazilian footballer call Luza is coming. You know the one. Every time he gets the ball the crowd all point at him and chant "Luza! Luza!" He's bringing his wife, Maria. She was Miss Brazil a few years back. Then we've got an actual foreign minister from a West African country. He's name Mozawinga.'

Gran was actually interested. 'Anthony Mozawinga? There was a John Smith story about him in the papers. It said he was using children to go down mines and make himself millions in diamonds. They're called blood diamonds, you know Thomas, because of the blood of the children that's shed to get them out. Some of them even die down his mines. They say he's got an army of child soldiers too. It sounds like your Ania Rose boss gets into bed with some dubious people.'

'I don't think she's going to go that far with him, Gran,' said Tom. 'She probably just wants to chat with him to tell him to stop his wicked ways. And the other guests include a Bollywood producer Ania's hoping will sign for us as a client and that awful Dr. Smith who keeps coming to give me medicals and what she calls cleansing enemas. Then there's my one and only client so far, Mandy Gilmore. The police are still searching for her husband for selling stuff to make nuclear weapons to North Korea. She must have gone to Dr. Lynn's clinic for liposuction or something because she's suddenly lost about twenty kilos and now only has one chin, oh, and Johnny Rockett...'

'**The** Johnny Rockett!' exclaimed Gran. 'Your Mum's got all his LPs. I thought he died of a drug overdose?'

'Apparently not, Gran. Johnny and the Rockets are making a comeback. Rose PR is their new manager. But I've saved the most important person until last... Rachel Duvall is coming!'

'Who?' asked Gran.

'Gran! Rachel Duvall! The actress... I mean actor... She was in the best film ever – Invaders from Esbos!'

'Never heard of it,' groaned Gran. 'Was it another one of those silly space films?'

'Yes! It's brilliant! She's brilliant! Ania is giving me the chance to have her.'

'Oh, I see! It's the sort of dinner party your granddad and I used to have in the 1960s, is it? Throw the car keys on the table and all that, eh? Can I come?'

'No, Gran, you can't. And I mean have her as a client and do her publicity. She hasn't made a film for ages, but I have a plan to make her into a superstar and Ania is being brilliant and backing me all the way, even though she thinks Rachel acts like a ten year old in a school play. Ania's just the best!'

'I'm sure she is, Thomas,' said Gran, sounding dubious. 'But she sounds a bit out of your league. Just like every other sane woman on the planet, but listen, Thomas... Maybe if you do okay in this contest some desperate spinster might be interested, eh? I thought your granddad was a real loser until he won a teddy bear at the fair, so you never know.'

'Thanks Gran,' groaned Tom, 'but I think this contest against these two other companies is a bit more serious than that.' He lowered his voice to the faintest whisper. 'Alice has told me not to say anything, but she's told me it's so important the other companies might actually send a ninja hit squad to try to kill me.'

Tom heard only silence, except for Gran's slightly asthmatic breathing. Gran said, 'I didn't hear that. You'll have to speak up. Never mind. I need to put the kettle on.'

Tom stared at the receiver as it buzzed in his hand. He replaced it on its cradle and stared at it. He looked up to see Alice standing in the doorway of his little office. As usual, she looked sad. She said, 'I promise to always protect you, Mr.

Benson, Sir. I promise no harm will come to you while a single breath remains in me.'

Tom Benson looked at Alice. He hung his head and looked at his frail fingers. He said, 'The other companies take this contest really seriously don't they, Alice?' He looked up to see Alice grimly nodding. With a deep sigh, Benson held an index finger aloft and said, 'Heavy the head that wears the crown, Alice. That's from…'

'Henry IV, part one, act three, scene one,' Alice finished. 'But the quote should really be uneasy lies the head, Tom. Now tell me more about this Star Wars…'

## 8. DAY 8. WEDNESDAY.

## COPELAND TAKES A TOUR.

Copeland woke up in the grand suite of Keira's Starr's Longbeck stately home estate having had a much better night's sleep than he had at his new flat in Slough the night before, when he had hardly slept a wink. After returning from the pub with Freya they'd had a couple of night-caps and Freya had taken his hand and said she would look into any thefts of anaesthetics by the pentagram murderers while he was away. Copeland was just nodding off when Freya crept into his room. Copeland knew she was obviously drunk, had used the bathroom and then gone into the wrong room by mistake. She had got into his bed, also clearly by mistake, and slid over towards him, obviously not knowing he was even there. Copeland had slid out the other side of the bed, grabbed his dressing gown and tried to sleep on the sofa.

Hoping Freya had avoided a hangover, Copeland hitched himself up and leaned back against the headboard. His room had been tidied while he slept. There was no sign of the dessert dish, the empty bottle of wine or the remnants of the cheeseboard, nor was there any sign of his camera tie-pin or his microphone watch. He knew he had left them on his bedside table right next to his glass of water and his packet of statins. He huffed and contented himself that at least he wouldn't have to wear a tie.

Breakfast was a single kipper and a slice of wholemeal toast on a silver tray delivered to his room by two young men in white shirts who, for some unknown reason, winked at Copeland and apologised for the staffing misunderstanding of the previous day and said they would be taking care of all his needs from now on. Trying to be friendly, Copeland winked back and gave them a thumbs-up.

Copeland loved kippers, but knew they hated him, so left the kipper and managed a bite of the toast before he needed to lengthily use the bathroom (which he blamed on the wriggling Korean tentacles he'd eaten the evening before).

Keira Starr soon appeared in a black velvet jerkin and calf-length skirt to personally give him his big tour. It was just as boring as all the stately home tours ex-wife Helen used to drag him on. Grand ballroom, grand library, grand this, grand that. Copeland had no idea why everything was called 'grand' when there was only one of them. Where was the 'not so grand ballroom', eh? He had already done the outside tour and seen the kennels with the dogs as big as tigers with their loud barks which did his headache no good at all and he had visited the stables, which smelled as bad as the kennels, and the hundreds of ninja types leaping around on the lawn looked just as boringly ludicrous as they had in Freya's photos. In contrast, the old restaurant and gift shop was a hive of meaningful activity with people pouring plastic tubs of ChewiVits into machines and people at the other end sitting at a conveyor belt and putting the packets of vitamin tablets into boxes ready for transport. Keira Starr showed him the space set aside for the necessary equipment to come from Butterburn so they could make the ChewiVits on site. When she gave him a couple of packets to try he pretended he had never tried them in case he got Beth Spencer into trouble for giving him freebies and commented on their honey taste as he chewed on one.

Copeland soon decided losing the tie pin and watch probably didn't matter. The East Wing was dull and the West Wing was really dull. Besides the ground floor cafeterias, they were both full of bedrooms and what Keira called common rooms with people in black clothes drinking coffee and playing snooker or darts or board games. It would have been like a university hall of residence except some of them were reading.

In the basement, Keira had to cajole Copeland from her well-stocked wine cellar to view rooms filled with oats used for luncheons and then on to the torture chamber. Keira explained the rack, the iron maiden and a very unusual looking seat. It was a stool with a large metal cone on top which Keira called the Judas Chair and explained how traitors would be sat on it and sometimes also had weights attached to their feet. Copeland felt his haemorrhoids twinge.

There was lots of other medieval paraphernalia. Keira Starr explained: 'The previous owners used to charge extra for visitors to come down here. Of course, it all used to be a wine cellar or something until they got into financial trouble and decided to try to attract more visitors by pretending it used to be a torture chamber. A few hundred years out of date for a Georgian stately home, of course. We got rid of the papier-mâché people they had here being tortured. It was all quite unseemly. Not remotely like the real thing at all. We rarely use it but no one wants to buy the torture stuff and we can't just throw it away. It's all heritage, isn't it, Inspector? And what else would we do with the room anyway?'

'Someone's put a dart board up,' Copeland pointed out. Then…without the slightest warning… he turned one hundred and eighty degrees, pointedly pointed with an extended arm and proclaimed, 'We missed that door, Miss Starr! What are you trying to hide in there, eh?' He was quite impressed with his tone and even the inner voice said, *Yes! That's put her on the spot!*

'The staff toilet?' queried Keira Starr. 'Bit of a corridor…'
She pushed the heavy wooden door open. 'Tut, keep meaning
to change that light so it's not on a timer.'

She pushed the light switch button in and Copeland trudged
dejectedly behind her down the narrow corridor to another
heavy wooden door at the end. It had a little man and a little
woman on it.

*It's unisex! Arrest them all, Copeland!*

Whoever was behind the door was clearly not well. Besides
a rather obnoxious odour, Copeland heard shrieks and cries
of, 'Oh, my God! My stomach! I can't take this!'

He thought he recognised the voice. 'That sounds a bit like
an Australian girl I met at the Butterburn place you fund near
Hadrian's Wall.'

Keira nodded. 'Yes, it's Kylie,' she said.

'Got it! It's Kylie!' Copeland exclaimed. 'She sounds like
she's eaten something she shouldn't have. Maybe she had the
wriggling Korean delicacy too?' he suggested. He felt
vindicated when he heard Kylie shout, 'It's moving! Oh, no!
It's coming out of my stomach! Help!'

Copeland tapped on the door and called, 'Don't worry
Kylie. It'll all be out soon. Trust me, I know.'

'Aaargh!' replied Kylie.

Copeland turned to Keira and said, 'Shall we move on?
Perhaps some fresh air outside? Ooops. The light's gone off
again. Bit scary down here isn't it?'

Keira took his hand and led him out and into the light, then
up the spiral stone stairs and on to the rear of the stately home
where Copeland looked at the gravel path running alongside
the long, oblong, ornamental lake and through the orderly
Capability Brown garden beyond, where it became a stony
path leading to the distant woods. He said, 'You can let go of
my hand now.'

Keira did and pointed beyond the team of gardeners to the distant woods. She said, 'This is just the main part of the estate. It stretches a few miles in each direction. The servants live in the estate village nearby. Some Dark Stars live in my home, but most Dark Stars live in accommodation I've had built beyond the woods, along with all the recruits. Most were once homeless. We offered them a new life and new purpose.'

'Selling drugs?' said Copeland gazing towards the woods.

'They run from their accommodation blocks to the front of the house for their self-defence training every day,' Keira Starr told him. 'It's only just over a kilometre. Let's go.'

Copeland reasoned thus: if Keira Starr was willing to show him the Dark Stars' accommodation then she was obviously not hiding anything illegal there and going there would be as big a waste of time as the rest of the morning had been.

*You think it's a long way to walk, don't you Copeland?* said a certain inner voice which had gone quiet since it had gone dark in the smelly corridor to the staff toilet. Copeland realised his inner voice was not omniscient. It was not at all because it was a long way to walk. It was really because it would mean at least another hour before lunch. 'Let's just go back inside,' said Copeland. 'It's getting very hot now it's nearly *lunch time.*'

Keira shrugged and said, 'Very well. You'll miss the Dark Stars' luxury apartments, the recruits mixed dormitories, the gyms, meditation halls and the re-education centre, but we'll just do the top floor of the main house. I have a very interesting antiques collection.'

Copeland grimaced. He popped another ChewiVit into his mouth and began to turn but his eyes fixed on the gravel path running beside the lake and through the tidy garden to the stony path beyond. He said, 'All those ninja people – I'm very up-to-date with modern terms you know – they do all their jumping about stuff barefoot. They do wear shoes when they run to their training don't they? Or do you believe suffering is good for the soles?' He grinned at his own pun.

Without looking at him, Keira shrugged again. She seemed to have got it down to a fine art. She said, 'My followers call it the Path of Devotion.'

***Do we detect perhaps a smidgeon of megalomania here, Copeland?***


## KIRSTY AND KURT.

Kirsty wore the black uniform with pride. The red armbands with the white circle containing a five pointed black pentagram were matched by the symbol on her black peaked cap. The spurs of her black boots rested on her desk as she leaned back on her swivel chair (which happened to be black) and flexed her horse whip. She stared as the bald visitor entered and sat down on the other side of her desk. She said, 'Hell is empty and the devils are all here.'

'Where?' asked Kurt, looking around.

'It's a quote from Shakespeare,' Kirsty enlightened him.

'Is she a writer?' asked Kurt. 'Sounds a bit spooky for me, though, Ginger-nut.'

'He wrote plays,' Kirsty informed him, guessing Kurt was having one of his not so good days.

'Ah, plays,' nodded Kurt. 'Didn't get much call for plays in the SAS. Did one at school, though. It was a bit weird. All about fairies and some guy name Oberon and was supposed to be set in some sort of dream in the middle of summer according to the title. I think it was written by one of the teachers who was taking some of those drugs we sell.'

Kirsty flexed her whip and smiled knowingly, as someone might smile at someone who was feeding a crocodile by offering them peanuts from their hand, and said, 'What can I do for you, Kurt? Do you have a personnel problem?'

'No I don't, thank you very much, Kirsty! I shower every day!' retorted an offended Kurt. He pointed and remarked, 'Whip and spurs, eh, Kirsty? Have we got another staff discipline problem, then?'

Kirsty snapped, 'How I administer staff discipline is up to me. Do you have a staff problem for me, Kurt?'

'It's more of an existential problem.'

Kirsty rolled her eyes, wishing she had never explained that word to Kurt. She knew what was about to come. 'Go on, Kurt,' she sighed, resignedly.

Kurt rubbed his prickly chin and said, 'Well, you know how we wear these uniforms that make us look like Nazis?'

'Yes, Kurt,' answered Kirsty, flexing the riding whip almost to breaking point.

'And,' went on Kurt, 'you know we expect our people to be totally loyal and obedient and if they have families they get taken away?'

'Yes, Kurt,' answered Kirsty, digging spurs into her desk.

'And you know how we expect drugs bosses to run away or we put their head in a box?' asked Kurt.

Kirsty closed her eyes and nodded.

'And,' said Kurt, 'you know the way we get money out of businesses and bribe police and drop people we don't like into pits and other stuff like that?'

'We do, Kurt,' answered Kirsty, starting to think of where she would like to put her spurs.

'And you know us Dark Stars sell drugs and we've got this new drug that will get everyone hooked so we make even more money?' asked Kurt.

Kirsty slammed the end of her whip down on the table. 'What's your point, Kurt?'

Kurt wiped his nose on his black sleeve and said, 'Well, I was wondering... We *are* the good guys, aren't we?'

'Kurt,' replied Kirsty as calmly as she could, 'we've had this conversation quite a few times before and I'll give you the same answer. Yes. We are the good guys. The world is broken. It will be a much better place when Keira Starr rules it, and I should know, I'm from Wolverhampton.'

'Wolverhampton, eh?' said Kurt, settling into his seat. 'You were lucky, you were! We lived in a cardboard box on the side of the motorway.'

Kirsty narrowed her eyes. 'We're not doing that one as well, Kurt.'

'Oh, go on! What about the dead parrot one then? Or the cheese shop sketch? Or the Spanish Inquisition? You like that one... No one expects the Spanish Inquisition! Remember?'

Kirsty was tempted but said, 'Maybe we can break up the monotony again tomorrow, but as you can see...' She cracked her whip across the table.

'Of course,' nodded Kurt. 'The staff discipline problem.'

Kirsty frowned. 'I'm going riding, Kurt!'


## MR. GREY HAS A MONEY SAVING IDEA.

Mr. Grey had opened his eyes to see Mr. Pink kneeling astride him. Mr. Pink did not look happy and had not brought Mr. Grey's usual morning coffee. Instead, Mr. Pink seemed to have brought a knife. The knife was uncomfortably close to Mr. Grey's throat. For a moment, Mr. Grey considered putting the same knife through Mr. Pink's eye socket, but that would lead to a lot of mess over his quilt, his new pyjamas probably getting ruined and the need for their equal opportunities employer Mr. White to advertise, interview, appoint and train a new Mr. Pink. Mr. Grey could not afford to wait for a new Mr. Pink when he needed the money to pay for another hit man (or woman) to kill Larry Copeland.

Mr. Grey looked up at Mr. Pink with his knife and asked, 'Is something wrong, Mr. Pink?'

'You took Valdis money!' cried an unhappy Mr. Pink. 'Valdis hid it good. In Tesco bag. Under Valdis bed. You tell Valdis where money is. Then Valdis kill you!'

Mr. Grey frowned and tried to surreptitiously free an arm from under Mr. Pink's knee. 'But, Mr. Pink, my dear friend, I told you about the money.'

A note of hesitation sounded in Mr. Pink's voice. 'When? When you tell Valdis about my money?'

'When we were watching that dancing programme on TV,' Mr. Grey said, sounding quite convincing. 'Don't tell me you weren't listening when you were watching all those scantily clad young women prancing around on the screen?'

'No. I mean yes,' said Mr. Pink. 'Where my money?'

'I told you how I'd invested your money along with mine and how it will make us rich,' said Mr. Grey, seeing Mr. Pink towering over him begin to waver. 'You said something about it making you enough money to become president of Estonia.'

'Latvia,' said Mr. Pink, looking left and right as if he was trying to remember.

'Yes, that's it. Latvia,' said Mr. Grey, unable to give an accompanying nod because of the knife point under his chin. 'Remember I said…' Mr. Grey knew his waking brain had hit the ground running just like it used to in the old days and, sure enough, it pinged the answer he was looking for. 'I said we were a good team and should start branching out.'

'Like tree?' said Mr. Pink.

'Yes, Mr. Pink,' smiled Mr. Grey, letting his new, hastily thought up brainwave take form in his head. 'We carry on getting money for doing these pentagram killings for Mr. White, but we take on some extra work of our own.'

'So where my money?' said Mr. Pink, pushing the point of the knife against Mr. Grey's neck. 'Oops, sorry. You now got bit of blood on your jam-jams.'

'Don't worry, my Latvian friend. I'm sure it's just a drop in the pond,' said Mr. Grey through clenched teeth. 'I used your money, and much, much more of my own, to buy into a hit-man advertising agency run by someone called The Broker. He'll get us contracts so we can kill people for a lot more money than we get for these pentagram murders. And we can just shoot them so there'll be none of this messy business putting things in freezer bags.'

Mr. Pink nodded while he thought about this. The knife slowly withdrew from Mr. Grey's neck. Mr. Pink climbed off Mr. Grey's chest and sat on the side of the bed. 'And no more heart bags delivered in car parks to old Mr. White? No more waiting around while he counts them and phones person he calls My Lady?'

'Soon there will be no more killing for Mr. White once the money starts pouring in,' said Mr. Grey, placing a hand on Mr. Pink's shoulder and thinking how Mr. Pink would never see a penny of the new money before he killed him. 'In fact, Mr. Pink,' Mr. Grey cheerily said, 'we already have our first contract. It's to kill a very nasty man called Larry Copeland.'

'OK,' said Mr. Pink. 'I get your morning coffee now.'

Smiling, Mr. Grey could not believe he had not thought of this plan before. The hit-man market was in need of more manpower and he could use The Broker to pay himself to assassinate Larry Copeland. The Broker's commission would be a small price to pay for the anonymity it granted him.

## COPELAND VISITS THE CONTROL ROOM.

Sometime after seeing cases full of antiques mainly from a place 'Lady' Keira called Mesopotamia, Copeland followed her to a further part of the third floor and a large metal door. After the retinal and palm print scans, Keira Starr tapped her code into the keypad and the airtight door hissed as it opened. 'I know,' said Keira, turning to face Copeland. 'I keep meaning to change it. 29031461 is the first number everyone thinks of, isn't it?'

'I suppose so,' said Copeland, moderately convincingly.

'Yes,' sighed Keira. 'It was after the battle of Towton that King Edward bestowed a lordship on my family, but that usurper Henry VII took it away again.'

Copeland said, 'That's sounds annoying, but why did you let me see the door code, Miss Starr?'

'One way or another, it won't matter soon,' she said, gesturing for him to precede her through the door. 'This is our control room, Inspector Copeland. No doubt this is what you *really* came to see.'

Copeland found himself at the back of a room with rows of screens and keyboard tapping Dark Stars. He thought it resembled a Hollywood version of CIA headquarters. The huge frame of Konrad hovered in a far corner. Copeland surveyed the scene as Keira sidled alongside him. Pointing over the heads of the black shirted Dark Stars seated at their keyboards and monitors, she pointed to big screen on the wall opposite and said, 'A map of my growing empire, Inspector.'

Copeland looked at it, did some sage nodding and said, 'You're only letting me see this because you're going to kill me, aren't you?'

Keira hooked her elbow through Copeland's and stared at the screen with him. She said, 'Bring up the statistics, Kevin.'

Three Kevins turned round from their monitors. One of them said, 'Does My Lady mean the drug sales figures? Or the business protection insurance takings? Or…'

Copeland felt Keira tense as she said, 'The crime rate figures, Kevin!'

'Oh, those…' said Kevin, blushing. 'I'm going on the naughty seat for that, aren't I, Lady Keira?'

'Just do it, Kevin,' said Keira. Leaning in towards Copeland she whispered, 'The naughty seat is like being sent to Coventry.'

Copeland nodded and looked at the screen. It took some time for him to work out what he was looking at.

Keira's arm through his pulled him a little closer as she said, 'The figures in white are just projected figures in the towns we've taken control of more recently.'

'I don't understand,' said Copeland, staring at the screen.

'Yes, you do,' said Keira Starr. 'We deal with criminals without the need for all that tedious business of evidence, lawyers and courts. We deliver a swifter form of justice. We're saving the taxpayer millions. We're fortunate to have some sympathetic friends among the police. Our surveys show local businesses feel they get their money's worth for the insurance premiums they pay us.'

Copeland nodded understandingly. 'I think you mean the police you bribe and the businesses paying you protection money, don't you, Miss Starr?'

Seeming to ignore him, and with her shoulder now pressed against his, Keira continued, 'And, of course, in all these towns and cities there are no drug-lords now, except for me, so there are no gang related attacks or murders. I sell drugs for virtually what I buy them for so they're far cheaper. Consequently there are fewer robberies committed to get money to buy them. We're trying to wean people off drugs like heroin and cocaine. We regard such addiction as a health problem. Our drugs profits are used to set up clinics and we incentivise addicts to attend them with cash payments.'

Copeland was not so easily dissuaded. 'But they still buy your new designer drugs.'

Keira shrugged. 'A necessary evil in the short term while there's still a demand. But our new drugs are safer, cheaper and, best of all, they're made locally. By not smuggling narcotics around the globe we'll have zero carbon emissions for the UK drug industry within two years.'

*That's great, Copeland! Greta Thunberg will be pleased!*

Copeland turned his face away from the big screen to look at Keira Starr. He almost got a mouthful of black hair and turned slightly away. He saw something. He cried, 'Wait!' and felt slightly guilty about possibly deafening Keira Starr. 'What's that?' he cried a little quieter, pointing to one of the monitors in the second row.

'That's just one of our live CCTV monitors in our underground crystal meth lab,' Keira informed him.

'No, that!' Copeland pointed at the monitor again.

'That's our incarceration facility,' said Keira. 'Basic by current standards – pits in the ground with gratings across...'

'No THAT!' demanded Copeland.

'Oh...That's information on a spy we're keeping tabs on,' Keira said. 'Her name is Freya Noyor. She's forty eight and a Norwegian national even though she was the daughter of someone in the Greek embassy in Oslo. We think she was spying here for a London drugs gang. We've sent a Dark Star called Kerry to...'

*Copeland! I can't believe it! Freya is forty eight! And I always said she was always a member of the fairer sex, didn't I? And YOU thought she was a...*

'She works for me,' said Copeland. 'She's my researcher. She goes a bit hands-on sometimes. She even came up here to get some photos.'

'She works for Department C?' asked Keira incredulously, craning her head forward and peering into Copeland's eyes. She stared, let go her gaze, and said, 'She's a lowly researcher? Problem solved, then. As a favour to you, Inspector Copeland, we'll leave her alone.'

'Good,' said Copeland. 'And now!' he said firmly, turning to Keira and determined to be unperturbed by her black hair in his mouth. 'About your locally produced designer drugs... Ptha! Bit of your hair there... Tell me about the new designer drugs you make down in the secret basement of your fake research facility up in Butterburn! You know, the one near Hadrian's Wall? The one where...'

Keira Starr turned to face him. As tall as him in her heeled ankle boots, their eyes were close. Almost as close as their noses. Copeland stopped talking. He knew this game. She was trying to stare him out. He was determined not to be intimidated. He could outlast anyone; unless it was lunchtime.

A voice inside Copeland's head raised a note of alarm with, *Watch out, Copeland! She's close enough to kiss you!*

She huskily whispered, 'Just say you'll join us, Larry. Join us and help us make the world a better place.'

Copeland narrowed his eyes and, in the most threatening whisper he could muster, asked, 'What's in the basement in that Butterburn place, Miss Starr?'

*This Keira Starr woman is really good at staring people out, isn't she Copeland?*

Unflinching, Keira whispered, 'How does a large seven figure salary, the best rooms in the house, your own servants and a personal chef sound, Inspector?'

*Don't be tempted, Copeland...But... A personal chef?*

Unflinching, Copeland whispered, 'First things first. Tell me what's in that basement or I'll arrest you for obstructing the course of justice, Miss Starr. Your hundreds of Dark Stars armed with swords and guns don't intimidate me!'

*Copeland! Don't be stupid! It's a personal chef!*

Keira slipped her arm from inside Copeland's and stepped back. She waved a hand into the air and shouted, 'Everyone out!' as she glowered around the room.

Copeland inwardly smiled. He might be about to die, but he'd won the staring contest.


## FREYA


Freya had only managed just one of her other tasks because getting clear images of the occupants in the van used in the anaesthetic robberies had proven impossible but, using the police database, it took Freya no time at all to trace the owner of the van. It was registered to Jimmy Mason. Jimmy 'Machete' Mason had several arrests and zero convictions for selling a complete range of class A and class B drugs, suspicion of some gruesome murders involving a sharp implement designed for cutting down jungle vines and a few forays into people trafficking which had not ended well for the people being trafficked. In short, he was not the sort of person you would invite round at Christmas. However, the fingerprints of the headless torso found near the Sunderland dockyard area ruled out Mr. Mason as being the current driver of the van, unless he had converted it into a driverless vehicle and his head was enjoying a tour around Britain.

Sunderland was now firmly in the grip of the Dark Stars. They had taken over Machete Mason's patch and had no doubt taken over his distribution centres and his other assets, including his vehicles. They had probably not sent the change of ownership information for the dirty white van to the vehicle licensing centre, perhaps because there wasn't an appropriate box to tick on the form to say the previous owner had been decapitated, but it was obvious to Freya which organisation the two shadowy figures sitting in the front seat on the traffic cam footage belonged to. But try as she might, a decent image of their faces eluded her. Most of the traffic cam images had light reflecting off the windscreen and the others were just as useless: the driver wore a baseball cap and the passenger always wore a hat that looked like a fedora.

What Freya had done was set an alert. If any traffic camera detected the van's number plate, then Copeland's laptop would instantaneously receive an image and a location. While she waited, Freya thought she might just browse the MI5 database again and have a little peek inside the file simply called Butterburn. She clicked on it.

In flashing red letters the screen said, 'Access Denied.' Freya upturned Copeland's laptop to see which sticker he had written his Butterburn password on. There were quite a few stickers, but none of them said 'Butterburn password', though she made a mental note of his Tesco online delivery password for future use. She turned the laptop upright again. She clicked on the Butterburn file icon again. The 'Access Denied' screen flashed three times before it was replaced with a warning. Apparently, trying to access the file required ultra top secret clearance and a third attempt to access the file would be considered an act of treason by HM Government.

Freya considered the message on the screen and decided it was probably time to go to the shops. She wanted to get a magazine to see if her story about Foreign Minister Mozawinga and his unscrupulous exploitation of African children to mine diamonds had been syndicated in full yet.

## COPELAND HAS A MEETING.

Shocked by what the CCTV cameras had shown in the basements of Keira Starr's Butterburn research labs, Copeland meekly followed Keira out of the control room. As Beth Spencer had told him, the basement beneath her trio of labs contained vats of crawling grubs waiting to be made into steak pies, but the basement below the hi-tech labs run by Cynthia Wood was where the real secret lay. Not just a secret, but an ultra top secret. Copeland thought he may have exaggerated his security clearance level...

*Exaggerated! You lied through your teeth Copeland!*

But his minor exaggeration had worked and Keira Starr had allowed him to see what was being hidden in the basement and it certainly wasn't anything to do with drugs.

'Pardon?' muttered Copeland as he trudged down the corridor behind Keira.

'I said,' said Keira, 'Beth and I have decided to get rid of the grubs. She's got a plan to turn fast growing lichen into meat substitute instead.'

'Sounds yummy,' replied Copeland, still thinking about what he had seen in the basement, the things which Keira had called the biggest secret in the world. But he wasn't thinking about it for long. As he followed Keira through a door at the end of the corridor his inner voice said, *Uh-oh...*

He had walked into a room dimly lit by five candles flickering in a candelabra as tall as a giant cactus he had recently poisoned. It was exactly the same room he had dreamt about when he had woken up in a sweat, except this room had the added macabre bonus of a high-backed black chair on a low pedestal.

'I dreamt of this room,' muttered Copeland. 'Except for the throne on the little stage. I dreamt of it. The stone table with the inscribed pentagram…everything. I dreamt you made me sit down right there and eat my own heart.'

'Probably too much cheese before bedtime,' Keira suggested. 'Please sit there, Inspector.'

'That one? With my back to the door? Right where you made me sit to eat my heart?' asked Copeland, but found himself drawn to the chair and sitting down. It had been a long morning.

*And we need lunch, Copeland, and, quite frankly, at this stage, I don't care what we eat.*

Keira Starr went to the door.

*She's gone to get the cauldron to serve you human hearts for lunch,* said an unhelpful inner voice. For once Copeland responded with, *That's really not what I wanted to hear.*

Keira returned with a tall, wide individual sporting a closely cropped blonde beard. Keira said, 'I think you've met Konrad.'

*Aha, Copeland! That was his name! Where's lunch?*

Copeland said nothing and watched as he saw Keira and Konrad sit across the table at two points of the inscribed pentagram. Previously on 'sit at a pentagram and eat your own heart', Copeland had been giving his full concentration to a certain sphincter muscle he happened to be sitting on. Konrad's appearance doubled Copeland's workload and he wondered if Kylie had finished in the staff toilet yet – somewhere secluded and remote would be appropriate.

'Relax, Inspector,' Keira said soothingly as she made a downward motion with her palms. Copeland allowed himself to relax a little, except for his sphincter.

'Firstly,' Keira said with her fingers interlocked and bowing to Copeland. 'Let me apologise. You know how it is, Inspector. Being a billionaire crime lord isn't all it's cracked up to be. You wouldn't believe how much there is to do and sometimes things get overlooked. I sincerely apologise for the servants and night guards we provided yesterday, but I trust the new male servants are acceptable for all your needs.'

Copeland nodded. 'They seem very nice young men,' he said, wondering why it mattered so much who was going to fetch scones and Danish pastries.

*Yes! Ask for Danish pastries, Copeland!*

Copeland thought his conscience was really starting to stray from its mission statement of reducing his cholesterol, which, as he understood it, was item 17a, sub-clause four, when it had awoken him one night in 1994 and recited a list it said it had been working on for five years.

'Inspector Copeland?' said Keira. 'You seem somewhat distracted. Are you alright?'

'Oh, fine,' said Copeland. 'This circular stone table with the pentagram..?'

Raising a dark eyebrow, Keira said, 'Do you know the pentagram dates back at least to ancient Greece and Babylonia? That Christians once used it as a symbol of the five wounds of Christ? That it was also a symbol of the five senses? Some attribute its origins to King Solomon. It was also the symbol of Sir Gawain in Arthurian legend to symbolise knightly virtue. Further back than any of that, in Greek myth, the pentagram's corners represented the five seeds that the original sentient being, Khronos, placed in the earth for the whole of the cosmos to appear. Even in the Renaissance it was a charm, like the one hung around my neck, to protect against evil forces. It is only recently that the pentagram has been associated with evil, and even that nonsense started as an inverted pentagram. Where a certain best-selling author got his ideas about pentagrams and woman power and da Vinci codes from I don't know. In short, the pentagram is *not* a symbol of evil. My Dark Stars and I are not evil, Inspector Copeland. We are misunderstood.' Keira Starr paused and waited. Fortunately she was good at waiting.

Eventually, Copeland said, 'Hmmm, yes…Pardon? I sort of phased out there thinking about…' Copeland almost leapt from his chair, but considered the effort involved and thought better of it. 'I've seen this before!' he exclaimed, pointing at the table. 'When I was a child, my father used to drag me to museums. This stone table was in one in… Somerset!' Copeland laughed. 'Yes! That's why I dreamt about it. It was in a little private museum in someone's house. The owner pestered my dad to buy stuff. I wanted him to buy Excalibur. The museum man had ten of them. He said this table was the original round table. You know, Miss Starr…King Arthur's round table!' Copeland laughed. 'All the knights of Camelot around this table? Ridiculous! It's only as long as a table tennis table.'

*You just* **had** *to do it again with the sporting comparison, didn't you, Copeland?*

'He died,' said Keira. 'The man who ran the museum. His money grabbing children sold off everything. I bought the round table. You are sitting where Sir Galahad sat, Inspector.'

Copeland lifted his chin and sat up straight. He was sitting where Sir Galahad once sat! Sir Galahad! The knight who was pure of heart!

*She's taking the piss, Copeland!*

Konrad shuffled and said, 'Ahem.'

Keira gave him a look, turned back to Copeland, leaned her elbows onto the table and said, 'So will you join us, Inspector Copeland? Join us to make the world a better place?'

Copeland rubbed his chin. The choice seemed clear. He could join the Dark Stars, become ridiculously wealthy, live in luxury and have all the really excellent cheese he wanted. Or he could probably never leave the room alive. It was a choice that merited some thought. As he stroked his chin his eyes narrowed and he made a decision. For once, he decided to be selfish. It was time to do something for himself. To have what **he** wanted. He said, 'Any chance of a Danish pastry?'

Keira Starr glared at him across the pentagram table and said, 'No. It'll spoil your lunch.'

*Doesn't know you very well, does she Copeland?*

Shrugging as he stared back at Keira, Copeland slipped a hand into his pocket, withdrew it again, moved it slowly over his protruding stomach and placed it over his mouth. He folded his arms and pretended he wasn't really chewing. It was the fourth ChewiVit he had eaten since Keira had handed him the two sample packets. What else was there to do while being dragged around on a boring stately home tour?

'OK, then,' Copeland said after tucking the ChewiVit aside into his cheek. 'Before I tell you whether I'll join your Dark Stars or not, tell me why you kill off your Dark Star failures.'

Keira turned her head to look at Konrad. It was Konrad's turn to shrug. With her dark eyebrows frowning she turned back to Copeland and said, 'What are you talking about, Inspector?'

'Ah-ha!' said Copeland, wagging a finger at Keira and then at Konrad. 'I caught you off-guard with that question, didn't I? Just like all the great detectives like Poirot and Columbo and... I can't think of any more... catch the criminals off-guard with the all-important question when they least expect it! Ah-ha!'

Keira Starr looked even more confused. 'What *are* you talking about?' she asked, shaking her head.

Copeland folded his arms and put his elbows on the pentagram table. 'It's obvious, Miss Starr. When your Dark Stars don't live up to expectations or leave, you have them killed before they tell others your dark secrets! You have someone knock at their door, inject them with anaesthetic, carve your pentagram symbol on their foreheads and remove their hearts so they don't tell anyone about your evil doings.'

*Evil doings? We need to work on your interrogation technique, Copeland.*

Keira and Konrad looked at each other. They looked back at Copeland. Konrad said, 'Remove their hearts? Are you saying people are being murdered, Inspector?'

'How many?' asked Keira.

'As if you don't know,' sneered Copeland. 'There's at least a dozen.'

'It's nothing to do with us, Inspector,' protested Keira, shaking her head. 'How could you think that of us? We may have disagreements with other criminals, but, for your information, any recruits who fail the initiation tests and any Dark Star who is found wanting is found employment with us. Where do you think all the servants, gardeners, cooks, cleaners and so on come from?'

Konrad added, 'There are some who need specialist mental support but they get that at our health centre in the village.'

Keira twiddled her pentagram pendant while adding, 'But full disclosure, Inspector… Those who are habitual criminals either end up back on the streets where we found them or spend a spell at our incarceration facility.'

'So,' said Copeland. 'You'd have me believe the only people you ever harm are people who may well deserve it and you have nothing to do with these pentagram murders?'

'That's correct, Inspector,' nodded Keira. 'It sounds like someone's trying to frame us.'

An icy silence followed. Copeland couldn't think of anything else to say.

Keira's dark eyes widened. She banged the sides of her clenched fists on the stone table. She closed her eyes, took a deep breath and calmly said, 'Inspector Copeland…When you visited my Butterburn research labs you had a folder in your car. It told you how to find its location – my security people up there found it and photographed it for me.' Her eyes opened and fixed on Copeland. 'Who gave you that folder, Inspector?'

'Er, it's a secret,' muttered Copeland, wondering if he was really supposed to have kept the folder in his car.

Keira pointed threateningly at him. 'Whoever gave you that file is setting me up. Don't you see, Inspector? They gave you that file so you would find my Butterburn labs. They knew you would find the pentagram was our symbol. They put me and my Dark Stars on your radar. They knew you were genius enough to join the dots and here you are, sitting there accusing me of being behind these murders!'

'Er, possibly,' said Copeland, thrown by being called a genius for the second time in his life.

But a voice in Copeland's head said, *Oh, come on Copeland! Why would Ania Rose try to frame this megalomaniac? She's denying the murders so you'll join her merry band of vigilante drug dealers and give her all your passwords to the police and MI5 databases, just like Director Miller guessed she would. Say no to her offer Copeland. Let her do her worst and torture the information out of you!*

## FREYA FINDS OUT SOME STUFF.

Several magazines were strewn across the floor of Copeland's lounge where Freya had thrown them. A few columns in a newspaper hardly paid the rent and sometimes Freya thought her agent dangled the lucrative prospect of syndicating a story in front of her before snatching it away again so she would carry on working her fingers to the bone. Not one of the many magazines she had bought was carrying her story about Mozawinga and the blood diamonds scandal. She walked over to the scattered magazines and was about to kick them further across the carpet when she noticed something. She sank to her knees and picked a magazine up. She read the advert, threw the magazine aside and picked up another. She flicked it open. The advert was there again, staring her in the face as soon as she turned the front cover.

She sat on the sofa behind the lounge door and flicked through more magazines. A third, then a fourth and a fifth all carried the same advert. All in the prime position to make sure the reader saw it. She had to admit it was a good advert. Anything with the word FREE emblazoned across the top was bound to attract the reader's attention. Tossing the magazine aside, Freya stood and paced the room. She stared out of the bay window. Her mind whirred until it remembered what Copeland had told her... She logged on to his Department C emails. She waded through the Tesco, Golf Club and La Sanza emails, thinking she might mention to Copeland he might consider having a separate email other than his Copeland @ department C dot MI5 one, and finally got to one sent by Director Miller.

True to her word, Director Miller had sent the ChewiVit® she had taken from Copeland off for analysis. Freya wondered if Director Miller had seen the full page adverts in all the magazines owned by Keira Starr and was as alarmed as she was that ChewiVits were being given away *free* for the next five days. (Available only at selected pharmacies and health food stores.) But Director Miller's email to Copeland said next to nothing, only how the initial analysis had confirmed what Copeland had been told by Dr. Beth Spencer – the tablets really were just vitamin tablets with an added boost of a naturally occurring, newly discovered enzyme, known in the scientific community as vit-transferase. Freya was disappointed until she got to the end of Director Miller's email: someone in the testing lab knew someone who knew someone who was researching the newly discovered vit-transferase enzyme and would let Director Miller know if anything else had been found out about it. Freya huffed. If reporters like her worked with the same urgency as scientists then news about WW II starting would be just hitting the headlines.

## 9. Day 8.5 or Wednesday, Continued.

<u>TOM PHONES HOME.</u>

'Yes, thanks, Mum,' said Tom into the white telephone receiver. 'I'm settled in well here. I've even got my Rachel Duvall poster up on the wall.'

'Oh, yes,' said Mum. 'The pornographic one.'

'She's wearing her SpaceForce uniform, Mum. It's not pornographic. It's cult.'

'Cult, eh? I was in a cult once, Tom. It was all sex, drugs and sex 24/7 except when we were eating porridge. Best five years of my life that was. We managed to sleep now and again, of course, otherwise we got those waking dreams that were like the worst acid trip ever. I only left because I got pregnant. I probably thought the LSD and the speed and the ecstasy I was swallowing were my contraceptive pills. I could have had an abortion, or had the baby and given it up for a sacrifice, but I chose to leave the cult and keep it. Worse decision I ever made.'

So... Mum...' said Tom Benson with some trepidation. 'Are you saying I have an older brother somewhere?'

Mum paused for a moment before replying, 'Let's put it this way, Tom... After I left the cult I met your dad and he thinks you were born four months early.'

Tom laughed. 'I should have guessed you were winding me up, Mum! *You* in *that* sort of cult! That's ridiculous... Mum? Mum?'

'She's gone Thomas,' said Gran's voice. 'She looks like you said something that offended her. I hope you didn't tell her your cult is better than the one she used to be in?'

'This is *not* a cult, Gran,' said Tom, tersely. 'The Roses are a mutual assistance commerce group. It's certainly not a sex and drugs cult like Mum was trying to wind me up with. It's yoga, meditation and **total** celibacy. As in **total** abstinence*!* Ania says I'm practising control of my body using my mind so that I can evolve into a better sort of human who has mastery over my body's hormones and electrical impulses.'

'Sounds like fun,' Gran said apathetically, 'but more importantly, how are the arrangements for the dinner party going and have you got me an invite yet?'

'Well, Gran, it's all go here,' enthused Tom. 'We're in full swing preparing for Saturday. Simon and Alice are teaching us how to be good waiters – us being me and a first year art student called Ingrid – she says that's her professional name because she hates her real name. I think she should call herself Britney. She looks a lot like a young Britney Spears. She's apparently made over thirty films since Christmas. Ingrid has – not Britney Spears. She says she's been a nurse, a teacher, a policewoman and has been a schoolgirl lots and lots of times.'

'I see,' sniffed Gran. 'Sounds like the sort of films your dad watches on his own in the shed on his laptop.'

'Really? He gets wi-fi that far from the house? Anyway, this Ingrid is also going to be my team mate representing Ania in that contest I was telling you about – which is starting to sound more like that programme called *I'm a Celebrity Get Me Out of Here*! HA! And she's taking over from Lucy next week as my personal trainer. Ania says Ingrid will be good at toughening me up.'

'This Ingrid will have to perform a miracle to do that, Thomas,' said Gran, distantly. 'So how is your training going for this meaningless competition against other companies?'

'To start with Gran, it's not meaningless,' whispered Tom into the phone. 'It's not just worth millions, but hundreds of millions! If we win then Ania will get the backing from the contest organisers to expand around the world – not just the

PR company but her hotels, gyms and everything else. She says if we win I could maybe run a new Rose PR office in Beverley Hills and have all the Hollywood stars as clients. So you can tell everyone your grandson is going to be a multi-millionaire! How about that?'

'That'll be nice,' said Gran, flatly. 'But you have to win first, don't you, Thomas? There's not much chance of that, is there?'

'Actually, Gran, Ania thinks there is a good chance, providing one of the opposition companies doesn't find us and send a ninja hit squad first. That's why I can't leave the house, in case they do. I never used to go out anyway. But Ania and I watch films together sometimes. We watched Rachel Duvall in "Invaders from Esbos" last night. It was the extended version which shows more about what happens when Rachel gets friendly with the purple alien woman. Ania said my self control is coming along very nicely through focusing my mind with meditation. That's despite Ania always going round the house in her short kimono robe and Alice wearing something called second skin when we do yoga.'

'And you had your warrior princess Lucy sharing a sauna with you and now you've got your Rachel Duvall poster on the wall... It must be hard, Thomas.'

'Gran! Don't be crude! ' retorted Tom. 'I told you, we're all *completely* celibate here. Absolute, *total* abstinence, remember? And I don't even think of *any* of them in *that* way at all. Honest.' A short silence was followed by, 'Uh-oh, upsy-daisy... Sorry, Gran. I need to go and meditate to get control of my electrical impulses and hormones now.'

# COPELAND GETS LUNCH.

Lunch had not been what Copeland had expected. While Keira and Konrad stayed seated at the round table, allegedly to discuss the news of the pentagram murders, a bald headed man smelling of dog mess took Copeland down to eat. Bald Kurt trained the recruits and was a man of the people and, to show his solidarity with the recruits who had hit each other with various lengths of wooden sticks all morning, he sat with them for lunch to lecture them on how to improve their martial arts killing techniques. A ladle of what Copeland could only think of as gruel was slopped into the bowl Copeland held out while the cook greasily grinned at him from the other side of the counter. Dessert was a ChewiVit wrapped in a serviette which had been used more than once as part of a recycle and save the planet campaign.

Seated at a long wooden table amid a host of sweaty recruits in white karate suits, Copeland lifted his tarnished spoon from the bowl and watched the gruel reluctantly splatter back into his bowl. He made do with the ChewiVit.

Worse was to follow. Copeland was planning on having an afternoon nap when a ginger haired woman with shoulders as wide as a door tapped his shoulder and told him she was his afternoon guide. Copeland had no idea why she was carrying a riding crop but took one look at her and grudgingly rose to his feet. He decided to ask Keira if he could go home soon.

At least the afternoon tour had little walking involved and his new guide, Kirsty, did not smell too bad and Copeland soon got used to her horsy odour. As he swallowed his ChewiVit dessert he even began to find the aroma quite earthy and uplifting. The black Range Rover was comfortable, the sun was shining, the estate's scenery enchanting – Copeland smiled and tapped a rhythm on the dashboard.

Kirsty drove him to what she called The Village to show him where the servants lived. The Village was more like a small town. The blocks of luxury apartments had a supermarket, leisure centre, theatre, library, medical centre, schools and a residential home for the elderly. There was not another car in sight. White shirted men and women of all ages were happily going about their off-duty business.

Copeland cheerfully asked if the two servants who had helped him unpack and bring him tea and scones lived there. Kirsty winced and said they did, but they were ashamed to have failed in their duties and had donated their day's pay to charity. Munching another ChewiVit and feeling quite invigorated, Copeland nodded his understanding – Ruth and Linda had indeed failed: they had served scones without jam and cream and put the milk in before the tea, but he was feeling in such a good mood he asked if they could be given another chance, perhaps along with the two guards who had escorted him back to his room the previous evening. Kirsty frowned but said she was sure it could be arranged and Copeland was mentally revising his plans to include more local cheese while she made a phone call, then she gave him her life story and interrupted his train of thought.

Copeland was soon ignoring the delights of The Village as it trundled by outside at ten miles an hour and was giving Kirsty his full attention. As she swung the car around to head back to the stately home, Copeland said, 'So, unlike these servants and recruits and Dark Stars you refer to as homeless scum, your real name is Angela Crump and you owned a riding stables that got into trouble so you joined a business group called The Roses and you got lots of new customers and their kids for your riding school but gave the Roses 20% of your increased profits then there was trouble because people said you mistreated the horses and the customers disappeared and you were going bust but someone called Ania offered to bail you out if you came here and did some spying for her and you got caught but after you were re-educated you joined Keira, passed the loyalty tests, became a Dark Star, got given a new name, rose up the ranks and became head of personnel which basically involves imparting what you call proper levels of discipline?'

'Pretty much,' nodded Kirsty, grinning at Copeland, who was encouragingly patting her shoulder. A moment later her grin became alarm as she asked, 'Are you eating another ChewiVit, Inspector? Is that your second today?'

'No,' smiled Copeland. 'It's about my...' He rummaged in his pocket to take out the two packets Keira had given him after they had toured her ChewiVit packaging depot in the old customer restaurant. 'Oops, that packet seems to be empty,' said Copeland, screwing up the wrapper and fishing the second packet out of his pocket.

Kirsty stopped the car and grabbed the packet off him. She waved it in front of his face. 'This is a ten pack! You've eaten a whole ten pack in one day?'

'And one after breakfast and the one I had with the gruel,' grinned Copeland with his thumb up.

'My God!' screamed Kirsty. She pointed to the pack she held in her hand. 'Look! It says one-a-day! They act like super vitamins to give you energy, well-being...Vitality! My God! You've had twelve since breakfast!'

'Yeah... Feeling good, uh-uh, like a young man should, uh-uh now,' sang Copeland. Staring wide-eyed at Kirsty he wiggled his hips and cried, 'Hey, Kirsty! I feel like a teenager again! I'm a man! You're a woman! You know what we should do?'

# KEIRA AND KONRAD DISCUSS THEIR DILEMMA.

As soon as Larry Copeland had risen from the circular, pentagram inscribed table and left the senior management conference room Konrad turned to Keira and asked, 'It's not us doing these murders, is it, Kee? There are *some* Dark Stars who leave and you tell me you take care of them...'

Keira glared at Konrad. 'Not by killing them! I find them employment. Do you think I'm arrogant enough to have them killed and have my symbol carved into their foreheads? Really, Konrad!' She sighed and fiddled with her pentagram pendant. 'I think I know what's going on,' she said, 'but I'd like to hear what you have to say.'

Konrad clasped his hands together and stared at them in the flickering candlelight. Taking a deep breath he said, 'If it's not us, then...We know Copeland works for this offshoot of MI5 called Department C. We know Department C is being sponsored by private businesses. We know Ania owns many of those businesses and probably has the owners of the others in her pocket as well. I suspect her so-called Roses are a source of information for this new Department C and Department C uses that information to swoop down on organised crime gangs and seize their assets to pay back the loans from the sponsors. In time, providing Department C can get its act together, sponsors like Ania will be making handsome profits on their investment.'

'And?' said Keira, standing and walking behind Konrad to place her hands on his broad shoulders.

'And Ania's seen a way to use her influence over Department C. She hires people to commit murders and leave a pentagram symbol carved into the victims' foreheads. She then gives Department C information about our Butterburn facility so they send someone to check it out. They see our pentagram symbol everywhere and suddenly we're the prime suspects behind a series of murders. But they have no proof.'

Massaging Konrad's shoulders, Keira said, 'So?'

Konrad thought. 'They'll get proof. It'll be something like a victim surviving and claiming he was a Dark Star who ran for his life from your evil organised crime empire – trying to silence him will appear to give us the motivation for the murders. Or they'll catch one of the killers. Or think they have. It'll be some stooge Ania has paid a fortune to. They'll be offered a deal if they name the person who hired them. They'll say it was you. You'll be arrested or…'

'Or what, my Viking friend?' Keira softly asked.

Konrad turned his head to look up at Keira. He removed her hands from his shoulders and stood to face her. '*Or*, My Lady, we could stand and fight!'

Keira took his face between her hands. 'We're not going to fight, Konrad. A gun battle with the police would play straight into Ania's hands. They would win. Do you remember me finding you near death near York, Konrad? Do you want to lose another battle? Besides, killing police officers is not a great foundation for the sort of future we're trying to build, is it? No. We need something to prove Ania is really behind these pentagram murders. We need all the information we can get so it's more important than ever we get into the security services computers. Inspector Copeland is still our key to that. Keep offering him every courtesy and make sure he doesn't leave, Konrad.'

'Understood, My…Are you going somewhere, Kee?'

Keira stroked Konrad's cheeks as she said, 'I need to get out. Get some exercise. Do something exciting. Ease some of the stress. I think I was as bored as Copeland on the tour I gave him this morning. I was so glad he didn't want to see the Dark Star luxury apartments, the gyms, the entertainment complex, or the recruits' mixed dormitories, the meditation halls, the re-education centre…I think I'll visit that child grooming gang we said we'd take care of.'

Konrad nodded. 'I'll assemble a couple of our kill teams to ride with you.'

'Don't bother, Konrad,' whispered Keira. 'There's only about fifteen of them. Just send a collection squad to take them to our incarceration facility. I've had some extra pits dug so we might as well use them. I'll have them hog-tied and ready for the collection squad.'

'It would be quicker to kill them, Kee,' Konrad whispered.

Keira smiled. 'You're just worried I won't get back until morning aren't you? Don't worry, they won't gather together until later so I can spare a couple of hours now before I go.'

Keira pulled Konrad's face closer to hers and, just before their lips met, Konrad whispered, 'Only a couple of hours?'


FREYA.


Freya also needed to de-stress so went for a run and spent the afternoon catching up on another investigation while she waited for a sighting of the pentagram killers dirty white van.

Even according to the MI5 database, Ania Rose had seemingly not existed until just over eight years previously when she had got planning permission to build a three storey super mansion north of Bricknall and adopted sixteen year old Karen Liddell. Freya knew Ania had told Copeland she had attended Cambridge, but a thorough search of their records failed to show Ania Rose had ever been there. At least there was some information for her adopted daughter, Karen Liddell. Her history was recorded briefly at an expensive, prestigious girls' school, from which she had been expelled at the age of fourteen, and a record of her being in a psychiatric institution for two years after that. Freya wondered where this twenty four year old woman was now and whether Ania Rose still had any contact with her, but thought her less than relevant and turned her search efforts back to Ania Rose, desperate to find even one single photograph of her.

Wading through the Dark Web into the Darker Web finally yielded a clue. According to a historian who had pompously given himself the online name-tag 'Tacitus', Ania Rose had been around for hundreds of years – or more accurately, women calling themselves Ania Rose had because *Ania Rose* was not a person, but a title, just like Beryl had the title 'Pickford' as head of the Pickfords. Ignoring the fact the historian calling himself *Tacitus* was probably a certifiable lunatic and had taken his own life by blowing out his brains, Freya recalled Beryl Pickford had said something that Copeland had picked up on. What was it? Yes! That was it. Beryl Pickford had said the Pickfords had found the Ania **Roses** helpful. Roses plural! Beryl Pickford had said it was a slip of the tongue, but it made sense. Ania Rose was not one person but the title given to the head honcho of The Roses. Freya had a new line of enquiry – The Roses. Freya read on and, according to the historian who had blown his brains out, The Roses had been involved in trade and had owned land since before the Roman invasion. Since *before* the Roman invasion? Since the first century? Unlikely, thought Freya, and diverted her searches to the dead historian.

Ten minutes later, Freya had her head in her hands. Even the most extreme conspiracy theorists known as the Truth Investigation Council, or the TICs for short, had written the historian *Tacitus* off as a complete head-case. There was even a condemnation from one Thomas Benson Esq., who argued conspiracies were a matter of fact (such as aliens building

Atlantis and JFK being assassinated by Elvis who was, incidentally and as a matter of fact, still alive and working in a fish and chip shop in Cardiff) and seekers of what Thomas Benson called The Truth should not be misled by charlatans like insane fake historians who blew their own brains out.

Oh, well, thought Freya, let's try a different approach. Copeland had been helpful after a few pints and had told Freya he was soon meeting with someone called Louise who could give him enough to get Keira Starr put away for a million years. Freya thought Copeland may have been exaggerating a little. She tried cross referencing Ania Rose with the name Louise. Nothing. She tried the Dark Web. Nothing. She tried the Darker Web. Nothing...except a suggestion she cross referenced the name Ania with the name Lou. By the gods, thought Freya: the Darker Web search engine makes Google look like an amateur! She did as suggested and got... Bloody historian hash-tag Tacitus again. Freya sighed. OK... Freya read what Mr. certifiably insane, conspiracy theory outcast, gun in the roof of the mouth and pull the trigger Tacitus had to say.

Freya read a very well argued and badly punctuated exposé about a contest. She told herself it couldn't be true. She told herself the historian was mad and some crazy contest simply couldn't be *that* important. She poured herself a large Scotch, followed by another and decided it was all garbage.


## Copeland. Sort of.

Poking his dishevelled haired head around the door of his master suite on the second floor of Keira Starr's stately home Copeland shouted, 'What?'

Tall blond-bearded Konrad shouted, 'Can you turn the music down?'

'What?' shouted Copeland.

Konrad pointed to his ear and made a turning motion with his hand.

Copeland responded with a cheesy grin and two fingers and shut the door.

Konrad turned to look at Kirsty. With her hands on her hips she sneeringly said, 'Told you! Ruth and Linda have been in there for nearly three hours. And that was after *I* was in there for an hour with him until they showed up. He's insatiable!'

Konrad gave her a benevolent smile and said, 'Do you still have the packet of ChewiVits you took off him?' Tapping her riding crop against her thigh, Kirsty handed them over. Konrad looked at them and said, 'So Lady Keira gave Copeland these as a gift and you took them off him?'

'I certainly did!' Kirsty replied proudly. 'He was overdosing and you know what…'

'So you stole them off him,' said Konrad.

Kirsty's face fell. 'I didn't steal…'

'Kirsty!' snapped Konrad. 'You of all people know our punishment for anyone caught stealing.'

'But, Konrad…' stuttered Kirsty, looking imploringly at Konrad.

'Report to Kurt,' ordered Konrad. 'Tell him you have admitted theft and accept whatever punishment he sees fit.'

Kirsty hands were clasped together. 'Konrad… Please…'

'And when your punishment is over, Kirsty, you will make recompense to Inspector Copeland by donating the next ten days of your ChewiVits ration to him.'

Kirsty was distraught. 'Konrad…No… Please…I'll do…'

'Go!' barked Konrad, pointing down the corridor.

With tears in her eyes, Kirsty slowly plodded away down the corridor. The two Dark Star guards started giggling. Konrad glared at them. They tried to stop. He smiled and winked at them and they let their laughter out. Konrad placed a hand on each of their shoulders. 'Kamille, Kamilla, you know what's expected of you?' he said. They bit their lips and nodded. Konrad turned and banged on Copeland's door again. He waited. He banged again. The door vibrated on its hinges. The door opened slightly to show Copeland's perspiring face.

'What now?' shouted Copeland's perspiring face. Konrad stepped back and pointed at Kamille and Kamilla. Copeland grinned and shouted, 'Oh! Right! Shift change. Good. I think I've worn these two out. Hang on!'

The door closed. Konrad waited, sensing Kamilla and Kamille behind him were becoming tense. He suspected one of them was nervously straightening her pentagram armband.

Finally, the music was turned down and Copeland opened the door wide. Servant-maids Linda and Ruth appeared, looking completely worse for wear and trying to fix their hair. Linda paused to hug Copeland and say, 'That was brilliant, Larry,' and Ruth paused to kiss Copeland's cheek and say, 'I've never known a man with so much energy!'

Copeland waved the dishevelled servant-maids goodbye as they wearily disappeared down the corridor and wiped his sweating forehead on his shirt sleeve before turning to smile at Kamille and Kamilla, raise his eyebrows and say, 'Ready for some fun girls?'

Konrad cried, 'Grab him!' and the two Dark Stars leapt forward to grab Copeland's arms.

'No!' screamed Copeland. 'I want to carry on dancing!'

## KURT VISITS THE NAUGHTY SEAT.

Master of Hounds Kurt stopped and leaned against the wall of the basement torture chamber. He lifted his shoe to view the latest occupational hazard stuck to the bottom. He didn't really mind. He was used to it and, besides, the stuff that came out of the dogs had led directly to increasing his influence and power. Besides being a chief martial arts trainer and Master of Hounds, Lady Keira had recently promoted him and given him the extra responsibility of being the one and only *official* Longbeck Estate pooper-scooper officer. He even had his own plastic gloves. After relishing the prestige of his new role, Kurt tried to remember why he had descended into the basement. Vaguely aware this was neither one of his good or bad days, Kurt remembered and clicked his fingers. Only a minor amount of brown goo sprayed from his plastic glove. Placing his sticky shoe back on the ground he crossed the corridor to open the door opposite. He pressed the button for the light timer and strolled down the staff toilet corridor.

The staff toilet door required the key Lady Keira had returned to him. He unlocked the door, put the key back in his pocket and took out the little torch he had, for once, remembered to bring. Kurt may have been used to what came out of the rear of dogs, but the stench assailing his nostrils when he opened the door was something else. 'Blimey, Kylie!' he said, heaving as he clenched his nose.

Kylie's entire body was trembling. A large droplet of water fell from the overhead cistern and splattered on the back of her cropped, wet head. She lifted her head. Another drop splattered on her face. She looked at Kurt, groaned, 'You're not real,' and let her head sag again.

'Fair enough,' said Kurt. 'I'll just leave you here then. You probably like being sat on an old toilet with your hands chained behind the downpipe while that rusty water drips from the cistern so you never go to sleep. Have the constant nightmares that keep coming while you're awake been interesting? The brain's a funny old thing, isn't it? Quite remarkable really. They say not sleeping means no dreaming so after a few days you dream while you're still awake otherwise the brain explodes or something. I had a lot of snakes crawling around my legs after my third day without sleep. You certainly learn all about your deepest fears on the naughty seat, don't you Kylie? Oh, dear. The corridor light's gone off. Pitch black down here, isn't it? Hang on I'll just try to find the switch on this torch. Can't see a thing…'

The torch came on. Light blasted into Kylie's eyes. 'Aargh! Turn it off!' she screamed. Kurt felt a little sympathetic and pointed it at the floor. 'So,' said Kurt, 'I hear you were hallucinating about something inside you clawing at your insides to get out. That must have hurt.'

Exhausted, Kylie muttered, 'You really are real? I can't tell anymore. I know Lady Keira was real. She helped me.'

'Really? How?' asked Kurt, curious.

'That thing inside me… I'm sure that was real. It was gnawing and clawing at my insides. Lady Keira helped me. She told me if I tore my intestines out and ate them then the thing in them would go away. It hurt like hell but it worked.'

'Oh, right,' nodded Kurt. 'The old eat the creature that's eating you trick, eh? I don't think that really happened, Kylie. Your hands have been handcuffed behind the downpipe the whole time. I know. I've still got the key. And I hate to be the bearer of bad news, but it looks like your stomach is still where it was when I put you down here.'

'NO!' growled Kylie. 'Keira came and saved me. My stomach came back because I ate it. I owe Keira everything. There's nothing I wouldn't do for her!'

'I understand, Kylie,' sighed Kurt. 'I suppose I've felt the same way since she helped me survive the venom all those snakes had bitten into me. It was pretty painful before that. Anyway, enough of this idle chit-chat, young lady. Keira sent me to get you out because she has a job for you. It seems some clever girl name Kylie put a tracker on that Copeland chap's car when he was up at our labs near Butterburn.'

'Butter... burn,' Kylie groaned as her head sagged again and water splashed on the back of it. 'I was burned alive twice yesterday. I know we're trained to ignore pain but it hurt.'

'Just another waking nightmare, Kylie,' Kurt assured her. 'You'll feel better once you finally get some sleep. You mark my words – it'll all be like a bad dream in a few years time. In fact, it will be exactly like a bad dream. You'll have it every night, and every morning you'll wake up worshipping Keira for saving you. Now, where was I? Yes, so this tracking device placed on Copeland's car was tracked going to a few different places and Lady Keira now thinks one of them might be the home of Ania Rose so she wants you to go there and...'

Kylie's head shot up. 'Go *there!* For God's sake leave me here!' she begged.

'Oh, come on Kylie,' soothed Kurt. 'You said you'd do anything Keira asked of you, and I'm sure Ania Rose and her Roses can't be as bad as all those rumours say. If she catches you spying on her house then I'm sure she'll just invite you in for a nice cup of tea and a chocolate muffin, so let's get those handcuffs off, get you all cleaned up and find you some clothes, shall we?'

'And I'll feel better? And I won't be imagining all these horrible spiders crawling all over my skin?'

Kurt winced. 'The spiders are actually real, Kylie.'

# COPELAND.

Also having problems distinguishing dreams and reality was a certain Inspector Larry Copeland. He didn't care though. He was happy. In fact, he was as happy as Larry. His dream failed to involve intestinal gnawing creatures, snakes, or even spiders, but he had felt like a sheep being dipped into a big bath and held underwater by two athletic Dark Stars and one Viking-like giant. He had wondered if the submergence dream symbolised some sort of Dark Star initiation ritual into their pentagram-loving Satanic cult, and his inner voice had eagerly agreed with, *Yeah, man! A weird Satanic cult that baptises people just like Christians do! Rock on, Copeland!* And the dream carried on with some shampoo, soap, a towel, fresh clothes and being manhandled down the grand staircase into a black Range Rover where, from the back seat, Copeland waved cheerily to Konrad as the car pulled away and Konrad went back into Longbeck House shaking his head.

The next thing Copeland was aware of was being very happy to be in a very yellow apartment with soft piano music and the smell of perfume and meeting Phil and Julie Redman. Phil claimed he had met Copeland once before when he had visited a crime scene in Dorset where Phil had been the copper on duty behind the police tape. It was the same day Phil had later given an interview to the press and afterwards got fired. Copeland gave "his old mate" Phil a hug that nearly snapped his spine. Phil had to steer Copeland away from doing the same to Julie. Copeland thought dyed blonde Julie was really dreamy – as in a character in a dream. Copeland further suspected Phil Redman was his devious subconscious inserting his ideal self into the dream: Phil was slim, handsome and, most importantly, thirty years younger.

Copeland's happy-dream theory was fully supported by other unusually bizarre events, such as the way his dream self ignored the steak and chips and instead piled his plate with tasty broccoli, drank orange juice instead of wine, and the weird refusal of apple crumble while patting his protruding stomach and telling his hosts he was trying to lose weight.

While engaged in eating the best broccoli mound he had ever tasted, Copeland clapped a lot and shouted 'Hurrah!' quite frequently as Phil Redman told him how he'd been a night club bouncer who couldn't pay the rent until he met Keira Starr, became a recruit and was soon to graduate as a Dark Starr in record time due to his black belts in lots of Japanese and Chinese words Copeland had never heard of (but 'Hurrahed' anyway) and had lasted longer sparring with Lady Starr than anyone else for months (Applause) and had the bruises to prove it (Eye of the tiger, Phil!). Phil explained he'd been re-educated (Learning lights the mind, Phil!) and had shown unswerving loyalty and willingness to do anything for the cause (Good for you!) and was really looking forward to his initiation ceremony to become a fully fledged Dark Star and 'sticking it to the bad guys' (HURRAH!), selling less harmful drugs (Well done Phil!) and giving businesses value for money for their protection insurance (You really are the main man, Phil!). Julie had been able to resume her career in marketing because the kids were boarding at The Star Prep School during the week and Julie's senile mother was now being cared for in The Star Care Home (Hurrah for Keira!), but Julie was thinking about trying to become a Dark Star herself because she liked the idea of slicing a bad guy's arm off with a samurai sword (You GO girl!). Both the Redmans agreed it would be simply great if the rumours were true and Mr. Copeland was going to be the next head of security now that the former head, Kato, had been summarily dismissed and was literally on gardening leave tending to the rose garden.

When the meal ended Phil tidied away while Julie made coffee and Copeland smiled at all the pretty yellows in the room and bobbed his head to the Beethoven sonata playing in the background while sniffing the perfume where Julie had been sitting. The coffee was accompanied by chocolate mints and ChewiVits. Julie smiled and said, 'We always have our daily ChewiVit after our evening coffee, Mr. Copeland, and we didn't know if you'd had one today so…'

Copeland stared longingly at the three ChewiVits on the saucer Julie Redman held tantalizingly out of reach. She seemed to hover them there for an eternity before placing the saucer down on the far end of the table.

*You're drooling, Copeland,* whispered an inner voice, *but it's alright 'cause this is all just a dream anyway…*

Phil joined them and said, 'We both take our ChewiVit at this regular time whether I'm here or in the recruits' mixed dormitory when I take it after our communal shower. ChewiVits are really good for giving you energy and once you've taken one regularly for about five days your senses really seem to come alive.'

'You really must try one after the coffee, Mr. Copeland,' urged Julie. 'Phil's right. Once you've had a few it's like all the senses are heightened. Colours are more striking, sounds and smells more pleasant, food tastes great and touch… well, touch is really, really heightened…'

With a broad smile, Phil looked lovingly at Julie and said, 'Some *other* sensations are really, really heightened too… Aren't they, Julie?'

Copeland was staring longingly at the saucer of ChewiVits.

Seemingly ignoring her husband's look, Julie said, 'But you should never take more than one a day. I took two the other day, accidentally of course, and I had so much energy I had to burn it off by, er, doing an extra dance class.'

Copeland muttered, 'I like dancing. Can we have…'

'Really? Perhaps you'd like to join my dance class tomorrow?' said Julie. 'But when I took two tablets, and it really was by accident – honest – besides having even more energy, my senses were so heightened everything, and I mean *everything*, was so overwhelmingly fantastically pleasurable I could hardly cope.'

'Hang on, Julie' said Phil, with a note of ire in his voice. 'If two a day are so overwhelmingly fantastic, then why are we only having one a day?'

Julie snapped, 'One a day is enough, Philip! My marketing department is geared for national distribution for one a day. There's an explicit warning on the pack. These vitamin tablets are *super* vitamin tablets. You know that, Philip. The added vit-transferase enzyme Dr. Beth Spencer's team found in human blood and has retro-synthesised make the vitamins work so well they boost all our bodily functions, including the endocrine system.'

'The what?' asked Phil Redman.

'Can we have the ChewiVits now?' groaned Copeland, starting to feel a bit down.

'The endocrine system, Philip!' huffed Julie. 'The endocrine system regulates our hormones – one reason the tablets make us feel good is because the boosted vitamins help stimulate the endocrine system so we make more feel-good hormones like dopamine, serotonin, and endorphins – that's why we want to, er, exercise more to keep up our endorphins – and, of course, we *all* know it boosts our oxytocin… hmmm… But doesn't change ones like insulin or glucagon, and it *definitely* doesn't boost hormones like testosterone, oestrogen, progesterone… Honest! Or we'd all be…erm… trying to make babies, wouldn't we?'

'Can we have..?' began Copeland, but lacked the will to finish the question.

'Hang on, Julie,' said Phil Redman with more ire. 'How do you know all this science stuff?'

Julie folded her arms, looked smug and said, 'I was going to tell you later, but Lady Keira has chosen me to be the new face of ChewiVits. She says I look trustworthy and I'm attractive on screen. Beth – that's Dr. Spencer to you – has been briefing me via video-link for when I'm on TV or giving interviews to magazines. That's why my hair is short and my nails are done… I have my own personal stylists now. Nice young men. ChewiVits hit the shops this weekend for their five day free trial. After that we've decided to sell them for £10 for a pack of five, which is only 500% profit, *and* you can get a pack for less with vouchers from Keira's magazines.'

Phil Redman said, 'You've had your hair done?'

Copeland muttered, 'Did you know Keira only makes ten pence profit from each magazine? But she sells… Forget it… Can we have our ChewiVits now?'

Phil scratched his head. 'I still don't get why we only have one a day, Julie, not if…'

'Bloody hell, Philip! Sometimes!' Julie shook her head in despair. 'Look, you know how it is if you're late taking your daily ChewiVit? And how it is if, God forbid, you actually *forget* to take it? Your body gets a vitamin slump and you feel awful and have bad dreams…'

'Nothing to do with all the feel-good hormones slumping then?' asked Phil.

'Idiot! Of course not!' snapped Julie. 'Serotonin is the happy hormone and lack of it makes you irritable. Am I irritable? No I am bloody not! Despite idiots like you Philip!

Listen, moron…Dopamine is a neurotransmitter, that's why our brain fully appreciates our senses and we experience heightened pleasures and the sodding endorphins, besides acting like an opioid in the brain to minimise pain, well, they create euphoria – am I anything less than euphoric because I haven't had my goddamn ChewiVit today after I took two yesterday – which was completely by accident just like the day before! No! I'm fine! I'm as euphoric as ever so sod off, Philip! And as for you *even inferring* that the oxytocin, the so-called love-drug, goes down and our libido falls from its usual dizzy heights…Well, Philip! You can just forget what we had planned for later tonight!' She slammed a hand on the table before grabbing the saucer, taking a ChewiVit and handing Copeland his.

'Hurrah! Hmmm… honey…' said Copeland as he chewed and Julie waved the saucer towards husband Phil before snatching the final tablet and throwing it into her mouth.

After the ChewiVit slid down his throat Copeland's dream became more bizarre. He sang 'I Want to Break Free' as the athletic Dark Star twins Kamille and Kamilla guided him into the really shiny black Land Rover and he hummed along with the car engine and stroked the lovely leather seat as they drove back to Longbeck House. He dreamt he was back in his room and his friend kind Konrad had put the packet of ChewiVits that nasty Kirsty had stolen from him back on his bed. After dreaming of sharing the ChewiVit packet for supper with Kamilla and Kamille, the dream became really, really strange. Both Kamille and Kamilla were in it.

# FREYA

Taking it all back about scientists working at the pace of a snail with a hernia, Freya read the email from Director Wendy Miller that popped into Inspector Larry Copeland's inbox just before midnight. It said:

Hello Larry,

I hope you have finally learned how to get your emails on your phone so you can read this. I also hope we were right about Keira Starr trying to bribe you to join her and she hasn't just got you there to kill you, in which case you probably won't be reading this even if you have learned to get emails on your phone. (Ha, ha!) Rest assured Larry, if you are killed we'll put a little plaque or something up to remind us how you died for God and country.

So, presuming you haven't been cut up into little pieces and scattered around Yorkshire, I thought you should know there have been some tests done on this vit-transferase enzyme thing your one-time acquaintance Dr. Spencer is putting into these new vitamin tablets.

But first things first. The enzyme really is found in human blood, just as Dr. Spencer claimed. Because the ingredients are all naturally occurring the tablets got speedy approval to go on sale. Except, Larry, the human blood other researchers have tested for this vit-transferase seems to only contain minute quantities of it. Some people's blood has none at all. One university lab had to use a hundred litres of blood to get five microlitres of this super-transferase stuff out of it. Now, I'm told a microlitre is a thousand times smaller than a millilitre, so it's not very much. The university lab injected the five microlitres into two volunteer test subjects, a male and female first year undergraduates. They didn't have enough for more subjects. The scientists say the two subjects appeared to remain quite cheerful and seemed able to perform simple problems very quickly, so no harm there. After a few hours the subjects are said to have reported everything seeming 'more alive', whatever that means. Unfortunately they had to stop the test when the test subjects became, how can I put this? They became very friendly with each other. (As in VERY friendly. You know – wink, wink, nudge, nudge friendly.) The medical watchdog people have dismissed the test because only two people were involved, because it was injected not swallowed, and because the test subjects were first year students anyway so what did the experimenters expect? The government scientists have said they confirm they believe, on balance, and taking all available statistical data into account, a ChewiVit with the added vitamin booster of the naturally occurring, newly discovered vit-transferase enzyme is completely safe. They say they believe ChewiVit vitamin tablets will improve the health of the nation and since each ChewiVit tablet contains two millilitres of super-transferase they expect public well being to improve significantly and put less pressure on the health service. Two millilitres may seem a lot when the other scientists needed a hundred litres of blood just to get a few thousandths of that amount but I think we have to go with the government scientists' advice on this one and assume the tablets are safe and are not some new synthetic, addictive wonder drug as I suspected.

Speaking of synthetic: the synthetic version of the vit-transferase enzyme Dr. Spencer has made to go in the ChewiVit things has been patented by Starr Enterprises. The patent office won't allow naturally occurring things to be patented but has accepted this is a synthetic version so they've okayed it. Keira Starr will have no competition for her new sort of vitamin tablet. I expect she'll make a fortune but it's legal and nothing to do with us so you need to find evidence of her selling proper drugs or making a designer drug that is illegal. Either that or hurry up and get some evidence tying Miss Starr to these pentagram murders. Otherwise you can look for another job.

All the best,
Director W. Miller.

P.S. Hi Larry. Janet here. Wendy dictated the above to me and I'm typing it so I just wanted to remind you about coming round to my house to see the latest gift you gave me for typing up your last report. How about Sunday evening? Shall we say about 6? I'll be ready and waiting.

PPS. Bring some of these new ChewiVit things if you can.

PPPS. And your handcuffs.

Freya found herself tapping her nails on the table top. She looked out of the bay window into the quiet street outside. One question burned in her mind. Who the heck was Janet?

After a large single malt Freya decided it was high time she phoned her agent. Freya knew her agent would still be awake. She always was. Freya felt it was time to confront her agent about why the Foreign Minister Mozawinga blood diamonds story had not been syndicated, and, after she had complained about that, just happen to mention the current story about an evil organised crime gang and a new designer drug was going nowhere. Freya knew she had hit a dead end, especially after she had been unable to find out what was really in the basement below Keira Starr's Butterburn research facility. And while she was admitting her failures to her agent, she may as well tell her how she had wasted her time investigating Ania Rose's tentacle-like business connections and Ania Rose's involvement in a high stakes, inter-company contest. That story was a bust too, unless she counted an insane historian who had committed suicide as a reliable source. While she was at it, Freya thought she might as well also tell her agent about the time she had wasted looking into the pentagram murders because there had not been a single hit on the van used in the anaesthetic robberies and the murders. Freya could guess why – Copeland had told Keira Starr she was a suspect and Keira had instructed her henchmen to lay low until she provided them with another vehicle. Freya tried not to consider Copeland had accepted Keira Starr's bribe and had told her everything.

Freya picked up her phone to call her agent and reconsidered. The trouble with phoning her agent to complain about the Mozawinga story's syndication and admit her failures was risky. Freya's agent was not just her agent. She was also technically her manager. Freya was under contract. It was one of those contracts Freya was locked into but her agent/ manager could tear up at anytime. Freya did not want to lose the contract. She had been out on her own, fending for herself before. It had ended with her in some forsaken corner of the world and surviving by eating insects and vermin. Freya thought she would still phone her agent, but merely politely enquire about the promised syndication of the Mozawinga story.

As she had suspected, her agent was indeed awake. A long conversation ensued. The call did not go as Freya had expected. When it ended Freya poured herself another large single malt. She thought she deserved to celebrate. She sipped and was visualising herself holding her Pulitzer Prize when the laptop pinged. A traffic camera near Watford had spotted the pentagram murderers' van heading north on the M1. Freya looked at the image on the laptop, smiled and wondered if anyone had ever won two Pulitzers.

## 10. Day 9. Thursday.

### KEIRA

Keira handed over her sword to be cleaned and let one of her most trusted Dark Stars take her Vincent Black Shadow to the garage, but kept her black leathers on as she strode across the courtyard in front of her home and around the corner of the west wing to the kennels to get what she needed.

The sun had barely risen but Keira knew Kurt would be there feeding the dogs which had toured the perimeter all night with their Dark Star handlers. Kurt believed in feeding the huge hounds three regular meals a day, mainly so they wouldn't get peckish and eat their handlers. They were fond of human meat.

In his black uniform and two red armbands with their black-on-white pentagram insignias, Kurt was kneeling with his back to her, mixing food into five dog-bowls in front of the wire mesh of one of the kennels. Four dogs were inside. One had its leg up, urinating in a corner, two lay half asleep, the fourth approached the wire mesh and growled at the approaching Keira Starr. Without breaking stride, Keira looked at the huge black hound snarling at her. She held a gloved hand out towards it, raised a single finger and dropped it again. The hound cowered back and sat whining with its head hung.

'My Lady!' said Kurt, standing, turning and dropping to one knee in front of Keira.

Halting in front of him Keira beckoned him to rise with, 'Get up, Kurt. We're all equal here.'

Kurt stood, tilted his head to one side and said, 'You and I both know that's not true, Keira. For a start, no one else can move as fast as you and take out six of my best trained Dark Stars without breaking sweat.'

Keira stared into his eyes. 'You're having one of your more lucid days, aren't you Kurt?'

Kurt laughed. 'I doubt it will last a whole day. A few hours perhaps,' he said.

Keira took his shoulders. 'Still, it must be good to have a few hours when you feel... like yourself.'

Kurt let out an ironic laugh and said, 'Not really. When my faculties are back, like now, I know they will go again. I know in a few hours time this me won't exist anymore. All I can do is hope I'll come back again someday.'

Keira smiled sympathetically, took his head between her hands and brought it down to press her forehead against his. She whispered, 'One day we'll find a way to get that bullet out of your brain without you becoming a vegetable, Kurt.'

'Whatever happens, and whoever I am, My Lady,' Kurt whispered, 'I am and will always remain your most loyal servant.' He stepped back and bowed.

Keira laughed. 'That's because I saved you from those snakes when you'd spent a week on the naughty seat! And exactly when *did* everyone start calling it the naughty seat?'

'It is a seat for people who've been naughty – as well as for putting people like me on. Don't get me wrong. I agree with your reasons. Unless we face the deepest, darkest fears lurking in our nightmares we can never overcome them and be truly free. But you know that's not the reason I'll always be loyal. And it's not because of your plan to take over and deliver justice and replace narcotics with the new tablets either. It's because when all I had was despair you were my saviour, Keira, just like you were for so many Dark Stars.'

Keira folded her black leather arms across her black leather chest. She knew there was another reason Kurt was so loyal.

She stared at him and said, 'The Dark Stars are growing powerful and you still want revenge, don't you Kurt?'

'Of course!' snapped Kurt. 'If I'd been some rich white bloke they would have found a way to get me off. You know how it is – some people even look at *you* a bit funny because you look a bit Arab. What chance had *I* got? None!'

'You did what you had to do, Kurt,' soothed Keira.

'Damn right I did. What else was I supposed to do? We'd already taken out over thirty Taliban and all my mates were dead. Only the Captain was still standing and he was holding his guts in. The last of the morphine had been pumped into Jonesy but there the Captain was, *standing* holding his guts in. We might teach the Dark Star recruits to ignore pain, Keira, but my SAS Captain was something else! He stayed on his feet covering me until I had the last of the Taliban tied up and on their knees, then he gave me his pistol, nodded and keeled over and died. I was alone in the middle of nowhere. What choice did I have? Then a month later I get a Taliban bullet in my head and they tell me I was lucky be alive. But it didn't stop them sending me on another two tours, did it? Then it's back to blighty for a court martial for war crimes.'

Keira placed a hand on his shoulder.

'Five years inside, I was,' continued Kurt, more calmly. 'Five years until they let me out with nothing but the clothes I was standing in. What was I to do? Who hires an ex SAS bloke convicted of war crimes who acts like an imbecile most of the time because he took a bullet for his country? Sometimes I think winter on the streets was harder than Afghanistan, Keira. If you hadn't come along I don't think I would have survived another one. It wasn't the cold, it was the utter despair... Of course I want revenge. I want to get my hands on all those privileged white blokes who sat there passing judgement on me when they didn't know the slightest thing about what it was like being shot at every day and watching what the Taliban did, even to their own people, let alone what they did to us if they took us alive. I want revenge on all those who sent us there but never had to look at the mutilated body of their best mate.'

'Your time will come, Kurt,' sighed Keira.

Kurt nodded grimly, then smiled and said, 'You do know you're covered in blood, don't you?'

Keira pulled forward some strands of her stained black hair to look at. 'I went to sort out another of those child grooming gangs. Some of the girls were there when I got there. What the men were doing with them wasn't nice. I may have been a little overenthusiastic, but most of them survived to be taken to the pits, minus the parts they would need to ever do that sort of thing again of course. If they're lucky they might not bleed out.'

'They'll wish they had after they've spent a few months living in their own filth and on scraps down the pits,' laughed Kurt. 'You know, My Lady, we should rotate the Dark Star guards up there more often. They must be bored with nothing to do except throw their leftovers down to the prisoners.'

'Good idea, Kurt,' agreed Keira. 'I'll get someone right on it, but first I wanted to ask you for… Kurt? Did you hear something?'

A weak, distant voice called, 'Help. Lady Keira. Please. Help.'

Keira looked about. 'That sounds like Kirsty,' she said. Keira looked inside the kennel. She pointed. She said, 'Kurt…Is that Kirsty?'

'Oh, yeah,' said Kurt, grinning. 'She unwisely chose to cower in *that* corner. It's where the dogs prefer to do most of their business. She spent the night in there with the day shift dogs. Now she's getting to know those from the night shift.'

'Help,' beseeched Kirsty, huddled with her arms wrapped around her knees in the corner.

One of the huge hounds plodded over to her and barred its teeth a few inches from her eyes. Keira knew it was Kirsty's eyes because it was the only part of Kirsty not covered with dark brown matter.

'Most of that is from when we threw her in,' explained Kurt, adding, 'I'd be quiet if I were you, Kirsty. They haven't had their breakfast yet. They may be a bit peckish and there's enough of you to feed them all for a week.'

Kirsty's eyes were firmly fixed on the long yellow teeth of the dog in front of her. She was silent. The dog chose not to eat her. Instead, it turned its head and lifted its leg.

Keira said, 'Oh, I can see her face now. That dog must have been holding that in for ages. Why is she in there, Kurt?'

'Theft,' replied Kurt. 'She took a packet of the ChewiVits you gave to Copeland away from him. She says she did it because he'd already eaten a whole pack and a fair few more, but Konrad said that was no excuse for stealing Copeland's ChewiVits and sent her to me to be punished for her thieving. My first idea was to see what happened if I didn't feed the dogs but I know you think she's useful for staff discipline so I suppose they get their usual... As will Kirsty. Unless you've brought back one of those child grooming blokes?'

Keira turned her eyes from Kirsty and grimaced. 'Sorry, Kurt, thought I'd better not,' she said. 'It might give our friend Inspector Copeland the wrong idea about us.'

Kurt said nothing. He turned to look into the kennel again. The dog had finished and was reconsidering sinking its teeth into Kirsty's thigh but was giving Kirsty the benefit of sniffing and drooling over her first. Slowly, Kurt said, 'I think my imbecile self thought Kirsty needed to revisit her humility and put her in there yesterday evening. Sometimes, I sort of get his memories like I've seen what I did on TV.'

Nodding her understanding, Keira called, 'Kirsty! If you carry on harming my horses when Kurt decides to let you out, we'll put you back in and give the dogs lots of ChewiVits. They won't be interested in eating you then, will they?'

Kirsty's cowering head nodded. Then she realised what Keira meant and her wide eyes bulged. Keira turned to Kurt and said, 'You can dissolve the tablets in warm water.'

'Good tip. Warm water. Thanks,' said Kurt.

'Right,' said Keira, turning away from Kirsty's shocked, bulging eyes and clapping her hands. 'The reason I came to see you Kurt is to get the key to the basement toilet so I can see how Kylie is getting on.'

Kurt looked puzzled. 'She's gone,' he said.

'Oh, dear,' said Keira. 'Surely she drank the dripping water? I know she was quite skinny, but she can't have starved to death in just a few days? Don't tell me her heart gave out? You know, Kurt, that's starting to happen too often. I blame all those trans-fats these people have stuffed into them when they were children.'

'She's not dead,' explained Kurt. 'She's gone. You told me to send her to see if the place Copeland had been tracked to was Ania Rose's home. She's gone there.'

Keira slapped a gloved palm onto her forehead. 'I didn't mean *that* Kylie, Kurt. Not the Australian Kylie. I meant the other one.'

'Oh! The one with the mole on her chin!'

'No! The *other* other Kylie! Damn. Maybe we do need to find some more names for Dark Stars like Kirsty keeps saying we should… But I can't believe you sent the Kylie who was on the naughty seat – her brain will still be Swiss cheese for at least a week. She's likely to do anything.'

Kurt laughed. 'I wouldn't worry. All she has to do is see who's going in and out of a house. How wrong can she get that? Besides, she's completely devoted to you. She says from now on she will worship you and call you goddess Keira.'

Quietly and with maximum menace, Keira said, 'If anyone *ever* calls me a goddess I will personally rip out their tongue and make them eat it! You'd better let Kylie know that when she gets back.' She sighed her sigh. 'Let's cheer ourselves up. Let's give the dogs lots of ChewiVits.'


## COPELAND.


Copeland woke and opened his eyes expecting to see the piano that had fallen on his head. There was no piano. He closed his eyes again.

An inner voice groaned, *What the hell we were drinking last night, Copeland? This is the worst hangover ever. And what was with all those weird dreams?*

Copeland tried hard to think about the last thing he could remember. That was it… That ginger haired woman built like a shot-putter named Kirsty had taken his packet of healthy vitamins off him. Damn thief! He hoped she someday got what she deserved. His muddled brain slowly recalled he had not, in fact, imbibed even a droplet of alcohol, or even beer for that matter. In a flash, Copeland realised what had happened; why he could hardly remember the day before; the way time had jumped; the significance of all those weird dreams; why he had ended up in bed without his stripy pyjamas on… It was obvious! He had sunstroke! All that walking around outside on the boring Keira Starr tour… Sunstroke! He was certain. He was certain because he'd had sunstroke before. Unlikely as it was, it had happened on holiday in Wales when he was ten. Near a place called Towyn, to be exact. A caravan holiday. It was the last holiday his little sister ever had. That sunstroke was all delirium, weird dreams and time jumping, just like yesterday. It had lasted for a whole day and night and afterwards he had felt just like he did now, like a piano had been dropped on his head and he had been drained of all his bodily fluids.

He felt relieved it was sunstroke and not a hangover – because that would mean years of drinking had not made him immune and the fear of a hangover might even make him want to drink less... Whew! Lucky escape, there! Thank goodness it's only sunstroke, he thought, and nodded off again.


## FREYA.


In contrast, Freya woke up from her usual four hours sleep feeling so alive she decided to go for an early morning run. Warming up with some stretching in Copeland's lounge, she switched the TV in the corner on. It was the usual diet of breakfast TV with the middle-aged husband and wife couple known affectionately as Richie and Jude. They sat on their sofa interviewing a healthy looking woman with short blonde hair who, Freya gathered, was name Julie Redman. Julie extolled the virtues of ChewiVits and asked interviewers Richie and Jude what they thought of them. Richie and Jude had apparently enjoyed their advance trial and agreed the ChewiVits had indeed made them feel 'more alive' and 'great' and 'like teenagers'. They asked Julie about side-effects. For some reason Richie went bright red and Jude started giggling and nudging her husband, leaving photogenic Julie Redman a free hand to promote the health benefits of

ChewiVits unchallenged. As Freya stretched and pulled an ankle to her spine, she was interested to learn of a possible ChewiVit side-effect – people seemed to prefer a healthier, balanced diet, and although Julie Redman's claim that ChewiVits could end the obesity epidemic seemed optimistic, Freya thought ChewiVits generally sounded like a good thing.

Freya switched off the unending free commercial and pounded the pavements, reflected on her night time musings and concluded that winning two Pulitzer prizes might be too ambitious. The pentagram murders story would be good, especially if the murders led to the arrest of billionaire Keira Starr, as Freya was confident they surely would, but it was the other story she was sure would win her the prestigious Pulitzer. She knew better than ask her agent how the information had come her way, but a young married couple and their baby had escaped the village in Serbia before the flesh-eating bio-weapon had got to them. Freya's theory was the villagers had been used as guinea pigs for the bio-weapon and if she could track down the young couple who had escaped they could tell her exactly what had happened and what had wiped out everyone else in their village. Freya felt herself increase her running speed the more excited she got about getting back to Serbia.

Every other story was irrelevant. Her agent had said she could have a few more days to see if she could wrap up the pentagram murders story – had she told her agent about billionaire Keira Starr's involvement? Freya thought she probably hadn't, but it didn't really matter, not as much as avoiding these people standing at the bus stop anyway. Freya thought it might be wise to slow down and resumed a more steady speed along the pavement once she had dodged through the crowd of commuters. So what if her agent had said she should forget all about Keira Starr's Dark Star organised crime empire? So what if her agent had said to forget all about Ania Rose and her manipulative business dealings to create her business empire of fawning followers pretentiously calling themselves The Roses? So what if her agent had said she was mad to even try to investigate a story about a contest between Ania Rose's companies and two others, even if they had bet millions on their own contestants winning? Apart from Copeland telling her about Tom Benson being 'a contestant', Freya had nothing to go on anyway except the ramblings of a dead lunatic historian so she could see her agent's point. None of those stories mattered. Serbia was the big one and Freya was more than willing to follow her agent's instructions, especially now she had assured Freya her story about the blood diamonds and corrupt African politician Anthony Mozawinga was being syndicated the following week and a large payment was already heading her way.

## MR. GREY AND MR. PINK.

The plans had changed. Mr. Grey knew they had to move more quickly than he had anticipated. As usual, he and Mr. Pink had gone to the rendezvous with Mr. White. It was in Sheffield, in the Morrisons car park, as usual. They had handed over the refuse sack containing what Mr. Pink continued to refer to as heart bones, as usual. As usual, Mr. White had looked into the refuse sack, nodded and handed over a Tesco bag full of cash. But Mr. Grey knew nothing about this had been *as usual*. Mr. White may have thought he was being clever but Mr. Grey had always known he was the smartest person in the room, or in this case in the Morrisons car park, and Mr. Grey saw the signs and knew this was no time to have all his eggs in the same shopping trolley.

Mr. Grey knew when assets were becoming a liability. He had ordered the liquidation of many assets in his time in the KGB and SVR and could read all the tell-tale signs the expendable assets had failed to read when their time was up. Mr. White had met them in the car park, as usual, but not in the usual place out of view of the store's security cameras, and Mr. White had conveniently kept his back to the camera even when he conspicuously sidestepped away. The wide brimmed hat sitting on top of Mr. White's white hair was another giveaway. True, it was a sunny day, but did Mr. White really need to keep it on until he was driving away? Mr. Grey had no doubt Mr. White was wearing the hat, which he had obviously bought on holiday in Mexico, to obscure his face from the cameras and make everyone think he was going to a fancy dress party as Speedy Gonzales. Mr. Grey considered that was actually possible since the wiry little Mr. White certainly had the nose to imitate a mouse, but Mr. Grey thought his other theory more likely and the sombrero was to hide Mr. White's face.

Besides shielding his face from the cameras while making sure Mr. Grey's and Mr. Pink's faces were not, Mr. White had made another, bigger give-away mistake. Mr. Grey knew Mr. White was simply a middle man. He was just a lackey. Mr. Grey knew there was a Big Boss lurking in the background somewhere. It was not unusual for Mr. White to take the heavy duty, carefully tied by the little yellow thing provided, plastic sack from them and immediately make a phone call to the ultimate Big Boss to report he had got the latest delivery from what Mr. White called 'the less than competent assassins'. Mr. Grey did not mind being publicly belittled and humiliated like that. He knew it was just Mr. White trying to motivate him and Mr. Pink to become better killers: back in his KGB/ SVR days, Mr. Grey had himself used the complete humiliation technique to foster increased commitment many times and it had always worked, right up until the highly motivated agent got himself killed taking one stupid risk too many a few weeks later. Mr. Grey thought, *C'est la vie, as the Italians say*. Where was he? Oh, the phone call. So, Mr. White often telephoned their ultimate, Big Boss employer as soon as the heart bone bag had been delivered, and, indeed, he often used the term 'My Lady' when talking to Big Boss. Mr. Grey had no qualms about working for a mere woman but the Big Boss being a member of the English aristocracy would have bothered him if she was not a long-term employer with her long list and, English aristocrat Lady or not, if she was paying him to kill people then she probably had a good reason to want them dead. After the first six kills, Mr. Grey had abandoned his theory that the victims were her ex-husbands. After twelve he had abandoned his theory they were her ex lovers. Not that Mr. Grey thought a woman having twelve or even, God forbid, thirteen lovers was a bad thing. He wasn't sexist. But some of the men they had performed the pentagram artwork on would have been lucky to have ever had even one lover. This had prompted theory three in Mr. Grey's brain. Their ultimate, big boss employer was a very old, rich, lonely, desperate, nymphomaniac woman – obviously titled or Mr. White would not have called her My Lady – and had put all these young and good-for-nothing ex-lovers in her will. Mr. Grey was painfully aware that English lawyers charged extortionate amounts, so it was probably cheaper for the old Duchess (or whatever) to hire people to kill the ex-lovers than hire lawyers to change her will. It made sense. That was why she wanted their hearts, so she could look at them on her mantelpiece and remember them with some fondness in her dying days. Either that, or 'My Lady' was just vindictive and wanted their removed hearts to gloat over. Mr. Grey could sympathise with that as well.

But now! Today! Mr White had not used the 'My Lady' but had actually used their employer's name. Out loud. Well within their hearing. Mr. White had phoned and, as usual, had the usual conversation…'Yes, the bag is pretty heavy…Yes, it looks like these dolts have met their quota…' BUT THEN!!! TODAY!!!! 'Yes, Miss Rose, I'll let them know their work was appreciated, don't worry about that Ania.'

What really clinched it for Mr. Grey, and made him sure he and Mr. Pink had become as disposable as a soiled nappy, was when Mr. White thanked them for their services, only adding he would see them soon as an afterthought.

As they drove out of Sheffield and Mr. Grey noticed Mr. Pink had taken the A61 route again and, as usual, was stopping every fifty metres for traffic lights – with bloody cameras! – Mr. Grey let out a huge sigh. He knew people only made the mistake of actually naming the **real** employer to employees if they had become expendable. And expendable usually meant being killed in the next 24 to 48 hours, though when Mr. Grey had been the unnamed employer in the good old days only a few months before an expendable lifespan was more like 24 to 48 minutes. Oh, hum, those were happy days, thought Mr. Grey as he tapped his phone to Google who this Ania Rose was. In its infinite, all-encompassing, God-like wisdom Google said 'The nearest florist to you is…'

'Why you punching car door?' asked Mr. Pink.

Mr. Grey thought this deserved a considered, measured and deeply philosophical response. He raised a finger and wisely proclaimed, 'Time and tide wait for no…' Bugger, what was it Copeland had told him the phrase was? Was it crabs? No. That was something Copeland said he'd once had after he'd been on holiday to Crete. Mermaids? That made sense.

Mermaids lived in the sea. The tides were to do with the sea…
No, not mermaids. Fishing trawlers? Probably not. It might
be… No, that's a bit rude. After some thought, Mr. Grey once
again realised his mind was not what it had once been, settled
on, 'Bugger off, Mr. Pink! I'm busy,' and returned to the
infinite wisdom of the all-knowing and, if it had its way, all-
seeing, Google and tapped until he got to page 23 where he
found the name of Ania Rose, who was apparently not a Lady
or a member of any sort of royalty at all (not even the Belgian
one). She was only mentioned on Google for owning an
insignificant public relations company outside London – not
even *in* London, and Ania Rose was so unimportant she did
not merit even a single photo of herself on the whole internet.

But Mr. Grey knew she was getting money from
somewhere to pay them. As if a light had come down from the
heavens, Mr. Grey had his road to Damascus moment, or
more accurately his road from Sheffield moment, and Mr.
Grey had an epiphany… Inheritance! This Ania Rose had
inherited wealth and the men they were killing – he used the
term loosely since his main job was passing Mr. Pink a large
freezer bag – these ex-lovers might contest old Ania Rose's
will when she probably wanted to leave everything to her cats.

This realisation did not change the fact that Big Boss Ania
Rose had decided he and Mr. Pink were now expendable,
probably because Mr. Pink had got the victims' addresses
wrong once too many times. Mr. Grey knew a change of
course was required, along with a change of name to go with
it. He wanted his new name to be a good, firm name, just like
Comrade President Khrushchev, who had tried so hard to start
a nuclear war with the despotic democratic USA in 1962. A
good, firm name, Khrushchev. Not like Putin. What sort of
name was that? Poo-tin? It sounded like metallic dog faeces.
Mr. Grey hated Putin. He hated Putin for fundamentally

ideological reasons – it had nothing to do with Putin ordering him to be sent to Siberia. Honest.

Mr. Grey put past differences behind him and focused on the present ones. He turned to Mr. Pink. 'Once you get on the motorway, and once you get past the seventeen miles of cones and non-existent road works, put your foot down and get to London. We need to start our new career and do our first job for The Broker,' said Mr. Grey as he thought, *And then your life very abruptly ends Mr. Pink.*

## FREYA

Despite the baseball cap worn by the taller man and the fedora hat worn by the shorter one (along with the dark overcoat despite the sweltering weather), it did not take Freya long to go through the video footage from the Morrisons car park security camera and have several grainy black and white images of the two men's faces. She sent them off to the Department C computer where she knew they would be shunted to the MI5 and police facial recognition database. Within minutes an answer to her query appeared on the laptop screen. It said: *Your custom is important to us. We have a high volume of enquiries at the moment and your request may take longer than usual. You are fifty second in the queue.*

Freya closed her eyes and gritted her teeth. She distracted herself for a while by re-examining the gifts she had bought online for Copeland. Then she went back to the Morrisons car park footage and went through it frame by frame, looking for the slightest glimpse of the face of the sombrero hat man who had handed over the money to pay the pentagram killers for their grisly murders of innocent men.

# MR. PINK AND MR. GREY

'So you say Valdis should drive to London?' said Mr. Pink. Mr. Grey nodded.

'Because if Valdis drive back to home in Birmingham then we die?' said Mr. Pink.

Mr. Grey nodded.

'That Mr. White or someone has put bomb in our nice flat now we expendable? See? Valdis learn new word you taught him. Ex-pen-da-bull,' said Mr. Pink.

Mr. Grey nodded.

'Mr. White stupid, eh? He say name of Lady Rose Ania, eh? He give away they plan kill us, eh?' said Mr. Pink.

Mr. Grey nodded.

'Good job you listen good, Mr. Grey. Valdis not listening. Valdis was looking at silly Mexican hat on Mr. White head,' said Mr. Pink.

Mr. Grey nodded and spoke. He said, 'Watch out! Der'mo! That was close! Keep your eyes on the road, Mr. Pink!'

'Valdis ask questions. You nod. Valdis have to look at you, Mr. Grey!' said Mr. Pink while keeping his eyes on the road.

Mr. Grey glared. 'Right, Mr. Pink,' he said. 'Let's go through it for the tenth time before we get to London, shall we? *Don't* look at me and nod when you're overtaking! Yes, Mr. White let the name of our employer slip when he called her Ania Rose. Before today he's always called her My Lady. So that means they don't care that we know who is hiring us and that means they don't care because we'll soon be dead so that means we definitely shouldn't go back to our rancid accommodation in Birmingham because they're either waiting for us there or they've done what I would do and rig a bomb to go off a few moments after we've gone in, or watch us go in and set it off with a phone device, so we need to forget about working for Mr. White and this Ania Rose and start our new hit man business straight away. We're going to London to fulfil our first contract and kill someone name Larry Copeland. Now, have you chosen a new name?'

Mr. Pink said, 'What rancid mean? Never mind. Valdis already learn one word today. Valdis new name is Ozola.'

Mr. Grey was impressed. 'Ozola? That's a good name. We will be Stalin and Ozola. But tell me, Mr. Pink, why have you chosen Ozola? Is Ozola your hero like Stalin is mine?'

Mr. Pink smiled, very pleased with himself. He said, 'Ozola my name. I am Valdis Ozola. It on passport.'

Mr. Grey would have put his face in his hands but knew he had to keep his eyes on the road in case he had to jerk the steering wheel again. Impassively looking straight ahead, he said, 'Let's just stick with Mr. Grey and Mr. Pink, shall we?'


## FREYA


The face of the mysterious sombrero man who had taken the plastic refuse sack from the pentagram murderers in the Morrisons car park and handed them a conspicuous Tesco bag in return had proven elusive. Despite her best efforts, all Freya had managed to get was a grainy image of the back of his neck, his right ear, right cheek, and a very long, almost mouse-like, nose. The shadow cast from the ridiculous, wide-rimmed sombrero he wore did not help, but at least she had a good idea of his height. She had extrapolated from the nearby cars and calculated he was quite short for a male and perhaps only as tall as she was. The cut of his expensive grey suit also said he was very much on the thin side. He had also sidled off sideways with a slight limp. Glimpses of his white hair had prompted Freya to conclude he was elderly. She had given the unknown man the title 'Mr. Sombrero'.

After three hours a flashing icon at the bottom of her screen told Freya the facial recognition software finally had a match. She clicked. It was the MI5 database. The message was titled 'Top Secret'. She read the probability of a match was over 90% for one of the men she was sure was a pentagram murderer. She read the information. She clasped her head and muttered, 'Skit'r,' which roughly translates as 'Poo' (though in no way connected to a small, furry bear of the same name). She clicked again and saw the second face had been recognised, amazingly enough, by passport control. Face number two belonged to a Latvian called Valdis Ozola. Poor Valdis had experienced a very troubled upbringing and extreme neglect as a child due to his parents being short of cash and unable to buy him a PlayStation. His anger had festered until it led to him feeding his parents into a wood chipper and fleeing the country. He had also despicably killed the family rabbit. The reason for this was unknown, except he was a complete psychopath. Interpol had a warrant out on him. So had the RSPCA.

## MR. GREY AND MR. PINK

Parking had been the cause of the first argument. Mr. Grey was adamant they should not park the dirty white van directly in front of the house where they were about to kill someone. Nosy neighbours would spot it, and possibly them. Mr. Pink countered this argument with logic: he had driven in circles around the surrounding one-way streets for nearly half an hour and this was the only parking space they had seen, and that was only because that red Ferrari sports car had left the space just as they approached it on their third lap around the streets of Leyton.

Then there was the argument about money. Mr. Grey had finally backed down and agreed Mr. Pink should get half the fee The Broker was paying them to kill Larry Copeland. At first, Mr. Grey had resented Mr. Pink asking for half, especially since it was really Mr. Grey's money, but he eventually relented when he remembered a good portion of the money he had paid The Broker to hire some hit-men (i.e. them) was in fact Mr. Pink's money from under his bed. Mr. Grey further concluded Mr. Pink's cut was irrelevant since Mr. Pink would be in a shallow grave long before he got any money anyway.

The current argument was more philosophical. Mr. Grey wanted to just knock on the door and shoot Larry Copeland. He had even purchased a revolver from a man at the pub especially for the task and wanted to get his money's worth. Mr. Pink would not hear of such blatant lack of artistry, not after he had spent weeks perfecting his pentagram carving skills. Fighting his inclination to always be right and kill anyone who disagreed with him, Mr. Grey eventually gritted his teeth and agreed with Mr. Pink – reasoning traitorous Larry Copeland would still be dead and he could still get value for money from his new second-hand revolver by using it on Mr. Pink.

With the details finally settled, Mr. Pink and Mr. Grey got out of the van to get their usual gear from the back.

'Why you drive?' asked Mr. Pink a short time later. 'Not Valdis fault we got wrong house this time.'

'It was the *right* house, Mr. Pink!' shouted Mr. Grey as he swerved round a corner. 'But that was not tubby Larry Copeland. Don't you get it?'

'No,' said Mr. Pink.

'Copeland has cheated us and moved house!' angrily said Mr. Grey. 'That lunatic has moved in.'

'Man knew you,' Mr. Pink said.

Squeezing the steering wheel, Mr. Grey counted to ten and said, 'He called me Mr. Pontius Pilate and he called you third Roman soldier from the left.'

'But he nice man,' said Mr. Pink. 'He said he forgive us for ruining his weekend by nailing him to cross even though him still bit annoyed he spend two weeks getting thorns out of his hair. What exorcism mean? Is it sort of biscuit? Mr. Jesus man say he'd take his tablets then give me exorcism and tea.'

'And you would have gone in to drink it too if I hadn't dragged you away!' shouted exasperated Mr. Grey. He counted to twenty and asked, 'What went wrong with the anaesthetic pen anyway?'

Mr. Pink took the pen from his tan overall breast pocket and looked at it. 'Valdis stuck it into nice Mr. Jesus man's leg when he took box, just like always. Valdis filled pen with more sleepy-time water so pen must be broken,' he said, shaking the anaesthetic pen before unscrewing one half from the other, fiddling with the spring and screwing it back together again. He clicked it a few times. 'It okay. Valdis fix pen,' he said and tested it. He said, 'Ow! Yes. It work fine now, Mr. Grey. Little needle went straight through Valdis's trousers and…' Mr. Pink's head fell against the side window.

Ignoring his comatose comrade, Mr. Grey squinted with determination at the road ahead and said, 'Larry Copeland may think he's got the better of me by moving house, but I will find him and then the shoe will be on the other sock!'

# TOM BENSON.

Tom Benson sat at the end of Ania's twelve seat dining table with his back to the door into the half-furnished sitting room and the dying cactus. Simon and Alice sat halfway down each side, watching. Tom lit a cigarette lighter and waved the flame about. His other hand swept across the flame, made a fist and flew into the air above his shoulder. He slowly turned his fist, opened his hand to reveal…Abracadabra! An empty hand! He held his other hand up…Voila! Empty hand!

Standing at the far end of the table near the door into the kitchen, Ania grinned and clapped enthusiastically. Simon nodded and applauded vigorously, shouting, 'Bravo, Mr. Benson, Sir! Bravo!'

Tom Benson grinned his toothy grin and said, 'Ania taught me that. That's real, magic, eh?'

'You did it very well, Tom,' said Ania, still clapping.

Alice said, 'He dropped it in his lap.'

'Did he?' said Simon, open mouthed mid-clap. 'No, he didn't! I would have seen it.'

'Simple distraction, Simon,' said Alice. 'He made you watch the other hand as it swept towards the flame and you kept watching it while he let the flame go out and drop the lighter into his lap.'

Ania snapped, 'Alice!'

Alice shrugged her slender shoulders. 'Well he did, Ma'am.'

Crestfallen, Benson took the lighter from his lap and placed it on the table. Glumly, he stood and announced, 'I'm going for a walk in the garden.' He turned on his heel and went through the dining room door.

'Alice!' snapped Ania again. 'I've been teaching him tricks like that for days and you ruin his confidence the first time he does one in public. And I was starting to think you liked him!'

Alice stood, flicked both sides of her soft cinnamon hair from her cheeks, carefully pushed her chair under the table, adjusted it a few centimetres to the left, stood behind it, turned to face Ania and said, 'I do like him, Ma'am. I admire the tenacity he displays trying to master his yoga. He always gets straight back up again no matter how hard he falls. But that's no reason not to be honest, is it?'

'Sometimes, Alice…' Ania began, stopped and looked the length of the table to where Tom Benson had sat to perform his trick. 'Where did he go?' she asked.

Frowning, and sure his employer had heard Tom Benson just as well as he had, Simon said, 'Er, he said he was going for a walk in the garden, Miss Rose.'

'He went through the door into the hall, not the one into the lounge,' said Ania Rose.

Alice's doleful hazel eyes widened. 'Oh!' she shouted and rushed towards the hall door.

Tom Benson kicked the pebbles across the drive and looked at the sunset. He was fed up with the rear garden. Despite the huge rectangular lawn requiring a small tractor mower, despite the surrounding variety of trees, despite the floodlit tennis court with the great oak beyond and the gardeners' sheds and greenhouses and the anthill and more trees beyond, Tom Benson felt the back garden was like a prison: a very spacious prison, but the high, electrified, barbed wire topped fence beyond the trees made it still *feel* like a prison. For once, he wanted to be in the garden at the front of the house. It still had the high fence and the electronic gate some way off at the end of the drive, but it was open and not closed in by trees, and right now it also had the last reds of sunset over the fields beyond the country road running in front of Ania's house. He wished he could, just once, go through the gates, stand on the low rampart of grass running down the other side of the road and look over the open fields to see the sunset, but he knew he could not. His contract said he could not. It said he could only leave the grounds of Ania's house if Ania said he could, just like he wasn't allowed to do *anything* unless Ania said he could. It was one of the prices he had agreed to pay when he signed the contract to become Ania's male representative in the high-stakes contest against the other companies, in return for getting his own clients, for getting his friend Brian a better place to live and proper mental health care, for getting his nephew and niece a scholarship and for getting Lucy out of 'the naughty seat' for ruining Ania's favourite rug. He was looking at the reddening evening sky and thinking about the special friendship he had developed after just a few days training with Lucy when he heard a soft thud. It was instantly followed by a loud crack. He looked down. The white shirt he had chosen to wear to do the disappearing flame trick seemed to have a stain on it. It was a red stain. The stain grew and seeped down into his sky blue trousers. Tom Benson felt faint. He tottered and fell.

Moments after Benson crashed sideways onto the gravel drive, Alice was kneeling at his side. She rolled him onto his back and tore his shirt open. She rammed her hand onto the seeping hole in Tom's side, where the bullet had struck him just above his belt. She placed her other hand on top of the first, pressing as hard as she could to stop the blood oozing from his unconscious body.

'Tom!' Alice screamed. 'No! Tom! Hang on!'

She heard the gravel crunching and turned to see Ania and Simon running towards her. With tears in her eyes she looked up at them and whimpered, 'He's been shot.'

Shocked, Simon said, 'She's touching him! She never...'

'Not now, Simon!' barked Ania.

'Right... I'll phone for an ambulance,' said Simon, turning back towards the house.

'Stop!' ordered Ania. 'You'll get whoever did this to him! Go in and open the gates, get swords for you and Alice and find the shooter. I'll get Benson into the house and summon medical aid. Go!'

Simon swallowed hard, nodded and sprinted back into the house. He slapped his hand on the button to open the gates and rushed into the gym. He threw open a wooden locker door and took two katanas from their mounts. He threw their sheaths aside and, with a samurai sword in each hand, ran back to the front garden.

He had to stop at the front door. Ania was coming up the steps with Benson in her arms. Simon stepped back to let her pass, staring at Benson's blood draining down Ania's white silk blouse and trousers. He watched, forlorn, as she carried Benson into the lounge, shook himself and leapt down the steps into the front garden. Alice was nowhere in sight.

'Alice!' shouted Simon, running across the gravel drive towards the open gates with a samurai sword in each hand. Reaching the road he bounded across and stopped on top of the waist-high grassy bank on the other side. At his feet lay an abandoned rifle with a telescopic sight. He angrily kicked it aside and looked across the field. In the distant twilight, far beyond the hedge, he caught sight of the white puffed sleeves of Alice's maid uniform and as his eyes grew accustomed to the growing gloom he could see the silhouette of Alice running.

Alice closed in on the black shirted, black trousered woman in front of her. Alice had seen the woman throw her rucksack aside and quicken her pace as soon as she spotted Alice running across the pasture after her. Alice caught up with her trying to find a way through the hedge at the far end of the field.

Alice slowed to a brisk walk as she approached the woman with the cropped blonde hair. She was a little shorter than Alice and even thinner, as if she had hardly eaten for days, and looked, like Alice, in her mid-twenties. Alice detected an Australian accent when the woman pointed a finger at her and said, 'Stay back, maid! I am trained to kill! My martial arts skills are beyond anything you could ever imagine! I have been trained by the best! I am Kylie and *I* am a Dark Star!'

Alice slowed her walk so she could stop a few metres from the black uniformed young woman. She said, 'Please wait,' and bent down, unbuckled her black shoes and kicked them off. She nodded to the Dark Star calling herself Kylie. 'Shall we?' asked Alice.

Dark Star Kylie took up a stance. Not the boring old Crane Stance, thought Alice, folding her arms and watching Dark Star Kylie go through a few motions. Probably intended to intimidate me and show me how she's going to sever my carotid artery, thought Alice, irritated by an itch on the end of her little nose and succumbing to the need to scratch it.

'Yaaaa!' screamed Kylie as she ran at her.

*Hmm*, thought Alice, *that's a pretty good flying head kick*. She stepped aside and watched Kylie fly past her shoulder. Kylie landed on her feet a few metres beyond Alice. She swiftly turned to rain a series of punches and kicks at Alice. Alice blocked, deflected, blocked. She caught Kylie's ankle as a foot swung at her head and pushed Kylie back.

Kylie retreated and panted. 'I'm not my usual self,' she gasped. 'I've had something inside me eating its way out for the last few days.'

Thinking it was starting to get a little chilly, Alice waited for Dark Star Kylie to attack again, moved to her right and side-kicked the side of her opponent's knee.

With fists raised, Kylie sneered, 'That didn't hurt at all, servant girl! We Dark Stars are trained to ignore pain!'

'Hmm,' said Alice. 'Are you trained to walk with torn knee ligaments and two broken bones in your other ankle?'

Moving forward to attack, Dark Star Kylie realised her left knee refused to bend and sagged when she had any weight on it. She shifted her weight. She felt her right ankle bones grind together. She hobbled forward and swung punches at Alice until something hit her ear. She staggered sideways and fell face first to the ground.

Alice was standing over unconscious Dark Star Kylie when Simon arrived. Alice said, 'Oh, good! Katana swords. Well done, Simon, but please don't touch mine ever again.'

Simon passed Alice her katana. 'It took me some time to run down to the field gate then catch you up,' he said, looking down at the motionless, stubble haired Dark Star. He winced and said, 'They don't go in for decent stylists up there do they? And she looks like she's not eaten for days, the poor brainwashed wretch.'

'Stop talking, Simon,' said Alice standing over her fallen adversary. She raised her sword high in both hands and bellowed, 'Off with her head!'

Simon was shocked. He'd never heard Alice bellow before.

# COPELAND

Larry Copeland would normally have regarded staying in bed all day as a perfect day. But not today. His head had gone from feeling like a piano had been dropped on it to feeling like a mountain had been dropped on it, probably somewhere from high orbit, and aches and cramps had spread through the rest of his body. Added to the crushed by a mountain feeling were hot sweats alternating with freezing shivers and stomach pains so severe he felt like some sort of alien creature was inside him trying to eat its way out. Throughout it all, Copeland lay in a daze, repeatedly muttering the words, 'Bloody sunstroke,' and all his inner voice could lamely suggest was, *Must get a hat, Copeland...* Maidservants Ruth and Linda were more helpful. One of them would frequently lift his head from the pillow while the other poured water into his mouth.

By late afternoon Copeland was able to be propped up with a few pillows behind him and drink some tea. He was still feeling too ill to complain when Linda poured the milk into the cup before the tea and silently endured a lecture by Ruth telling him the stomach cramps could be a sign of vitamin overdose: although still convinced it was sunstroke, Copeland vowed he would never take another vitamin tablet ever again.

As Ruth was clearing the tea and the full plate of untouched biscuits away, Kamille and Kamilla appeared and ushered the servants from Copeland's room so they could have a private word with him. They stood at the foot of Copeland's convalescent bed and after glancing hesitantly at each other a few times they informed Copeland they wished to be part of his personal bodyguard when he started working for Keira.

*Just nod, Copeland,* suggested an inner voice. *The sooner they leave the sooner we can get back to sleep.* Copeland nodded. The two Kams were thrilled.

Copeland had privately begun to call the tall hovering Dark Stars the two Kams, mainly because he had no idea which was which, just as he had never been able to work out which was Ant and which was Dec. One of them – one of the 2Kams, not Ant or Dec, because they weren't in his room – glanced over her shoulder at the closed door behind her, got a nod of approval from her twin and hesitantly sidled along the side of the bed to tell Copeland how they wanted to be his personal guards because of the incredible bonding experiences they had shared the previous night. Other Kam nodded enthusiastically as bedside Kam told Copeland they were amazed by his energy and thought they had probably got away unnoticed with their swim in the lake, though they still could not work out where he had got the traffic cone from.

Copeland didn't know either. He couldn't remember a thing. He managed a tired smile and a half raised thumb before he nodded off again.


## ANIA


By the time Alice found her shoes and she and Simon returned to Ania's three floor, Olympic swimming pool size mansion with its tennis court size lounge, soccer stadium size back garden and curling sheet size conservatory there was a car they recognised in front of the goal post high marble pillars flanking the front door, which was not as big as a snooker table. Alice and Simon looked at each other quizzically and marched down the long gravel drive. Once inside, Alice hit the button to close the electronic gates before they went into the lounge.

With Ania kneeling beside him, Tom Benson lay on Ania's favourite white rug. It was the same as her previous favourite white rug which Lucy had spilled something on. The new favourite white rug was somewhat bloodstained.

'Ow!' shouted Tom Benson as Dr. Smith threaded a needle through his skin, shook her head and said, 'I've frozen it with a spray. It's completely numb. The pain is all in your head, Benson. Just look away and think of England!'

'Ow!' shouted Tom again as Ania stood and approached her shocked servants, standing frozen in the doorway. 'It was just a nick,' she said. 'He must be one of those people who bleeds a lot. Doctor Smith says he probably passed out through shock. Once I got him in here I laid him on the rug and looked at his wound. It was obvious it was only minor so I used some superglue then called Dr. Smith. Ambulances don't need to waste their time with minor scrapes, do they?'

Benson shouted, 'Superglue? You stuck my skin together with superglue?'

Ania shook her head and turned her long neck to frown over her shoulder at Tom Benson. 'The Americans invented it during the Vietnam war. It's designed for wounds. Why do you think it sticks your fingers together better than it sticks your sole back onto your shoe, Tom?'

Tom resignedly said, 'Oh, okay, Ania, I suppose my body is legally yours anyway,' and lay back down to stare at the white ceiling while Dr. Smith pulled through another stitch. Tom Benson said, 'I think that freezing spray has finally worked... Hey! You're not going to give me another one of your cleansing enemas while you're here are you, Doc?'

'Enemas are good for you,' replied Dr. Smith. 'People pay a lot of money at our Uroboros Rejuvenation clinic for them.'

Simon and Alice looked at each other with raised eyebrows.

Frowning, Alice said, 'Sorry, Ma'am… but all that blood was because of a flesh wound? I could have sworn…'

'He was lucky,' said Ania, combing her blood stained fingers back through her long red hair. 'Completely ruined my blouse and my new favourite rug, though,' she laughed. 'So is that the would-be assassin over your shoulder Simon?'

'Yes, Miss Rose,' ventured Simon hesitantly. 'Apparently she's one of Keira Starr's Dark Stars. She told Alice her name is Kylie.'

Curtseying, Alice said, 'We found her sniper rifle as well, Ma'am. It was almost directly opposite our gates. I left it in the hall. I'm sorry to say I nearly made the mistake of killing her, but Simon blocked my katana just in time and quite rightly suggested you may want to question her first.'

'Yes,' said Simon. 'Alice bested this Dark Starr and was about to slice her head off after she shouted "*Off with her head*," Miss Rose.'

Alice wondered why Ania and Simon exchanged a look.

Swiftly turning away from her servants, Ania clapped her hands together, raised both hands in the air and cried, 'Well done one and all! Wait here!' She squeezed past Simon, Alice and unconscious Kylie and bounded up the stairs.

After ten minutes, Simon said, 'I think this Dark Star is waking up.'

Alice looked into Kylie's fluttering eyes and nodded. She slapped Kylie's ear again. Kylie's eyes stopped fluttering. Simon said, 'You'll have to teach me that one, Alice.'

# TOM BENSON TALKS TO HIS FAMILY

'Yes, Dad, really,' said Tom into the white phone receiver.

'Once again, I'm afraid I don't believe you Thomas,' Dad said in his flat monotone. 'You're just attention seeking again, just like you cried and cried when you were six and fell out of your bedroom window.'

'Honestly, Dad,' Tom Benson said imploringly, 'I really was shot. About two hours ago.'

'So you're in hospital, then, are you Thomas?' asked sceptical Dad.

'Well, er, no,' said Benson. 'My waist was nicked. But there was lots of blood. It was all over Ania's favourite rug.'

'Hmm, I see,' said Dad, 'so with all that blood loss you feel tired, I suppose. Do you feel tired, Thomas? You're phoning well after your usual nine o'clock bedtime.'

'I don't feel at all tired, Dad,' sighed Benson. 'I feel pretty good actually since the Doc injected painkiller into me. But Alice and Simon said they were sure the bullet had hit me and I'd bleed to death!'

'But it didn't, did it Thomas?' persisted Dad. 'Three stitches is less than I had when I cut my eyebrow falling out of the loft the other day. And who are Alice and Simon?'

'Servants, Dad. I told you about them. I told you they both spoke really posh.'

'I never bother to really listen when you're talking Thomas. Now, let's talk about something more important before your mother comes in from her gardening.'

'Mum's gardening? It's dark outside.'

'She's messing with her herbs again. She's picking some hemlock to put in a cake for the neighbours. She says she's fed up with them moaning about their missing dog.'

Tom laughed at his father's dry sense of humour.

'The thing is Thomas,' whispered Dad, 'I've got a problem with my laptop. Things keep popping up on the screen when I'm watching Netflix.'

'Adverts?' asked Tom.

'Yes, Thomas. I just told you that!' snappily whispered Dad. 'Adverts inviting me to video-chat, whatever that is. And I've never seen any of these women before. Your Mum will think I'm, you know, breaking our marriage vows if she sees them. Some of them want to give me their address. It says they live locally so they must already know where I live, mustn't they? The thing is, these ladies on the adverts are dressed a bit provocativ… Oh, here's your Gran. She wants a word.'

'Hello, Thomas,' said Gran. 'How's it going? You don't need to tell me you were shot and bled on your boss's rug. Your dad has to have the phone on loudspeaker to hear it. And even when he whispers he shouts. I could hear every word you both said. Oh, he's shouting something now… He says he'll ask your brother about the pop-up adverts because you probably wouldn't be able to help because of you being a bit of a total failure and all.'

'Well, Gran,' said Tom, 'after I was shot at…'

'Probably just someone shooting their gun by accident, Thomas,' Gran said in her usual Gran-knows-best way. 'I mean, be honest Thomas – who'd waste a bullet on you? I suppose it might have been one of the neighbours mistaking you for one of those evil little goblins out of Lord of the Rings, though. They were bald as well.'

Tom gave up. He had always held out the hope that at least his Gran listened to him. Obviously not. He said, 'Ania gave us all a present for our bravery afterwards. She gave Simon a little gold lion. He was thrilled. He said it was Etruscan. He knows about that sort of stuff. He said the Etruscans lived in

Italy before the Romans took over. Alice got something Simon says is Roman. It's a really chunky gold necklace.'

'Gold, eh?' said Gran as if she had been listening. 'What did you get for your present from Ania, Thomas?'

'Well, Gran… She gave me the bill for a new rug. Did you know rugs could cost over twenty thousand pounds?'

'No, I didn't. I'm going to help your Mum make a cake now, Thomas. Bye.' Click.


Tom Benson replaced the phone receiver. Leaning against the door frame of Tom Benson's compact office, Ania said, 'It's always so touching when you phone home, Tom.'

Tom Benson stared at the phone, raised an index finger and said, 'The fool doth think he is wise but the wise man knows himself to be a fool.'

Ania tilted her head. *'As You Like It?* What's Shakespeare got to do with this, Tom?' she asked.

Benson mirrored Ania's folded arms with his own, looked hard at her and said, 'I'm just a decoy, aren't I?'

'Pardon?' came Ania's reply.

'Well,' sighed Benson. 'I'm supposed to be one of your contestants – what you call your Champions – in this inter-company competition thing and we all know at least one of the other two companies seems willing to do anything to win, apparently including shooting me. Yet we're telling everyone I'm going to be your Champion. The cleaners, gardeners and every visitor gets told I'm going to be entering the contest for Rose PR and I'm betting everyone at work knows as well. Please don't say where you live is a secret, because it isn't. You even invited Larry Copeland here the day after he came back from that Butterburn place up north. No doubt they put a tracker on his phone or his car, but you invited him here anyway. You're the smartest person I've ever met Ania, so you must have wanted these Dark Star people to find this place, and me. I think your *real* Champions are hiding somewhere else.'

Ania shuffled uneasily in the doorway, folded her arms tighter and stared at Tom Benson.

'I mean,' went on Benson, 'I'm not exactly Mr. Universe am I? And who are you telling everyone your female Champion is? Ingrid the big-mouthed Britney Spears lookalike porn star!'

Ania sniffed, 'She's hardly a star. She just needs the money.'

'Yeah!' sneered Benson. 'I reckon she'd do anything for money. She's probably told everyone in her tower block she's going to be your Champion by now. The others will soon be after her as well, not that I care. She's mean.'

'Hmm,' said Ania. 'You seemed to like her well enough when we watched her little films together. Is the reason you don't like her so much now because she calls you monkey-man? You shouldn't be so sensitive about your looks and lack of height, Tom.'

Behind his desk, Benson folded his arms tighter as well. 'I should've known,' he muttered, shaking his balding head. 'All those strange questions you asked me when I brought Mandy Gilmore's file over and stayed for dinner!'

'You said yes to all of them,' Ania reminded him. 'Including whether you'd bungee jump off a three hundred metre high bridge, eat live cockroaches and not blink if someone was throwing knives a hairs breadth from you head.'

'I was just trying to impress you!' Benson cried, arms wide. 'Oh, I see now... They were some of the tasks in previous contests weren't they?'

'We call it the Game, with a capital G. Just like we call the contenders Champions with a capital C,' Ania informed him.

Exasperated, Benson put his hands on his balding head and groaned, 'They were trying to **kill** me!'

Ania tutted. 'Of course they weren't, Tom. Killing opposition Champions is frowned upon. Kylie was aiming at your stomach, not your heart. They were just trying to ruin your training schedule.'

'Oh, that's okay then! Good job she was three inches left and not three inches up!' said Benson ironically. He raised a finger. 'Meanwhile, your **real** Champion continues training in secret, eh?'

Ania's crystal green eyes narrowed. 'Are you saying you want to pull out of the contract?'

'Of course not,' sighed Tom. His shoulders slumped as he leaned onto the desk. 'How can I? I know I've signed total control of my body over to you for a few months but if I break the contract Lucy would lose all her clients, Brian would be homeless without his meds, Tim's kids would lose their scholarships and I'd be out of a job. Plus there's that clause that says if I want my body back you get to keep certain parts permanently.'

Ania laughed heartily, said, 'I'd make it quick and painless, Tom,' then became more serious and said, 'But you're missing the fact you'll become a millionaire if you can successfully promote the clients I give you.' Seeing Benson look sceptical she added, 'If we get the Bollywood studio you can run their UK publicity too.'

Benson's squinty eyes widened. His gnome-like face beamed. 'Gosh! Thanks, Ania!' He grinned his rabbit teeth.

Ania smiled her wide, full-lip, Julia Roberts smile and said, 'I believe in rewarding loyalty, Tom, and you are sticking to your contract extremely well.'

Benson's momentary beaming face fell again. He looked down at the desk and moaned, 'It's hard though, Ania, having you contractually in charge of my body. I understand I'm trying to learn self-discipline and control with all the kung-fu, yoga and meditation, but, the thing is…I'm getting frustrated.'

'Oh, dear,' said Ania, as she pushed her shoulder away from the door frame and theatrically placed her palms on her cheeks. 'Do you have that itch on the end of your nose again, Tom? Do you want permission to scratch it?'

'I didn't mean an itch, I meant… Well, now you've said it I do have an itch, right on the end of my nose, but what I meant was…It's this abstinence thing and, well, I have… It doesn't help you going round in that short kimono robe thing.'

Ania lowered her hands and shrugged. 'I just got out of the shower. It is my home, Tom. Surely I can go around my own house in nothing but my robe… Oh! Are you saying it's been a week since..?'

'You have a CCTV camera in every room so you know the answer to that, Ania, and you had me working all hours for weeks before that, so it's been…a lot longer.' Tom swallowed hard. 'I'm not sure I can control myself much longer, Ania. Inside this little body, I'm still a red-blooded male.'

Ania nodded, slowly walked round to Benson's side of the desk and sat on it. She extended a red nail and softly scratched the end of his nose. 'Poor, Tom. It must be so, so hard…to have an itch and not be able to scratch it. But you can't, can you? Your contract is airtight. You have to ask yourself, would it stand up in court?'

'It probably would! That's the problem!' Tom sarcastically smiled. Ania wrinkled her nose, flicked his ear and crossed her legs. Looking at the ceiling, Tom said, 'And even when you're at work there's Alice and…'

'You have designs on my daughter?' asked Ania quietly.

Stunned, Benson's piggy eyes looked at her. 'But she's twenty four and you're only just over thirty!'

Ania placed a finger on his lips, smiled her enigmatic smile and said, 'That's so flattering of you, Tom. But she's my adopted daughter. She is legally Alice Rose. I adopted her when she was sixteen. She'd been expelled from a top public school for violent conduct – very violent conduct. She spent two years receiving some extremely poor treatment in an institution before I adopted her. When she was eighteen she insisted on earning her keep and she became a servant. She was too anxious to even leave the house anyway so I reluctantly agreed. She's a genius with numbers so she runs all my business accounts as well. All was well until just over two years ago, shortly after Simon came, and she had another episode. It was as if her anger took her over and she became a different person. We had to double her medication. She's been unable to touch anyone since that last episode. That's why I'm telling you this. Tonight was a breakthrough. When she thought that bullet had gone into your gut she actually put pressure on what she thought was your wound while you were unconscious. She actually *touched* you. Then, for the first time in eight years, she actually left the house. She ran out of the gates after that Kylie person who shot at you. Then she apparently also touched Kylie – to break her ankle, rip her knee ligaments and knock her out. Alice usually has to use a sword or something. Perhaps she should carry a knife?'

Behind Ania's finger, Benson said, 'Maybe give her a broom handle? Giving a knife to someone with anger management issues may not be a good idea.'

'Shush!' shushed Ania, placing a finger on his lips. 'Alice has been working to control her emotions and tonight she channelled her anger and didn't let it control her – at least up until she was going to slice the poor woman's head off and Simon stopped her. But it was still a breakthrough, and we owe it all to you Tom. She likes you. You're not *that* much older than she is. And now she's touched you once, perhaps, in time, your physical relationship could grow into something more... intimate.'

Tom Benson thought about this. Thinking about it didn't help his abstinence any more than Ania sitting cross legged on his desk in her short kimono did. He said, 'Gulp!'

'In the meantime,' Ania said scratching the tip of Benson's snub nose again, 'we need to help you with your self-control so you can resist your urges, at least until you learn enough to control your body to resist your hormones. I'll get Dr. Smith to come round early in the morning.' She gave one final scratch and stood up. Benson had to close his eyes.

'Er, Ania,' he said with a scrunched, disapproving face, 'will Doc Smith be giving me some sort of drug?'

'Oh, no, Tom,' laughed Ania. 'No drugs. I'll tell Dr. Smith to bring a few cans of that freezing stuff she numbed your side with when she stitched you up. We'll keep you well sprayed. That should work. But tonight we'll do something temporary to help you resist all those troublesome hormones. It's getting late, so let's go. I've still got our captive Dark Star shooter to interrogate – I tied her to a bed as well.'

# 11. DAY 10. FRIDAY.

## COPELAND

If he was going for a final walk with Keira Starr then Copeland knew he would definitely need a hat. Linda went to find a suitable one while Copeland tried to explain to Ruth why the milk needed to go in *after* the tea.

Flushed with the success of a new tea convert, Copeland considered the hats Linda brought back. The Panama looked stylish but, to really be on the safe side from another dose of sunstroke, Copeland wanted one with a really wide brim. He chose the sombrero.

Keira was waiting for him at the rear of the house on the wide gravel path alongside the narrow oblong lake, where the lines of trees running down each side offered some protection from the mid-morning sun, but not much. She turned, she looked at his hat, she raised an eyebrow. Walking up to him, she took both his hands in hers and kissed his cheeks. 'How are you feeling today, Larry?' she asked, squeezing his hands.

'Not fully recovered and still couldn't face eating, but better,' he said. 'Thanks for asking, Keira. And thanks for coming to see me yesterday and giving me that drink of honey in warm water, it really perked me up.' He kissed her cheeks.

'I'm glad you came to the ball last night,' said Keira.

'Well,' smiled Copeland, 'you were very…'

'Persuasive?' suggested Keira.

Copeland laughed. 'I was going to say persistent! But everything you said to convince me sounded reasonable and the ball was in my honour, so I could hardly carry on lying in bed, could I?'

'I didn't know you could dance so well, Larry,' Keira said, releasing his hands, moving alongside him and putting her arm through his.

'All those lessons with my ex-wife,' said Copeland. 'It was like riding a bike the way it all came back. You can dance pretty well yourself. And I should know after three hours dancing with you! My feet are still sore.'

Slowly setting off down the path with her arm hooked through his, and still smiling, Keira said, 'You could have said no when I kept suggesting one more dance, Larry.'

'You were very...persuasive,' laughed Copeland. He stopped. 'And it was interesting to discuss your plan to have a thousand years of Dark Star domination without any crime or street drugs, your ideas on what we used to call free love and whether the milk should go in before the tea. But...You're shorter! Have you got any shoes on under that skirt?'

Leaning against Copeland, Keira lifted a foot to show him.

Astonished Copeland gasped, 'You can't walk on this gravel barefoot, Keira! It's sharp!'

Keira kissed his cheek again, did one of her half shrugs and said, 'Pain is all in the mind, Larry. It's what every recruit has to learn before he or she becomes a Dark Star. It's only gravel. It's not like it's broken glass those TV magicians walk over, is it? We save that for Dark Star initiations. Let's stroll. We need to talk frankly before you leave.'

'Before I leave? I thought this was just a final chat to give me one more chance before you handed me over to be tortured. What are you offering this time, Keira? Is it head of security again, something like becoming your new crime lord governor of Grimsby or just a straightforward bribe? It won't do any good you know. Director Miller and I guessed you were inviting me up here to get my passwords for the security services databases. Except for the police and MI5 ones I'm already locked out of everything. If you try to go into the MI5 database through the Department C server using my log-ins it won't work. It would have to be from one specific laptop. If it's not from that one laptop then instead of you having a back door into the Department C and MI5 databases, they'll have a backdoor into yours. The computer virus is just waiting for you to try to log-on as me.'

Keira sighed as she looked across the lake. 'Thanks for your honesty, Larry, but I guessed you'd guessed we'd got you here for your pass-codes – I guessed it the first night you were here, when you said you thought you were here so I could bribe you. But why are you telling me you knew what I wanted and about a virus waiting to infect our computers?'

'I don't particularly want to be tortured,' said Copeland. 'And even though I know they've all been blocked, I still wouldn't tell you my passwords even after a year of torture.'

Keira was sceptical. 'To do that you would have to resist pain better than any Dark Star, Larry.'

'Not exactly,' said Copeland, adjusting his sombrero. 'I don't actually know any of my passwords. I have to write them down. I suppose Director Miller's plan to get into your computers might have worked if she hadn't assumed I actually *knew* my passwords. If you tortured me for long enough I might possibly remember my password for my Tesco online deliveries.'

'I don't intend to torture you, Larry,' Keira laughed as they gradually approached the mid-point of the lake. 'Konrad suggested it when he had the idea to invite you here to get all your login details so we could plant spyware and more in the security services computers, just as you guessed. But what *I* want to do is to still offer you a job.'

'What?' said Copeland. 'You still want to? Why would you...Oh, I see! You let me go back to London, they reactivate all my passwords and stuff again and then I sneak back here to take up a job I can't refuse and I give you all my passwords before they realise what's going on. You're in their computers before they know it. And the next day I'm found dead with a pentagram carved on my forehead.'

They walked a few steps in silence before Keira moved in front of Copeland and said, 'While you have been here, Larry, I hope you've learned we stand for justice – *swift* justice. Some may accuse me of being judge, jury and, yes, from time to time, executioner. But we only punish the guilty. Always and severely. Very severely. And if I could get my hands on whoever is killing these innocent men and trying to frame me by carving my pentagram sign on their heads then a swift death would be too good for them…Let's continue our walk.'

With her arm hooked back into his they continued their slow stroll in silence until Keira suddenly laughed. She turned Copeland to face the lake and, pointing at it, said, 'Look at that lake, Larry. It's a man-made, ornamental lake. Heaven knows what lurks in there. Cholera? Typhoid? Who knows? Yet I've heard three people were actually swimming in it the night before last. Can you believe it? No one knows who they were, or how that traffic cone appeared over the other side of the lake. Most of the recruits and Dark Stars are young and few have ever had any sort of real family. They need guidance, Larry. I don't want you to join us as head of security or to run a town but…' Keira faltered.

'To be a father figure?' asked Copeland, stunned.

Keira winced. 'More of a grandfather figure,' she said. 'A figure who does not instil fear, but someone they can look up to and respect. Someone who can give them advice and guidance so they don't do silly things like swim in a germ infested lake!'

Copeland stood, shocked to the core while his inner voice said, *Er, Copeland...Are the symptoms of cholera anything like sunstroke? Bugger it! Forget that – just ask her about the salary and if you still get a personal chef.*

## FREYA FINDS THE MISSING LINK

Freya had hardly slept. She knew she was lying to herself about the real reason but told herself she couldn't sleep because she was disappointed the image of the sombrero wearing, pentagram killers' paymaster was not clearer. She had fed the best image she had found of sombrero man into the facial recognition software and it had soon told her there was not enough of his face to get a match. Freya was certain this man must work for Keira Starr and she had evidence of him handing over a Tesco bag to the pentagram killers. At least she now knew *their* identities. She also knew the police were sure the saliva found at the scene of the murder of Rupert Jennings belonged to one of his killers. Once the two killers were found, Freya was sure the DNA of the saliva and the DNA of one of the killers would match. It would be an open and shut case for any jury. Copeland would get the credit for their arrests and save his job and she would have her story.

There were just a few small problems. The white van used by the killers had seemingly disappeared from the face of the earth. It had not been recorded by any traffic camera since the previous evening, when it had been spotted driving north from east London. Another problem was although she now knew the identities of the killers, she certainly could not let the police know directly or there would be questions about how she had got the information and she didn't really want to be imprisoned for breaking the official secrets act. She knew she had to work through Copeland but dare not phone him while he was still at Keira Starr's Longbeck Estate. In fact, Freya was growing concerned Copeland might not come back at all. What if Keira Starr had successfully bribed him? What if she had fed him to her huge black dogs? What if she had imprisoned him? What if..? Freya stopped thinking about it. She knew all she could do was wait. He had told her he expected to be away two or three nights, so she wouldn't start worrying yet.

Knowing she needed to do something to keep herself busy, Freya had stopped tossing and turning in bed and got up to search for a link between the pentagram murder victims. She knew DCI Ross had undoubtedly tasked people to do just that and they had obviously come up with nothing, but it would give her something to do.

By seven she was thinking it was an impossible puzzle to solve. There *was* no link between the victims. They lived in different parts of the country and had attended different schools. Her theory they had all once been Dark Stars who had turned their backs on Keira Starr began to dissolve. If they had been Dark Stars and Keira Starr wanted them dead because they had information about her illegal activities, or even because she wanted to make a point about anyone daring to turn their back on her, it didn't add up. *When* had they been Dark Stars? *When* had they even trained to become a Dark Star? All the victims had a full history of education, employment and unemployment, information about their rental agreements or mortgages – DCI Ross had even had their credit card histories analysed. There was nothing to suggest they had ever worked for Keira Starr, and nothing to suggest the murdered men had *anything* in common.

With a banana in one hand and a glass of water in the other, Freya played her final card. The victims' computer records would have been one of the first things the police looked at, along with the victims' phones, so she knew trawling through them would be a waste of time, but trawl through them she did, not knowing whether it was something she'd seen that provoked it or whether it was the nagging question of how the killers knew they would find victims who lived alone. (Except for poor Mr. Jennings and Widow Jennings, but Copeland had said he thought Mr. Jennings was a mistake.) Freya took Mr. Jennings out of the equation, and scanned the computer records again. Damn! Freya had hoped all the single, lonely men living in a variety of places and a variety of accommodations had the common denominator of an online dating web site. No doubt DCI Ross had once had the same idea and found exactly what she had found – there was no dating site in common. The victims all used different ones. Freya stopped halfway through a banana bite. They *all* used different ones!

Tossing the banana skin aside, Freya went into one dating site after another. She was sure Copeland wouldn't mind her using his credit card to register him for almost every dating site in the country. By mid-morning Freya had got around the firewalls of the first site and was looking at the online dating record of one of the victims, Mr. Will Jones. She jotted down the names of everyone he had contacted using the site. Of course, dating agencies had strict guidelines about members giving their addresses to each other but it didn't stop them talking on the phone did it? Every victim could have divulged his address over the phone to someone, not knowing the person they spoke to was really Keira Starr or one of her trusted minions. So… Who had murder victim Mr. Will Jones asked for the number of? Freya sighed. Mr. Jones had requested the phone number of almost every woman on the dating site. Fortunately, very few had given it to him.

By lunchtime Freya had hacked into the fifth site and was on the verge of giving up when another thought struck her. She had been looking for the names of the women the victims had contacted and got phone numbers from, but what if Keira Starr had used a different name and number for herself on each site? Freya began to despair but thought she would try one last Hail Mary longshot. If Keira Starr was using different names on each site then she was bound to be using different photos, but Freya thought it was worth a go, especially since there was nothing else to do… By this time Freya was so absorbed by the challenge for its own sake it did not cross her mind that Keira Starr had no reason to kill this wide variety of solitary men who had clearly never been Dark Stars and probably had no idea who Keira Starr even was.

Going back through the sites and the contacts, Freya went through screen after screen of dating site women who had given their phone number to the murdered men. Freya soon stopped. One photograph stood out. As soon as Freya had seen what the woman looked like she had wondered why someone who looked like that needed to use a dating agency, then thought how unfair that thought was – this poor woman was probably hounded if she stepped into a bar or onto a dance floor. In anyone's opinion, the woman was stunning. Freya soon realised she was the common denominator. She checked and, yes, there she was, under different names, but she had been contacted by all the murdered men Freya had got the dating site histories of so far. She could see how easy it was for the woman pictured on the screen to attract men. Freya was sure this woman would turn out to be a Dark Star and be under the spell of Keira Starr and then it would be game set and match. And how hard could it be to find the woman on the web-sites photos? Tall, a figure and cheekbones to die for, skin as smooth as marble, long red hair, a flawlessly straight Greek nose, eyes as green as emeralds and a Julia Roberts smile. Freya pressed print screen and immediately rolled her eyes and slapped her forehead. How could she be so naïve? It was obvious who this woman was. This wasn't a real person at all! Keira Starr had concocted this fake woman with a Photoshop expert. No real woman could be *that* perfect.

Freya gave up, and as she wondered into the kitchen to make toast she finally realised Keira Starr had no motive to have the victims killed. She lost her temper and threw the nearest thing to hand at the kitchen window. Fortunately, the bread bounced off and Freya finally admitted to herself what was making her so tense. It was *the* question she really needed the answer to – why hadn't Copeland told her about Janet before she felt this way about him?

## COPELAND.

Copeland had almost gone onto autopilot and driven back to his little semi-detached in Leyton before he remembered he now lived in Slough and someone was paying him a huge monthly rent to live in his old place. And here he was, at his new home, where parking was much easier than in Leyton. He parked directly in front of his new, ground floor flat, climbed out of his car and was about to get his things from the boot when he noticed someone running towards him at speed.

***Good grief, Copeland! There must be a dog chasing her!***

Pounding to a halt in front of him in her red vest and red shorts, Freya took a few deep breaths and panted, 'Hi, Larry. Lost weight? Glad you're…whew…back safe. Just a sec.'

Copeland smiled and gave Freya her requested moment and waited while she leaned her hands against the side of his car and stretched. Then, while bent holding her ankles, she laughingly said, 'Brand new BMW, eh? So you've taken a bribe from Keira Starr after all, then?'

Copeland leaned back against the side of his new car and laughed too. 'It's not a bribe. We did an exchange. That little Nissan was technically mine. Director Miller took the £800 pounds for it from my bonus. Keira and I just swapped cars.'

'That's alright then?' questioned Freya, standing upright and looking at him hard.

'Glad you think so,' said Copeland, having learned how to take questions as statements, when it suited, from an expert. 'It's an electric hybrid,' he proudly said and, as Freya began bouncing up and down, added, 'You look good Freya…'

Finishing her eye rolling and pony tail shaking, Freya looked at Copeland aghast and said, 'I'm really sweaty and I shouldn't be! They say ladies should glow, not sweat! Ha! I need a shower and then I'll show you who the pentagram killers are! I found out! Let's get your stuff in from your car.'

While Freya showered Copeland unpacked and made much needed tea, with the milk quite rightly going in after the tea. He was about to take his first sip when Freya appeared at the kitchen door wearing clothes similar to the red ones she had been running in, except these were white.

*Yep, Copeland… Definitely a female of the species. Just like I always said she was, didn't I?*

Copeland sipped his tea and decided he would wait for another time to tell Freya she was off the hook with Keira Starr and could move back to her home in Wimbledon. He thought Freya looked as if she was going to say something, or perhaps waiting for him to say something? He worked out what it was. He said, 'I've had sunstroke. I was thinking. Perhaps we could… Damn phone!'

He put his tea down and took his phone from his trouser pocket. It was a WhatsApp call. The phone screen informed him it was Beth Spencer. Copeland showed Freya the screen before he answered the call.

He said, 'Dr. Spencer! Beth! Hello there! How's things up there at Butterburn? Cured cancer or made better synthetic skin yet?'

'Where are you, Larry?' whispered Beth Spencer, furtively.

'Er, at home,' Copeland informed her, frowning across the kitchen to Freya listening at the kitchen doorway.

'Are you alone?' whispered Beth.

'Er… Yes,' answered Copeland. 'I'm quite alone, Beth.' Looking at Freya, he put his finger on his lips.

'Put me on video call, Larry,' Beth whispered.

'Er, okay,' said Copeland, looking at Freya with panic on his face. She stepped across the narrow kitchen, leaned over his arm and pointed to where he had to press. He waited while she stepped back.

'There we are,' said Copeland. 'Hey! I can see you! Amazing! Erm, are you alright, Beth? You look…Are you in a bathroom? I wondered what the background noise was.'

'Hey, Larry, you've lost weight! You only look six months pregnant now. Yes, I'm in a bathroom. The taps are on because of the listening devices they put everywhere here. I told you they're paranoid about leaks to other companies. Point the phone around,' whispered Beth.

'Er, sure,' said Copeland, waiting a moment while Freya dropped to the floor before he scanned the phone around and said, 'I'm in my kitchen having some tea with the milk…'

'Show me every room,' hissed Beth, 'and then outside.'

'Why?' asked Copeland, quite reasonably he thought.

Looking over her shoulder and then, according to the image on the phone screen, apparently getting under a sink, Beth hissed, 'I heard you'd left Keira Starr's Longbeck Estate, Larry, but I want to be sure she hasn't still got you there and has released false information. Show me you're not there.'

'Fair enough,' said Copeland, and took the phone on a tour of his ground floor flat and then into the street outside. All Beth said was, 'Small flat, Larry,' and 'That's a nice BMW parked outside.'

Back in his lounge, Copeland sat on his sofa while Freya sat out of sight at the small round table in the bay window. 'So, Dr. Spencer,' said Copeland, 'tell me what Inspector Larry Copeland of Department C, sort of MI5, can do for you? Have you just turned the taps up so they're louder?'

'Yes!' snapped Beth before whispering, 'You did get my clue, didn't you? When you came up here last weekend? Please tell me you did and you've followed up on it, Larry! Please say you did! Oh, God! Please!'

Finding himself whispering, Copeland said, 'Yes, Beth. I got your clue. You tipped me off about Butterburn having a basement. They'd hidden the lifts behind the storage stuff hadn't they? Well, I found out what's in the basement, but you're worrying unnecessarily.' On Copeland's phone screen, Beth's face had an open mouth. Copeland knew why: Beth was shocked he had been able to find out about something the Department of Defence classified as ultra top secret. He continued, 'The robotic combat suits Dr. Wood's team are making are being built for the British Army. The Americans already have them. Probably the Chinese too. The Russians have some but they're probably fake, just like the robot they sent to that robotics convention last year. Did you see that? It was on YouTube. It was just a man in a robot suit! Hilarious!'

Louder than she had been, Beth screamed, 'Not the bloody robots! I told you about the basement because of the grubs being made into meat substitute so you'd know what you'd eaten wasn't vegetarian. Disgraceful, isn't it? Grubs are still helpless animals aren't they? Who cares about the damn robots? The clue I gave you was the ChewiVit vitamin tablets I left on your car seat!'

'Oh, *that* clue!' said Copeland, trying not to look at Freya.

'Yes!' snapped Beth. 'Remember I had to leave you at dinner and I told you I'd spent half the night sorting out a problem with the production of the ChewiVits? We found the regulation of the vit-transferase enzyme had been changed. Each vitamin tablet was getting almost a thousand times more than it was supposed to. I thought it was an accident at first, but then realised it wasn't! And they've moved the production from here now so I can't change it. That sort of dosage will send the endocrine system into overdrive and massive amounts of certain hormones will flood through the body. If people take one tablet a day it should be fine, two is risking it depending on body size, but three or more... Disaster! People will feel *so* good they'll never stop taking them. And more than three ChewiVits then... I don't even want to think about it... People would soon be *more active* than Tom and I used to be and that's saying something! Even one a day over a prolonged period of time may have effects I can't even contemplate. Please tell me you've sent the ChewiVits I gave you to be tested so the authorities who regulate these things can pull the plug on them.'

Copeland nodded sagely. He was good at doing that when he had no idea what to say. 'Don't worry, Beth,' he said at length. 'It's all in hand. The ChewiVits have been tested and we know they have a really high dose in them compared to the amount found naturally in human blood. The authorities are considering their response but you know how slow these bureaucrats can be. But if you're saying the ChewiVits are as bad as heroin or cocaine or...'

'Don't be stupid, Larry,' hissed Beth. 'Of course not. They may be a bit addictive in massive or prolonged doses, and may even cause a few mild withdrawal symptoms, but they're not like narcotics or anything!'

'Okay, Beth, leave it with me,' Copeland soothed. 'I'll send a strongly worded email to the government scientists to chivvy them along. Just hang in there.'

'I'm going to resign,' said Beth, not bothering to whisper. 'I'm going to become an ordinary hospital consultant again.'

'No!' protested Copeland. 'You can't, Beth! You can cure cancer, make artificial skin for burns victims, find out how astronauts can survive long enough to go to infinity and beyond! No one else could do that, Beth. Only you are that smart!'

Beth was silent for a moment. 'Thanks, Larry,' she calmly said. 'I always thought you were perceptive. That means a lot. I suppose I have to stay, don't I?'

'Yes,' affirmed Copeland. 'And you can phone and tell me about anything illegal they get up to up there. Such as selling those robot combat suits to the Russians and not to our army.'

'Sure,' said Beth. 'Er, while we're talking… Have you seen Tom?'

'Actually, yes,' said Copeland with a broad smile. He tried to think how to tell Beth that Tom Benson had effectively signed over his body so it could be trained to be in tip top shape for a contest worth millions against other companies.

*Tom Benson in tip top shape? Are you kidding Copeland? That would take forever! Look, Copeland, I've been quiet while you've made Beth into your informant, but don't lie to her about Tom Benson. It would break her heart!*

Copeland liked Beth. She may have currently looked like she had been dragged through a hedge backwards upside down and in dire need of a few ChewiVits to lift her spirits, but he did not want to upset her. He said, 'Tom is living with a really beautiful younger woman in her three storey mansion in grounds as big as Wembley stadium. He seems okay.'

*You complete bastard Copeland,* groaned Copeland's inner voice. *You just HAD to get a sport comparison in there somewhere, didn't you!*

'Whaaat?' said Copeland, looking at Freya.

'She was crying when she hung up,' said Freya.

'She has to let go, Freya,' said Copeland with a deep sigh. 'She can't have her past with Tom Benson eating her up forever. Believe me, I know.'

Freya said nothing. She leaned on her elbow on the table and said nothing. She nodded and said, 'I suppose we all have to let go of the past sooner or later.'

Copeland sagely nodded and finally slipped his phone in his pocket. He said, 'So, as I said before, I was thinking. Perhaps this evening we could go out for a really nice meal together. I've had sunstroke. I've hardly eaten for days, so…'

'A nice meal, is it?' said Freya, sharply, adding a glare for good measure. 'Humph! I gather from what you told Dr. Spencer that you've seen the email from Director Miller telling you the ChewiVits are deemed safe despite having a high amount of this super enzyme Dr. Spencer is so worried about. We both know the truth about ChewiVits, don't we?'

Copeland said, 'Didn't you want to tell me something about finding the identities of the pentagram killers?'

'This is more important! Answer my question. Have you seen the email?' demanded Freya, swivelling towards Copeland and tightly folding her arms across her white vest.

Flopping back against the back of his sofa, Copeland said, 'Yes, I read it. Before I left Longbeck, Keira gave me my phone back and…'

Leaning forward, Freya cut in. 'And I've noticed we seem to be on first name terms with *Keira* after spending three *nights* with her!'

'We seemed to get on okay,' said Copeland, a little puzzled at the aggressive tone in Freya's voice. 'Oh, I see. Don't' worry, Freya. I haven't turned my back on the law in favour of her ideas of swift justice. I told her that before I left. I told her I'd think about it though. And I'm pretty sure... Well, somewhere just over fifty percent sure, she's not behind the pentagram murders. She's just a drug lord... Or should it be drug lady? Ha! Hmm, okay, yes... Kee, er, Keira Starr showed me the email on my phone. Did you know you can get your emails on your phone? I didn't! Keira seemed quite pleased about the ChewiVits not being recalled or anything. Actually, she was more interested in who Janet was.'

'So am I!' Freya said, quite loudly in Copeland's opinion.

'Well,' shrugged Copeland, 'I'll tell you what I told Keira. Janet is Director Miller's personal assistant, the current head of personnel at Department C, our office manager and administration manager and types all my reports for me because I can't type – my old school friends tell me I'm just crap at spelling, but they're just typos, honest – yes, Janet is Director Miller's right hand woman, giving her all the relevant reports from all the other branches of the security services. Her husband was eaten by lions, you know.'

'And...' said Freya. 'I suppose she has a particular interest in studying the influences of ChewiVits and is some sort of student of different types of handcuffs? That's why she asked you to go round to her house with both when she shows you the latest gift you got for her!'

Copeland looked hard at Freya. He slowly said, 'Freya, you are an absolute genius. I've been trying to work out why she wanted me to take ChewiVits and handcuffs round to her house. I would have never guessed. Well worked out, Freya.'

Softening, Freya rolled her eyes and asked, 'And showing you the gift you sent her?'

Copeland scratched his head and said, 'I get her gifts for typing my reports for me. I've been trying to think what the last gift was. Did I tell you I had really bad sunstroke while I was away? It's left me a bit befuddled at the moment, but, what keeps popping into my mind is a giant cactus. I think I got Janet a giant cactus. It sounds about right. I hate to say it, but Janet is a bit of an old fuddy-duddy who refuses to retire. She's someone who would think a cactus is actually exciting, believe it or not.'

'Oh,' said Freya, embarrassed and shuffling on the dining chair. 'I thought Janet was…Never mind…Yes, in that case… I'd love to go for a romantic meal with you…'

*Hang on, Copeland! Who said it was a* **romantic** *meal!*

'Shut up!' Copeland snapped.

'Pardon?' said Freya, taken aback.

'Oh, right…' Copeland floundered and had to do a bit of his sage nodding. 'Er, I thought I heard my phone go again. My mistake. About this meal… Shall we go to the pub again?'

Not knowing whether to nod, shake her head or roll eyes, Freya simply said, 'I think I'll just show you who the pentagram killers are now. Then you can put out an all points bulletin or whatever you call it so they can be arrested. I printed off their photos too. Hang on.'

Pointing, Copeland said, 'Isn't that one on the printer next to you?'

Freya looked down at the printed picture of the stunning redhead she had thought might be the link between the murder victims. She looked at it, sighed, turned back to Copeland and said, 'No, that's just another dead end. The killers' printouts are in my bedroom.'

Copeland smiled and watched her leave the room. He stood, went over to the table where the printer sat next to the laptop and looked at its latest printout. He thought, *Oh, good for Freya. She finally found an online picture of Ania Rose. Nice bikini too, what there is of it.*

Freya gave Copeland a brief synopsis of her activities while he was at Keira's Longbeck Estate and she finally admitted she saw no connection between the murder victims and Keira Starr's Dark Stars before laying out three A4 printout photos on the table in front of him. She said, 'Have you booked a restaurant for us yet? Larry..?'

Coldly, Copeland ignored her, pointed and asked, 'Who's this one?'

'Valdis Ozola,' replied Freya. 'Latvian. Interpol warrant for murdering his parents. And this one is…'

'Vasily Goraya,' said Copeland. 'Former KGB, Order of Lenin, Order of the Red Star, and also known as The Kamchatka Killer. Latterly General Goraya of the Russian SVR.'

'General?' queried Freya. 'The MI5 database said he was a colonel.'

'Hefty promotion to general,' said Copeland. 'Just before the Kremlin ordered him to be sent to Siberia. That's where he's supposed to be. Just wait until I get my hands on Beryl Pickford!' Copeland stood motionless. Then he picked up a dining chair and threw it at the sofa.

'Larry…?' said Freya, as Copeland followed the chair and started punching a cushion on his sofa. 'Larry!' shouted Freya, 'That's your favourite cushion!'

Copeland threw the cushion down and whirled to face Freya. He looked at her. Tugging the side of his silver hair, he turned and paced back and forth across the room. It didn't take long: it was a small room. Angrily he paced and snarled, 'Vasily Goraya threatened to kill my daughter, Freya. Yes, I have a daughter. I haven't seen her since she was three. I wasn't allowed any contact...For her safety...Too late now. She's a post-grad art student. A sculptress. I'm told...I'm told by her partner that she's really good with bronze...'

'Larry, calm down,' said Freya. She soon wished she hadn't. Copeland's finger was waving in her face.

'Calm down! She's my daughter, Freya!' shouted Copeland. 'Vasily threatened to kill her!' He lowered his finger and stared at the floor. 'He's like a bad penny, Freya. It's him...' Copeland buried his face in the side of Freya's hair. She hugged him. On the verge of tears, Copeland said, 'He'll kill my Emily. He must know I was involved in... Just a minute...' Copeland stood, wiped a shirt sleeve across his eyes and said, 'Why is he one of the pentagram murderers?' He smiled. 'Ha! Yes! He's down on his luck and has to keep a low profile! He's hiding from the Russian SVR and from Beryl and her Pickfords. If he was going to kill Emily to get revenge on me, he'd have done it by now.'

Freya watched Copeland clench a fist in the air, shudder, and turn back to the pictures on the table. Pointing at sombrero man he said, 'Who's this one?'

Freya grimaced. 'Don't know. There's not enough for the facial recognition software to identify him, even if he is in the MI5 database.'

Copeland glumly replaced the thrown dining chair and sat on the sofa. 'Big problem,' he groaned. 'In my last two cases I failed to get the big fish. I don't want that to happen again. I'd like to keep my job. If we find and arrest Vasily Goraya and this…'

'Valdis Ozola,' said Freya.

'If we arrest them,' continued Copeland, 'they may or may not tell us who our sombrero man is. Even if they do, we may or may not find him. And even if we do find him, he may or may not tell who is *really* behind the murders, providing the money or tell us the things that are really bothering both of us… *Why* are these men being killed? *Why* is the pentagram carved on their foreheads? *Why* the gruesome removal of their hearts? We may have thought we knew the answers when we thought the murders all pointed to Keira Starr, but now we both doubt she's the one behind it all those *whys* are back.'

Freya stared at him. Copeland stared back. The nature of the mutual stare changed into something softer. Freya said, 'Larry… I need to tell you something… It's work. I have to go to…' Copeland's phone pinged. He ignored it. Freya said, 'Take it.'

Reluctantly, Copeland took his phone from his pocket, read the text message and put the phone back. He looked at his watch. He looked at Freya. He said, 'Sorry, Freya, it was a message from Ania Rose. I think our romantic dinner has to be postponed. I have two hours to get to a meeting with Keira Starr's sister, Louise. Let's hope she has some answers.'

## COPELAND MEETS A SOURCE.

The inaptly named Manchester Docks public house near a village just west of Birmingham was frequented by many customers over its one hundred and fifty year history, usually at a rate of about one per week. Consequently, it was not hard for Copeland to guess which of the patrons his new informant Louise was when he rushed into the otherwise empty pub.

Ania Rose had texted him where and when to meet Louise. The when being within the next two hours or Louise would leave and any chance he had of obtaining evidence on Keira Starr would disappear like a coin in a magician's hand. After the quickest shower and change of his life, Copeland had sped towards Birmingham.

'You're late,' was the first thing informant Louise said when he burst into the less than charming pub. The second thing was, 'I'll have a pint and a double whiskey. I've opened a tab so you can pay.'

Noticing there were several empty glasses already on the old rectangular wooden table, Copeland said, 'Sorry you've been waiting.'

'Nearly twenty minutes,' said Louise. 'You are Inspector Copeland, aren't you? Good. Call me Lou. Order me a pie and chips while you're at the bar. I'll wait until later for my usual bottle of red.'

*Aaaah...* said the inner voice. *At last you've found a kindred spirit, Copeland... Your one true soul mate...*

Copeland rang the little bell on the bar and waited. He turned to look at Lou and gave her a smile. He could see the resemblance to Lou's elder half-sister, Keira Starr. Lou had the same jet black hair, the same Mediterranean olive skin. Apart from also having two arms and two legs, the resemblance ended there. Lou was even shorter than Tom

Benson and was, well, round. And while her hair was indeed very black it sat on her head like a mouldy cauliflower. An impeccable eye for colour was demonstrated by Lou's dress sense – orange trainers and a woolly lime green poncho resembling a tent over her baggy red jogging bottoms. She was the first younger sister Copeland had ever seen who looked significantly older than her sibling.

A barmaid finally appeared and said, 'Yow oright luv? Getcha summat ta drink? Sem agin fer yower lil leddie ist?'

The Peaky Blinders sounded cultured in comparison, but Copeland interpreted the word 'drink' and gave his order. The pies came out of the rusty warmer and the chips emerged from the microwave before the second pint was poured and Copeland's credit card had been tapped.

'So,' said Lou after downing her double whiskey and half draining her pint. 'You want to know about big sister Keira, eh? Ania tells me she's having people bumped off and carving her pentagram into their foreheads like she's leaving her mark on them.'

Copeland nodded eagerly and took his notepad from his jacket inside pocket. He was impressed he'd remembered it.

'Well, Inspector Copeland,' said Lou. 'I don't know anything about any murders.'

'Oh,' said Copeland.

'But I do know where she cooks up her meth,' smiled Lou. 'Is that right? Cooks up her meth? Does that mean makes her methamphetamine? The beer and pie are good aren't they, Inspector?'

Copeland nodded, even though he thought the pie looked as if it had once been burned by Alfred the Great along with his cakes and reheated many times since, and the equally vintage beer had possibly sat motionless in the pipes since the Norman Conquest.

Lou took his notepad and pencil from him, wrote down an address and said, 'There you go. Keira's crystal meth lab. It's under a laundry at that address near York. She got the idea of building it under a laundry from a TV programme. The laundry is in her name so… There you go! One search warrant and Keira's crime empire falls like a pack of cards!'

Lou handed him the notepad back, swigged the remnants of her pint and engulfed a mouthful of pastry (because the pie's content was just air).

'Tell me, Lou,' said Copeland, 'she's your sister and…'

'Half sister,' corrected Lou, spraying pastry flakes from her mouth.

'Er, quite,' said Copeland, brushing his jacket and wishing he had not sat opposite Lou. 'Keira is your half sister, so why are you giving me information to arrest her? I've met her and she seems quite…'

'My glasses are empty,' Lou said, pointing at glasses that were indeed empty. 'Forget the double whisky this time, Inspector. Just bring a bottle back. Don't worry. I'm not driving.' Lou's cheeks wobbled as she giggled. So did her chins.

Copeland went to the bar, rang the bell and, while waiting for the barmaid to appear, surreptitiously switched on his phone's Google translate.

'Nuvver sem egin luv,' said the stout barmaid, which Copeland thought may or may not have been a question. He glanced at his phone. Squiggly lines appeared on the screen as Google translate had a nervous breakdown. Sighing, Copeland said, 'A pint of best and a bottle of whiskey, please.'

'Yow spake posh dowya,' replied the barmaid. 'Yow orta bin ere Winsdee fer tha quiz niyt luv. Yowda wun. Nuwun else in ere.'

Copeland nodded and smiled a lot before returning with a pint and a bottle of Famous Grouse, which Lou poured into one of her empty pint glasses. 'This'll keep me going for a bit,' she told Copeland, reassuringly. 'So why am I shopping Keira? Is that what you call it, Inspector? Shopping someone? Do you think I drink too much?'

'Yes, no,' said Copeland, wanting to just excuse himself to phone Director Miller. He had phoned her earlier and told her of he was going to meet Louise and Wendy Miller had a judge on standby to issue search and/ or arrests warrants for Keira Starr and/ or Dark Stars as necessary, and the location of the meth lab Lou had just given him would be a good start.

'I'm shopping Keira because Ania paid me,' said Lou.

'What?' said Copeland.

'Ania paid me to tell you something to get Keira arrested. Thirty million. It'll pay some of my debts. Petty cash for Ania, that is, Inspector, but not for me. I'm worse than broke.'

Copeland noticed the whiskey was being consumed as if it was beer, though not his beer, which sat as flat as dishwater in his glass. 'Why would Ania Rose pay you so much to get Keira arrested, Lou?' asked Copeland. 'What's she got against Keira anyway? It seems personal.'

When she stopped giggling Lou leaned forward, put her finger on her lips and said, 'It's because of the Game.'

'The Game?' queried Copeland.

Lou imitated Copeland's sage nodding and said, 'The Game is a competition – a contest – between us. It started when our grandparents gave us lots of money and…'

'Hang on,' interrupted Copeland. 'You mean yours and Keira's grandparents.'

Lou almost choked on her whiskey. She screwed her chubby round face and said, 'Naaa…I mean OUR grandparents. I'm Ania's sister too. No, that's not right… I'm her step sister, half sister, I'm getting a bit muddled, Inspector.'

'So, 'said Copeland, '…if you're Keira's half-sister and you're also Ania's half sister then that means…'

*Hells bells! You haven't even had anything to drink! Keep up, Copeland!*

Sniggering, Lou whispered. 'Don't tell Ania I told you, okay? They hate each other. As I was saying, what was your name again? Doesn't matter. Our grandparents gave us oodles of money and we started a logistics business together. I've no idea what logistics actually is, but it was doing pretty well and Ania and Keira were always bickering about who was in charge. So… Might need another bottle soon… So, to decide who should run the business they decided to have a little competition. They sort of included me as their little sister even though they knew I couldn't find my way out of a paper bag even when I was sober. Their nickname for me was Loopy. Loopy Lou, that's me… Inspector! That's it! Your name is Inspector, isn't it? Bloody funny name, that, Inspector. Are you sure you don't think I drink too much?'

Shaking his head, Copeland said, 'Of course not, Lou.'

*This is wrong, Copeland,* snapped Copeland's inner voice going into conscience mode. *She's drunk and you're taking advantage of the poor little woman by getting totally irrelevant information out of her. Shame on you! And all those calories probably aren't improving her figure either.*

Copeland responded to his inner conscience by waving to the barmaid and pointing to the empty bottle of Famous Grouse. While Lou stared at her many empty glasses she said, 'So working out the contest thing was just more arguments until they decided it should be a test of loyalty. They said whoever was the boss should inspire the most loyalty. We all thought up a sort of loyalty test. Mine was who could go and fetch some booze the quickest. We all had to pick two of the staff to represent us. Can you *actually* believe I *actually* had a man and woman who *actually* volunteered to *actually* be on my team? Ania's Champions won – that's what we called them, our Champions, with a capital C of course. Where was I? Oh, yeah... Ania won and took over everything but then after all the contracts had been signed and stuff, Keira found out Ania had cheated. She'd bribed all the other contestants. Well, Keira's Champions, not mine. Mine were rubbish anyway. Mine always are.'

Copeland was glad he had not even sipped his beer. He said, 'I don't get this. You, Ania and Keira are half sisters. Your grandparents gave you a heap of money. You started a business together. You argued about who was in charge. You had a competition. Whichever of you could prove you inspired the most loyalty in the staff got to take over the business. Ania won by bribing Keira's Champions. Keira found out but it was too late to change the contracts so Ania got everything.'

Lou nodded, almost fell onto the table and mumbled, 'Nearly everything. Keira and I got a few crumbs to try to start our own businesses. Of course, Ania wasn't Ania Rose back then.'

'Wasn't Ania Rose?' said Copeland, despairingly placing a hand on top of his head. 'What do you mean, Lou?'

Lou sat up, swayed a little and said, 'OooH! Look! She's brought a new bottle of whiskey! Do you think I drink too much? Did I ask you that already? Ania? Who's Ania? Oh, Ania! She only became Ania Rose when she took over that you scratch my back I'll scratch your back and let's make oodles of money together Roses sect. Ania Rose is her title, not her name. She became the new Ania Rose and she was all, like, there's been Ania Roses since like the year dot and I'm the new one now so I'm really, really important.'

Copeland thought what Beryl Pickford had said when she had said she had misspoken. Beryl had said The Pickfords had always got on with the Ania Roses... NOT Ania Rose, but the *Ania Roses*! Copeland realised 'The Roses' may well have existed for almost as long as The Pickfords, give or take a couple of hundred years. Perhaps The Roses went as far back as the time when The Pickfords had called themselves Ye Honourable Friends of Ye Crown, and The Roses leader had always inherited the title of Ania Rose. Perhaps. But surely some learned historian would have found that out...

Copeland said, 'So Keira hates Ania Rose, or whatever her name was back then, because she cheated at this competition Game with a capital G thing and took over the company your grandparents had given you money to set up, but I know an acquaintance of mine is training to be Ania's Champion chap. Is there going to be some sort of rematch, Lou?'

*Who cares? Let's go back home to Freya and have... I didn't say that! Forget I'm here!*

'Rematch? Naaa. Yeah. Rematch,' Lou slowly said as she waved an intoxicated finger across the table at Copeland. 'The Game is because... Hang on, let me try and remember... Oh, yesh. These business people... Are they business people? Yes, I think so. They're financiers and bankers and own mashive electronic companies and shipping and who knows what elsh. Pour me another, Inshpeshterr. Thanksh. Well, they shaid, *"Hey, babe, you wanna join an organisation that controls the world?"* and Ania said, 'Well, sure," and Keira said, "Hey, scumbag redhead bitch, you cheated when you got our company," and these control the world people sorta said, "Ooh, we don't want arguments, do we? Let's make it fair. We'll organise another competition for you gals" and I said,

"Can I play as well?" and they said "OK" and they organised another competition. That's the gist of it. We had another competition. Shall we have another pint? Mine's a whishkey.'

Copeland was desperate enough to take a mouthful of the scum floating on top of his lifeless pint of beer. He spat it back. Grimacing, he said, 'And...?'

Lou tried to focus on him. She said, 'And what?'

Hands wide, Copeland asked, 'And...You had another competition...Who won that one?'

Lou looked at him as if he was insane. 'Who won? Who won? Who won the Game to take over everything that Keira, Ania and I own and join these people who say they control the world? Who won? No one has ever *won*, Inshpeshtor. All the Champions always fail at leasht one of the loyalty teshts. No one has ever *won*. Thatsh why us keeps having them, year in year out... Your mate is training for the nexsht one.'

Copeland stared at his full pint of beer. He swished it around the glass. The floating scum stubbornly stayed put. Still looking at it, he said, 'Lou, when you say everything... You mean whoever wins this contest – this Game – gets *everything* you other two own? The winner takes it all?'

'*The loser standing small*,' Lou sang, bursting into the Abba song with gusto. She was not a great singer. Thankfully it was only the chorus. When she finished, Copeland thought her head might topple off her chubby neck when she did very high and very low nods and replied, 'Yep! Winner gets everything! Right down to the last braid of glass, Inshpeshtor... I think I mean braid of grass. Blade of grass. Is your name really Inshpeshtor? Course, I've got bugger all left for Ania and Keira to win anyway. Just a couple of little companies that are going busht any day now. Even sold my mansion. Moving into a run-down place in the middle of nowhere, I am. Haven't even got enough to hire two people to enter the Game for me. I'm broke, Mr. Inshpeshtor…'

Lou put her face in her hands and started sobbing. Copeland winced and moved round the table to sit beside her. He carefully placed a consoling arm lightly round her shoulder. She half fell onto him and cried down his jacket. He gave her a gentle squeeze and whispered, 'Sorry, Lou, but I have to ask… Do you think Ania might have people killed and make it look like Keira was behind the killings so she couldn't take part in this contest you call the Game?'

Lou wiped her nose on his shoulder before she sat upright, swayed, looked at him, frowned and said, 'What game? Oh, the Game game. Would Ania..?' She stopped and looked around the decaying bar. She stared at Copeland and said, 'What was the question? Oh, no! Ania wouldn't… Not to win the Game thing and take over all Keira's… No, she wouldn't… Would she? We *have* to be there, you know, when our Champions do the challenges for the Game. It's a rule. We lose if we're not there. So if Keira got arrested and was in the clink… Would Ania frame Keira for murder? Never! Don't know. Maybe. Feel a bit sick now Inshpeshtor…'

## 12. Day 11. SATURDAY, SATURDAY!

Freya watched the disheartened Copeland apathetically spoon his cornflakes around his bowl. Sitting beside him at the bay window dining table, she placed a hand on his shoulder and said, 'So you got Keira Starr's drunken sister Louise outside where she threw up on the pub's steps, then again in the car park while you held her up and waited for the taxi you called for her?'

Copeland lifted cornflakes on his spoon, turned the spoon over and let them flop back into his bowl. 'Then I phoned Director Miller. She was waiting for my call. She got a search warrant for Keira's crystal meth lab that Louise gave me the address for and phoned North Yorkshire Police. They were raiding the place within two hours of my call.'

'It's not your fault, Larry. We know it wasn't you so it must have been one of the police who tipped off Keira Starr,' suggested Freya, stroking Copeland's shoulder.

Copeland sighed deep and long. 'Whoever it was the Dark Stars must have acted fast. By the time the police got there the fire-fighters were fighting a losing battle. The fire chief thinks it must have been the dry cleaning chemicals that caused the fire to get so hot, but I suspect the chemicals they were using to make their crystal meth helped. Nothing was left. It even melted the glass in the laundry shop's windows. I was almost back in London when I got the call to say the evidence we thought we were going to get to arrest Keira Starr had literally gone up in smoke. I stopped at a service station and stared into a cup of black coffee for I don't know how long.' Another spoonful of cornflakes slopped back into his bowl.

Freya looked out of the bay window. She looked at Copeland's soggy cornflakes. She looked at the laptop and printer he'd moved to the far side of the table so he could place his phone and his mug of now cold tea next to his bowl. She leaned forward so she could turn her head and look the disconsolate Copeland in the face. Squeezing his shoulder, she said, 'You should have woken me up, Larry.'

Under her palm, Copeland's shoulder shrugged. 'I knew you were tired after your late nights spent discovering the identities of the pentagram murderers.'

Freya repeated, 'You should have woken me, Larry. I really wouldn't have minded. I could have... consoled you. I care about you, Larry. Really care.'

Copeland dropped his spoon into the bowl and leaned back on the dining chair. He looked Freya in the eye and said, 'I'm not sure how I feel, Freya.'

Freya felt her heart tighten in her chest. A hard, cold stone grew in her throat as she whispered, 'It's okay, Larry.'

Copeland shook his head. 'It's not okay at all, Freya. I shouldn't feel this way but I sort of admire Keira Starr. Part of me thinks she really is trying to make the world a better place. True, she's a megalomaniac who demands total obedience from her private army of Dark Stars, a dangerous vigilante who puts criminals in holes in the ground to deliver her own justice, a billionaire drugs lord lady who slices the heads off her rivals and is so utterly ruthless she even puts one of her top Dark Star lieutenants in with her oversized dogs as a punishment.'

Shocked, Freya sat back, grimacing with hands clasped. 'What did the Dark Star lieutenant do to deserve that?'

'Stole my ChewiVits off me,' huffed Copeland. 'Maybe a bit harsh to put Kirsty in there with the dogs for a whole week, but that's Keira I suppose. She may have her faults, but she believes in justice and wherever Keira Starr has taken over things are getting better. There's less crime, more drug rehabilitation and no homeless, and she's funding that

Butterburn research place so super-smart people like Beth Spencer can cure cancer and stuff. I guess she's *technically* breaking the law by selling drugs and killing other drug lords and so on but... Anyway, we have nothing on her anymore, and meanwhile our new number one suspect behind the pentagram murders is Ania Rose, close confidant of Director Miller, Department C's super-informant and, I strongly suspect, the main person behind the private finance sponsorship money funding Department C. Like I told you before my cornflakes went soggy, it's all about this stupid winner takes all contest they're having. Ania Rose stands to lose absolutely everything including her Roses organisation if Keira wins so, I'm afraid to say, it makes sense for Ania to try to frame her half-sister by hiring killers and leaving Keira's pentagram symbol carved into the victims' foreheads so all fingers point at Keira Starr. Like I said, according to Lou, the rules of this Game contest thing say they *must* to be there when their so-called Champions compete. Devious Ania Rose wins everything even if Keira Starr only ends up in police custody! Do sisters always squabble as badly as this?'

Freya stared at Copeland for a few moments then gazed out of the window as she said, 'I only had a brother. He's long gone...' After a long sigh she looked back at Copeland and asked, 'Did your informant Lou tell you who these financiers, bankers, multi-national company owners and so on actually are? You know, the name of this organisation which claims it controls the world and wants the winner of this contest to join them?'

Copeland shook his head. 'Lou said they just called them the organisers – because they organise the contest – The Game... I still can't believe someone like Tom Benson could ever be considered a Champion with a capital C!' Copeland laughed and pushed away his cornflakes bowl.

Glad of some levity, Freya joined in with Copeland's laughter. 'Ha! Thomas Benson Esquire! The *not* so famous writer of several conspiracy theory articles for *Gloom and Doom Monthly*! You'd better not tell him about these so-called organisers, he'll be telling you they're the ones he banged on about in one of those articles I told you about. I've forgotten their name, now. What were they called?'

'The Family,' laughed Copeland. 'He calls them the Family, or when he's really got you pinned against a wall he gets in your face and says they're really called the Fyli, which Tom says means family in Greek, but I looked it up and...' Copeland put his hands up. 'OK. I have to be honest, Freya, I did actually ask Lou if the organisers of their contest were called the Family... And, do you know what?' He lowered his hands and looked at Freya very seriously.

'What? What!' demanded Freya. 'Don't tell me she said they were!'

Copeland burst out laughing. 'She looked at me like I was speaking Dutch and threw up in the car park again!'

Following another mirthful moment, and still smiling, Copeland looked at his cornflakes and said, 'I even put honey on them. I really had a craving for honey, but my appetite still hasn't come back after my awful sunstroke. Anyway, cheer up Freya! Keira Starr may have slipped through our fingers and we've no way of identifying Sombrero Man so there's no way we'll ever prove whether Ania Rose was or wasn't the evil genius using him to pay the pentagram murderers.' He stood up, bowl in hand, and gave Freya a grim smile. 'I suppose all that's left to do is to distribute the photos of my old acquaintance Vasily Goraya and his new sidekick Valdis Ozola and hope the police eventually pick them up. Ha! I'm back to getting the insignificant little fish arrested and letting the big fish like Ania Rose go scot-free. I suppose I can say goodbye to Department C and vegetate watching daytime TV.' Half heartedly gesturing towards the printer, he smiled and added, 'At least you can do your article about the Roses now I've told you Ania Rose is just her title as their leader and you've found a photo of her.'

'Pardon?' said Freya, who had been only half listening, thinking about her long-dead brother and how she was glad at least some killers like Vasily Goraya would eventually be brought to justice. She realised what Copeland meant, grabbed the photo off the printer, leapt up and thrust the photo between Copeland's nose and his cornflake bowl. Incredulous, she said, '*This* is Ania Rose?'

Copeland found it a little difficult to tear his eyes from the idyllic clifftop photo of azure sea and white sands. The redhead in a micro-bikini had nothing to do with it. But he looked at Freya and said, 'Er, yes…'

Grinning broadly, Freya said, 'Put the kettle on Larry while I get dressed! I can't go round in this old tee shirt all day.'

*Why not?* asked an inner voice.

Freya wore clothes, mugs of tea were emptied and Copeland eventually grasped why he had become a fully paid up member of some reputable dating websites, and lots of not so reputable ones. He supposed in her line of work as an investigative reporter, Freya had learned how to hack into the sensitive files of any commercial website once she had got through their front door, and the front door of these dating websites was entered by officially registering on them (by using Copeland's credit card and putting his profile in). Yet despite the holiday photo of Ania Rose being linked to pentagram murder victims, the names accompanying the photograph were all different and all not hers. Even so, Copeland resolved he would confront Ania Rose with the photographs of the pentagram killers Vasily Goraya and Valdis Ozola, along with the fuzzy photo of the unknown Mr. Sombrero Man, tell her he knew about her plan to frame Keira Starr so Keira would be arrested and Ania could win The Game, seize all Keira's assets and join an invisible organisation of billionaires secretly running the world! He would not go down without a fight, he told Freya, slapping his hand on the tabletop and suggesting another mug of tea first.

'Aha!' grinned Freya as the doorbell rang. 'Good. Your presents have arrived! I had to order more by express delivery when I saw you'd lost weight. Just a mo!'

*Presents! Great! How nice… Er… Whose credit card has she bought them with?*

Copeland didn't care how Freya had paid. He knew it was the thought that counted and was smiling to himself when Freya came back into the lounge carrying a large cardboard box. His smile faded somewhat when he saw a revolver following close behind her head and a delivery man dressed in a tan uniform and black fedora hat, who looked remarkably like…Copeland got up so fast he went a bit giddy.

'Sit down on your sofa again, Comrade Larry,' ordered Vasily Goraya, Order of Lenin, Order of the Red Star, former member of the KGB and SVR, also known as The Kamchatka Killer and, more recently, as Mr. Grey.

'Good,' said Vasily Goraya as Copeland slowly sat. He poked Freya in the back with his revolver. 'Now you sit on the far end of the sofa next to him. Then there will be much less mess when I shoot you both.'

After giving Freya a feeble smile as she sat next to him, Copeland watched Vasily sit down at the little round dining table in the bay window and – what a nerve! – help himself to the biscuits Freya had just fetched. 'Have I upset you in some way, Vasily?' asked Copeland, nodding at the revolver pointing at him.

'Aha!' said Vasily, waving his pistol barrel in Copeland's general direction. 'You tried to get me sent to a Siberian salt mine. But I still had friends in the Russian mafia I could pay with my last few roubles. I walked out of the embassy in handcuffs but someone else got on the plane to Russia.'

Leaning forward, Freya balanced the large cardboard box on one hand. With it wobbling precariously on her palm she lowered it down and slid it onto the floor. She leaned forward and peeled off the tape. Vasily Goraya frowned, shook his head and said, 'I found that on your doorstep. It is from someone called Ann Summers.'

Leaning forward, Freya put one hand in the box and, one by one, pulled out the contents and laid them on the floor. Copeland and Vasily stared as each one came out of the box. A voice asked, *Now do you remember it wasn't a cactus you bought Janet for typing your report, Copeland?*

Vasily said, 'I have that red satin set at home. I'm wearing black at the moment. But they are all too big for you. More Comrade Larry's size.' He pointed with the revolver barrel. 'Except for that very naughty one.'

Freya sat back, smiling at Vasily Goraya. 'Yes, that one is for me. But you were telling us about your escape, Mr. Goraya. Didn't the people on the plane to the Siberian salt mines recognise it wasn't you?'

Tearing his eyes from the array laid on the carpet, Vasily used his hand not holding a gun and pointed to his head. 'With black bags on our heads all prisoners tend to look the same. For a small extra fee, my mafia friends got someone who was about the same height and looked a bit like me. The Dorchester had to appoint a new doorman the next day. So here I am for my revenge. Aha! Revenge! Revenge is a dish best served lukewarm, eh, Comrade Larry?'

'Pardon?' said Freya.

Ignoring Vasily, Copeland explained, 'Vasily and I used to drink together and I taught him some common English sayings. He mastered them well.'

Vasily laughed, 'There is no time like the past, eh, Comrade? Now, before I shoot you and your housekeeper…'

Freya protested, 'I'm not his housekeeper!' She thrust a leg in Vasily's direction. 'Would a housekeeper wear designer jeans?' She pulled the shoulder of her blouse in Vasily's general direction. 'Would a housekeeper wear a Giambattista Vali floral lace cape blouse? Or these Jimmy Choos? I don't think so!'

*Let's hope Vasily shoots you before you get your credit card bill, Copeland.*

Freya wasn't finished. 'I'm not his housekeeper! I'm Freya Noyor and I'm… his…his… His lover!'

Copeland almost choked, but thought he recovered well by doing a bit of sage nodding and saying, 'As a point of information, Comrade Vasily, we haven't sort of actually consummated the relationship as yet, as it were.'

Freya joined in with a bit of sage nodding of her own and said, 'Perhaps you could give us a couple of hours before you shoot us, Comrade Goraya?'

'A couple of hours?' retorted Copeland, no longer sagely nodding and staring aghast at Freya.

Vasily laughed. He said, 'I think I'll just shoot you now before you have some sort of marital argument. As Larry once told me, there is an English saying… Time and tide wait for no woman! Aha! I remembered it! But to be honest, I never understood that one. Now, Comrade Larry, my old friend, before I kill you, I have to tell you this secret…'

310

*Excellent! You'll finally learn something before you die, Copeland.*

Copeland didn't mind his inner voice interrupting. Vasily had paused for a quick demonic cackle before leaning forward on his dining chair and gloating, 'All those nights we spent in the pub when you thought we were friends... I was using you! I was extracting information from you! You fool! You gave me many secrets after two pints of ale, Comrade.'

'Well...' Copeland said, pulling a hate-to-tell-you-this you evil gloating Russian spy face, which, to be fair, was not the sort of face commonly used by the general public, so it was understandable Vasily looked slightly bewildered when he heard Copeland say, '*We* were actually using *you*, Vasily. True, I gave you low level information we decided you could have to gain your trust, but all the rest was rubbish. We just made it look true. *We* were interested in the questions you asked. If you asked about it, then you didn't know the answer did you? We found out what you did and didn't know about from the questions you asked. Don't you Russians ever read any spy books?' Copeland turned to Freya. 'Good film that as well... Sean Connery, Michelle Pfeiffer... She's nice... You could dye your hair Freya and...'

'I'm not dying my hair!' snapped Freya. She sighed, looked into Copeland's eyes and softly said, 'I want you to love me as I am, Larry.'

Vasily waved his gun at them and said, 'Look! Time and tide wait for... Have I done that one? What were we saying? I have to tell you, Comrade Larry, I sometimes get a bit confused these days... I think I'll kill your housekeeper first, then you, if that's alright.'

'And then what Vasily?' asked Copeland. 'Go back to killing people, carving a pentagram on their forehead and taking their hearts out so you can prove they are dead and get your payment? We have proof it was you. Photos of you and your partner, the Latvian Valdis Ozola, have already been circulated to every police force in Europe. Honest!'

'Hum,' hummed Vasily. 'Hummm… No they haven't. You said honest at the end then. I know that means you're lying. I read an article about it. It was in a magazine I read regularly. It's called Doom and Gloom Monthly. The article was written by… No, it's gone again… A frequent writer… Aha! Written by Ben Tomson!'

'Tom Benson?' suggested Freya.

Vasily said, 'Could be.'

Freya and Copeland looked at each other and winced. Copeland nodded sagely, turned back to Vasily and clapped his hands. 'So, Comrade Vasily, you haven't said what your plan is after you kill us. Freya, stop elbowing me. Save it for later. More pentagram murders is it, Comrade? More killing lonely men for a few thousand pounds a time? More blood money from Ania Rose?'

'Ha-ha, Comrade!' said Vasily. 'So you also know Ania Rose is paying us for these murders? Poor woman…wanting the hearts of all the very numerous ex-lovers who spurned her.' Vasily sighed. It was probably the first time he'd ever done that. 'My days of handing a sealable freezer bag to poor Mr. Pink are over. Oh, Mr. Pink was Valdis Ozola.'

Pointing an accusatory finger at Vasily Goraya, ex KGB, ex SVR, etcetera… Freya said, 'The police have his DNA from the saliva at Mr. Jennings' house. They'll get you, you evil scum!'

Copeland said, 'She's a very emotional home help,' then winced as he groaned, 'That elbow was really sharp, Freya.'

Appearing as if he had somewhere lost the thread of the conversation and intended to shoot the TV, Vasily said,

'Valdis is as dead a doorknob. His saliva is just a drop in the lake now.'

*Quite close, that one, eh, Copeland?*

Back to waving the gun at Copeland and Freya, Vasily said, 'I knew Mr. White was going to double cross us when he gave us our cash and phoned our Big Boss and used her real name. So I'm not killing any more people for Ania Rose. Neither is Mr. Pink. He's dead. Shame really, he'd just perfected his carving a pentagram into a forehead technique.'

Shocked, Freya said, 'You've killed Valdis Ozola?'

Vasily grinned and waved his revolver. 'I shot him when he went behind a tree to relieve himself. I left his body in the woods. Along with the man whose car I'm driving. So before I start my new job as a contract killer for hire, I thought I would tie up loose ends and kill you Comrade Larry. Finding you was easy. My new employer – The Broker – provides addresses for victims for a small extra fee.' Taking another biscuit, Vasily stood and pointed his revolver at Freya. 'Any last requests, home-help lady? Apart from two more hours of life, or anything else for that matter.'

'Who is Mr. White?' asked Freya, staring into the barrel of the gun. 'We call him Sombrero Man because…' She stopped because Vasily laughed loudly.

'Yes,' said Vasily when he stopped laughing. 'Mr. White was wearing a sombrero last time, when he gave away the identity of our employer by calling her Ania and Miss Rose instead of "My Lady" like he usually did. A short wiry fellow with white hair and a nose like a rodent! I don't know who Mr. White really is, so I'm afraid, Freya Noyor, I can't answer your dying question. Sorry. I will be shooting you in just a moment Comrade Larry, so hang on to your horse chestnuts, but first…Time to die, Miss Noyor…'

*Copeland! Do something! Save Freya! Throw yourself in front of the gun!*

Copeland had time to see Freya turn to look at him with panic in her eyes before he heard Vasily click back the hammer of his revolver. 'Wait!' Copeland shouted. 'Let's do a deal, Vasily!'

Vasily stared down at him. 'You took away my power and all my offshore bank accounts, comrade. There will be no deal. It is no good closing the stable door after the horse has run away!'

'What if…' said Copeland, nodding sagely as he leaned forward between the gun barrel and Freya. 'What if I could get you a job with all the power you could ever want? All the money you could ever want? And a free mansion with your own servants, including a personal chef!'

'A personal chef?' Vasily said as his gun began to waver for a moment. But only a moment. 'No!' Vasily shouted. 'You have tricked me before, Comrade Larry.'

Copeland held up his hands. 'This is no trick. I promise I can get you this job – *if* you spare our lives, Vasily. I just need to make one phone call. You can point your gun at me and shoot if I say anything you don't like. What have you got to lose, except a life on the run as a hit man? Sit down and change your life forever… Pass me my phone and I'll make the call.'

Vasily looked suspiciously at Copeland but carefully lowered the hammer of his revolver and pointed the barrel at the far arm of the sofa next to Freya. 'There's your phone, there,' he said.

Copeland looked at the phone and back at Vasily. 'Comrade Vasily, my phone does not have a pink case. My phone is on the table by the bowl of soggy cornflakes.'

Vasily nodded, passed Copeland his phone and sat back on the wooden dining chair with his gun pointing squarely at Copeland.

Copeland rang a number from his speed dial list. Smiling, he said, 'Hi Keira... Yes, I'm fine thanks. Sorry to say this call is business and not pleasure... Of course I'll phone just to have a proper chat soon... Really? The dogs did that? That's hilarious! Poor Kirsty, eh? Ha!... Now, you know you're looking for a new head of security for your *organised crime* headquarters up there on your Longbeck Estate? I think I've got the ideal person sitting right here with me now. He even has his own gun... Yes, really. I can see down the barrel right now. He's willing to start straight away and I'm sure your head of personnel, Kirsty, would get on with him really well, but I know you won't let him start until you have a written reference so I'll email you one tomorrow. I'll pass him the phone and you can tell him what's on offer and he can tell you all he's done. I'm sure you'll agree you have an ideal place for him... Yes, Keira. Kiss, kiss to you too. Just a sec, I'll pass him the phone.'

Vasily whispered, 'Organised crime?'

Copeland whispered, 'Just between us, Comrade, I'm really in the pay of the biggest crime gang in England. You must have heard of the Dark Stars. Oh, good – you have. I feed them information about the police and security services, rival gangs and so on. You get the picture. Keira is our leader. She's paying me ten times more than Department C. Have you seen the new BMW outside? She gave me that yesterday. Sorry to keep you Keira, here he is now...'


Leaning on the small dining table to look through the bay window, Copeland and Freya watched Vasily Goraya drive away before they stood looking into each other's eyes. Copeland didn't even see the punch coming before Freya's knuckles connected.

'What was that for?' asked Copeland, rubbing his jaw.

'What was it for?' shouted Freya. 'I guessed a genius like you would have a plan to save us from being shot, but I didn't know you were working for Keira Starr! You traitor!'

***Traitor? Possibly. Genius? Never… Look out, Copeland!***

Copeland saw the second punch coming and stepped back. 'I'm not!' he cried. 'Stop trying to hit me, Freya! I let Vasily think that so he thought he had something on me to get his revenge. I know what he's thinking. Once I send his reference to Keira and his job is secure, he'll let Director Miller know I'm in the service of Keira and her Dark Star army. But what do you think Keira will do after he's just told her about why he's so qualified to work for her?'

'Give him the damn job, of course!' shouted Freya, taking another swing at Copeland's head. 'And he won't need to tell Wendy Miller anything. I'll send her a copy of the recording.'

Copeland had manoeuvred around the room and had grabbed his favourite cushion as he retreated past the sofa. He held the cushion like a shield and asked, 'What recording?'

'Stand still you lying piece of skit'r! The recording I made when I took my phone from my pocket and switched it on. I wanted us to get him to talk. Why do you think I kept elbowing you?'

'Phones can record things? Really? How about that!' said Copeland, being forced back into the hallway with only a blue cushion for protection. 'Mind my cushion, Freya. You'll knock the stuffing out. I didn't see you touch your phone.'

'Simple distraction, like this,' said Freya aiming a punch while landing a kick on Copeland's shin. 'You and Goraya had your eyes glued on the slinky underwear stuff I was taking from the box. Neither of you noticed what my other hand was doing with my phone.'

Dropping his cushion and bending to rub his shin, Copeland looked up at Freya and said, 'I surrender.'

'Good,' said Freya, fist poised. 'Now where are your handcuffs so I can chain you to the bed?'

Copeland looked quizzically at her and said, 'Can't we do that later, after our romantic meal? I've already booked the... Ow! You can really punch, Freya. My arm's numb now.'

'I'm going to handcuff you and phone Beryl Pickford so she can have you carted away and put in a deep hole somewhere! Why is that funny, Mr. Copeland?'

Copeland stopped grinning and sat on his hall floor to rub his shoulder and shin as simultaneously as he could. Looking up at Freya hovering over him with clenched fists he said, 'You saying I'll be in a deep hole is funny because that's where Vasily will be by tomorrow. If he's lucky. He's just told Keira what he's done and Keira is probably already getting the antiques in her torture chamber ready for him. Keira is a stickler for justice and Vasily Goraya has just confessed to not only killing innocent, lonely men but also to countless other killings, including wiping out a whole village in Kamchatka.' Copeland smiled again.

Freya slowly lowered her fists. 'You set him up? You knew without Valdis Ozola linking them to the saliva's DNA there wasn't enough evidence. You sent him to Keira Starr to deliver her own sort of justice!'

'And I swear to you Freya – I'm not working for her. We just got on well... As friends!' grinned Copeland.

Hesitantly, Freya knelt. Not so hesitantly, she kissed him.

Copeland would have enjoyed the kiss more if his jaw wasn't hurting and his inner voice had kept quiet instead of saying, *So, Copeland, you're not saying anything about Keira Starr owing you a big favour then?*


Inspector Larry Copeland of Department C closed the door of his new, black BMW saloon and looked at the front door of Ania Rose's home. He thought it looked…

*Don't you dare even THINK any sports comparisons, Copeland! You're not in my good books at the moment! I might even… What do these crazy sisters call being sent to Coventry? Something about a seat, wasn't it? No, it's gone… Just watch it, OK?*

Copeland was watching. He was watching the electronic gates close with a spark of electricity shooting between them while reflecting on the fact that only just over an hour ago Vasily Goraya had put his revolver in his pocket. Now here he was outside Ania Rose's home in one of his recently cleaned dark blue suits (thanks to maid Rose). He carried a blue manila document folder containing four photos in his hand and a copied recording of Vasily Goraya confessing everything on his phone. Copeland was determined to present the evidence to Ania Rose and arrest her for hiring the pentagram murderers in an attempt to frame Keira Starr. He felt more confident now than he had when he had kissed Freya goodbye and assured her he would be back in plenty of time for their (romantic) dinner date.

Copeland knew their dinner together was now more important than ever. Freya had told him she needed to risk going back to her house in South Wimbledon to get her passport and Copeland had finally remembered to tell Freya why she was no longer in danger from Keira Starr. Then Copeland had felt worse than he had when he'd had his sunstroke – because Freya had told him she was flying to

Serbia tomorrow to get her Pulitzer Prize winning story, and telling him she'd return in a month or so hadn't really helped.

With this news weighing heavily, Copeland had got into his new BMW and had been promptly blinded by the sun. Fortunately, he had found some Cartier sunglasses in the glove compartment, right next to some packets of ChewiVits. His craving for honey had been diminished by two ChewiVits swallowed on the twelve mile journey to Ania Rose's. He knew he'd vowed he wouldn't take vitamins again in case he overdosed and got stomach cramps, but that was then, and right now he was sure the stomach cramps had been another symptom of his sunstroke and besides, he had reasoned, *just* two ChewiVits wouldn't do any harm, would they? And he had been right. They hadn't done any harm at all. In fact, they were making him feel quite good. He walked boldly towards the house with a confident spring in his step and the flimsy folder containing the photographs in his hand.

Every teenage girl's pin-up boy Simon held the front door open as Copeland scrunched across the gravel. Simon did not move out of the way when Copeland reached the steps, but stood resolutely blocking the doorway in his pristine white shirt and said, 'I'm sorry, Inspector Copeland, Sir, but this is not a good time for you to see either Miss Rose or Mr. Benson. Everyone is busy. The cleaners are in and the caterers are already in the kitchen preparing for tonight's dinner party. I'm sure you can speak to Miss Rose then, or wait until after Mr. Benson has finished his waiter duties to speak to him.'

In a dilemma, Copeland stopped at the bottom of the steps and stared up at Simon. He had forgotten he was invited to a dinner party where he could see, first hand, how Ania Rose sometimes got her information, stay the night in a luxury bedroom and arrest someone who could earn him a few million pounds bonus.

*Be honest Copeland! You didn't forget the dinner party. How you were going to spend two million pounds has been on your mind all week. You just forgot today was Saturday! Let's go home, get the tuxedo on and arrest Ania Rose tomorrow when we're a few million pounds better off, eh?*

Copeland looked at Simon and said: 'I'm not coming this evening, Simon. In fact, no one will be!' He resolutely mounted the first step and handed Simon the folder. 'Hold this a minute while I find my Department C warrant card…Thanks …Just bear with me. I'm sure it's in one of these pockets… There!' He flashed his official ID card in its new leather wallet and said, 'Inspector Copeland, Department C and sort of MI5. This is official business! Stand aside young man! Can I have my folder back please?'

Simon handed back the flimsy folder and, open mouthed, stood aside as Copeland bounded up the steps into the house. Pretty Alice was striding down the hall towards him with her soft cinnamon hair bouncing in her wake. She was in her usual black satin dress with short, white, puffed sleeves. She was carrying a sword. Copeland noticed it was a very shiny sword before the tip was promptly placed at his throat.

*Two people wanting to kill you in the same day, eh, Copeland? There's probably a queue somewhere.*

Lifting his chin before he had a closer shave than he really needed, Copeland said, 'Hello, Alice. Nice sword.'

'It's not a *sword*. It's my katana,' Alice corrected.

'Alice!' cried Simon, recovering his composure. 'What the hell are you doing?'

'Search him, Simon,' commanded Alice sternly. Changing her tone she said, 'Sorry about this, Inspector Copeland, Sir, but a Dark Star called Kylie shot Tom Benson and you've been under the influence of Keira Starr for three days…and nights. We can't take any chances.'

'Benson was shot!' exclaimed Copeland, receiving a nasty scratch from a samurai katana sword as payment for his concern. He thought it might be a good idea not to move his head again.

Simon, who had reluctantly begun searching Copeland from behind, said, 'Mr. Benson only sustained a scratch, Sir. Some superglue and three stitches in his side and he was fine. The inspector has lost weight but he hasn't got a gun, Alice.'

'You knew that, Simon. You just saw me go through all my jacket pockets,' Copeland pointed out.

'Do a proper, ***thorough*** search, Simon,' ordered Alice. 'We don't want our male Champion's life put at risk, do we?'

Simon huffed and began his ***thorough*** search.

'Bloody hell, Simon!' said Copeland, wide eyed. 'What do you think you're going to find down there? Ow! That's not a pistol barrel!'

'He's clean,' announced Simon standing up.

Alice nodded and said, 'Good. He still might have a bomb. Let's do an internal search.'

'What?' simultaneously shouted Simon and Copeland.

'Stop making a fuss, both of you,' said Alice. 'I'll keep my katana at his throat while you strip him, Simon. We can bend him over a chair. If you're squeamish, Simon, there are some rubber gloves under the sink. Oh, sorry to say, Inspector Copeland, Sir, but we may be out of lubricant. Doctor Smith used the last few drops on Mr. Benson this morning for his cleansing enema.'

'Hang on, Alice,' Simon and Copeland simultaneously said. They looked at each other. Simon said, 'After you, Sir.'

'Thank you, Simon,' said Copeland, wishing he hadn't turned to look at Simon and sure a droplet of blood was about to stain the collar of his light blue shirt. 'Let's just rewind here. Benson was shot by a Dark Star name Kylie? Australian

Kylie?' Alice and Simon simultaneously nodded. 'I know her,' continued Copeland. 'Poor girl was stuck on a toilet with an upset stomach, shouting about things eating their way out from inside her.' Alice and Simon shot each other a look. 'I'll tell you this, Alice, and you, Simon... Don't ever eat a Korean delicacy if it's still wriggling its tentacles on your plate!' He risked an emphatic finger. 'So, I take it Kylie Dark Star is in police custody?'

'Ania let her go,' said Simon, who seemed to be checking again to see if Copeland had any hidden weapons secretly stashed in his groin area. 'You really have lost weight, Sir,' he said, flatteringly. 'You feel quite... healthy.'

'Yes! Ania let Kylie go!' snapped Alice as she forced Copeland's head back with her katana tip. 'Ania said Kylie said she didn't shoot at Benson so she did some sort of deal with Keira Starr and let her go. Humph! I still think she shot poor Mr. Benson. I would have peeled off her skin then sliced off her head!'

'Er... Quite,' agreed Copeland, beginning to believe there might be another side to Alice he had not previously noticed.

*I think you should focus more on getting out of having an internal body search, Copeland*, suggested a wise voice.

From the other end of what Copeland thought was at least a badminton court length hallway, *(Copeland! No!)* Ania Rose shouted, 'By all the wretched gods! What's going on?'

'Hello, Ania' said Copeland with a little finger wave as Alice turned and the sword point made another nick.

*Oh, dear! Bet that one needs a stitch, Copeland.*

Rapidly clicking down the wooden floored hallway in quite high heels and her favourite white silk kimono robe, Ania almost grabbed Alice's sword holding hand, thought better of it and used a finger to carefully push the katana point away from Copeland's neck. With some gravitas, Ania looked hard at Alice and said, 'Get Larry some tissues, Alice.'

'Yes, Ma'am,' said Alice, who did her little curtsey with one hand (because she was holding a sword in the other) and hurried off.

Ania said, 'And you can stop searching him for hidden weapons now, Simon,' and Simon gave a nod and hurried off. Alone at last in the hallway by the front door to Ania's Olympic swimming pool size house... Oops, sorry... Ania placed a finger on Copeland's worst minor cut.

*Told you so, Copeland! Very touchy-feely sort of person.*

Ania smiled and said, 'What brings you here, Larry? Come to check out the cheeseboard and get a wine list preview?'

Copeland said, 'You're taller than me in heels... Oh, yes... What brings me here! You may well ask! Well, Ania Rose! There will be no wine! There will be no cheeseboard! Ania Rose, you're under arrest!'

Ania raised her perfect eyebrows and said, 'Really! You never cease to surprise me, Larry, and, believe me, only you and Tom Benson have done that for a *very* long time. Let's go into the conservatory and talk about it. Please don't argue or I'll call Alice back and let Simon do an internal search.'

In the conservatory, which ran the whole length of the two blue whales long house, Copeland put his jacket on the back of a white wicker armchair and sat at a square, glass topped table facing Ania Rose. He dabbed tissue on his neck, looked down the twenty elephant lengths lawn and asked, 'Why is Tom Benson walking back and forth across your lawn carrying a glass full of water on a tray and a book balanced on his head?' Ania Rose told him it was necessary last minute training for Tom to be a good waiter at her dinner party, which also explained why Tom Benson was dressed in full penguin-like waiter uniform, so Copeland asked, 'And why is that young woman dressed as a maid flapping one of her pigtails in his face while he dodges around the cones?' Ania Rose explained Tom Benson may have to deliver cocktails while dodging other guests and Ingrid was simply taking a time out from her elocution training with Simon and trying to distract Benson just like other dinner party guests might. So Copeland said, 'Your maid Ingrid's uniform looks, er...too small for her. Is it one of Alice's? Actually, she looks a bit familiar.' Ania Rose told Copeland a lot of people thought Ingrid looked a lot like a younger Britney Spears, not that Britney Spears had aged badly of course, but it was also possible he may have seen young Ingrid in one of her many short films. Copeland nodded sagely while considering this. After watching Benson and Ingrid for some time he said, 'I hear one of Keira's Dark Stars name Kylie took a shot at Tom Benson but you let her go.'

'She didn't shoot at Benson,' said Ania. 'That must have been someone else. I know because after she and I had a little chat I got Benson in the room with her. He has the uncanny skill of being able to tell if someone is being truthful or not.'

Copeland laughed as he continued to watch Benson perfecting his waiter skills. 'I've known Tom for years. He reads books about that sort of stuff – how to read micro body language and how stage magicians use it.'

Ania said, 'I did a deal with Keira Starr. I let her Dark Star go in exchange for someone else.'

'Someone else? Who?' asked Copeland, looking at Ania.

'You,' said Ania.

Copeland laughed. 'That wasn't necessary. As a matter of fact, Keira and I got on very well.'

'She would have tortured you to get information.'

'I didn't have any. I told her my passwords wouldn't work while I was there. She got you to release Kylie under false pretences, Miss Rose.'

'Oh,' said Ania, now watching Tom Benson balance his tray. 'So no matter how much she threatened or tortured you, you wouldn't have been able to tell her The Pickfords headquarters are above a bank in Kensington, what they used to be called, or anything else? You worked for the Pickfords for three years Larry. You know more than you think you do. What if she found out about your daughter?'

Copeland swallowed hard. 'Keira's not like that.'

Ania sneered, 'So you don't think she's ruthless enough to do *anything* to get what she wants, Inspector?'

Copeland thought about this. Eventually, he said, 'Thanks for arranging the exchange, Ania.'

'Don't mention it,' said Ania Rose. 'Let's have some refreshments before you arrest me, shall we?'

Alice had arrived minus her katana but with refreshments.

Copeland ate and drank and gazed into the garden wondering how he could have forgotten Keira Starr was, for all her charm, a ruthless crime lord. He was beginning to suspect the ChewiVits he'd consumed had somehow had an adverse effect on his razor sharp mental capacities.

*Which previously only needed meat pie topped pizzas and a couple of bottles of red wine to stay razor sharp, didn't they, Copeland?*

'Ahem! Inspector?' Ania Rose eventually said after they had finished quietly enjoying their tea and Danish pastries. 'You're going to arrest me for something aren't you?'

'Quite so!' said Copeland brushing flakes of pastry from his lap. 'That pastry was really good and I could eat another. I'm famished. Did you know I had sunstroke? But back to business...I'm here to arrest you, Ania Rose!' Copeland stood, stared down at her in as much of an intimidating way as he could and flipped open his blue manila document folder. Dramatically, he pulled out a photograph, slammed it on the glass tabletop, glared Ania Rose in the eye and said, 'I have a recorded confession from *this* man which says you're responsible for... Hang on. That's the wrong photo. That's the one the other one shot and left dead in a wood somewhere... Aha!' He slammed another photo on the table. '*This* man says...'

'Why do you do this, Larry?' asked Ania. 'Why do you always play the bumbling Inspector when I know you only do that to throw people off guard?'

*I'd never noticed that, Copeland.*

Copeland said, 'Stop trying to evade, Miss Rose! Your mind game sleight of hand tricks won't work on me! I know all about what you're trying to do. All about the importance of this nonsensical contest between you and your **two** half sisters! Louise is not only Keira's half sister, but is **your** half sister too! Aha! I can see the surprise on your face! You are Keira Starr's half sister and you want to take over her Dark Star empire – and her magazines – by winning the contest you pretentiously call The Game and joining the international billionaires running the world, don't you? You hired people like these two...' Copeland pointed at the photographs laid on the table... 'To kill people and carve a pentagram on their foreheads so Keira Starr got the blame and got arrested. Then she wouldn't be there at this Game contest thingy and by not sticking to the organisers rules requiring her to attend in person she would forfeit everything to you! Aha!'

Ania said: 'You seem unusually animated, Inspector. You haven't been eating these new ChewiVit tablets, have you?'

'Errrr... No... Honest,' said Copeland.

'Good,' responded Ania. 'They can make one somewhat energetic, as it were...' She laughed. 'So... It seems Lou was her usual loopy self. I knew meeting you in a pub was a bad idea. I suppose she got drunk.'

Copeland said, 'She threw up on the pub steps and twice in the car park...And...Don't try and change the subject! You're under arrest. You have the right to...'

'I get one phone call, don't I?' said Ania with her Julia Roberts grin. 'Now, should I call my lawyer, or your boss Wendy Miller, or our mutual friend Beryl Pickford?'

Copeland stayed focused. He withdrew another photograph from his blue manila folder and demanded, 'Tell me who this sombrero wearing man is, Miss Rose! Oh... that's you on holiday in a bikini... Sorry... Let me just...'

Going even paler than usual, Ania Rose placed her hand on her own photograph, looked at Copeland, shuddered and quietly asked, 'Where did you get this photograph of me?'

*She knows darn well you got it from dating websites she was using to locate men who lived alone, Copeland. Show her the photo of Mr. Sombrero Man White and she'll confess to everything... Possibly!*

Holding Ania Roses' gaze, Copeland sat down. He said, 'You've worked hard to keep your digital footprint invisible since you took over as leader of the mutual-aid business group you call the Roses. There's not a single photo of you anywhere on the internet. I suspect this one of you on holiday in your bikini was taken before you became the Roses leader and changed your name from Starr to Rose. I have an associate who is at this very moment researching your background, Ania **Starr**!'

Ania pulled the hem of her short white kimono across her thigh and smiled. 'I'll be honest with you. You're half right, Inspector. My name has always been Ania. But I was never a

Starr. Elder sister Keira, younger sister Lou and I all have different fathers. I did become Ania Rose to lead the Roses. But the next leader won't have to change her name. My adopted daughter is already Alice Ania Rose. Here she comes to clear away our pastry plates. She likes to earn her keep. I think your phone is vibrating in your pocket, Inspector.'

Alice did her curtsey and began tidying the table. She pretended not to look at the photographs, but gave Ania a puzzled look when she saw one of them was of her.

Recovering from learning Alice was Ania's daughter, Copeland withdrew his vibrating phone from his pocket. He had ignored it twice, expecting it was Director Miller calling to pester him about doing his report on his Keira Starr visit, but saw it was Freya calling. 'Excuse me,' he said, half turning his back on Ania to take the call.

He said, 'What's up, Freya?' and then listened, tapped and swiped his phone, looked at it, put it back to his mouth and said, 'Yes.' He listened again before saying, 'Okay. I understand. What's that Norwegian swear word you use? Okay. Skit'r! See you later.' Shaking his head he turned back to face Ania and put his phone on the glass tabletop, now clear except for the three A4 size photographs. Ania waited while Copeland stared distantly into the garden where Tom Benson was still practising on his own; Ingrid was presumably somewhere with Simon and her elocution.

Still staring into the garden, Copeland said, 'He'll get sunstroke dressed like that in this weather. Did I tell you I had sunstroke when I was staying at your sister's?' He stopped garden gazing and picked up the photo of Ania Rose, looked at it and placed it down on the table in front of Ania. He said, 'My associate found this photograph of you on several dating websites. This man...' Copeland pointed to the photo of fedora wearing Vasily Goraya. 'This man is Vasily Goraya, an ex senior officer in Russian foreign intelligence. I have a recording of him on my phone claiming a man he calls Mr. White used your name when he was handing over money to him and his deceased partner...' Copeland pointed to the photo of Valdis Ozola. 'The money was to pay them for committing the pentagram murders. Because of the pentagram connection, we thought Keira Starr was behind it at first. We thought the victims were once part of her Dark Stars who had left so she was having them killed and leaving her pentagram mark as a warning to other Dark Stars who might think about leaving.'

'So did I. Kee is arrogant enough to do that,' conceded Ania, listening intently.

'Then,' sighed Copeland, 'we thought it was you trying to frame Keira so you could get her out of the way and win your contest, take over everything she owns and join your mysterious contest organisers who apparently, according to Lou, claim they run the world.'

'Lou told you that?' Ania put her head in her hands. She shook her head and looked up at Copeland. 'They don't say that at all. They are simply a group of business people who work together. That's why they call themselves Fyli. In Greek it means group, as in clan.'

*Oh, it's pronounced feeli, Copeland. You should tell Benson...*

'So,' said Copeland, 'this group acts pretty much like your Roses do, but on a bigger scale?'

'Correct, Inspector, despite what conspiracy theorists say about them,' said Ania. 'And if it wasn't for Keira falsely claiming I bribed her contestants when we had our original contest the Fyli wouldn't be insisting on us having these tedious rematches before they let the winner join them, but they seem to like games and we are where we are.'

'Hmm...' said Copeland, sensing there was more than he was being told. 'Lou told me you three used to own a logistics company together but it became fractious so you each thought up a staff loyalty test to decide who should be the sole owner.'

Ania nodded confirmation. 'That first contest seems an age ago... But you're talking now as if you don't think I'm the chief suspect who paid these men to kill others.'

Resignedly sighing again, Copeland stared into the garden and said, 'No. My associate called to say she had found older photos on the dating websites used to contact the victims. The older photos had been replaced by your photo. This is the photograph that was there on every dating website before yours was.' He picked his phone up, tapped a few times and handed his phone across to Ania.

Ania looked at the photo and said, 'It's Keira! In a bikini...' She pointed the phone at Copeland and turned the photo of herself round so he could see it the right way up. Copeland looked at the photo of Keira, he looked at the photo of Ania, he looked at the photo of Keira again. He said, 'You're both standing in exactly the same place, on a clifftop overlooking a very blue sea.'

Urgently, Ania said, 'Look harder, Inspector Copeland.'

Copeland looked harder. He said, 'I see...'

Nodding, Ania said, 'Well spotted, Larry. It's not **exactly** the same place is it? Kee and I were standing next to each other when that photo was taken. It's been doctored so both Kee and I appear to be on our own.'

*You hadn't got a clue had you Copeland? You were going to say something about the tiny white and black bikinis being similar, weren't you?*

Copeland had a little think and said, 'So why would Keira put a photo of herself on countless dating websites and then change the photo to one of you a few days ago?'

Ania said nothing. She sat back in her white wicker chair and waited.

Copeland had another little think. It took a third little think before he said, 'Are there any more Danish..? Got it! You don't have any photos of you on the internet! Neither does Keira. Both of you keep images of yourselves very, very private...You keep them in the family...If you and Keira were both on the original photo, then who took..? Oh, no!'

'Show me the photo of your unknown intermediary, Inspector,' Ania said.

Copeland took the photo from the folder. Placing it on the table he said, 'You can't see much because of the sombrero, but Vasily Goraya let slip he's got white hair and a nose like a...'

'Rodent,' Ania finished. 'It's Harry Hudson. He used to work here doing Simon's job until I fired him for... Let's not put too fine a point on it...He sexually assaulted my daughter. Alice had a mental breakdown a few months later because of what he'd done. It was two years ago and, as you know, she still can't bear touching anyone. Hudson got another similar job but he's recently been trying to ingratiate himself with me by doing things like...'

'Sending you information,' finished Copeland. 'He's the HRH who sent you the file about Keira's Butterburn research place near Hadrian's Wall that got me involved in this case to start with, isn't he?'

Ania nodded.

Copeland nodded as well. 'He knew someone would go up there and see all the pentagrams and link them to the murders, which is exactly what I did, and Keira Starr became the chief suspect behind the pentagram murders so we would eventually arrest her...' Copeland slapped his forehead. He pointed to the photo of Vasily Goraya. 'Vasily said Mr. White used to refer to the big boss as "my lady", and only called her Ania and Miss Rose the last time they met a few days ago, and the dating website photo of Keira was changed to one of you a few days ago as well...Because Keira was about to be arrested for something else, such as her crystal meth lab near York! And I was about to arrest you for being behind the pentagram murders to frame Keira. You would have both been in detention awaiting trial for months...'

Ania said, 'And neither of us would have been able to attend The Game and we would have lost by default. The only remaining person would have won and got everything both Keira and I own. You can guess who Harry Hudson – your Mr. White – works for now. I suspect Hudson was also the person who shot at Tom Benson. Hudson and his little drone probably knew Kylie Dark Star was watching my house and thought she'd get the blame, driving another wedge between Keira and me. Do you want an address for him and his boss, Larry? I really should tell Tom Benson to stop before he passes out through exhaustion.'

After making a phone call to Director Miller so she could send armed officers to the address Ania had given him, Copeland set off home.

Watching Copeland leave with Alice by her side, Ania said, 'He's not coming to the dinner party this evening. He says he has something more important to do than become a millionaire. I'll phone Wendy Miller. I'm sure she'll be keen to take his place. Oh, and Alice...Find out every last detail you can about the person who rang Copeland. She's possibly Norwegian. She told Copeland *"skit'r"* was a Norwegian swear word, but that pronunciation is old Norse. Her name is Freya. Call Beryl Pickford as well and find out what The Pickfords know about her, but tread carefully.'

'Of course, Ma'am,' said Alice as she curtsied.

Ania waited for Alice to go into the third floor office and close the door before she went to her private quarters to make a call of her own. It began, 'Hi, Kee. Our little sister has been her loopy self again. Now don't get annoyed, but...'

Copeland stopped off to buy flowers. Freya liked them. Copeland liked the case of wine waiting in his hallway. It looked suspiciously like the £4000 a bottle wine he had enjoyed at Keira Starr's. His deduction was confirmed by a note Freya handed to him as she told him the case had arrived by special courier only moments before. The note read:

*Dear Larry,*

*I'm in London so I've sent this wine to thank you for clearing my name regarding what you called the pentagram murders. Ania just phoned and told me you'd worked it out. As you may have guessed, our little sister Lou is loopy. But that's no excuse, is it? By the way, Lou's last name is Hart, so I think the removal of the victims' organs was her private joke. As I said, she is loopy.*

*Thank you also for your gift of Comrade Vasily Goraya. I let Kirsty out of the kennel so she could have some R and R with him. She's letting him have a nice sit down on the Judas chair at the moment.*

*Please be assured I would have considered you important enough to have kept you for further 'discussions' if you hadn't told me about the password changes, but it just wasn't worth it without them so I exchanged you for Kylie. We stand by our own.*

*If you want a job with me anytime, my offer still stands.*

*Regards,*

*Keira. X*

## 12b.  DAY 12. SUNDAY. THE END.

As it often does, the day after the night before arrived.

Tom Benson was happy. Rachel Duvall was his new client and she had a lead part in heart-throb actor George's next romantic comedy where she would play a single soccer mom working in a diner, which heart-throb George just happened to go into to fall in love with her when his flash sports car broke down. George had agreed to Rachel getting the part because Tom had proposed she did it for free and George got her pay cheque. Tom also got the publicity contract for the Bollywood studio. During their tea together in Ania's garden, Tom had impressed Mithali, whom everyone thought was the PA to the elder studio boss, but was really the real studio boss all along and she was, as Mithali put it, "using the man as a more acceptable face in a patriarchal society." Tom phoned home with the good news and happened to mention The Game had been postponed for a few more months for some reason, but his contract giving Ania absolute and total control of his physical self covered that eventuality and could continue indefinitely, so no worries there.

Director Wendy Miller was happy. Being personally five million pounds better off and securing enough funds to revamp Department C's temporary offices had something to do with it. She had stayed the night at Ania's, as had Foreign Minister Anthony Mozawinga. Director Miller had made the early morning arrest of Foreign Minister Mozawinga thanks to his country's President wanting Mozawinga gone, thanks to Mozawinga being impressed by young Ingrid, and thanks to hidden cameras with recording devices in Mozawinga's bedroom. Mozawinga had boasted about quite a few things to Ingrid, including his exploitation of children and how he would soon overthrow his own president. Even so, the three judges took some time to agree to the seizing of Mozawinga's ill gotten gains. They had apparently needed to watch the recording of his boastful confession to Ingrid in full several times.

Ingrid was happy. Ania paid her much more than she usually got for making films.

Louise Hart was not unhappy. True, Harry Hudson had been arrested and some of her belongings were still at her old house when the armed police stormed it, but Louise was safely sipping whiskey in her new home knowing no one would suspect she was living in the clubhouse of a remote, abandoned golf course. She had the money she had from selling her house and businesses plus the thirty million she had suckered Ania into giving her. She had always played the part of a drunkard quite convincingly and for a small sum the barmaid at The Manchester had been helpful by filling whiskey bottles with cold tea. The stale pie making her sick was an unexpected bonus. Louise knew her sisters might be a bit miffed with her for a while for trying to get them arrested so she could win The Game and take over everything they owned but, all in all, Louise thought they might respect her more now they had seen she could play in the major league just as well as they could, though it was a shame Mr. Grey and Mr. Pink had disappeared and could not be arrested in the act of forehead pentagram carving and give Ania's name to the police, as planned. Louise slightly regretted changing her plan and wished she had stuck to getting Keira arrested for the murders then framing Ania for tax fraud as she had originally planned, but Ania and Copeland had presented her with a golden opportunity to have Keira arrested for her crystal meth lab and frame Ania for the murders without all the extra work needed to set up a fake tax fraud. Louise was disappointed that Copeland had somehow worked out Ania was not behind the murders and equally disappointed someone had tipped Keira off about the police raid on the lab. It meant she would have to try to find contestants for The Game again.

Dr. Beth Spencer was finally happy. She made the breakthrough with the new synthetic skin and knew they could finally start using it for the robots. The ones Copeland *hadn't* seen in the basement of the Butterburn lab.

A lot of people in the whole country were happy, providing their local pharmacies and health shops had not sold out of ChewiVits. This made Keira Starr happy. She knew this was just the start of the healthier ChewiVits replacing all those harmful street drugs, just as she had told Copeland while they waltzed. She knew he had finally seen how her long term plan would make things better. Why else would he have phoned her to warn her about the raid on her crystal meth factory? Keira was also happy because she had been able to recruit someone who had the codes to get into all the security service's computers.

Janet was very happy to escape from the damp Department C office and from typing Copeland's reports. She was happy with her new salary, her luxury apartment, her attentive servants and her personal chef, and even though she had needed to relocate to a stately home somewhere near Sheffield she had unlimited lingerie and handcuffs.

Ania was pleased to have found out Freya was a journalist, but still suspected she was something else as well.

Vasily Goraya was not happy. Kirsty was.

Larry Copeland did not know how to feel. Part of him was annoyed the only arrest had been that of Harry Hudson (aka Mr. Sombrero Man, aka Mr. White). The main perpetrator, Louise Hart, had vanished into thin air and the only assets available to be seized barely gave Copeland enough bonus money to pay for the tie-pin camera and transmitter watch he had lost. But it did not detract from memories of a wonderful evening with Freya, who was thrilled to have the pentagram murders story to write up and had agreed to finally try a few ChewiVits before they went for their (romantic) meal at an expensive restaurant. It hadn't cost as much as Copeland thought it would, mainly because Freya dragged him out of the restaurant after the starter. Copeland was glad to get home and take the women's underwear off. He'd had to wear it to prove to Freya it really was a cactus he'd given to Janet.

It had been after another ChewiVit and sometime around dawn when Copeland's fingers ran across the slight lump between Freya's shoulder blades and Freya told him it was a subcutaneous GPS transmitter her publishing agent could track her with. Copeland knew Freya went to some scary places and thought a tracker sounded like a good idea in case she was abducted. It made him worry a little less about Freya going back to Serbia, though he did tell her not to touch anyone who had symptoms of this new bio-weapon called Nosoi she was going there to investigate. Curious, she had lifted her head from his chest and narrowed her blue eyes. He told her she should get a gas mask as well.

On the plus side, Freya had fetched her passport the day before and her flight was not until early evening so they had a whole day together. The ChewiVit packets were empty before Copeland checked his blood pressure and they left for the airport.

Their goodbye at the airport was reminiscent of *Casablanca*, except there was no fog and it wasn't in black and white, and although it was Freya getting on the plane, he was playing the part of teary Ingrid Bergman. It didn't help when Freya kissed him and whispered, 'Whatever happens, Larry… We'll always have Slough.'

Printed in Great Britain
by Amazon